BLACK CURSES BREWING

WILDE WITCHES - BOOK 3

ERIN RICHARDS

Midnight Muse
PUBLISHING

BLACK CURSES BREWING
Erin Richards

Digital ISBN: 978-1943800230
Print ISBN: 978-1943800247

Cover Designer: Book Cover Artistry by Heather Hamilton-Senter

Praise for
Erin Richards' Books

"I loved this book [*Chasing Shadows*] and it never faltered from its action and suspense." ~*Night Owl Reviews* (NOR 5-Star Top Pick)

"The suspense will keep you turning the pages... The characters are complex and well-developed and there is never a dull moment in the story [*Chasing Shadows*]. If you love your romance with suspense, this is one book you need to read! 5 stars all the way!" ~*The Romance Reviews*

"*Stealing Twilight* by Erin Richards is completely enthralling with its addicting characters, unique plot, and satisfying ending." ~*Amazon 5-Star Review*

"*Seducing Darkness* is fast-paced and action-packed. It is well-written with vivid imagery that allowed me to get lost in the story. It offers drama, intrigue, and romance with a hint of humor that kept me entertained throughout." ~*Amazon 5-Star Review*

"Full of adventure, romance and two wonderfully heroic characters. The descriptions of the island are beautiful and the passion between Morgan and Ryan leaves you turning the pages to see if they can finally come together. A great book [*Wicked Paradise*]." ~*5-Stars, Paranormal Romance Guild*

"Perfect for fans of Julie Kagawa & Alyssa Rose Ivy. Loved this book [*Forbidden Thirteen*]! The plot was unique in a genre where everything has been done before. Just the perfect balance of action, supernatural and hot romance. Bring on book 2!" ~*5-Star Amazon Review*

Books by
Erin Richards

Psychic Justice Series
Chasing Shadows, Book 1
Twilight Rising, Book 2
Stealing Twilight, Book 3
Seducing Darkness, Book 4
Tempting Midnight, Book 5

Forbidden Legacy Series
Forbidden Thirteen, Book 1

Wilde Witches Series
Igniting the Witch, Prequel
Black Magic Rising, Book 1
Black Warlocks Prowling, Book 2
Black Curses Brewing, Book 3

Wicked Paradise

Young Adult
Vigilante Nights
Dragonfly Nightmare
Bittersweet Wreckage

See updated book list at:
www.erinrichards.com/booklist.htm

BLACK CURSES
BREWING

Chapter 1

Aspen Wilde held a spoon over a fat candle flame, melting fishing weights into oblivion. Molten lead spread across the spoon, and she dripped the contents into a spelling pot. The lead hit the cold water, sizzling and popping. Excitement sped up her heartbeat. Her first lead casting shattered the monotony of her day, an escape from her uber secret magic brewing. Both created an escape from the boredom of her luxury prison.

The door kicked open, and her cousin Brianne plopped onto a rolling stool, exhaling an exaggerated sigh. Aspen hunched over the copper pot and blew out the candle, hiding it from Brianne. Aspen, Brianne, and Brianne's twin sister, Marina, had all grown up together on the Wilde covenstead. More than cousins or sisters, they were best friends. Since Brianne was a water witch like Aspen, the pair held more in common than other witches on the covenstead. Except Brianne had no natural inclination toward herbs or brewing magic.

Her cousin twisted strands of her long blonde hair around her fingers, something Marina did when nervous, not Brianne. Aspen gave her the hairy eyeball. Her cousin flipped her hair behind her shoulders. "Give me something to do before I go cray cray." She leaned forward, scrunched up her face. "What are you hiding?"

"Nothing." Aspen looked away, avoiding eye contact. At least she'd stashed her black magic books. Brianne would have a field day if she understood the real magic Aspen brewed. Rio, her seagull familiar, squawked derisively from its nest atop her bank of cabinets near the ceiling. She shot Rio a death-ray stare.

"Baloney. You have all the fun in your mad science lab. Why didn't I inherit your alchemy and healing abilities? Instead, I can make rain." Water sprinkled from below the ceiling and misted their hair. "Big whoop." She peered in the pot Aspen attempted to cover. "Unpack it for me. That doesn't look like a potion or a gummy. Holy hell, I need a super energy gummy. Or CBD. *Something!*" She flailed her arms above her head and water misted the entire room.

Thank the goddess Aspen wasn't brewing a black curse. "Fresh out. Can't leave for supplies. So much for two-day deliveries. And I have webstore orders to fulfill that'll be late." Curiosity besting her, Aspen pulled away from the tiny cauldron on her stove. Two hard blobs of lead floated around the edges in the pot. "What do they look like?"

Brianne tapped a fingertip on her chin and pointed at the lead on the right. "Kinda resembles a tiny layer cake."

"Really?" The lead resembled a blob. But Aspen could make out a cake if she squinted hard and twisted her head to the side.

"What's it supposed to be?"

"Beats me. I'm getting weird vibes in my dreams, symbols of vines and purple flowers and stuff. I'm trying this ancient divination to see if anything meshes with the dreams. The lead shapes are supposed to mean *something*." She stuck her spoon in the pot and swished the blobs around. "The other one looks like an old-fashioned bomb." She leafed through her notebook. "A cake means a festivity is coming."

"I wish." Brianne slouched on the stool again. "No Spring Solstice festival since we're on lockdown."

"Sucks green donkey ass." Aspen snapped a photo of the lead blobs. "Give it time to manifest. Maybe Sage will bend her orders on the lockdown. Party time. Here we come." She snapped her fingers in Brianne's face. "Think positive."

Brianne grinned and tapped the lead. "Did you dream of gorging on cake?"

"Nope." Aspen refused to confess her actual nightmares, or how she bolted awake, her heart thundering in her chest, sweat dripping off her neck every other morning over the last month. The fear was so palpable, she'd set extra wards at her bedroom windows and door. Especially after her nightmares revealed the shadowy image of a man, and plants and vines growing rampant in the backyard.

With the tip of her finger, Brianne swirled the water into a tiny whirlpool, her magic keeping it spinning. The lead blobs spun around the pot's perimeter. "What does a bomb mean? Gotta be bad." She pulled her hand up into a claw shape and lifted the claw. Water rose with it, then waterfalled into the pot with a splash.

Aspen stuck her finger in the pot to stop the water. She examined the round lead ball, a tiny ignition wick sticking off to the side. She scrolled down the list in her notebook, and her fingers trembled. "A bomb means escaping danger."

"Great. You'll escape danger at our next party in the year 3001 if Sage has her way." Brianne snorted, and Aspen had to stop her from misting the room again. "I can't believe you're making fake prophecies."

Wiping the water drops off her face, Aspen nudged her gladiator sandal against Brianne's foot. "Beats moping around like a lame duck."

"I need to escape this covenstead. I'm dying without the ocean."

Aspen hung her head. "Yeah. Me too. Water witches need their water. I need the grounding and cleansing from actual salt water before my spells kick me back to Sunday."

"Exactly. Can't you talk *your* sister into bending her rules? It's been a month since Imelda kicked the bucket and disbursed her black warlock minions. No more black warlock attacks, and that turd Andre Charlemagne's imprisoned here. No one can get in or out, or anywhere near him. This lockdown's gonna kill us."

"It's the 'out' she's worried about. There *have* been minor skirmishes with other covens and black warlocks."

"But you need supplies." Brianne buried her face in her hands. "*We* need water."

"She'll kick us to the creek and tell me to order online." Aspen sank to the floor and crossed her legs. Not all her supplies were available online. She needed to visit her favorite local compounding pharmacy and apothecary shop. The creek didn't always cut it, especially during California drought-land days. At least the water flowed deeper and faster than a trickle this year from a good winter rainfall. But the lack of salt water provided little relief to a water witch who needed the cleansing of negativity the ocean provided.

"Then we all gang up on her. I'm for real having water withdrawals. That mist you saw minutes ago. That's all I can muster." Brianne pulled her phone out of her pocket and texted, nearly punching her finger through the phone hitting the send button.

"What did you do?" Alarm skittered across Aspen's shoulders. She didn't want Brianne to mess up her own plans of escape, two weeks in the making.

"Rallied the troops. We're going full smackdown on your big sis if she doesn't unlock the gates. I don't care if she sicks Rafael on us. Willow gets to leave whenever she wants, and she's toting a bum ankle. You and I are hitting the beach if it kills us." She sucked on her bottom lip. "Have there really been black warlock attacks?" Fear grabbed hold and weakened her voice.

"Willow's allowed to leave because she's bonded to a freaking black warlock." Aspen huffed out a breath. Hell to the no. Black warlocks weren't necessary in her life. No warlock period. Not after Marty. She sniffed her grief. Her one and only warlock had died a month ago during their skirmishes with the Helwig coven. His aunt Imelda had him killed to prove her badass-ness. Even though Aspen and Marty weren't romantically involved, they'd enjoyed a fun friendship, and he was a decent, if scatterbrained, warlock. She stroked the tail feather of Marty's former bonding familiar, Rico, as it fluttered in tattoo form on her arm. The seagull's eyes had quit leaking its sorrow just this week.

"The San Francisco and Silicon Valley covens have reported recent attacks, including black curses," she continued. "Nothing major, but they're escalating. Like black warlocks are testing the witchworld waters, seeing where they can infiltrate, the way they infiltrated the Helwig coven." She smirked at Brianne. "Uh, sorry. Did I just roll my eyes out loud? Weren't you paying attention to the council briefing last week?" Aspen knew Brianne had suffered a hangover after boredom prompted them to a challenge on who could create the best mixed cocktail.

Her cousin stuck her tongue out at Aspen. "I'm tired of hearing about the black warlocks."

"Well, you better buckle up, buttercup."

Witches had abolished the black warlocks over a

hundred years ago during the Witches and Warlocks War. Black warlocks held innate magic and didn't need witches to bond them to gain magic. A black warlock spell could mark a witch, boot her under his dominance for life, and stop a witch from using magic. He could coerce a witch to do anything at his discretion, all the while strengthening his magic with hers. Some black warlocks had survived the war, and their bloodlines had made a recent resurgence. Their leader, Andre Charlemagne, had tried to kidnap and bond Willow, among other dastardly deeds. The reason the Wildes had incarcerated him on their covenstead. It was one of the safest covens in the U.S. because of the ley lines running beneath the earth that aided in their ability to protect the property. Although, the lines and wards had fallen when the stupid Helwigs aligned with black warlocks and attacked the Wildes a month ago.

Chaos had targeted the witchworld, and everyone teetered on the edge of paranoia.

"Why can't we recruit more Ravenwood warlocks or their minions? Another Ethan or Evan Ravenwood for me." Brianne licked her lips, plumped her not-so-insignificant breasts.

"Eww. No, thanks. Sage and Willow can have the Ravenwoods or any black warlock, for that matter." She preferred the old ways where witches dominated black warlocks, instead of the new equality Willow and Evan Ravenwood were touting. With Marty's recent demise, she wasn't ready for another warlock, and certainly didn't want a love connection with one. Or a hit-and-run as Brianne alluded to. She had too much to do in building her healing and alchemy knowledge before she allowed love to interfere. And learning more about black curses and how to defeat them.

"Dude." Brianne's eyes rounded. "A warlock's a warlock, if you know what I mean. They all possess the same appendage. And I'm dying for one. The appendage at least."

"Jeez, Louise. What's gotten into you? You need a freaking lot." Aspen tossed a towel over her copper pot and accessories. "Let's gang up on Sage." Anything to distract Brianne and get her off Aspen's tail.

Rio swooped down and landed on her shoulder, dissolved into a tattoo, and took a perch on the skin of her neck. She grabbed her stuffed fanny pack, and after one last scan of her sanctuary, she locked and warded the door behind them. Didn't need anyone snooping around. *Danger, Will Robinson, danger.*

Brianne flicked her fanny pack. "I like how you're projecting our escape into the universe."

"You never know." Regardless if Sage grants them permission to leave or not, Aspen was escaping. She had things to do, see, and, more importantly, buy. And she didn't need her tagalong cousins.

They met Marina and the twins' older sister, Eden, in the hallway outside Sage's office. Not one of the four witches had a bonded warlock. An unnatural conundrum Sage was desperate to fix. Only thing, not enough warlocks in their sphere, and they feared a door to the black warlocks would open if they invited *any* warlocks in. Already happened once when Evan Ravenwood infiltrated the Wilde coven, gained Sage's trust to the point she bonded him, and then he revealed his identity. Good news, he was trying to protect Aspen's sister Willow, instead of handing her over to Andre, the Black Tide leader. The Ravenwoods sat on the good side of the black warlock coin. Other good black warlocks existed, but Sage was uber paranoid. Any new warlock in their midst now needed vetting to the nth degree by Sage, Rafael, *and* the Ravenwoods.

"What are you three doing if Sage grants you a hall

pass?" Eden asked. Eden would pay to hole up on the covenstead until they pried her fingers off her keyboard or off a book. But she'd expressed a desire to surround herself with books at the library or a bookstore. As a successful novelist, Eden's jam was none other than books.

"I'm hitting the beach," Brianne replied. "Aspen and I need the ocean and not that stupid babbling trickle."

Marina shrugged. "I wanted to follow a ley line that extends past the property line and try a few spells on it. Rafael said he'd hang with me, but Sage didn't want her head security witch and warlock off the grounds together in case crap tipped sideways." As an earth witch, Marina had an affinity to the ley lines. They were one of the few covens in California on such hallowed ground.

Footsteps intruded upon their moment. "Trouble times four." Rafael approached from behind. "What do I need to fix?" Sage's First Warlock, fiancé, and second-in-coven-command stood tall and gorgeous in his dark business suit, which he wore when meeting clients on the outside. Aspen fanned the heat blooming on her face. She'd always carried the hots for Rafael, as did most witches in the coven. But none would ever make a play for him, since he and Sage were starstruck over each other. And engaged.

"Why do you get to leave the covenstead and we don't?" Brianne rounded on Rafael.

"You're going there again." Rafael twisted the knob on Sage's office door. "Try that line on someone who isn't a black warlock and can hold his own."

"Did you just insult us?" Eden whacked Rafael's shoulder. "And you're a black warlock newbie. So don't get all ego-centric with us experienced witches."

"Yep. Insult." Brianne wiggled her fingers, and water misted Rafael's slick, dark hair.

He opened the door, trying to deflect the water with his newfound powers of air magic. "Sage, call your witches off me." A tiny typhoon whipped the mist into a decorative bowl on a sideboard in a mini whirlpool.

Sage sat behind the desk and laughed. "You're good with your air magic, my love." Aspen's blonde-bombshell sister and coven leader rose from her chair behind their mother's former desk and gave her attention to Aspen.

"Don't look at me." Aspen waved her hands in front of her face. "Look at the other blondie. Brianne's the one ready to fly over the cuckoo's nest." Brianne and Marina weren't identical twins, and Brianne had lost the Wilde auburn-hair gene to the shimmering gold and blonde Sage also sported. Although Marina had darkened her hair to a shade of night.

Rafael sidled around the desk and kissed Sage's cheek, gloved her hand in his own. "They want out. Should we take them on a field trip?"

Sage scowled. "No."

"Come on, Sage!" Brianne blasted her. "Marina can kill the gate ward and let us out. Would you rather we went on a jailbreak?"

Sage sighed and melted against Rafael. "I wish you all had warlocks for protection."

Marina scoffed. "A witch's magic is stronger than a warlock. How 'bout we agree to pair up, sign in and out, three-hour increments?"

Brianne beamed sunshine bright. "Now I can wrap my head around that."

Sage straightened, pushed away from Rafael. "Two gone at one time, and on-the-hour text check-ins."

The whoops and screams deafened, and Aspen covered her ears.

"Come on, Aspen, let's hit it." Brianne bulldozed through the noise.

"Wait, what about me?" Marina stood, hands on her hips, the light freckles on the bridge of her nose deepening.

"You two go," Aspen shot out, her glee racing her heart. "I'll go next. I just got a delivery message from the gate, and I'm gonna make energy gummies."

"Please make your cherry gummies." Rafael drooled at the gummy mention. He'd eat them like candy if she let him.

"Go." Sage waved her hand through the air. "Before I change my mind. Stay safe, stay together, and watch your backs. Don't use magic."

Brianne and Marina scattered like embers on a windy day.

"Our turn tomorrow." Eden hooked her arm in Aspen's, and they left Sage's office.

"Sure," Aspen said, and they parted in the hallway. She waited for Eden's footsteps to drift up the stairs before she bolted toward the kitchen. She raised a thin water curtain to hide behind and dashed through the kitchen to the side door before any kitchen staff caught a sniff of her. They might find a few puddles on the floor in her wake.

Aspen scurried into the perimeter woods where she'd stashed her motorcycle in an old garden shed four days ago, along with her helmet and empty saddlebags, ready and waiting for just this moment.

She rolled the bike through uneven terrain and onto an ill-used path cutting through the woods. Rocks scattered the path, and weeds and ruts made it uneven. Took a moment for tiny beads of sweat to pop on her neck, leaving her panting like a marathon runner. But her excitement to leave the grounds cut through any pain or exhaustion. The idea of zooming down the road on her bike, wind cutting around her, fueled her needs. She stuck her earbuds in her ears and cranked up her favorite alternative rock music.

By the time she reached the old emergency gate at the ill-used side of the property, she paused for a breather. She gathered her thoughts to slice through the wards protecting the property without killing herself or alerting the entire coven. A moment to remember the black magic spell she'd memorized.

The protective ward on the perimeter fence and gate crackled against her. As she stepped closer to the gate, a solid weight pushed on her lungs and drove the air out of her.

Chapter 2

Gasping, Aspen sucked in deep breaths through murky air, fighting the ward's push against her lungs. Magic enveloped her and her hands shook. Not enough to impede her escape, but holy hell.

She'd worked on her escape spell and tested it at least a half dozen times. First three times, she'd caused a blip on the ley lines and it alerted Marina. Rafael and Sage swallowed Marina's explanation that the lines blip all the time without affecting the wards. Marina had no clue Aspen caused it. The idea and chance to escape house arrest were too enticing. No one on the covenstead ever went to the old gardening shed, not with all the other defined paths and hiking trails. Marina never checked the old, rusty gate for the blip.

Had Marina beefed up her wards? The magic shimmered over her, and she voiced a counter-spell, regaining her composure. A few moments later, the pressure of the ward lessened. Grinning, she slipped on her helmet, braces, and gloves for her getaway and for protection if her spells went assbackwards. Incanting another counter-spell to pause the protective wards, she skimmed her fingers over the gate railings to impart her magic. She dribbled a counter-spell potion on the lock, and the lock clicked, slid open, and dangled in place. She recited the final spell to kill the ward, which guaranteed a microscopic blip on the ley line. With Marina gone, the sole witch tied to the lines, no one else would feel it. Sage would go full-on medieval if she discovered Aspen was brewing black curses and using them to break their wards. Aspen craved a way to contribute to the impending war with the black warlocks, and learning to defeat them by potions, charms, and curses dumped her front and center in the game. No one else in the coven possessed her unique abilities to brew curses and practice alchemy.

"So mote it be," she whispered. The sizzling magic surrounding her receded. "Yeah, baby!" She mentally high-fived herself. After steering her bike through the gate, she locked it behind her. To re-stitch the break she made, she invoked a warding spell and walked along the fence line for ten feet in each direction to spread her spell outward.

Halfway to the main road from the old fire road, she hit the ignition on her bike and jetted off the property. Wind whistled around her, a rush she'd missed. The thrum of the motorcycle between her legs was almost as good as sex. Sage once said it was the only action Aspen got. She'd take it! No relationship repercussions on a bike.

Aspen whooped and hollered. The power and speed trampled all her guilt and inhibitions. Exhilaration filled her internal tank after a boring month-long lockdown. But the month in her lab brewing potions and learning curses was a month she'd never regret. No one knew of her research, a big reason she didn't want Brianne or anyone else shadowing her in town.

The farther she sped down the twisty road through the hills to the coastal town of Santa Cruz, the more the sun peeked through the clearing fog. She reveled in the sun on her despite her motorcycle garb covering her from head to toe. By the time she reached town limits, joy and energy had refueled her body, mind, and soul. The rush of adrenaline thumped in her ears.

She parked at the side of the Sand Dollar Pharmacy near downtown, which contained an apothecary and herb shop. The place catered to witches, but the owner didn't promote it to the general public. Although witches didn't have to hide from the world, non-magicals were paranoid of them. Dr. Lorenzo, the shop owner, always seemed discreet and friendly to witches. His shop carried unusual witch paraphernalia that other places didn't, including herbs Aspen couldn't order online. And a witch sometimes had a hankering to sniff and touch the goods.

As she stowed her protective gear, she opened her senses to gauge magic in the air, on the ground, anywhere in her proximity. A fishy, briny tinge accompanied the breeze, the seaside town's natural elements. Not a skosh of magic tingled her senses. The ocean beckoned her witch-water element, but instead of the compulsion to the boardwalk and wharf, business swayed her. The ocean wasn't going anywhere. Plus, she didn't want to risk running into Brianne and Marina, knowing they'd headed straight to the boardwalk for their favorite amusement park foods and Brianne's dip in the ocean.

The bell above the door tinkled, announcing her arrival. The attention the tinkle caused squirmed through Aspen. Not that she needed to hide from people, she didn't want word to reach Sage. A few people shopped the shelves of over-the-counter meds, snacks, and touristy gifts. Aspen headed straight to the open door to the left, into the herb room.

"Hey, Miss Aspen. Long time no see," Dr. Lorenzo called to her from behind the pharmacy counter where he was helping another customer. "Let me know if you need help."

"Hiya, Doc. Will do." The moment she slipped into the herb shop, myriad scents filled her senses, energized her like nothing else in the world except the ocean. In her element, she wandered the room, touching the pouches, jars, and packaged items, checked out new and exclusive stock behind the glass counter.

As she snagged a canvas shopping tote, magic fringed her aura and teased her witch-water. Water spritzed from her fingers, and she flung off the drops in a random pattern, not wanting to leave puddles in the shop. Bad customer. The magic strengthened, and she backed against a far wall behind a rack of local herbs. Witch-fire. More than witch magic, or more than one witch. A black warlock? Subtle magic, but dynamic, like a new bonded warlock learning his bonding witch's powers. Yet, there wasn't another customer in the alcove. She dropped the tote on the floor to free her hands and cleared her mind to induce her defensive witch-water.

Two colorful surfboards bracketed a sailor's net dotted with all variety of shells on the far shiplap wall in harmony with the coastal town. A recent addition since she'd shopped there last. The door opened behind the counter, and an aura blast slammed her, frazzling her nerves.

He walked through, and the door shut behind him. Aspen's heart skipped a couple of beats. Goddess, he was the most beautiful man. As handsome as Rafael and the Ravenwood brothers, all gods among men, turning heads wherever they went. Why hadn't she noticed his good looks when she'd spied him last month for the first time since high school graduation? He possessed an aura that leant him an ethereal light, enhancing every feature of his chiseled face. About six feet tall, he stood with a firm, lanky build in a red T-shirt and board shorts covered by a black shop apron. The store logo, a sand dollar in sea grass, emblazoned the front of the apron. Lucky Lorenzo had changed so much since high school. Once a boy, now all sculpted, gorgeous, and confident man. She licked her lips, smoothed her hands down her leather jacket.

Despite Sage's forced lockdown, Aspen found life good, working in her lab, running her webstore, living on the covenstead. But the minute she spied Lucky, the second time since high school graduation, she had an odd feeling the gates sprang open to her real life. The sensation consumed her, and she almost stopped breathing. She'd never experienced this reaction to Lucky in high school. She'd liked and admired him from afar, but he steered clear of the witches. They ran in way different cliques.

"Can I help you?" He toted a self-possessed air about him, but as he addressed her, it faltered. His face remained passive, no smile, no grimace, just blank. Did he not recognize her? Had she changed so much since high school?

Aspen startled from his reaction and the magic drifting off him. She thought she knew of all the witches in Santa Cruz and their warlocks. Who had bonded him? Where had the witch hidden him? Or was there a new witch in town? She'd seen him a month ago from a distance in the pharmacy and sensed magic wafting off him like an unbonded warlock. But today, no way. A witch had bonded him since. Or was he a black warlock? In high school, she'd sensed no magic about him. But then, she didn't excel at sensing warlocks by their auras like Sage.

"Hey," she greeted. "Loading up on supplies." She acted nonchalant, let the chips fall as they fell. "Do you work here?" *Duh, mental forehead smack.* She pointed to the surfboards. "You surf?"

"My dad's the owner. Yeah, I'm easing back into surfing."

"Oh. I've been shopping here for years. Never seen you."

A healthy coastal tan glowed on his clean-shaven face and strong jawline. His wavy, highlighted brown hair fell to the top of his stiff shoulders. "Guess you can't know everyone in the world, right?" He turned away from her.

"Guess not." His animosity caused Aspen's defensive witch-water to rise. Guess he didn't remember her. "I'll finish my shopping and hit it." Before she reached for her shopping tote where it'd fallen, he'd skirted the counter, picked up the tote, and handed it to her. Water spritzed off their skin where they touched, and he jerked his hand away.

"Sorry." Was he a black warlock who held his own magic and had hidden it? Maybe that's why he appeared in the shop at the same time they'd captured the leader of the Black Tide. Rafael even had a sparse, non-illuminating dossier on him.

He returned to stand behind the counter, putting maximum distance between them in the cramped room. "Let me know if you need help," he said in a grumpy grumble.

Aspen darted down the aisles of the store and stuffed her bag, checking her list on her phone to ensure she snagged everything. Who knew when she'd escape the covenstead again? If she got caught, Sage would plunk a chain and lock on her door. The last items on the list required him to fill from cannisters behind the counter. Swallowing hard, she approached the counter where he sat reading an old leather-bound book. Her curiosity perked up. Old research books were her thing, especially ones on certain topics, like brewing potions and herbal remedies. He stood and hid the book on the floor as if she'd caught him holding stolen goods.

Two browsing women entered the room. Non-witches. Pagan wannabes. Aspen couldn't recite the items on the list without giving herself away and showed him her screen. "I need the last four items on the list in the quantity noted." Her spine went rigid as she waited for the expected horror or backlash.

Concentrating and face bland, he measured the herbs into plastic zip bags, labeled, and handed them to her. "Anything else?" he asked.

"What were you reading?" She couldn't resist the press of her curiosity.

He reddened. "Nothing. An old book from the attic."

Aspen sensed she'd overstepped. She paid for her items and took the sack he handed her.

"Thanks for your business. Come again." A callous afterthought.

"Sure. See ya." An uneasy feeling bogged her down as she sidled out of the store, unable to pinpoint if his brusque nature or the magic he exuded caused her the willies. More magic than an unbonded warlock's powerful aura.

The moment she finished securing her items in her saddlebags, magic slammed her, powerful and intense. A ring of blue fire encapsulated her and her bike, securing her in an inescapable fiery cocoon. She spun around but didn't see anyone along the side alley where she'd parked. When she raised her witch-water and sprayed the ring, the fire sputtered and reignited. Despite invoking a counter-spell to kill the fire magic, the fire ring thickened and dried her magic.

Black magic.

Goosebumps erupted on her skin, each raising a tremor of impending disaster. Sage had locked down the covenstead because of black magic and black warlocks. *Dammit all to Hades in a freaking handbasket.* Because of Lucky preoccupying her and her excitement at gathering fresh supplies, she'd forgotten to scope her surroundings for magic. *Keep your shit together, stupid witch.*

Rio, her seagull familiar, dove up her neck from her

chest and launched off her shoulder, trailing threads of water magic in its webbed feet. The familiar escaped the ring of fire before the ring encompassed her completely. The water threads were no match against the black warlock.

"Who's there? What do you want?" Her voice quavered.

A man stepped from behind the rear of the pharmacy. Blond highlighted the tips of his spikey black hair, framing a too-dark tanned face. If he didn't curb his tanning, he'd sport leather skin in another ten years. Although short and stocky, Aspen was no physical match to fight him.

"No need to trade names. I want a piece of the Wilde pie. Two birds. One pie today." Grinning, he scrubbed his hands together. How did he know her identity? Did the Wildes exude a unique scent or aura? She almost dipped her head to sniff her pits. "I can knock you out and carry you, or you can come willingly. Your choice." His grin widened. "You're the score of the year so far. No one's caught hide nor hair of a Wilde witch for over a month."

Why'd she ever decide to defy Sage? Sage was the Wilde High Priestess, leader of the Wilde coven and the entire western region for a reason. Her sister had called it. The Wildes sat at the top of the Black Tide's hit list. No doubt the dude was a charter member of Andre Charlemagne's stupid-ass group of fierce black warlocks.

"I don't have a beef with you. Take a hike, and I'll pretend I never laid eyes on you. Never heard you threaten me." As a water witch, she used witchcraft to power water to do her bidding, and she used magic-infused water to create potent potions and magical charms. But her dabbling in black magic hadn't reached prime time.

Wait, what? The black magic potion she used to open the lock might work to halt his magic enough to escape on her bike. She'd have to report the incident to Sage, so she didn't need the potion to sneak through the gate. And what did he mean by two birds? She glanced around. Not another soul near the pharmacy. Rio hid in a cypress tree near the warlock, and Aspen felt the familiar's pluck on her witch-water, ready to do her bidding or fly to her aid. The warlock hadn't yet added a ward to his fire ring, and she still had use of her magic.

The man grinned and advanced a step. "Is the fire addling your brain, Aspen Wilde? Your family stole from us. We want *him* back."

"Us? We?" Aspen gestured around her, then gripped her fanny pack. "Where are your friends?"

"I think you know what I mean." As he moved a few steps closer to her, his grin never faltered.

The fire ring expanded, and sweat formed beneath her breasts. She wanted to mist her broiling face but couldn't afford to use magic on herself. Magic use came with a price, and she must conserve her funds to spend on him when the door opened. She flicked a glimpse at Rio, and their bond vibrated in her chest.

Aspen eased open the rear zipper pocket on her fanny pack. "So, you think retrieving *him* will help you? Don't ya think controlling the Black Tide without him gives you more street cred and power?" She fisted the potion bottle. "Or do you need him to call the shots because you little minions haven't found a clue on how to operate?"

His wide grin slowly faded away, replaced by a flicker of uncertainty. She'd hit a nerve. Which meant the Black Tide needed Andre. A lightbulb flicked on in her brain. Were they bound to Andre? *Holy freaking hell on earth.* Their magic was less potent with Andre's magic tied in knots. The crazy idea stuttered her thoughts.

"Or do you need his magic?" She uncorked the vial, clenching the cork in her fist.

He lunged toward her, stopping short of the fire ring. Mark hit, and boy had she grabbed the brass ring of brass rings.

"You don't know what you're talking about. Keep your questions and theories to yourself, you dumb witch."

Despite the fire ring's heat, Aspen shivered. How had they not thought of this conundrum? Whether Andre's black warlocks, if bonded to him, would need his magic for full strength. Their allies, the Ravenwoods, had revealed nothing about it. But Andre practiced earth and water. This dude used fire, so fire was his own magic. Not all panned out in her theory.

"Just so you know, your fire is keeping you from me as much as it's holding me hostage," she quipped. "A punishable offense by human laws, not only the witchworld."

Before she blinked, the fire ring splintered. Blue sparks showered the air, and the warlock lunged for her. Water spouted off her, drenching them both. A wave tried to separate them, but his arms latched around her waist from behind. She inched her hand holding the vial from his locked arms. Using good old-fashioned self-defense, she back-kicked his shin, and he yelped, but didn't release his hold. Dancing blue flames flickered and spit off him.

Rio joined the fray and wrapped the warlock in water, dampening his fire before it scorched Aspen. She thrust wave after wave of water, but it did nothing against his black magic holding her magic at bay. Countering with his own waves of water, he proved her point that he may be bonded to Andre and using Andre's water magic. So much water, she sputtered.

"You're shit out of luck, girl," he spat in her wet face. "Give it up now, and I'll go easy on you."

"Screw you and the asshole you hitched a ride in on." Aspen cut the spigot to her water and sprinkled the contents of the vial on his left arm. The potion sizzled and burned through his shirt. An acidic scent of charred cotton mixed with the herbs rose into the air.

He bellowed and released her, bloody murder bulging the muscles in his neck. "What did you do?" He gripped his arm to his torso. His fire magic sizzled in the wake of his evaporating water magic.

Aspen sprinted toward her bike, the wind rushing through her ears. His thumping footsteps chased. She hopped on her bike, gunned it, popping a wheely in her haste that left her shuddering as her butt hit the seat. Flying over her head, Rio caught up to her when she had to wait for a few pedestrians on the sidewalk.

"Come on! Come on!" Running over people never hit her bucket list. The warlock shoved her from behind, and she toppled to the pavement, snapping her leg out from beneath her bike before it landed on top of her. Although a small bike, it still had a damaging heft.

With a powerful leap, Aspen soared into the sky, leaving behind a spinning cyclone of water. Rio snatched the magic and flew in a circle to enhance and hustle the water's movement. Her whirlpool sucked the warlock into the vortex and slammed him against the building next to the pharmacy. Soaked, he slumped to the ground and conked out.

By the time Aspen's vision cleared, the pedestrians had scattered, and Lucky was zip-tying the warlock's hands behind his back. He tugged the man against the wall of the pharmacy and zip-tied him to a steel fence post. She prodded her fingers beneath her blouse, and they landed on Rio's tail feathers. Safe and unharmed.

"Should I call nine-one-one?" Lucky asked. "Damn, you're one fierce witch." Intelligence and a trace of humor sparkled in his deep, teal-blue eyes. Why hadn't she noticed the unique color before? And why hadn't she noticed his full and inviting lips below his straight, well-proportioned nose? High school memories arose, and she recalled her paranoia of locking eyes with him, each time diverting her gaze before she lost herself in the fantasy of him. She was as sunk now as she was then.

Examining the broken handle on her bike, she fought her gathering tears.

"Need a ride?" His voice soothed, a far cry from his earlier Grumpy McGrumpy.

She crouched beside her bike and wiped a hand across her eyes. Her other hand ached from hitting the ground, and she gave up unbuckling her saddlebag and rubbed her palm.

He squatted next to her. "Here." He took her hand in his firm, smooth grip. "Let me see."

Aspen let him, and his touch electrified her, sending jolts through her entire body. A total about-face from his attitude in the store.

"No broken skin. I'll clean it and take you home. We'll load your bike in my truck."

"Can you load that jerk too? My coven leader will want to interrogate him."

He hesitated, considering. "If you want. Better than leaving him tied up here."

Still holding her hand, he helped her stand on her noodle legs. She hefted her bags over her shoulder, swept her wet hair back.

"By the way, I'm Lucky Lorenzo."

"I know. I'm Aspen Wilde."

"I know."

"Do you remember we went to high school together?" She squinted, waited for his response.

"When I read your name on your credit card, I remembered."

"Liar."

He shrugged, grinned. "Yeah, I remember. We didn't exactly run in the same circles."

"So, Lucky, how lucky are you?" Resistance was futile.

"Up to you, I guess." He guided her through the rear door of the shop, and she blinked back her surprise and curiosity.

He grinned his swoon-worthy grin again. "Do you know how many times people have used that line on me?"

She sat on the stool he gestured to, dumping her bags at her feet on the glossy cement floor. "Oh, thought I was one of a kind. Bummer."

"Believe me, you *are* one of a kind," he said in her ear, drew back, his face red and discomfited. "I want to apologize for my prior 'tude. Just an adverse reaction."

"To me?"

"It's complicated." He busied himself doctoring her hand.

An awkward, but not uncomfortable silence reigned until they returned to the alley. Aspen helped him load her bike and the grousing, kicking warlock into his truck bed. They tied the warlock's legs together and taped his mouth.

"Do you always carry zip ties in your back pocket?"

Lucky chuckled, and Aspen wanted to drown in the infectious sound. "A new bag of ties sat on the back stoop, which I meant to stash in the garage."

Like a perfect gentleman, he opened the passenger door and helped her hike up into the tall pickup. The truck interior smelled of spice and the sea. Like him. She picked up his leather motorcycle jacket and sniffed it. As he slid into the driver's side, she tossed the soft, worn jacket on the center console.

Once they hit the road, Aspen realized she'd allowed a near stranger to drive her home and no red flags flapped in the wind. And she didn't need to tell him where she lived by the direction he drove. Did the Wilde name mean something to everyone? Or had he stalked her since their high school days? Was she leading a nightmare or two to the covenstead?

Chapter 3

A spen hadn't noticed the calls and text messages blowing up her phone until lulled by the drone of the truck engine in the quiet cab. She dreaded Sage's disappointment and let the calls roll to voicemail. Every mile Lucky drove toward the covenstead, her head told her she'd made the right decision in leaving the grounds and bringing Lucky and the warlock to Sage. Both possessed magic not on the Wildes' radar. One was an Andre Charlemagne minion who might help them ferret out Andre's plans within the Black Tide. Plus, Sage was the best magic and warlock detector. She may get to the root of Lucky's magic and identity if he refuses to give them the four-one-one.

Aspen finger-combed her long, damp hair. She'd lost an earbud and stuck the other in her fanny pack, anything to distract herself from the man sitting beside her. When Lucky turned onto the street leading to the covenstead, she cast him a sidelong glance. "How do you know where I live?"

He white-knuckled the steering wheel, his skin a stark

contrast to the black leather. "Everyone in town knows where the Wilde covenstead's located."

"Bull. We're not famous."

Sweat peppered his temples. "My father keeps tabs on the witches in the area, you know, for business purposes. You're on his mailing list."

"Try again. We don't receive snail mail from the pharmacy." Aspen readied her witch-water, unsure where the conversation headed. Magic roiled inside her, and water dripped off her index finger to the floorboard.

Before they hit the periphery of the short driveway to the gate, he pulled alongside the road, and turned to her. "For real, I was on a bike ride years ago when I stopped in your driveway and saw the Wilde name scrolled in the wrought iron. An elaborate gothic gate containing a fortress. You don't see that around here."

"Why didn't you say so in the first place?" Aspen sensed him holding back, but she didn't want to press him toward an aggressive situation. Who knew what kind of magic he wielded?

"Didn't want you to think I was stalking you." He tapped his blunt fingertips on the dash. His fingernails had a straight trim, rather than gnawed stubs like many men Aspen met.

The warlock beneath the tarp in the truck bed banged against the sidewalls. Since they'd muffled him, he used his body for attention.

"Knock it off," Lucky pounded the rear window. "Are we safe from his magic?"

"I used a spell to bind his magic but it won't last much longer." Aspen gestured at him. "Pull up to the gate." She texted security at their new pre-fab gatehouse inside the locked and warded gate. They now maintained witches on twenty-four-seven gate duty. After the Helwig witches and their black warlock minions stormed the covenstead a few weeks ago, the Wildes had remained on high alert.

Lucky drove forward and parked in front of the closed gate. "Why the security?"

Aspen settled her attention on the side of his head, liking the way his wavy hair feathered in all the right places. "It's complicated." She threw his words back at him.

Ricky and his wife, Leah, approached the gate without opening it. Ricky had been Sage's warlock six years ago when she'd first met Rafael. A year afterward, Rafael became her First Warlock. Sage had to break her bond to Ricky so he could marry Leah, an earth witch, perfect for ground security.

"Hang tight." Aspen jumped out of the truck and strode to the gate. "How mad is Sage?"

"It's not Sage you need to kowtow to, it's Rafael," Ricky said. "Who's the warlock?"

Aspen gasped. "He's not a warlock." Who was she kidding? "He's Dr. Lorenzo's son, the man who owns the Sand Dollar Pharmacy and Apothecary."

Ricky landed a look on Aspen, leaving little to the imagination on the stupid meter. "He's a warlock. Jeez, even I can sense magic on him. Maybe *he* doesn't know it."

"Guess so. Are you gonna open the gate or what?"

The warlock in the cargo engaged in another ruckus, rolling and hitting the sidewalls.

"What the hell, Aspen?" Ricky shouted. Leah's earth magic coalesced into ivy vines sprouting from the sides of the driveway and surrounding the truck. Defense or capture. Didn't matter. The goon was toast when Leah invoked her ivy. "What's going on?"

Leaving tons of plot holes, Aspen related what'd happened in town. "Sage will want to interrogate the black warlock. You know she will."

"I want to interrogate the asshole myself." Ricky hit the remote on the gate. "Then I want you to tell me how you escaped the property with no one knowing. Rafael's jumping off the rails."

"Yep." Leah touched Ricky's arm to calm him, her skin stark white against his multicolor-tattoo arm sleeve. "You left a security hole. I'll work with Marina to plug it." She called Rafael on the two-way radio and told him to arrange a team to meet the truck.

Shame roasted Aspen's cheeks. "I plugged the hole."

Leah rolled her eyes. "You can't plug Marina's wards completely. No one can."

Ricky approached the driver's door, and Lucky rolled down his window. "One wrong move and you're a dead man. Got it?"

"Yeah. Figured the lay of the land."

"Follow the driveway to the front of the house and take the left fork at the circle. A security team will meet you." Ricky glared at Aspen. "Get in the truck, ward yourself, and watch him."

Aspen returned to the truck cab, sans ward, and Lucky drove through the gate at the pace of a snail. "They gonna off me?" he asked.

"No, but you'll need to spend cycles explaining who you are to our coven leader's First Warlock and head of security, Rafael Reyes."

His death grip on the steering wheel intensified. "I'm a normal dude. Can't I drop you off and go?"

"A normal dude." She snickered. "You really think you're normal?"

He coughed. "No different from high school. Older, more educated."

And so much more gorgeous. She stretched her arm over the center console and rested her fingers on his bare forearm, loving the strength beneath. "No, Lucky. You're more. Haven't you felt it? You've changed since high school. I sense magic in you I didn't then."

He sped up the truck a smidge to reach the house faster. The uncomfortable truth lingered, another lost warlock among the human world.

Witches and warlocks waited by the side of the house that led to the security suite in the basement. Lucky parked but didn't budge from his seat.

"I suppose they're not gonna let me leave, are they?"

The gang surrounded the truck, and two warlocks removed the tarp off the truck bed.

"They won't hurt you unless you threaten me or them. This is my family." Aspen gripped the door handle.

"Can you really sense my magic, or whatever it is?"

"Sure can."

He picked at the hem of his shirt. "I have to confess. We've connected in a way I've never connected to another witch, and I've been near a lot of witches in the store."

Aspen's eyelids blinked up a breeze. "What?" Had she sensed a connection or had she merely chalked it up to randomness? If he held magic, he was no doubt a black warlock.

He'd changed his clothes before they'd left the pharmacy, and he plucked a sachet of herbs from his pants pocket. "I masked the connection once I realized it." He stuffed the tiny bag in the ashtray.

The warlock in the bed fought the warlocks dragging him out, but didn't deter Aspen from continuing her conversation, despite Sage scowling at her by the basement door.

The scents permeating the sachet confirmed his truth. Aspen had used such rudimentary herbology during her learning years. "Why haven't I seen you in the shop before now?" she asked. "Where'd you go after high school?"

"Berkeley. Just finished my master's in chemical engineering."

Chemical engineering was the perfect background for

an apothecarist. But she'd dwell on that tantalizing tidbit later. A slew of glowering witches converged upon the truck.

"Stick with me and I'll protect you. Don't tell anyone you contain magic. Sage and a few witches will sense it even through the herbs. Don't use magic or they'll know you're a black warlock." She shoved the herbal bag at him.

He stuck the sachet back in his pocket. "I'm not a black warlock." His voice was like ice shards scraping against stone. "I can't be."

"Then you're bonded to a witch?" Aspen locked the door to prevent the witches outside from opening it.

"No." He raked his hand through his hair.

"Lucky," she pleaded. "Do you want to know who you are?"

"I don't know. It's complicated."

"Life's complicated." She squeezed his hand lying on his thigh. "Let's get this witch hunt over with, then you can decide. Or leave and never look back."

Aspen opened her door and motioned Rafael closer. His dark mask primed to kill her, Lucky, or something. "This is Lucky Lorenzo." Rafael did a double take. Lucky was already on Rafael's radar after the first time Aspen saw him before the lockdown. "He wants to talk to you and Sage alone."

"And you," Lucky added. "I won't talk without you."

"That's a given," she tossed over her shoulder. "Rafael, get everyone to back off. He's not a danger."

"You know we're restricting people on the covenstead," Rafael grumbled. He gripped her arm, and Lucky growled at him.

"Rafael, love." Sage approached. "Let her go. I'll deal with her."

Rafael's jaw clenched and unclenched. He released his grip and massaged her arm over her jacket. "Sorry."

She sniffed. "Chill, dude. Sheesh." She pushed past him and Sage and skirted the front of the truck to stand beside Lucky, now surrounded by six witches and warlocks. "Back off, feral people. Been so long since you've seen an outsider, you gotta attack the first one you see? Jeez, Louise." After surveying her motorcycle, making sure the warlocks treated it well, she led Lucky toward the basement door. She breathed in the clean evergreen and pine scents of the surrounding woods. One last lungful of freedom.

Lucky kinked his head to the side. "Who was that man who manhandled you?"

"He's my sister's warlock and fiancé, Rafael, head of security. She's the High Priestess of the entire western region."

"Well, he shouldn't touch you like that," Lucky groused, following her down the stairs, a tail of witches and warlocks behind them.

Emotion swamped Aspen, and she wanted to whisk Lucky away and talk without the angry mob. No boy, man, or warlock had ever considered or catered to her feelings. An eye-opening moment she wanted to savor.

"I'll pay him back with a nasty digestive potion in his drink later."

Lucky winced. "Hate to get on your bad side."

"I doubt you'll ever land there." Aspen reached the large open space in the center of the basement.

As they waited for Rafael and Sage, the angry mob surrounded them. Warlocks carted the kicking and fighting mystery warlock inside the cell Andre Charlemagne had occupied when they'd first bagged him. A band of witch-air muffled his mouth.

Magic connected to Lucky from all angles like nothing he'd ever experienced, a conduit to all the witches in the room. His untapped magic instigated and unleased a minor storm. Water misted the room, fire and wind drying it and blowing it away.

"Cut the magic." Rafael joined the group. "Unless you're warding the black warlock."

A chorus of "not my magic" and other denials rang out. All heads swiveled in Lucky's direction. Water funneled again and swished above their heads, the basement boiling as the water drizzled upon them. Heat rolled over Aspen. She jerked away from Lucky, but he held her gaze and then his gaze bounced to every person in the room.

In a surrendering gesture, Lucky raised his hands, wide-eyed fear in his expression. "I can explain." How could he when he didn't know what he did? He bolted toward the stairs. Two witches tried to stop him, and he shoved through them and took the stairs three at a time. He barreled straight into Sage on the landing blocking the door to the outside.

Chapter 4

Sparks and wind funneled off the witch blocking his path. The coven High Priestess. Lucky floundered and knocked into her as he caught himself on the banister. They fell in a tangled heap on the landing. Before he could lift away from her, Rafael yanked him off Sage, his brute strength something to behold.

"Off my witch, asshole." Rafael's voice was a low menacing growl. Literal steam billowed from his collar.

Panting, Lucky hung his head, gathered his thoughts. "I'm sorry. I didn't mean to hurt her... you." He nodded at Sage.

"Ben, stow him in the other cell. Set a protective ward." He nudged Lucky toward an older warlock. "If I see you raise one hair of magic again, you're a dead man." Rafael ensured Sage was in one piece, kissing away her frown.

The noise in Lucky's head killed the thoughts pinging his brain. The fire magic streaming off him lambasted him. He'd never experienced the like. The moment he'd entered the room, magic hit him from all sides, connecting deep in his core, and he lost his tightly held control. Something he vowed never to allow happen, the reason he steered clear of witches and warlocks, once he'd determined he held his own magic. Magic he hated with all his might.

Ben wrenched his arms behind his back, and a witch tied his wrists together in a solid band of air. The air band felt like a thick, unrelenting rubber strap. He ranted against the manhandling, but no sound erupted from his mouth. Air muzzled him, but at least he could hear. The words flowing into his head iced his blood. Ominous words of imprisonment, protective wards, isolation.

"Please," he tried to say. "Let me explain." His desperate gaze pinned Aspen in place. A tremor of fear crossed her face, like a shadow blocking the moonlight. He'd lost her too, the only person who might've helped him. They'd connected, a comfortable connection, not like the caustic magic in the basement from the now antagonistic Wilde witches and their warlocks. The same faint thread that'd tethered them in high school. One reason he'd avoided her, despite wanting to know *everything* about her. The herbal sachet was useless now. Every witch in the room had witnessed his dumb impulsive mistake.

Ben dumped him in a small room, rocking two straight-backed steel chairs and a twin bed. A half-ajar door hid a small bathroom. An older witch with Ben removed the muzzle, but not the band on his wrists. They split from the room and closed the door on the bleach-tinged space. The oppressiveness in the air weighed on his lungs. The ward altered his normally adrenalized veins and limbs into sluggish snails. If he possessed magic entering the room, it had fled. No big loss. He didn't want it. Or did he? The surge he'd created gave way to an inner excitement despite his abhorrence.

He scoped the room, little more than a large closet. Not even a window cut through the cement-block walls or steel door. He shook his head, flinging off his thoughts. No way did he expect to spend the night. For one, his dad would search for him if he didn't call or return home for dinner, a weeknight routine they'd established. Although twenty-six, he'd returned home to help this dad after he completed his long stint at Berkeley. Time for payback for all his father's support and tuition.

A thump knocked the door, and Lucky jumped in his chair, his arm jamming into the steel-framed back. Stars accompanied the pain he couldn't rub away. The door flung open, and Rafael barreled through, shutting it behind him, a loud thud vibrating the doorframe.

The fierce warlock hulked near the door, a storm roiling on his swarthy face. "Who are you, Luciano Lucky Lorenzo?"

"You know. You got the name right."

"I researched you when you hit our radar a month ago. Where'd you come from?"

Indignation swirled through Lucky. Rafael rowed up crap creek on the information waterways. "Where's Aspen? Is she okay?"

"She's not your business."

"Is. She. okay?" His indignation morphed into passionate fury.

Rafael seemed taken aback. "She's fine. Now tell me who you are and where you came from?"

"If you've done your research, you tell me what you know."

Rafael crossed his arms and adopted a defensive stance blocking the door. As if Lucky had a chance to escape. He seemed to mull over his next he-man outburst. "You attended Berkeley. What degree?"

"Chemical engineering. Bachelor's and master's."

Arms loosening, Rafael nodded. "Your father has owned the Sand Dollar since it opened in the nineties, which meant you attended school in Santa Cruz."

"Ninety-two. And big deal. Lot of people attended school in town."

"You were in high school with some of the Wilde witches."

"Again, where's the crime?"

"Your father's not from a family of witches. No intel on your mother's maiden name. Who is she?"

Grief so strong assaulted Lucky, a white haze fringed his vision for a second. Someone had killed Lucky's mother when he was twelve, but the police never identified the suspect. A hit-and-run when she was on her morning run. Anger took control again. So much for a welcoming committee. Why'd he think Aspen Wilde might help him figure out his life? Why'd he ever believe the lure toward the Wilde covenstead a month ago was so real he couldn't resist it? What could these witches want from him or his lame magic?

"Can you release the band on my wrists?" he asked, contrite and controlled. "Whatever magic you sense... I don't know. I mean, it's random. Comes and goes. I don't have control over it."

"No." Rafael flexed his arm muscles, a sign and a threat. "Fool me once."

The door opened a few inches, knocking into Rafael. "Let me in," a woman's authoritative and sultry tone ordered.

Rafael opened the door for Sage Wilde, the High Priestess of the entire western region. Aside from Aspen, she was the most beautiful woman he'd ever seen, although, he gravitated toward women with brown or red hair. Like Aspen's hair.

"Rafael." She gave him a blank stare. "You have a gun." She waggled her fingers in Lucky's direction, and the opaque band dissipated, enabling him to separate his wrists. She spun in a circle and uttered words he couldn't hear. "The room's warded."

He rubbed his wrists where the air bands had cut into his skin. Who'd thunk it that air could hurt?

"Hello, Lucky. I'm Sage Wilde." She didn't bother extending her hand for a shake. Her warlock—shooting mystical bullets from his eyes—would toss her over his shoulder and cart her to his cave if she tried. Lucky dipped his head in greeting. "We've experienced black warlock attacks against witches in the western region. I'm sure you can understand why we're cautious when strangers enter our midst. Anyone raising magic against us goes on our hit-list." She wanded her hands in the air. "Sorry if you got caught in the crosshairs. But you need to understand our position."

"And you'll remain here until we're satisfied with your answers," Rafael growled at him. "Or longer if we don't like your answers."

Spine steel-rod straight against the chair, he replied, "Are you kidding me? You're holding me against my will. I'm damn sure witches and warlocks answer to the same laws the world does. I can have you brought up on charges so fast, your heads will spin into the Pacific. Let me go, and I'll reconsider calling the cops."

Sage twisted a tendril of her long, lustrous gold hair around her finger. "There's a law you're probably not aware of since it doesn't affect non-magicals." She did air quotes around the words "non-magicals." "Bottom line, if a witch or warlock raises magic against another for ill-intent or harm, depending on the severity, it's a felony or misdemeanor. After the witchworld penalties, of course."

"Yep." Rafael grinned, his even, white teeth sparkling and salivating over Lucky as if prepping for his next meal. "I'd say you threatened bodily harm on multiple people today using your magic. Which is a felony charge. I have a dozen witnesses."

"Oh, so you've already called the cops on the warlock who attacked Aspen?" he asked, countering Rafael's smirk. "Cool. They're on their way." Rafael didn't utter a word. "Yeah, that's what I guessed. You're not gonna hold me here." Lucky rose from the chair, stretching out his cramped legs.

Rafael pulled his gun from his shoulder harness and aimed it at his chest. "Magic may be dead in this room, but this gun's housing real bullets. I suggest you sit your ass down."

Bristling for several long seconds, Lucky's butt met the seat, the cushion so thin, the cold of the steel beneath the foam chilled his bones. For over a month, he'd wanted on the Wilde covenstead, but didn't have a reason or invitation. Since he'd arrived, he needed to cool his jets to get what he wanted and figure out his strange lure to the property. Divine intervention intruded upon his day. Why fight it?

Rafael stuck his gun into his holster and propped his shoulder against the door. "Who's your mother? Who's the black warlock in your bloodlines?"

"I don't come from black warlocks or witches." He narrowed his eyes at Rafael. "Is that what you think?"

"It's what we know." Sage absently smoothed nonexistent wrinkles in her skintight leggings that left little to the imagination. "Magic radiates off you. Your aura's so dense with it, even Aspen recognized it when most witches can't sense magic from an unbonded warlock. I already know you're not bonded. I'd sense your witch's magic if one had bonded you. You possess black warlock traits fringing your aura colors. Need I say more?" She flipped up her hands, let them fall.

Lucky folded his arms across his chest, as if to hide the magic Sage alluded to. Hell, she more than alluded. She scored a hole in one. He'd tried to bury it all his life. Hid his limited abilities from his mother and father. Maybe his mother had known. She'd asked questions he had a hard time answering. His father always skirted the issue. Lucky tried to run from it by burying his head in his books and lab work, his dabbling in alchemy. Apparently, the herbs he'd stuffed in his pocket didn't work on Sage. Plus, he'd already given himself away even if he didn't know how it had happened.

Witches and warlocks had remained on the fringes of his life, toying with him. But no one ever took it further and had retreated after his denials. They mostly steered clear of him, which was what he wanted. Being a "magical" meant more than being a witch or a warlock. It meant his entire life was an epic lie. A lie he never wanted to confront until he'd returned to Santa Cruz and realized he couldn't flip the page to the next chapter of his life until he understood the preceding chapters. The lack of knowledge had eaten away at him since the moment he'd gained the ability to think on his own. Now he needed answers. Not as the target of a bullet or random witchcraft, though.

When Aspen stepped into the apothecary earlier, avoidance had fled the building. Everything about her hit buttons on his wish list in a woman. Vibrant, smart, and so beautiful, he couldn't not see her again, despite her origins. When the black warlock attacked her, he refused to stand by. Reality whacked him upside the head. Aspen Wilde became the catalyst to a life he needed to explore. Damn the consequences.

He hooked a lock of his long, wavy hair behind his ear. "I'm not here to cause trouble." Raw pain leaked through every word.

Sage stepped toward him, and Rafael tried to grab her. She brushed Rafael away and caught Lucky's right hand, closing her eyes.

Her magic hit him hard in the chest, forcing his

heartbeat into an erratic rhythm. It seemed to connect with the hidden magic inside him, a lifetime of magic buried deep, begging for his commands. Even with the wards in the room, her magic lived powerful and purposeful. Something more connected to him, a weave to another aura. Not Rafael or Sage. Most definitely not Aspen's sweet, soothing aura. He shook off the strange allure. He'd explore it later.

"I'm in a protective bubble, which is why the wards don't affect me," she explained. "You don't know who you are, do you?"

Capitulating, he shook his head, squeezed her hand so hard her bones creaked. But she held on.

"Rafael, he reminds me of you when we first met. Remember those days?"

"I remember." Rafael sagged against the door. "Were you adopted?"

"Nope."

"Who's your mother? Where is she?" Sage asked.

Anguish contorted Lucky's face. "Murdered when I was twelve."

"Oh, I'm so sorry." Sage dropped his hand and wiped hers against her thigh, as if she wanted to rid her skin of his anguish. "Once you hit our radar, we found no intel on her."

Lucky inclined back in his chair. He'd heard stories about how black warlocks had re-emerged after witches had killed them off in a long-ago magical war. How the witches, including the Wildes, fought to prevent another war. He didn't want to be involved on either side. Being here this day meant taking a side. He didn't know how he could play Switzerland. No way could he shake Aspen Wilde out of his head. Sure, he could take a hike and pretend the day never happened. Live his life in disconcerted agony. If his untapped magic didn't kill him first. Exposing his heritage complicated it all.

"Anything you say, Lucky, stays here among us three, unless you give us permission to discuss among the coven or our allies, the Ravenwoods. I promise on my role as High Priestess of the Wilde coven." Sage slid a black opal ring off her right hand and handed it to him. Lucky refused to take it. "This ring represents my promises to you."

"Keep your ring. I accept your promises. Doesn't appear as if I have much choice." He let the chips fall where they lay splintering across the cement floor. "My mother was a Ravenwood witch."

Chapter 5

Lucky could hear a pin drop after he detonated his bomb regarding his connection to the Ravenwood black warlocks. Far as he knew, the Ravenwood witches were all dead. After his mother passed and he'd found her journal, he understood why his parents had moved to Santa Cruz. He loved the community, missed it like crazy while at Berkeley. But he'd never met or missed the Ravenwoods. Sure, he'd "stalked" them and the Wildes. And as the saying goes, "today was his lucky day." *No pun intended.*

"A game changer," Sage said after she'd recovered from her surprise.

"Bull." Rafael tugged his phone out of his back pocket and scrolled through several screens. "There're no Lorenzos on the Ravenwood list of family members. No Lorenzo, and no other witch who could be your mother."

Lucky's lips curled under. "Like you know where every drop of Ravenwood blood lies? Where'd you get your golden list?" *Man, I wish I had that list.*

"A trusted Ravenwood source." Sage approached him,

strong magic shimmering off her. So strong it lifted the hair on his arms. "We need more information."

He stated the one thing he'd wanted forever. "I'll explain it all to Ethan Ravenwood. I suspect he'll want to talk to me."

"We're done here. Bind him." Rafael marched to the door.

Sage laid her hand on Rafael's arm. The gesture so intimate, it seemed to calm the warlock. Would Lucky ever meet a woman whose mere touch created such warmth, security, and loyalty? And love? Was that woman Aspen Wilde? The thought of being immersed in the witchworld with her fired a jolt through him. A world he'd shunned with a dedicated purpose since he'd discovered his origins, hidden from him by his mother and father.

Rafael swung around. "If I call Ravenwood, will you tell us who you are and why you're here? Other than aiding Aspen."

Lucky cleared the emotions clogging his throat. "I'll talk to Ravenwood alone... with Aspen." Had he killed a potential friendship with her?

"No—" Rafael said.

Sage interrupted him. "Deal." She elbowed Rafael's side. "Text him. I'll give Aspen the four-one-one." She left Rafael glowering at him before his phone screen received the brunt of his frustration.

"You can drop the ward," Lucky suggested.

"Like hell."

"Like I said, I'm not trained in magic." The ward pressed on his lungs, popping against his magic like sparklers lighting up his insides. Breathing was like sucking in molasses. Almost made him capable of commanding real magic. If he only knew how to use the wards in his favor.

"Dude, you already used magic. Until you've proven

you're not here to hurt the Wilde coven, then you'll remain under lock and ward." Rafael grinned and spread the left side of his jacket to reveal his gun. "Like we said. We have the right to hold you."

"My father will see the altercation on the pharmacy security cameras. You know... the system your company installed a few weeks ago. He'll come for me with or without the sheriff."

The door squeaked open, and he assumed Sage returned but couldn't see anyone behind Rafael's hulk.

Deep creases marred Rafael's forehead. "So you know who I am. Did you hire my firm deliberately?"

Lucky's lips edged up, short of a grin. "Easy suggestion to my dad."

"You've been stalking us? Son of a witch's tit," Rafael growled out. "Why tell us—" His words cut off as Aspen thrust her way from behind him. Her stormy red face contrasted with her gorgeous auburn hair, now secured in a loose bun atop her head.

"Answer the man." The storm exploded. Rafael held her back from launching herself at him. "Did you plan the attack on me to breach our coven?"

"No." How could he make her understand his ulterior motives, but not his ill intent toward her? The optics looked bad any way he looked at it.

Rafael's phone rang, and he tugged Aspen closer to the door as he answered. "Ethan. You need to get your ass in gear." He paused a moment, then punched his speakerphone button.

A man's deep voice cut through the rustling in the room. "I want you all to hear this," Ethan said. "If Lucky Lorenzo's a Ravenwood by blood, his mother, sister to my dad and uncle Richard, was Andre's mistress, sycophant, call it what you will. She turned on the Ravenwoods when she sided with Andre decades ago." A crackling on the phone cut him off. "I'm at the front door." He hung up, but he'd said enough.

"You piece of shit, Lucky. Ethan will cut through your lies." Aspen hurried from the room straight to Sage standing outside the door.

The wards severed whatever weird connection to her he'd felt in the pharmacy. In fact, his connection had dwindled from the moment he entered the house, mansion, castle, whatever you wanted to call the structure drooling gold coins.

"Aspen, stay."

"Sage!" Aspen slammed her boot on the cement floor. "We have other pressing matters. Let this rat scuttle out of here." She spun toward him, her face mottled red and so beautiful he wanted to die in her tempest. "Your apothecary has seen the last of my patronage. The last Wilde dollar." She escaped the room in a rush.

Ethan Ravenwood pushed his way through the doorway. Lucky had spied Ethan from a distance a few times in town. But Ethan up close and personal drove shock waves through him. The eyes, the hair color, the nose, albeit in a smaller form, belonged to his mother. Why had she never told him of their connection to the Ravenwoods? Why had his father hidden him away from family since the Ravenwoods moved to the area ten years ago?

Ethan froze in the doorway. He closed his eyes, opened them. Lucky settled in his chair again, needing to take a leak, but not wanting to lose the one moment that may define the rest of his life.

Ethan advanced a step, waving Sage away. "You resemble the Kenley I knew as a kid."

"I knew her by the name of Leigh." He stuck his index finger toward Ethan. "Need a DNA test."

The corners of Ethan's eyes dipped downward, the

glint fading to a steely resolve. "Maybe. Later." He shifted to Rafael and Sage. "Leave now. Kill the ward."

"What?" Sage said. "Are you sure?"

"I won't talk without Aspen," Lucky reiterated, not sure why he felt such a compulsion for her to bear witness to his story.

"Hell to the no!" Aspen shouted from down the hall.

"Please, Aspen," Sage cajoled. "Ethan needs your magic 'case things go sideways."

Clomping boots advanced toward the door. "Fine, what-the-fuck-ever. I can drown his ass if—"

The loud booming clunk of a door slamming cut off her last words. Wind gusted through the hallway outside his room, and more doors slammed shut or banged against walls. With a flick of her hand, Sage reinstated the bindings tying him to the chair. Everyone hurried into the central room, leaving him alone. Shouting and scuffling ensued. Bound to the chair, Lucky fought the wards in the room. At least the wards worked on any witch or warlock, preventing them from using it against him. Still made him a sitting duck.

Shouting and magic approached his doorway, and the ruckus elevated. Water funnels drenched everything outside the room. Stars detonated and drifted from the ceiling, landing on the fireproof cement floor. Air whooshed and dispersed the water funnels and exploding fireballs. Ivy crept toward the door from outside, shrinking back as they touched the wards, and continued their journey away from the room. A rivulet of brown mud snaked from beneath the baseboards near the door in his room, powerful magic undeterred by the wards. A second and third mud snake approached him. He was powerless to stop them. The scuffle shifted farther away, and no one approached his cell again.

A half dozen brown, headless mud snakes slithered up

his chair legs, roving up the back chair frame. Surrounding him. He moved his legs as far from the metal chair legs as his bindings allowed, which wasn't much. *Damn witches!*

Plant stems sprouted from the mud streams, expanding until they grew the size of his pinky, touching him, exploring. Not harming. Yet.

The green shoots grew tiny, hairy fibers that morphed into leaves. The vines crawled over his arms and down his torso, binding his legs to the chair.

"Hello!" he shouted. "A little help in here!" For all he knew, the magic intended to strengthen his shackles while the Wildes took care of their other problems.

Aspen ducked her head into the room, her hair flying in all directions, damp from her water magic. She cupped a hand over her mouth. "Did you do that?"

"Do I look like I can do that? Isn't there a ward on the room?" Anger took a spin at Lucky's voice. "And why is that your first question?"

With a casual gesture, Aspen brushed her fingers through her tousled hair before fully entering the room. A seagull flew over her head and crapped on the floor. He had to jerk his foot to the side to avoid the splat. The bird managed to perch on the slim doorframe to the bathroom. "Not anymore. Your pal decimated them. We're trying to determine what happened."

"Should you be revealing that? Aren't I the bad guy?" Lucky flexed his arms against the vines, but the threads tightened. "And he's not my pal."

"Yeah. Whatever." She scrutinized him. The seagull screeched, echoing Aspen's words. "Are you in pain? Do you feel magic from the mud and vines?"

"No. Feels like mud and vines."

Aspen scratched her head, her fingers trailing down to tap her chin.

"Are you gonna just stand there?" His frustration hit

level ten.

"What do you want me to do?" The gull made a cackling sound as if it laughed at him. "I'm thinking."

"The gull's your familiar?" He groaned low in his throat. "Why a sky rat of all creatures?"

As if she'd explained herself a million times, Aspen huffed impatiently. She ran a finger along one vine and snatched her hand away. "Ow. It bit me. Are they biting you?"

"No. They feel weirdly comforting, like they're hugging me and don't want to let go."

"I don't know whose magic it is." She sat on her knees on the floor, far enough away where he couldn't touch her. "I can't counter-spell it until I understand the source and makeup of magic."

"Yeah, didn't think so." He nodded his head toward the open door. The chaotic magic died down but hadn't dissipated. A puddle of water remained outside the door feeding the vines from afar. "What's going on?"

Aspen bit her bottom lip, paused for a long moment. "I don't know. Something triggered all our magic to cut loose. That black warlock may have mad skills."

"So, you think the vines and mud belong to him?" Stems cut into his skin for a millisecond, a tiny sting as if to warn him of something.

"Doubt it. He's a fire warlock with a water kicker." She sat back on her delectable rear, drew her bent legs up to her chest, and propped her chin on her right knee. "Did you play me? Is that asswipe working with you?"

Lucky's mood and face softened, glad that she hadn't abandoned him. "No. I'm not lying about him."

"But you're lying about other things?" She snorted. "Freaking fantastic."

"It's not what you think. I withheld information."

"Well, *Luciano*, you know what they say about a lie by

omission, right?"

"I'll make things clear to Ethan. Will you let me make it up to you?"

"Nope. You've lost those privileges." A smile teased the corners of her plump, kissable lips.

"Point taken." His gaze drifted to the puddle where a vine grew from a ball of mud. The creeper slithered toward the mud snakes now attached to his legs and fed them. He shuddered so hard his teeth clacked together. "Tell me about your familiar."

"Suppose you know about familiars," Aspen gloated. "You tell me what your familiar is."

Lucky flinched at a vine inching toward his neck. "Um, can you get help? I don't know what this thing's gonna do."

"Familiar first."

Lucky groaned. "I don't have a familiar. I'm not... at least I don't think I'm a black warlock."

"Really?" Aspen drawled.

"I swear by all that is holy." Anguish accompanied his words. "I don't know what I am." He hung his head, and the vine glided up his left cheek. "Please, Aspen."

She leaped up and tapped a vine, withdrew. "Crap on a toasty cracker." Ducking her head out the door, she called for Sage. "We've got a problem, Houston. Get Ethan too."

A bedraggled, wet and wind-wild Sage entered the room, Rafael and Ethan on her heels. True wingmen. Warlocks who loved their witch. Yet he understood Ethan wasn't Sage's warlock. A story existed there. Maybe he'd hear it one day. Someone called to Rafael, and he left Sage in Ethan's guard.

"Holy mother of the goddess." Sage reached toward a vine on Lucky's arm, and Aspen knocked her hand away. Fire had singed Sage's T-shirt leaving black holes exposing the honeyed skin of her flat abs. Lucky licked his lips. It'd been too long since he'd had a woman, and meeting Aspen had stirred up his desire... and desperation.

"Don't touch them," Aspen warned.

Sage clasped her hands together. "Did that black warlock do this too?" She spun on Ethan. "Who is Lucky to you?"

"From what he says, and the resemblance is there, he's Kenley Ravenwood's son, aka Leigh Lorenzo's son. I didn't know her as Leigh. Kenley was my father's youngest sibling."

"Gee, thanks for the history lesson, cous," Lucky shot out. "Do you all think you can get me out of this alive? Then we can have a kumbaya sesh."

"It's earth magic," Sage mused.

"What magic do you practice, Lucky?" Ethan asked.

"I don't." So many years hiding his magic potential ended that day. He heaved out an epic release of the tension he'd carried on his shoulders like an eight-hundred-pound whale.

"Well, guess what? He *said* he's not a black warlock." Aspen sneered, her lip curling with contempt.

"Hate to burst your bubble, but you are." Rafael entered the room, wringing the water out of his jacket. "Everything's under control. We've triple-warded our other guest. His magic's cut off, so this scene doesn't jive if you think it's him."

"Did you ward the two exterior doors?" Aspen asked.

"Yep. No magic's entering and none's coming from him."

"Magic's seeping to him and Lucky." Sage finger-combed the wet snarls in her hair. "We had problems setting a ward."

"By the way, his name's Pierre Charlemagne," Ethan added. "He's one of Andre's bastard sons."

"What?" Sage and Rafael exploded together, rounding on Ethan.

Ethan gave them his palms to forestall their rants. Lucky relaxed beneath the vines, enjoying the show, trying to prevent his heart from shearing his ribs and blasting through his chest. More than his anxiety triggered his racing heart. The name "Andre Charlemagne" held so many connotations in his emotions. So much he'd read about the man in his mother's writings.

"Table it," Aspen ground out. "Can we kill this magic attacking Lucky or not?"

"What are you thinking?" Sage asked.

"Snag Eden and the other earth witches," Rafael interrupted, adopting his he-man stance behind and so close to Sage they were almost one.

Aspen opened her fanny pack still latched around her hips, none the worse for wear. She slipped out a multi-purpose pocket knife and opened the longest blade. The steel glistened in the overhead light, the blade sharp and clean.

"Wait, you need a protective ward," Sage admonished. She mumbled words and waggled her fingers in Aspen's direction.

"You think it'll go sideways?" Rafael asked.

"One way to find out." Ethan scrutinized Lucky's face as if imprinting his features on his brain. As if he still didn't trust if Leigh—Kenley—was his mother.

"Are you insane?" Lucky said. "What if it covers my face and smothers me?"

"Cocoon!" Aspen shouted, bright gold flecks in the green depths of her eyes. "That's what this is. It's cocooning you to protect you, not harm you. Oh my goddess." She closed the blade on the knife. "Sage, whose earth magic does it feel like to you? I have a hunch, but you're better at ID'ing magic."

Sage stepped toward Lucky, avoiding the vines and mud snakes. She spoke words of a spell Lucky couldn't understand. Latin maybe?

Eyes rounding in horror, Sage gasped. "The magic feels like Andre's earth magic from when he attacked Willow at her apartment."

"Exactly," Aspen said. "He was jailed in this room at one point. His magic is lingering. A delayed spell, maybe?"

Ethan gripped Sage's shoulders and eased her away from Lucky. "I couldn't identify it at first, but you're right. I should've known since I'd spent years in his presence."

"Did Andre escape?" Air turned into razor blades in Aspen's lungs, each breath a slice of terror. "He was always warded in the basement. How could his magic linger?"

Rafael's fingers flew on his phone. "I haven't heard from anyone upstairs since we came down here. Leah's not answering, nor is Marina. Our best earth witches should be able to solve the puzzle. Where the hell are they?"

Had Lucky doomed everyone by coming onto the Wilde covenstead? Had he doomed his salvation as well?

Chapter 6

A spen's nose twitched as she sniffed the room. The vines had little to no scent. Another vine sprouted from the mud rivers and climbed Lucky's right leg. It grew as thick as Aspen's thumb and snaked up his torso until it found purchase around his neck. Aspen longed to cut the vines off his too calm body. Maybe his calm kept the plants chill since they now traversed over seventy-five percent of him. Testing the unknown might gamble with a death sentence.

Remorse filled her, strong and silent, throbbing in her head, beating against her rib cage. Had she caused this magic to assault him? If that warlock goon hadn't jumped her, or she hadn't left the grounds, none of this would've happened. A niggling doubt surfaced as she recalled the attack. The goon said something about two birds. *What did the neanderthal mean? Was he targeting both of them?* Her head and heart ached too much to tackle the line of thought.

Ethan, Sage, and Rafael left to survey the covenstead. Sage told her not to leave Lucky alone.

"I'm sorry," Aspen said.

His eyes softened. "Whatever." The vines tightened over his taut shoulders. "Not your fault. You're not an earth witch."

She jerked up her head. "How do you know? Earth witches can be healers and mix potions."

"Most earth witches grow their own herbs, not buy them. You already displayed your witch-water."

"Oh. Yeah. Right." She gnawed on her bottom lip and propped her shoulder against the wall. "Are you thirsty? I can scrounge up a straw."

"Nah. I already need to take a leak. Don't want to make it worse."

"Oh, Lucky. This is horrible." She reached to touch his cheek, froze. "What can I do?"

"Touch my face." A deeper shade of crimson painted his cheeks.

"I'm afraid. What if the vines smother you?"

"I've a hunch they're not meant to kill or hurt me." He lifted two free fingers a skosh and stroked the deep green leaves. The leaves quivered and feathered his hand in a soothing way.

"What if they attack me?" Aspen was dying to touch him. Dying to see how the vines reacted. Something between them connected earlier, and she needed to explore it. The way she'd wanted to explore it in high school when he'd wanted nothing to do with witches. Instead, he hung with the science geek squad and she with her witch clique, which included her three cousins. A force no one dared traverse.

Before a second thought, she slid her index finger toward his face. A vine unfurled from his left arm and snapped around her wrist. "Oww. Son of a vine bitch!" The stem tightened and dug into her wrist. "Let me go. I'll back away." In response, the vine broke skin. "Please. Stop. I'll leave you alone." The vine unfurled where it settled in a loose clasp around Lucky's arm, after stealing several drops of her blood. It exhaled a little puff of air, its leaves flapping as if to scold her.

Aspen wiped the residual blood on her T-shirt beneath her leather moto-jacket and retreated to the wall, despite an inclination to run far and fast. But she refused to leave Lucky alone in a mess of her creation.

"I'm sorry. It's not me, I swear. I'd never do this to you."

"Why not?" She hiccupped down a sob, more from frustration and guilt than pain. "You don't know me."

His composure crackled across his face for a split second. "I know you're a good, compassionate person."

"I'm a healer. Compassion is in my nature." She sniffed disdainfully. "I'm still pissed at you." High school memories flooded her mind. All the times she'd spied him, drooled over his cute surfer looks, and he shunned her. Never acknowledged her as they passed in the hallways or sat in the same classes.

"You've every right."

"Will you explain yourself?" She wiped more blood off on her shirt. She scrounged in her fanny pack for an alcohol wipe. A light film of perspiration dotted her forehead and heat escalated over her body. Fog glazed her eyes, and the two alcohol wipes slipped from her hand before her knees crumpled and dumped her on the cement. The pain of hitting the floor didn't make a dent in the strange lethargy overcoming her. "I think the vine poisoned me. I'm just gonna lie here for a sec." She slid to her side against the wall, fighting an overwhelming sleepiness. "Need Sage." As her throat thickened, her voice was but a whisper. Not enough to worry it might close, but enough to notice.

"Aspen?" A voice, faint as a desert wind, rustled the leaves on Lucky. "Sage!" Lucky yelled, struggling against the relentless creepers holding him to the chair. "Aspen needs help."

Willow, Aspen's younger sister, limped into the room and crouched next to Aspen. "What did you do to her?"

"She tried to touch me. The vine attacked. Punctured her wrist."

"Wills, snag a counter-spell potion," Aspen croaked. "Red topper, labeled, in fridge. Grab a few. Pain gummies in my secret stash."

"I don't want to leave you. Not like this. Not with him." Willow stretched Aspen out on her back, tore off her hoodie and bunched it beneath Aspen's head. The hoodie smelled of both Willow and Evan, a soothing scent of spices and vanilla.

"Go. Before it gets worse." Pain lanced her stomach, and she choked down bile, preventing her lunch from staging a comeback. "Lucky, how lucky are you. Far as I see, you're a nightmare that just keeps on giving. The goddess giveth, and the goddess taketh away. Is it a full moon tonight? Moon Goddess, don't forsake me." She was babbling nonsense, random thoughts popping into her head. "You were but a dream in high school."

"Aspen?" Lucky said, his mouth muffled.

The sucker living on her blood slid away from Lucky and skulked up the wall behind him. Other tiny vines branched off it, all carrying a microscopic drop of Aspen's blood. Creepers crisscrossed Lucky's face as if protecting him. Or maybe they planned to kill him, death by vines. Death by suffocation. Death.

"The vines..." Her voice drifted away as it became too difficult to speak. An ache formed at the base of her skull and mushroomed down her temples. If she closed her eyes, would sleep claim her? She tried it, but nothing happened. "Damn... sleep."

"Don't go to sleep, Aspen," Lucky said through his leafy muzzle.

"Can you breathe?" she asked, her fingers lifting a tad before drooping back down.

"Yeah. Talk to me."

"Is Lucky your real name?" Who called their child Lucky?

"Nickname. Real name is Luciano."

"Oh, I love that. Why the nickname?"

"Hated being confined, and I used to climb out of my crib. Each time, I'd land on something soft, never once hurt myself. It astounded my parents how I didn't break every bone in my body. Mom gave me the nickname, it stuck, and I kept it after she died. Keeps her alive within me."

Witches and warlocks converged upon the room. The gasps and exclamations solidified the severity of the situation.

"Back off!" Willow shouted. "Let me through."

Her sisters knelt by her side, and she managed a smile. "I—"

"Shush, don't talk." Sage smoothed the pain lines creasing Aspen's forehead. "Can you drink the potion?"

"Sure." Her witch-water drained away, and she couldn't raise a spitball in the desert to save her life.

"I brought pain potions and spelled charms," Willow replied. "Where does it hurt?"

"Where doesn't it hurt?" A coughing fit hit Aspen until someone held a straw to her lips, and she slurped a few sips of electrolyte water. "Hit me."

Willow uncorked a tiny vial and dripped the potion onto Aspen's tongue. The viscous counter-spell trickled down her throat until she consumed the entire vial. Willow attached an activated pain amulet on a leather band to her wrist, and the pain subsided.

"What do you want me to do?" Willow asked.

"Let me hang here." Aspen clutched her wrist, afraid to show her sisters the punctures. Something grew out of her skin, and she feared looking at it. Or was she hallucinating?

Rolling to her side, Aspen pushed her back against the wall, and pulled her knees up. Vines now covered most of Lucky's face, keeping his nose and eyes clear. When he fought the constricting suckers, more shoots grew and cocooned him.

"Fucking disaster." Anger and anguish fought for dominance on Rafael's mottled face. "What else can we do?"

Sage rose from her crouch next to Aspen. "I've tried several voiced counter-spells on Lucky. We can't find the source of the magic. Our two best earth witches are also stumped." She pried Aspen's hand off her wrist. "Aspen! Why didn't you say anything? Mother of the goddess."

"What is it?" she croaked out, her throat loosening up, making it easier to speak.

"Oh. My. Goddess. Tiny vines are sprouting from your wrist," Willow replied. "What the bejeezus should I snag from your infirmary?"

"Hell if I know. Give me another counter-spell."

Willow popped the cork on another vial. "How's your pain?"

"Tolerable." An idea bloomed in her head. "Sprinkle a potion on Lucky. It worked on the gate lock earlier." A flush worked up her neck.

He swung his head back and forth. "No. You might make the vines mad."

"Try it on a new sprout."

"You first," Willow said. "Drink up, buttercup." Aspen drank the potion much easier than the first one.

With the subsiding pain, Aspen's water magic aerated her body once again. As the well sprung, she realized how dry she'd become while the foreign magic attacked her. Even the tiny vine shoots quit growing out of the scratch on her wrist, although the ones that remained alternated between tickling and stinging her skin. "Try one drop on a new tiny shoot on Lucky's cocoon."

Sage uncorked the vial, and Lucky struggled in the chair. "Stop fidgeting, you're making it worse," Sage demanded. She dabbed a drop of the potion on her finger and patted a fresh shoot growing from a vine orbiting Lucky's arm.

With Willow's help, Aspen sat up on her knees. They waited for the potion to exact its revenge against the magic attacking Lucky. Took a few moments, but the tiny shoot shriveled and sifted to the floor, brown and dead.

"Give him the potion." Relief propelled her to stand, but she sank back to the floor, her legs unable to support her.

"Stay." Willow braced an arm around Aspen's shoulders.

"I need to brew more counter-spell. There's not enough." Her strength returned in dribs and drabs, but her water magic had depleted again, every drop needed to aerate her body's natural functions.

"How will the potion work on him if the magic's external?" Sage asked.

"Should stop the magic from penetrating." She leaned against Willow's arm. "I'll spray it on the vines."

"How fast can you brew more?" Willow asked, a dose of skepticism layering her voice. "Your potions take a while."

Aspen muttered something incomprehensible. "Just get me to my lab."

"Aspen?" Sage rounded on her. "What's going on? What magic have you been playing with?"

"Nothing." Heat blossomed on her cheeks.

"I knew it!" Willow exclaimed. "You're brewing black curses! This isn't normal magic. We all believe it's black magic, so your normal potions shouldn't have worked."

"Thanks for the vote," she said.

Sage crossed her arms over her breasts. "Are you dabbling in black magic?"

"Ah, hello," Lucky's muted voice interrupted. "I'm still dying by suffocation here."

"Get the guy some relief. Does it matter whether it's white or black magic?" Rafael lashed out. "Bad guy or not, I can't see him bound like this any longer."

"How do ya think I feel," Lucky replied.

Sage helped Aspen stand. "We're not done with this conversation."

"Yeah, whatever." Aspen stood, braced on each side by her sisters. She uncorked the vial Willow handed her and stepped toward Lucky. "Do you trust me? I drank it and I'm still kicking it."

"Don't have much choice, do I?"

"Nope." She stuck the vial between branches and leaves to his lips, and he slurped it down. "Willow, dab drops of the last vial at key points to stop the vines from covering more of his bare skin. I'm heading to my lab. Won't take long."

She had already brewed a jug of the base ingredients and stowed it in her fridge. She needed to add a few key herbs to activate it, boil it for a half hour, and then it would be ready to rumble. Aspen had worked on her experiment for months once they'd learned black warlocks had infringed upon the witchworld. About time she got to use the fruits of her genius.

Chapter 7

Rafael walked Aspen to the stairs and appointed Aunt Jessica and Jessica's husband and warlock, Ben, to escort her to her lab on the first floor. He didn't trust her stability. *Go freaking figure.*

Asking for their silence, she didn't want to explain herself to her deceased mother's twin. Once Jessica had abdicated her leadership of the Wilde coven to Sage, Jessica had no say in the magic Aspen conducted, unless she invoked the "I'm your former guardian, so do what I say" thing. Sage would slap her silly and disconnect her stove. Aspen must prove to Sage that black curses and the ancient magic she'd worked on during their forced lockdown was important, helpful, and necessary against the new witchworld they faced.

On wobbly legs, she walked and brainstormed in her head on how best to use her counter-spell potion on Lucky. First, she'd dilute her potion in half, spray it on the muddy streams, and gauge its effectiveness. Then she'd tackle the vines. By the time she reached her lab, her energy returned, and an eagerness to stop this madness fired her up. She waved her escorts away and locked the door.

Aspen dug into her pants pocket for the vial she'd saved after ingesting the potion. She had enough left to dab on her wrist. She rolled up her jacket sleeve, cringing at her first clear view of her wrist. Tiny vines grew out of the punctures. They'd quit growing after she drank the potion but remained green and listless. Holding her breath, she patted the liquid on the wound. Within seconds, the tiny threads wilted, browned, and fell away from her skin. Definitely black magic. If the magic hadn't stemmed from her attacker, then Lucky was the culprit, whether or not he believed. With a sigh of relief, she carefully cleaned the wound and wrapped her wrist in gauze. But the moment she covered the wound, the puncture scorched her skin, and she unwound the bandage, leaving the wound exposed. The burning pain didn't bode well. Already, two new vines had pushed up through the punctures. "Son of a vine bitch."

Energy gummies and ice water to re-hydrate her waning witch-water lent her the final energy boost she needed for her task. She set the detritus from her morning's experiments in her sink and dug into her cabinet for fresh, consecrated copper spelling pots.

She'd hidden the two herbs needed to add to her base ingredients in the rear of her locked cabinet in containers marked 1 and 2. No one would dare touch them without a real identifying label. Witches didn't typically use these herbs for what the witchworld referred to as "white" magic. She'd found an old black magic alchemy book in an obscure used bookstore in San Francisco two years ago. The bookstore owner had no clue where he'd gotten the book since he'd inherited the shop from his mother and grandmother. Aspen purchased the score of the century for less than a song. No one in the coven knew she possessed it. Well, until now.

"Damn Lucky Lorenzo," she groused. If not for him, she

could've hidden her new talent of brewing archaic and black curses until prime time called.

Measuring the two herbs, she set them to brewing in separate pots in distilled water. Then she dumped her base ingredient mixture in her large pot and set the burner on high. Two hours later, she'd brewed her counter-spell and diluted the potion in a spray bottle. She stuffed the half dozen vials and the spray bottle in her healer's bag. Never left home without it. Except on days she planned an escape. *I ought to just go play with a porcupine.*

She stuck skull-and-crossbones stickers on the containers and locked them in her fridge. Much too perilous for grabby hands, especially Brianne who liked to play with Aspen's concoctions to everyone's detriment.

Scents of too many herbs to identify followed her into the hallway. She swished her hand over her nose to dispel the pungency. When her eyes lit on the blond-haired warlock, Matthew, her smile faded.

"What are you doing here?" she asked her youngest aunt's warlock. Aunt Juliette was gallivanting around Europe collecting intel on black warlocks. Juliette was twelve years younger than Jessica and wasn't ready to settle down to a life in the witchworld. Random traveling ceased when she'd accepted Sage's orders to determine the black warlock presence across the pond.

"Sage assigned me to you." He held out his hand. "Do you want me to carry that?" Without proximity to the witch who'd bonded a warlock, the warlock still linked to the witch's magic, but it wasn't at peak performance.

"I'm good."

Aspen hated that Sage had assigned a warlock to guard her. But the blame game landed squarely on herself. "When is Juliette coming home?" She gave him a break. A good and loyal warlock, he wanted only to please the coven and his witch. He hated that Juliette refused to allow him to travel with her. They weren't romantically involved, but no witch in this day should travel alone. Too many black warlocks popping out of thin air. Like today. *Le sigh.*

"She doesn't run her itinerary by me."

"She should've taken you with her."

"Every time I mention joining her, she says she can't let me tie her down." His footsteps slowed, and he scratched his head, leaving his blond locks in a tousle.

"I'm sorry." Aspen faltered at the door to the basement, tripping on her own sluggish feet.

Matthew caught her elbow. "Easy there."

The door reader wouldn't read her and she banged her forehead against the steel panel. She had no energy for this day. "What's wrong with this blasted thing?" She tried again to no avail.

"Hang tight." Matthew's thumbs flew on his phone screen. "Rafael locked all the readers. Try again."

Third time was indeed the charm. Matthew held the door open for her. She could use nice guys in her life. Although good-looking and one of the nicest guys she knew, she didn't go for blonds. Except for surfer-dude types with blond highlights. Like Lucky. She flung the thought out of her head, ratcheting up the ache brewing at the base of her skull. Maybe Brianne should take Matthew for a spin if her boredom hadn't already sent her to his bed.

"What's it like not having your bonded witch nearby?" Not trusting her waning strength, Aspen clung to the stair rail and slowed her roll down the steps.

"Not much different," his slight nasally voice intoned behind her. "I can raise fireballs and blast things into smithereens, just can't do too much before my power's shot to shit."

"Can you feel Juliette use magic?" Aspen hit the bottom step in a small vestibule. One more door to trip through.

"When she uses powerful magic. But she's used little." His boots slogged down the stairs behind her and halted when she engaged another reader. This time, she punched in the code.

"She must be safe if she hasn't used magic," Aspen continued, keeping her mind off Lucky and her nebulous solution to his problem.

Matthew winced. "You know Jules, she likes her stun gun."

Aspen laughed. "Yeah, along with pepper sprays and real guns."

"And knives."

Sage and Rafael stood outside the door to Lucky's room. Aspen willed her heart to stop the sudden galloping. "Did my potion work to slow the spread?"

"Yes," Sage replied. "But he passed out."

Aspen lunged for the doorway. "Did you check his pulse?" she demanded, her mind jumping from one thought to another.

"Of course. That's why I'm lounging on this cold-ass floor resting my bum ankle against the hard cement." Willow rose and wiggled her ankle, the cast recently removed after she broke it during the coven's altercation in capturing Andre Charlemagne.

Aspen clenched the full spray bottle, the liquid warming her palm. "Well, hell's bells. He can't drink the counter-spell potion."

"Why does he need it?" Sage asked. "The vine hasn't broken his skin."

"How do you know?" Aspen stamped her foot on the cement, the motion vibrating up her leg. Everything was her fault, and she craved a trip through a time warp. "This is the freaking *best* day ever."

"Give it to him when he wakes up, sis." Willow shot Sage a glare.

"No shit, Sherlock." Aspen slipped on goggles, a mask, and gloves she'd brought from her lab. "Everyone out. Now!"

She examined the spots on Lucky's left sneaker where Willow had dribbled the potion. The vines had shriveled, and golden-brown bits littered the gray-painted, cement floor. Satisfied, she set the sprayer to a fine mist and sprayed the narrow mud rivers stemming from beneath the baseboards near the doorway. Without confirming her handiwork, she sprayed all vines to the point they encased Lucky's legs.

The brown streams shrieked; a sound destined to irritate Rafael's black lab familiar. "Rafael, you may want to split. The sound will bother Shadow."

"I hear nothing." Rafael's lab familiar leaped off his arm in a blob of ink, morphed into his black lab shape, and scrambled from the room. Rafael bolted after his familiar, both so new to the witchworld familiar game, they were still training each other.

Every ounce of Aspen's energy focused on her task. The mud dried and splintered into dust, and the musty scent of decay joined the dead bits. Dust sifted off Lucky as though she'd just discovered him sitting in the attic after decades. The vines attached to the mud rivers shriveled. She snuck a finger between vines and leaves and checked Lucky's wrist pulse. A strong beat.

Aspen wiped her hand on her pants as if the plants carried a plague. For all she knew, they did. "It's working."

A sharp arch rose above Sage's eyes. "We need to have a long talk."

As the temptation to stick her tongue out at her coven leader arose, Aspen suppressed it by biting down. Blood welled and she forced herself to swallow, the coppery taste coating her throat. "Whatever," she drawled. "There's a method and reason to my madness, and you'll never stop my creations." She looked her sister square in the eyes. "I'm following in Mom's footsteps." In more ways than anyone knew, not even her sisters.

"I'll take your madness over Andre Charlemagne's any day, sis. You have epic skills in the lab, whether or not you're brewing black magic." Willow backed away from the doorway to avoid over-spray.

Ignoring her sisters and the other witches and hulking warlocks waiting outside the room, she worked on the vines detached from the mud streams. They already yellowed, no longer joined to their life source. A light coating of the spray on the main vines hosting the hundred baby vines did the trick. Finished, she waited for the magic to complete its job. The last vine holding Lucky to the chair fell to the floor and evaporated to dust.

Aspen stripped off her protective gear and tossed it all in a pile. "Rafael, Matthew, stretch Lucky out on the bed. He's gonna slide to the floor."

Skirting piles of debris, the warlocks did her bidding. Lucky still hadn't awoken. Aspen used a soft, microfiber towel to brush the remains off him, examining him for puncture marks. Nothing visible, and her heart settled into a normal rhythm. No dealing with lingering issues. Her own cut was another story. It itched and burned on her wrist despite her counter-spell. The wound scared her. Something inside her core of magic felt like the tiny vines bound her to something unnatural and unholy. Lucky? Or her attacker in the other room? Nothing made sense. What had they done with her drops of blood?

Lucky's pulse remained steady, and his heart rate and oxygen levels read normal.

"Do you want me to spell him awake?" Sage asked.

"Let him awaken on his own. We don't know what magic attacked him or if there's a residual effect."

"Then what?" Willow stood tentatively on her heel to

test out her bum ankle before standing on it again. "Where'd Ethan go? I thought Lucky wanted to talk to him."

"Wasn't sure if we were under attack, so I put him on guard detail with Eden at Andre's room." Rafael smirked, no doubt about sending a black warlock coven leader to do a menial job. But then no one on the premises knew Andre better than his former Black Tide member, Ethan Ravenwood.

As a psychic warlock, he and Eden, who was also psychic, babysat Andre to find any pinprick into the black warlock's mind that might allow them inside. Sage had tried a truth serum on him, but Andre's magic fought it and won. They'd been working on a permanent binding spell to bind Andre's magic. Tedious work with hiccups that set them back a step for every two they took forward. Andre's magic was just too strong and stubborn, and they used archaic witch spells on a black warlock. The Wildes had their work cut out for them to better secure the warlock and ferret information out of his head.

Lucky stirred and groaned. His eyes popped open, blue-green orbs swimming in a pale sea. He slapped at his arms and legs, swiping at the nonexistent vines and leaves.

"Whoa, dude. Don't kill yourself." Rafael approached the bed and caught Lucky's wrists to hold him steady. "Stop moving. Let Aspen examine you."

"Get away from me," Lucky spat out. "You people are insane. This house is a fucking asylum." He tried to sit up, but Rafael's ironclad grip pushed him to the mattress. He hauled back his knee and shoved it in Rafael's chest. "I swear to *my* God and your stupid goddess that I'm gonna call the hounds of hell upon you all for what you've done to me today."

Rafael backed off, and Lucky sat up, lurching sideways, but resisting their efforts to help. Willow handed him a cold bottle of water, and he gulped it down.

Aspen handed him a counter-spell vial. "Take this. It'll help if the magic's inside you."

"The vine didn't breach my skin."

"Take it," Sage demanded. "Despite our first impressions, we didn't do this to you. We don't know the source of this magic. Far as we know, *you* cursed us."

"Screw you and the broomstick you rode in on," Lucky lashed out, but he took the potion and stuck it in his pants pocket. "I'm leaving."

Hands held up in surrender, Sage stepped away. "Rafael, escort our guest to his truck and ensure he leaves our property."

"Sage!" Rafael cracked his knuckles, signifying his readiness to crack some heads. "I'm not done interrogating him." Shadow approached Lucky, a growl emanating from her throat. She sat on her haunches between Rafael and Lucky, her beady eyes never drifting from Lucky.

"Oh, you're done." Lucky rose off the narrow bed, swaying for a moment before his spine straightened. "Whatever information I have for Ethan Ravenwood sits in a crypt now." He walked between Willow and Aspen, his fingers brushing her hand. The intense worry swirling in her mind caused her to almost overlook Lucky's subtle sign. A sign that gave her hope they'd unravel the enigma he presented.

"Thanks for the assist and the ride today." She shrank in on herself waiting for his retort.

"You're welcome," he whispered for her ears only.

Rafael escorted a slow-moving Lucky to the stairs. A tiny part of her seemed to wither like the brown vines sifting to grains on the floor. Any idea she possessed of reconnecting with him also turned to dust. A tiny part of her heart lay buried among the debris he left behind.

Flames of hope existed in the brush of his hand against hers.

Chapter 8

Aspen slumped in a chair in front of Sage's desk, waiting for her sister's reprimand. Everyone else had scattered, paranoid of Sage's wrath, but she didn't have such luxury.

The door opened behind her, and she smelled Rafael's cologne before he sat beside her. Shadow peeked out from his T-shirt and gave her googly eyes. The familiar loved her since she'd brought Rafael from the brink of a magic-induced death. Might also be the special dog treats she baked.

Dim lights glowing in all four corners of the room erased the early afternoon shadows created from the trees surrounding the front yard. A soothing ambiance to ease the afternoon's beyond-bizarre events. She held her tote close to her middle as if to protect herself from the wrath of Sage. She also hid her wound that offered no sign it wanted to heal.

"Are you okay?" Empathy spilled from Sage's eyes, shocking Aspen. Not that her sister was an ogre, but she demanded obedience as a coven leader, especially in the current precarious witchworld with black warlocks on the prowl.

Fighting her hollow desolation, she nodded. "I'm sorry. I thought I could get my herbs and return with no fuss. I never expected this clusterfuck."

"Not even in my wildest dreams." Rafael raked his hand through his thick hair.

"So how did you slip through that old gate? Leah found the breach later."

"You could've at least warded it again," Rafael said.

"I *did* ward it." Aspen scratched her itching wrist without alerting Sage and Rafael to her wound. They'd flip out if they saw it in full light. "I can't connect the ward to the ley lines like Marina can. I figured she'd think it was a blip caused by a line disturbance and reset it during her regular evening checks."

"The counter-spell you used was too strong. It was more than a blip." Sage kicked off her sandals and padded around the desk to pace the wool rug. She stopped by Aspen's chair. "Was it black magic? Same as what you used on Lucky?" Aspen nodded. "When did you start practicing black magic?"

"After black warlocks attacked the witchworld."

"Are you following formulas?" Rafael stretched out his long legs and crossed his ankles. Settling in for the long haul. So not good.

Aspen stifled a groan. She didn't need the interrogation after her suck-ass day. She fiddled with the straps on her tote, avoiding their gazes. "I found a book and other written documents."

"Did Ethan vet them? Are they real?" Sage clasped her neck and red bloomed up her throat. Angry red? Or?

"You saw the results. You tell me if they're real." She sniffed and crinkled her nose.

Sage shot daggers at her. "Why? What's your

motivation? You know black magic is dangerous, and most black spells are curses, right?"

"They're not all curses." In a burst of anger, Aspen jumped up, dumping her tote on top of her boots. She nudged it aside, granting her a moment to decide on spilling the truth. "Mom dabbled in black magic." There, she exposed the elephant in the room.

"Get real. Mom was as white a witch as they come." Sage shook her head, acting like Aspen had besmirched their deceased mother's name, reputation, her entire life.

"I found her witch's bible on her laptop, jammed with black magic recipes, curses, spells, potions, charms, everything under the sun in the witchworld. What she didn't document, she pointed to a source. Some she possessed and others from a list of obscure books she wanted to snag. I found one."

"What?" The blood drained down Sage's face. "I don't understand."

"There's nothing to understand. Mom hid secrets. Grams hid secrets. The Wildes have dabbled in black magic for centuries. We're not as lily white as everyone believes."

"Whoa." Rafael stalked to Sage. "Babe, you okay? Do you need to sit?"

"No. I need a damn bottle of tequila." Sage caressed his chest. "Love, please snag us some drinks."

"Wine?" Skepticism glimmered on his brow, knowing Sage had quit hard liquor years ago. She waggled her head, and he split.

"Why didn't you tell me?" Sage returned to her chair, elbows on the desktop, head clasped between her hands.

"Mom knew you'd go off the rails, and she didn't want it distracting you from ruling. She'd assumed you'd be ruling at the time I found everything. She left explicit instructions that I maintain her secret until necessary to divulge."

"Why now?"

Aspen held out her left wrist, revealing the puncture mark covered by dried, rusty blood. "It's necessary. I'm connected to whoever instigated this mess. A black warlock, I presume." She slumped into her chair, resting her wrist on her thigh.

Rafael entered the tense, silent room, bearing gifts of the grape kind. He poured three glasses of his and Sage's favorite Bordeaux and handed them out.

"What'd I miss?" He sat again and guzzled half his glass.

Sighing, Aspen performed her newest circus trick again. Tiny shoots regrew out of the punctures. "I might need a regimen of the counter-spell to kill this for good."

"What do you mean you're connected to the black warlock who caused this?" Sage set her glass down, all emotion absent in her all-business façade.

"My magic's different. Earthy, weighty, not restricted, though. I have the sensation of being bonded, although I don't have a true understanding of what reverse bonding feels like. The magic mingles with my witch-water, makes it sluggish." Aspen swigged her wine, wishing the alcohol would kill the thing inside her. If this was what it felt like to bond with a black warlock, screw it. She'd never bond another warlock again. If she survived this shitshow.

"If you're bonded, no counter-spell in the world will help you." Her sister meant bonded to a black warlock. A witch can't bond another witch. Now that black warlocks walked among them again after the Witches and Warlocks War killed them off over a century ago, a black warlock could bond a witch. Between witch and regular warlock, a bond must be consensual. Apparently, not so with a black warlock.

Rafael leaned forward, elbows on his thighs. "How? You didn't accept a bond or bond a warlock yourself. Was it that asshole who *isn't* a black warlock, Lucky?" He couldn't hide the snark in his tone.

"Oh, he's a black warlock all right." Sage's eyes narrowed to dangerous slits, her nostrils flaring. "Did he bond you against your will?"

"No. No! I don't know." Aspen sobbed, uncontrollable emotions she'd tried to check the moment the vine punctured her and foreign magic dominated her witch-water. She bowed her head and studied her black motorcycle boots.

Sage patted down Aspen's tangled hair. "Talk to me, sis. What happened? The sooner you get this on the table, the sooner we can rectify the situation. If Lucky did it, we'll force him to break the illegal bond."

"Then I'll kill the fucker." Rafael stroked the gun in his shoulder harness. "Or I might just kill him first and save us all the trouble. That'll break the bond." Rafael had suffered from an illegal bond from Sage's adversary when they'd first discovered he was a warlock. It had nearly destroyed him. The sole methods to break a bond is by the witch, or in this case black warlock, rescinding the bond, or death of the bonder.

Or by her death. Hating the sight of her wound, she buried her wrist against her middle.

"Let me see." Sage squeezed between the two guest chairs to kneel at Aspen's side.

Aspen hesitated, then spun her left wrist and extended it for Sage's examination. The puncture had grown to the size of an inch on the inside of her wrist. Tiny, pale green vine shoots remained stunted, not dying, not growing, but waving in the circulating air blowing from the ceiling vent. She shoved up the sleeve of her blouse. Purple and blue bruising extended up her arm in an intricate pattern, like a tribal tattoo. It morphed and changed direction. Aspen dragged her sleeve down again as if hiding the discoloration erased it.

"I've never seen the like." Sage sat back on her heels, and Rafael plunked a soothing hand on her shoulder. For not the first time, Aspen wished Rafael was her warlock. Not like she'd ever chase after her sister's fiancé, but he portrayed traits she'd eventually want in a warlock, even the romantic traits. But again, warlocks were so not on her Christmas wish list this year.

"When did the coloring emerge?" A shadow of frustration played across Sage's forehead, a contrast to the calm she projected.

"Noticed when I mixed the counter-spell." Aspen rubbed her arms. "Doesn't hurt. Just tickles."

"When did you take your last dose?" Rafael asked. "Has the pattern grown since then?"

"Took a dose when I left my lab with the counter-spell spray. It's grown." Aspen scratched her arm, wishing to scratch the pattern into obscurity.

"Anything in Mom's notes or in the books you found explain this?" Sage scrubbed her eyes. "This day... will it ever end?"

"I need to research." Aspen wilted in her seat. "I'll space out the counter-spell doses every four hours, and see if it helps."

"I'll review the *Book of Ink and Shadows* that Ethan loaned me to learn about black warlocks and their magic," Rafael offered. "Maybe Ethan's healer can help since she's worked with black magic." He slipped his phone out of his pocket and thumbed his message to Ethan, waited, and read the response. "He's coming from Andre's room. All's secure. Eden will remain in the atrium in a warded bubble. They're not picking any telepathic thoughts out of Andre today. Same old, same old."

A minute later, Ethan entered the room. Aspen did her show-and-tell, and he backed away as if she carried the zombie plague. "We shouldn't have let Lorenzo go. What if he skips town?"

Rafael snickered. "I installed a tracker on his phone."

"How'd you do that?" Aspen's eyes widened.

"He left his phone in his truck. You know I have epic security skills."

Rafael owned his own security firm and had beefed up the covenstead defense with state-of-the-art cameras, motion detectors, sound detectors and every kind of sensor available. Except all the witch and human security let her bypass an obscure gate in the back garden. Aspen wanted to wither beneath her chair and disappear under the dense wool rug.

"Did Marina and Brianne come home?" she asked.

"Yes. Thank the goddess." Sage returned to her chair, wheeling it close to her desk to prop her elbows on it. "Now you see why I didn't want anyone leaving. I gave in to you four today against my better judgment."

"It's my fault. I planned this before." Aspen's hand fluttered to her lap. "I needed to get to the herb shop to snag stuff I can't order online."

"Doesn't matter right now," Rafael groused. "Let's work on this black magic. Ethan, can you ask Marjorie to research this? Or do you have any idea what this could be?"

"It's not magic I've ever seen." He pointed his phone at Aspen's wrist. "Do you mind if I snap photos and send to Marjorie?"

Aspen agreed and Ethan sent the photos to Marjorie Magellan, a free agent who didn't belong to any coven. She slid under the radar, but owed her allegiance to the Ravenwoods. She'd helped Aspen with Rafael when he'd recently discovered he was a black warlock and got blasted with Sage's aether magic during their siege against the Helwig coven.

Silent, they waited for a reply from Marjorie, an

anecdote, something. A flame danced off Sage's pointer finger, and she lit a candle under a brass bowl of calming, lavender-infused water on her desk. She lit more calming candles to absorb the tension in the room. Aspen dipped her finger in the bowl and set the water boiling. She breathed in the lavender, held it in her lungs, expelled, and did it again until calm centered her.

When Ethan's phone rang, alarm rebloomed in the tense atmosphere. The call came too quick. They only heard Ethan's end of the conversation. "Okay. Talk to Aspen." He hit speaker and handed her the phone.

"Tell me what you're feeling?" the witch asked, her tone imbued with the compassion and empathy of a true healer.

"Do you know what this is?" Aspen asked.

"Not quite. I'll need to research."

"It's invasive and moves inside me, like an internal scope. Doesn't hurt per se, but bogs down my magic, like it's sipping my magic and studying it. I just did a water spell, and it didn't interfere." Aspen paused, bathed her senses with the lavender again. "Hard to describe."

"That's how I felt when Zelda Helwig bonded me without my permission," Rafael said.

"Any pain?" Marjorie asked.

"A slight tingling and a headache. I took a black magic counter-spell potion." The admission came freely now that the world knew she dabbled in black magic alchemy.

"Is it helping?"

"I don't know."

"Don't take another dose. I want to see what happens." Marjorie paused. "Don't ingest any potion or use any spell except over-the-counter pain relievers."

"What about the wound?" Sage returned to Aspen's side and twisted her wrist.

"Leave it alone," Marjorie replied.

"And the others... are they tattoos?" Apprehension choked up Aspen's voice.

"Photograph them now and each hour. Then we'll assess once I've done my research."

"Is it black magic?" Ethan asked.

"An ancient form." Marjorie paused again. "Before the war, black warlocks knew how to bond a witch without permission, similar to what Helwig did to Rafael, with magic, not herbs. One of many reasons we eradicated them in the war. The knowledge was spreading, and it was too risky to witches." She paused. "Identify anyone you've come in direct contact with over the last few days."

Aspen swept her gaze over the group in the room. "I've ID'd them. We have one black warlock locked in our basement."

"And Lucky Lorenzo," Sage added. "We don't know what he is. He swears he's not a warlock."

"But he's a Ravenwood by blood," Ethan replied.

"Yes. Yes. There's a story there," Marjorie said as if she already knew. "Keep him there."

"Too late. We let him go." Rafael paced the room, his footsteps a soft thud on the rug.

"Find him. I'll be in touch." Marjorie clicked off.

Rafael engaged his tracking app. Aspen sprawled in her seat. All she wanted was time-travel to the morning, wishing for an epic do-over.

"He's at the beach." His teeth ground together, a silent snapping of frustration. "No, he's on the Walton Lighthouse jetty. Let's go." Ethan and Rafael sprinted from the room, not a moment too soon before Aspen burst into tears.

Sage handed her a wad of tissues, forcing her to end her meltdown. "Let's photograph the tattoos."

"In my bedroom. The light's better this time of day."

They retreated to Aspen's bedroom on the second floor

and locked the door. Aspen stripped to her bra and panties. The purple and black tattoo had formed into green vines. The tattoo vines growing from the puncture site trailed around her arm to two inches down the back of her shoulder blades. Seeing the tattoo in the mirror sent a tortuous itch trailing the tattoo's path. She scratched her arm, her nails digging into her skin trying to scrape it off.

"Stop," Sage demanded. "You're making it worse."

The colors brightened, and a purple flower sprouted on the vine at her wrist, like a corsage for a hellish prom she never agreed to attend.

Chapter 9

Legs dangling above the boulders, Lucky sat at the end of the jetty jutting out from the lighthouse on the Santa Cruz Harbor. The end of the world across the blue waters of the Pacific arrested his attention, an unknown calm that promised obscurity, complete opposite of the witchworld. The ocean lapped at the rocks surrounding the lighthouse, swamping the voices in his head. He'd texted his dad and told him he was hanging with friends. Didn't want him to trip out over his long absence. But he needed solitude. He needed to grapple with his life flipping into an inevitable freak show.

Even though he'd bided his time for a Ravenwood showdown, and sought answers to a million questions, he wasn't ready to hear the truth. The truth his parents hid from him. They had their reasons, but the time had arrived for his dad to fess up. Reading the bits and pieces of his mother's secret notebooks led to many unanswered questions. Questions his father may know, and others the Ravenwoods may know. Most of all, questions Andre Charlemagne, the man incarcerated on the Wilde covenstead, could answer.

Lucky's plan failed in some ways, and in others, he celebrated internally. He now had an in with the Wildes and a path forward to Andre.

"Lucky."

The loud voice broke over the waves crashing onto shore and killed his solitude. Another notch of frustration punched his emotional belt.

He groaned and glanced over his shoulder. Rafael Reyes and Ethan Ravenwood hung in the long shadows of the lighthouse.

"You asked me to leave. I left." He inhaled the cleansing, salty air, and his gaze drank in the ocean, imprinting both on his senses. "Are you tracking me?"

Rafael spread his hands, palms up. "We have our ways."

"We want you to return to the covenstead," Ethan said. "You agreed to talk to me."

"That was before."

"Before what?" Rafael asked. "Far as we know, you brought this negative-ass magic to our covenstead."

Fury gushed through Lucky, and his spine straightened. He leaped to his feet and confronted the two warlocks. "If I brought the magic, then it's gone. A big 'if.' Why would I attack myself with magic?"

"It's not gone." Rafael's pitch dipped an octave. "It's latched on to Aspen."

The evening breeze kicked up and blew his hair around his face. A tic formed in Lucky's jaw, and he swept his hair back. "Is she okay?" Concern erased his anger, and he dug his fists in his front pockets. "I swear it's not my magic. I'd never hurt her."

"Remains to be seen," Ethan replied. "First, we need your help to contain this before more shit hits the fan. My healer wants to examine anyone in contact with Aspen today."

"Am I suspect number one?"

"Or two." Rafael took a step closer. "We'll treat you as a guest until circumstances prove otherwise."

Lucky snorted. "Right. I already witnessed firsthand how you treat your guests."

Ethan held up his hands to forestall further talk. "Let's go chat."

Lucky texted his dad again, this time telling him he was spending the night at a friend's house, and he'd catch his normal shift tomorrow. He'd returned home from Berkeley to help his dad in the shop for the spring and summer, and he had no plans to renege on his duties. "I'm bringing my truck, or rangers will tag it after the parking lot closes."

"I'll ride shotgun," Rafael offered. "No funny business."

Although the two warlocks were semi-kidnapping him, they hadn't nicked his phone, and they gave him freedom to drive his truck. But then, that status might change the moment they landed on the covenstead. He stuck his hand under the floorboard beneath the driver's seat and tapped his handgun.

Once on the road, Ethan leading the way in a black SUV, a dense silence enveloped the cab until Lucky cut through it. "How do you know Aspen hasn't been in contact with other witches or warlocks over the past week? Anyone could've done this to her. Can't someone trigger or time-release spells?"

"Aspen hasn't left the compound in a month, and she traveled straight to your shop. You and that other asshole are the only people she's had direct contact with outside the coven."

"Are you holding her prisoner, too? She said something about sneaking out."

"It's none of your business."

Lucky blinked back his surprise. He glanced in the rearview mirror. A nondescript white sedan tailed them from the lighthouse parking lot, driver and a passenger in the front seat. Paranoia jiggered the bit of nerves in his gut that hadn't already tripped off the rails. Were they boxing him in?

"Are those your warlocks behind us?"

Rafael peeked in the passenger side rearview. "Nope. We didn't bring anyone. Why?"

"They've tailed us since the parking lot. I have a bad feeling." Lucky maintained his speed behind Ethan. "If I veer off, will Ethan trip?"

Rafael called Ethan, relayed the situation, and put him on speakerphone. "Do what you think is right to see if they're following. Ethan will hold his own."

Taking the next right. The road led to town and a more congested area. Lucky flicked his blinker on, and the white sedan did the same. Both cars made the turn. Houses on large tree-shaded lots sat far off the road but grew closer together the farther he drove.

"Keep on the same road, and I'll take a different route," Ethan said. "At least he's not following me."

"Thanks, asshole. Means they're following Lucky, or me. Or it's a coincidence."

Lucky bit his tongue. He had a lot to say but didn't want to incur Rafael's wrath. One flick of his finger and the warlock could fry him in his seat.

He made four random turns down streets where the houses sat on quarter-acre lots, maintaining three miles over the speed limit. The sedan followed. "No coincidence."

"Son of a witch," Rafael grumbled and hung up on Ethan.

Magic prickled in the cab's air, like tiptoeing through a minor electrical field. The hairs on Lucky's arm stood on end. "Dude, dial down the magic."

"Sorry. Sage has powerful witch-fire. Makes it uncomfortable around other witches and *warlocks*." He gave the side of Lucky's head a long perusal. "Dude, we know you're a warlock."

"Well, it's more than I know." Lucky's jaw tightened.

"Point taken. I've been there myself." Rafael scanned the area. "Pull into the parking lot of the Church of the Pines up ahead. Should be empty this time of day."

"Then what?"

"You have a gun. Get in some target practice."

"Figures you saw that." Lucky knocked his fist on the steering wheel.

"No. But you just verified it." Rafael texted Ethan their location. "Ethan's not far, coming from the opposite direction. Drive around the church, act like you're lost or something. We'll stall them until he arrives."

Acting like he was searching for a location, Lucky slowed the truck, drove forward, and crawled by a building. The sedan did the same, even though it had room to pass them on the left. The church rolled into sight, and he turned into the first driveway of the massive empty parking lot.

"Does the whole town attend this church?"

"It's non-denominational. They like everyone and every religion."

"Even yours?"

Rafael scowled. "Being a witch or a warlock isn't a religion."

"People have recognized paganism as a world religious sect."

"Witches and warlocks are not pagan, so to speak, idiot." Rafael's witch-fire sizzled in the air. "Pagan believers think it's the ancestral religion of the whole of humanity. This church is just non-denominational, not aligned with any religion or sect. You have a lot to learn.

What'd you get your master's in? Building sandcastles?"

Lucky ignored Rafael's dig and drove close to the church schedule posted on signage by the double doors. The sedan followed, not bothering to hide, remaining close to the second exit, easy for them to block Lucky from leaving. "Now what?"

"Now tell me why they're following you." Rafael stared him down.

He thought long and hard about his month since leaving Berkeley. "Why do you think they're following me? You're the badass warlock, guard dog to the top witch in the entire western region."

"Because someone attacked Aspen outside your pharmacy. No one followed her there. Pierre was already there, tracking you," Rafael countered. "Now these goons are following us. *You.* It's your truck. They didn't take off after Ethan. Their car was in the lighthouse parking lot when Ethan and I arrived."

Screw me now. Lucky drove to the side of the large one-story church. The sedan moved again in a slow roll. "I don't know who they are. Pierre showed up at the pharmacy a few days ago. He's been scoping it out since. Thought he was hunting witches. Not me. I'm a nobody. I had no clue of his identity until today."

Rafael busted out in a cynical laugh and slapped his palm on his thigh. "Are you for real? You already admitted you're a Ravenwood. Until recently, the Ravenwoods were working for Andre Charlemagne, the leader of the Black Tide, the biggest, baddest group of black warlocks in the world. Resurrected warlocks from the Witches and Warlocks War. But you don't know any of that. Do you?"

Chilly slashes caressed Lucky's spine. "Would you believe me if I said I don't know other than what I've found on the internet?"

"As a matter of fact, everything about you feels

authentic, except for the bits and pieces you haven't told us." Rafael's voice softened. "But you want to, right?"

Lucky parked his truck near the rear double doors of the church. "You have no idea how I need to understand who I am." He'd always fought the light and darkness within himself without understanding a thing.

"I understand. I was in the same boat six years ago. Until I met Sage."

"So the warlock outside the pharmacy was waiting for a chance to snag me? I don't understand why he attacked Aspen."

"Because every black warlock wants to snag a Wilde witch. We kidnapped their leader." Rafael studied the sedan in the rearview mirror. "Table this conversation. Ethan's here now. We'll approach the sedan from opposite sides." He studied Lucky. "You stay here. Use the gun if things go sideways. Shoot them, not me or Ethan. Call Sage, not the police."

"No shit, Dexter." Lucky slipped his hand under the seat and flicked off the safety catch on his small revolver. He'd gotten his carry permit just before he'd returned to the witchworld Mecca of Santa Cruz.

With a swift motion, Rafael placed a business card on the console. It had nothing more printed on it except a number. "This is our emergency line. Any Wilde witch or warlock will answer, but speak to Sage. No one else."

Rafael jumped out of the truck, leaving Lucky feeling like an incompetent idiot, needing protection from badass he-men. But when it came to magic, they outnumbered him by far. He hated it. Hated that he'd dumped Aspen in jeopardy because of his own ignorance and a bit of cowardice, truth be told. Convincing himself he could help this situation, he eased out of the driver's side, his phone and the card in his rear pocket. The card may as well be useless. If Ethan and Rafael fell to the two black warlocks, he was a dead man too.

Although he'd left the covenstead earlier to sort through the emotions barraging his head, he refused to foist these men off on another. Lucky had barged through the door to the witchworld and must accept the consequences, good or bad.

A dandelion popped through a gap in the tarmac. He kicked the offensive weed, hating his lame magic. The yellow dandelion head opened. Too bad he couldn't use the weed to defend himself. Unless... He snapped his fingers and concentrated. An earthy, aromatic magic seemed to envelop him. More dandelions sprouted through the cracks in the parking lot until a field of yellow smirking flowers waved in the breeze. A mysterious magic had swamped him when those vines almost smothered him earlier. His bit of innate magic awakened and raised flags to grab the attention of that foreign earth magic. They both frolicked inside him like long-lost buds. It scared the life out of him. But he sensed he could do magical things now when he never could before. Other than light the occasional candle. Another magical ability he couldn't identify as an earth warlock.

Halfway to the sedan, Rafael stomped on the new weeds in his path, crushing them under his boots. The warlock didn't turn in Lucky's direction, but he sensed the eyeballs ogling him from the back of Rafael's head.

While Rafael figured Lucky had created the field of yellow weeds, he wouldn't know the dandelions were root linked. Lucky's arms grew leaden. He hoped he could control his untrained magic from injuring Ethan and Rafael. He also hoped he didn't sign his death warrant by magic or otherwise. His strength depleted, and he staggered. Magic use cost the user big-time. A new conundrum.

The sedan doors opened, and two men in their late

twenties scrambled out. They carried no weapons, convincing evidence of their warlock status.

"Why're you following us?" Rafael pulled no punches. "We're enjoying the town and minding our own business." Ethan skirted the car from a distance and halted next to Rafael.

"You have something we want," said Bald and Burly. He sported a trim black goatee, a black T-shirt, and khakis.

Ethan crossed his arms over his chest. "Doubt it. We took nothing belonging to you."

"No one said you *took* anything, Ravenwood," said burly man number two with cropped brown hair. His craggy cheeks had courted too many drugs in his youth.

"Do I know you?" Ethan asked.

"You would if you'd remained on the right side of the warlock fence," Baldy said.

"Your man, Pierre, attacked one of my witches today." Rafael skid right past "go." "We'll send him home when we're done working him over."

Relief oozed through a knot in Lucky's shoulder. The dudes didn't want him. Everyone in the witchworld knew the Wildes had abducted Andre Charlemagne. A war hovered on the horizon if something didn't give between the Wildes and the Black Tide. Even though Lucky had shied away from the witchworld, he'd kept his eyes and ears wide open, more so since returning home. Waiting and biding his time. The dark witch web helped keep him in the know.

Both men chortled as if Rafael had taken center stage at a Comic-Con.

"You think we want Pierre? Screw that asshole. He's just another one of Andre's bastards. He'll return home," Baldy, the ringleader, said. "Make no mistake."

"Well, you can't have Andre. Take a hike," Ethan piped up. "Or suffer the consequences."

"Consequences? Like this?" Buzz-cut wound up his

arm and threw a series of baseball-sized fireballs at Rafael and Ethan. The orange and yellow fire hissed as it whizzed through the air.

Wind gusts slammed into the fireballs, sending sparks and blue embers floating away on the natural sea breeze. There was nothing natural about the gusts of wind Ethan emitted. An air warlock. Lucky logged the tidbit into his memory crypts. He already knew Rafael wielded fire magic, either his own or Sage's. Lucky didn't know how it worked when a witch and warlock were bonded. He needed to scour the dark web for more intel.

Vines grew from the root formation of the dandelions and snaked toward the two men. Without knowing how, the intertwined weeds wrenched on his magic, and he heaved in draughts of air to replace his emptying lungs. Fireballs, air, and waterspouts erupted into a magical maelstrom as the warlocks fought. Every iota of his magic emptied onto the tarmac. Tilting to the side, he found the ground closing the gap to his head. He landed hard, crushing the dandelions beneath him. Unable to move a muscle, his mind clouded. Bleary-eyed, he watched the fight continue until the air stilled and an eerie silence fell.

Chapter 10

A boot jabbed his thigh. The fog in Lucky's head began to clear, and the boot tapped his thigh again. "Hey, man, you okay?"

Lucky's muddled head made out the words. Something tied him to the ground, but he realized his own exhaustion rooted him to the tarmac. As the clouds drifted from his vision, he scanned the parking lot, his gaze landing on two man-shaped lumps swaddled in dandelions by the sedan.

He swallowed hard. "Did I do that?"

"You betcha," Rafael said. "Now you gonna tell us what those men wanted from you?"

Ethan Ravenwood stuck out a hand. He grasped the firm grip and let Ethan haul him to a sitting position, his back against the front wheel. He clenched his head in his hands, needing a moment to recover from exhausting magic he didn't know existed.

"Come on. We don't have time to waste." Rafael helped Lucky stand.

Lucky's legs wobbled, but he steadied himself against the front fender. "I'm fine."

"You don't look fine." Concern rode Ethan's voice.

"Get in." Rafael hopped into the driver's seat.

The dandelions evolved to puff balls, the leaves already yellowing. Lucky staggered to the passenger side, feeling like a royal screwup.

The drive to the Wilde compound remained hushed, but a renewed interrogation was on the horizon. "Who were those two guys? What's gonna happen to them?" he asked.

"They'll live. Your weeds were unfurling as we left. They're Black Tide members, Andre's men, according to Ethan."

When they reached the Wilde gates, the security team in the gatehouse sprang to action, and the gate slid open, fluid and silent. Seemed like the Wildes operated a well-oiled security machine. Who'd kicked their puppies?

Rafael drove to the far side of the house and parked in a visitor spot in front of a four-car garage. Right back where Lucky started. After he stumbled out of the truck, hanging on to the door, he expected Rafael and Ethan to take his phone, but they didn't. Unnoticed by either man or perhaps disregarded, he shifted his handgun in his waistband. Unsure if he'd ever possess usable magic again, he was determined not to enter the lion's den unarmed. He even dropped a pin on his father's phone just in case, something they had been doing since pins became a thing. His dad liked to go on weekend golfing trips with his buds, and Lucky hiked, biked, and spent time in nature. *And I'm digressing, thinking about the mundane when shit has and will hit the proverbial fan.*

Before he stepped through the back doorway, bracketed between the two warlocks, his phone rang. "Hey, Dad. What's up?"

"Why are you in the hills?"

"Hiking with... a friend." The Wildes were so far from friends. Ethan, who knew? Aspen, well, hope floated.

"Do you know where you're at?" The message in his father's gruff question startled him.

"Uh, yeah. Property owned by the Wildes."

"The Wildes are witches. You have no business involving yourself with witches," his father yelled. "We cater to them at the store, that's it. Easy money."

"Whoa, Dad. I know what I'm doing." The lie oozed through his clamped teeth. A heavy hand landed on Lucky's back, and Ethan guided him through the doorway. Cinnamon-apple permeated his senses, stemming from bowls of potpourri scattered on a chest or table here and there. The inside of the mansion soothed every bone in this body, more so than the scent that reminded him of his mother in autumn.

"No, I don't think you do. I don't want you involved with those people."

No doubt because his father held secrets from him. A strong determination to learn why the Wildes and Ethan believed he was a warlock set up shop and reinvigorated him. *Believed? Hell, he proved it today.* Or why he'd manipulated real magic for the first time in his life. And more determined to look Andre Charlemagne in the eye.

"Sorry, Dad. I'm a grown-ass man. See you tomorrow. It seems we'll have plenty to discuss." He stuffed his phone in his pocket. "Sorry. He's paranoid."

"Because he knows more than he's told you." An angry tic flicked in Ethan's jaw. "I'd love to pick his brain about your mother."

"Why do you care about her? You didn't know her," Lucky blasted, his determination turning into Plymouth Rock. They stood in a large, industrial-style kitchen, activities of meal-preparation on the stainless-steel surfaces. Garlic bread baking and Italian sauces flooded the kitchen, and Lucky's stomach rumbled. Depleting his magic and skipping lunch didn't appease the empty cavern in his middle.

Rafael guided him through the kitchen, and he salivated with every step. "Planning to feed your prisoners?" he asked.

"You're not a prisoner," Ethan responded.

Rafael jabbed Lucky's shoulder past a tray of steaming garlic bread. "We'll feed you, don't worry."

His hunger to see Aspen eclipsed the rioting in his stomach. Thoughts of her overshadowed everything in his crap-ass day. But how would she feel about him now, the scourge of the witchworld for reasons he didn't comprehend? Especially after the frosty treatment he'd handed her in high school. Except for one small moment of weakness. Oh, and the other glaring action he'd never live down. He'd tried to dig out of his own head and cozy up to her in high school and failed miserably. Failure was no longer an option.

The Wildes had decorated the mansion in eclectic, but traditional styles in creams, greens, and pale grays. Everything meshed and created a homey atmosphere that rendered Aspen's so-called prison a luxury resort. They took a short walk along a hallway and entered a small laboratory and office. Beyond the immaculate space, another room housed two single medical beds, ready for their next victims. A stack of stuffed padded envelopes on the floor teetered toward the wall, ready for mailing. Lucky had already seen Aspen's webstore and knew she created and sold herbal and spell-casting goods catering to witches.

Aspen strode out of a bathroom attached to the patient room, drying her hands on paper towels. "Oh. You again." She huffed out a breath.

"Can you examine him?" Rafael asked. "He depleted a ton of magic."

Her sculpted eyebrows hiked up her smooth forehead to her radiant auburn hair. "What magic? He doesn't *have* magic." Her snark was so much overkill.

Adding his two cents to the conversation, Ethan said, "He does now. He's a Ravenwood warlock. And I want answers. Give him whatever he needs for energy, pain, whatever. Then send him to the dining room."

Aspen twisted her mouth in the cutest sneer Lucky had ever seen. "You calling the shots now, Ethan?" She turned to Rafael. "Is that what you want?"

"Yeah." Rafael's mouth curved up at the corners. "It's a Ravenwood matter as much as a Wilde matter."

"Not really. It's my matter, and I don't need to tell you shit." Lucky had no energy to add force to his words.

Rafael advanced on Lucky, and Aspen slipped between them. "Is that how you want this to go down, Lucky? We hold the upper hand."

Aspen pressed her hands against Rafael's beefy chest. "Go. I'll bring him to the dining room."

The scent of heaven rolled off Aspen. He breathed in the myriad herbs and her own natural perfume, imprinting her scent on his brain. Orange blossoms, sweet and fruity. What magic had she wrought upon him? Until he'd spied her in the shop today, he'd wanted nothing to do with the Wilde witches, despite his high school crush. Now, all he wanted was... screw it. He wanted Aspen Wilde. The rest of the crew could take a hike off a short pier for all he cared.

Without another caveman grunt, Rafael and Ethan left, but not before Rafael plucked the handgun from Lucky's waistband. Screw him and the broomstick he hitched a ride on.

"What now?" he asked.

"Sit on the examination table."

He drew his phone from his back pocket and set it on the cushioned exam table. As he complied, he spied black, green and purple tattoo colors peeking out from Aspen's long-sleeve silky T-shirt. They hadn't existed earlier. She rolled a cart close to him, the top tray holding instruments and potions. He grabbed her arm to stop her, shoving up her sleeve in one slick move. The vine tattoo wound around her arm. He gasped, ogling the markings.

She wrenched her arm from him. "Don't touch me."

"Those weren't there before." Tiny live vine shoots grew out of the puncture on her wrist and fluttered in the air blowing from the ceiling vents. Turning away, he edged his butt onto the exam table.

"What did you do to me?" she asked, making a hissing sound.

"I swear I didn't do this, at least not intentionally. I'm affected too. Whatever has gotten its claws into me from the attack in town, caused me to sprout a field of dandelions."

Aspen's eyes slivered. "What do you mean, attacked?"

He told her everything, leaving out how he'd felt inside. He couldn't form words for his own discernment.

Aspen plopped onto her rolling stool. "Is this why you're being compliant and not fighting Rafael or me tooth and nail?"

He hung his head and twisted a colorful bead bracelet around his wrist. "I need to understand what's happening to me. I think the Wildes—you—can help."

"Is it spelled?" She touched a couple of the beads, the softness and warmth of her skin trickling into him. He wanted her touching him more than anything. She calmed the fiery, earthy storm brewing inside him. When she withdrew, a frigid blast swept over him, and the storm ratcheted up a notch.

"Not that I'm aware. After I taught my niece how to make the bracelets, she painted the beads and gifted it to me."

"Is she a witch?"

"She's ten." He chuckled. "Dad's side of the fam. Maybe

she's a witch to her mother, but not me."

"Don't mistake bitch for witch." Aspen rolled her instrument tray closer. "She's talented. I could use her to make our spelled charms prettier. We use plain old wooden beads. Witches would gobble these up from my online store."

"What do your charms do?" Mundane conversation calmed Lucky. But his curiosity never abated. The more he learned about the witchworld, the better for living the rest of his life either inside or outside the fold.

"We use charms for healing, energy, no-doze, protection spells, you name it. It's one way we use magic. They can also provide a witch or warlock with magic they don't possess. The spelled charms don't detract from their magic but might enhance it with whatever magic a witch spelled the charms with." She pointed a digital thermometer at his forehead and registered his temperature on her iPad. "One hundred. Are you feverish?"

"Warmer than usual. Started when the vines attacked me. You too?"

"Yeah." Aspen sucked in her upper lip.

"For what it's worth, I'm sorry." He stretched his arm to her, but the fire in her brilliant green eyes forced him to drag his arm to his side. "Are you in pain from—"

"From the vines tattooing their way across my body? From the puncture on my wrist that won't react to healing magic? The vines rooted beneath my skin? What do you think?" She sagged forward, head bowed, her body shaking.

Lucky pulled her into his embrace. To his surprise, she wrapped her arms around his waist and rested her head on his chest, her angst and sobs stealing her common sense against enemy number one. But the soft, warmth of her in his arms undid him. He'd do anything to erase her pain and restore her to the witch—the woman—she was before she'd entered the pharmacy. What had he unleashed upon this beautiful woman, upon this next-level day?

He kissed the top of her head, the fresh scent of her hair infusing his senses. "I wish I could erase this day." She sniffed hard against his shirt, her breath searing his flesh. "I'll do anything to take your pain away. Tell me what to do."

"You really don't know?" she asked.

"I swear I don't." He tightened his arms around her. Her lack of resistance told him a ton.

"Why did you kiss me just now? We don't even like each other." She drew in her stomach.

"You needed comfort."

She patted him, her warm fingers lingering longer than necessary. He never wanted her to stop touching him. "Whatever. Thanks. Let's figure out this bitch. Together."

The comforting moment evaporated, and he planted his butt again on the exam table. "I can't work with someone who doesn't like me."

"Get used to it." Aspen snatched bottles and vials out of her refrigerator, hiding her face from him. "Now, tell me what ails you, Lucky Lorenzo."

He slivered his eyes at the three bottles. "Any poison there?"

"Did you want poison?" She quirked her cute eyebrows.

"Just checking." He laughed. His phone buzzed for the fourth time, and he glanced at the screen. His dad threatening to send the hounds of Hades after him. Laughter fell flat, and somberness eclipsed his momentary cheer.

"Trouble?"

"My dad's not keen on me being here."

"Among the badass Wilde witches."

"How'd you know?"

"*Wild* guess." She shrugged. "He's always nice to me at the pharmacy." She uncorked a bottle and doled out a spoonful of the golden viscous liquid. "This will calm you and help you deal with the changes going on inside you."

Lucky's head whipped up. "Why do you think I have changes going on?"

"This isn't my first rodeo dealing with a warlock who doesn't know he's a warlock, or a black warlock. Case in point, Rafael."

"He hinted about that." Lucky opened his mouth and Aspen jammed the spoon inside. He swallowed the honey-sweetened, flowery potion.

"I bet he said little. He's not much of a talker until he gets to know you. And trust you." She poured another potion in the spoon. "This one's bitter. But it'll curb the heat roasting you from the inside out."

"Jeez. You *have* ridden in the rodeo." Grimacing, Lucky smacked his lips, and the vile concoction slithered down his throat. A calmness already slowed his heart rate. "Pain next?"

"You betcha."

Aspen finished administering her potions, and a normalness centered him, more normal than he'd felt since he first noticed the buzzing, earthy strangeness after he'd turned sixteen.

"You're a miracle worker." He ignored his phone vibrating again, this time a call.

"Tell him you're okay."

"I already did."

"Tell him again. We won't hurt you. We just need to understand what's happening to you, me. The dude in the basement."

Lucky whipped his head back again. "What's his prob?"

"The vines are guarding his doorway. No one can enter. We're not sure how to feed him."

"Oh."

"Oh, is right." Aspen finished lining her potions in

impeccable order in her cupboard. "Now do you see why Rafael and Ethan snagged you?"

A tangled web of unease filtered through his new languidness. Again, what had he unleashed upon that day? Or had the man in the basement instigated the trainwreck?

Chapter 11

Why had Aspen let Lucky—a black warlock to boot—hold her? One part of her melted in his arms, while the other part remained angry at him for helping to foist this disastrous day upon them. But who'd defied Sage's orders and escaped the covenstead? *Jeez, Louise, was that only this morning?*

The door to her lab flung inward, and Brianne barreled inside. She wrapped Aspen in a bear hug. "Are you okay, cous?" Brianne dropped her arms to examine her from head to toe.

"Not really. How much have you heard?"

"Sage unloaded on Marina and me when we returned from town. We're grounded again. Thanks to you."

"I'm sorry." No guilt framed her words, nor lingered inside her. Well, maybe a little for Brianne who'd never let her live it down. After what'd happened, Sage's lockdown edict was right on the money.

Brianne inspected Aspen's wrist and the tattoos on her shoulder. "Sage said to measure them again." Her cousin eased her head back and perused Lucky's full length.

"Lucky Lorenzo, I presume?" Brianne licked her lips, a bright gleam in her pale green eyes. "If you weren't the bad guy, I'd love to see how lucky you are."

Aspen whacked Brianne's arm. "The jury's still out on whether he's the good or bad guy."

"Well, in that case." Brianne trailed her fingers up Lucky's arm and squeezed his biceps. He reddened, and he flicked her hand away from touching his face.

"Do you mind?" he asked. "I'm not property."

Brianne winked. "You could be."

"Wow. You treat your warlocks like chattel?" Indignation kindled in his exotic teal eyes, turning them dark and stormy. "No, thanks."

Aspen nudged Brianne out of the way. "My cousin, *Brianne*, is kidding. If you stick around, get used to her. We've all learned to tolerate her."

"As if." Brianne popped a squat on Aspen's rolling stool. "Now I'm playing healer. Strip it, Aspen, so I can photograph your tattoos. I want to see those bad boys." She swept her gaze over Lucky in a slow perusal. "You strip too. I bet you're hiding an eyeful."

"I didn't check." He scrubbed a hand over his face.

No tattoos inked his bare arms, but what did he hide beneath his red polo? Aspen feathered her fingers across his wrist. "You really didn't do this, did you?"

"I'm telling the truth." He gloved Aspen's hand on his wrist before moving to the hem of his shirt, a bit frayed at the side seams.

Dying to see him without his shirt, but unable to see his marred skin, she spun around. A sense of impending doom weighed on her chest. "Brianne, you check him."

Her cousin clapped and grinned. "Thought you'd never ask. Today's your lucky day, Lucky."

"Today has so not been my lucky day." He fisted his hands at his thighs. "I'll strip when Aspen strips." His voice shifted to a tease.

Excitement fringed her disdain and horror. She faced him again. "Fat chance. You're still Wilde coven enemy number one. Do you want us to check or not? Are you feeling anything?" She reached around and scratched her back. "Mine tickles and stings like a light sunburn."

"Been feeling creepy crawlies since I landed on your property."

"For real? Now I'm mega curious." Brianne pinched Lucky's shirt.

"Close your mouth. Flies are gathering," Aspen said to Brianne.

In one slick move, Lucky drew his shirt over his head. His sinful flat stomach, defined abs, and a tan worthy of summer dried up her retort.

Brianne fake-swooned. "My fingers need a closer inspection."

Aspen bumped her cousin out of the way. "Your chest and arms are fine. Turn." Before he'd turned all the way, she spied the black-edged purple flowers centered on his upper back. A gasp escaped her, and she cupped her mouth. Green vines crawled over his shoulder blades. "Did you have a tattoo before today?"

"No." He tossed a glance over his shoulder. "What is it?"

"The same flower and vine inked on me." Aspen tapped her temple, her mouth forming an "O." "A morning glory. Their seeds cause hallucinations, like taking LSD." She held up a small hand mirror for Lucky to see, while she held another one behind him.

"I'm not planning on licking my back." He examined his body in the mirror.

"You don't have to *lick* it. However, I might," Brianne teased. "But for real, the vines are a conduit of magic. The tattoo can take on the properties of a real morning glory.

Whoever cast the spell could penetrate your skin with the effects of the seeds. But no seeds until the flower dies and leaves behind a seed pod. Ingesting the flower will send you spewing *and* give you the squirts."

Lucky slammed the hand mirror on the counter. "Can I see your tattoo?"

Aspen unbuttoned her blouse, not caring if Lucky saw her sexy pink lacy bra. She stripped off her blouse, revealing the tattoos creeping down her left arm, halfway across her shoulders, and partway down her back. "Brianne, take photos." She cocked her head to see if they'd grown farther. Maybe a half inch. The growth stemmed from the wound on her left wrist.

Lucky stepped around her, the heat of his body seeping into her. "May I touch?"

"You can touch *me*," Brianne replied. "Let me strip first." Aspen shot her a death-ray stare. "Kidding." She took photos of Aspen's and Lucky's tattoos. "I'll take these to Sage. You two can touch each other to your heart's content."

"Send me the photos."

Brianne saluted her, took one last perusal of Lucky's physique, fanning her face, and left the lab.

"What does it feel like?" Lucky traced the vines and flowers across the upper half of her back. So delicate and comforting that Aspen wanted him touching her other side. Wanted what she shouldn't from this virtual stranger. And warlock. Black warlock.

"Your skin's so soft." His fingers traveled down her left arm, warm and tingly. "There's no distinction between the tattoos and your skin. They *are* your skin."

Aspen ran her hand up her arm until she met Lucky's fingers. She hesitated, withdrew, and rotated around him. She traced the vines and the three flowers, his soft skin over the firmness of his muscles beneath tethered them together.

"Same." She withdrew her hand. "You're on fire."

"Thanks." He chuckled, not budging an inch.

"I mean you're burning up." She shook off his cooties. Maybe he was contagious. She rummaged in her medicine cabinet and handed him two acetaminophen caplets and a bottle of water. "Good old-fashioned pain and fever reducer."

After he popped the pills, she took his temperature again. "Hundred and two. It's climbing."

As if on cue, he listed to the side and sank into himself. "I don't feel so hot." He started a slow slide to the floor.

Aspen lunged for him and assisted him to a bed in the other room. No sooner had his head hit the pillow and he was out like a light. She swept the hair off his face, his feverish skin burning into her. Reciting a water spell on a thin blanket, she cooled it to sixty-two degrees and draped it over him. Pondering her options, she debated on who to call. A medical doctor couldn't help him. A lightbulb flashed in her head, and she made the call to the Ravenwood healer.

"Marjorie," she greeted the witch, then responded to her instant question. "Yes, the tattoo is growing." She explained Lucky's situation, and Marjorie promised to head to the covenstead from her residence closer to the heart of Santa Cruz.

She returned to Lucky and forced herself not to kiss his worry lines away. With the security cameras turned on, she rushed to the dining room. Concern replaced her appetite. But she hadn't eaten since breakfast, and she'd plow through a meal the moment her eyes glommed onto a loaded plate. All attention shifted to her from the table where her family enjoyed their dinner. No one ever waited on anyone on the covenstead unless they'd scheduled a meal together. Their norm.

"Sage. Did you see the photos?"

"Did you leave Lucky alone in your lab?" Rafael jumped up, his chair clattering backward to the tile floor, the sound silencing the room.

She held up a hand. "His fever's climbing and he passed out. Marjorie's on her way." She set her phone next to her plate. Rafael texted gate security.

"Did you treat him?" Ethan asked.

"As best I know how. We don't know what we're dealing with." She tapped her phone, checked her camera. Still zonked.

"How are *you* feeling, cous?" Marina asked.

"Yeah, do we need to nurse you?" Brianne chimed in.

Sounded like everyone was in the loop. She rested the back of her hand on her own forehead. "A tad warm. I need to eat."

Uncle Ben loaded a plate with lasagna, garlic bread, and baked parmesan asparagus. The sight and scents of the Italian dinner assailed her hollow senses, and her belly rumbled. She dug into the meal to refuel her needs, which went way beyond the physical. A kitchen witch rolled in a dessert cart holding individual chocolate mousse cups topped with whipped cream. Her absolute favorite dessert.

"Ethan? Heard anything from Marjorie's research?" On normal days, they'd scatter to comfortable seating in the great room with their desserts, but tonight no one left the table while she continued to gorge on her lasagna. She noticed her sister Willow and boyfriend, Evan Ravenwood, were absent. Most likely both were doing homework for their respective law and grad schools. Her oldest cousin, Eden, was also absent, not unusual since she tended to hide from Ethan. The two played hide-and-seek since they'd discovered the other had psychic abilities. The mundane of keeping tabs on her family members kept her mind off the tattoo inching down her back in a more aware skitter.

"No. But Sage"—Ethan tipped his chin at her sister across the table—"found obscure black magic spells on the dark witch web that might've caused this curse on both you and Lucky. We're verifying their authenticity."

Aspen's fork clanked to her plate. "What are they? Did Andre's son do this?" To ease the constant itch of the tattoo, she rubbed her shoulders from side to side on the wooden back of her chair.

"I don't know," Sage answered. "I'd like Marjorie's assessment. She knows more about black magic than all of us combined."

Except maybe for their mother. Aspen ate a bite of garlic bread and tossed the rest on her plate. Apparently, their mother had conducted tons of research and dabbled in black magic behind their backs. Why? Had she foreseen the rise of black warlocks? Or just a curious cat? Or did she recognize value in black magic to work alongside "white" magic? Aspen wished her mother were present to explain herself.

She sucked down half a glass of lemon water. "Going to the lab." She grabbed a mousse and spoon, eager to read more in her mother's journal. Mom had alluded to at least one more text she'd hidden away, too treacherous for the average witch or warlock. Could it be on the grounds? Or another hidden file on her old laptop?

"Do you need me?" Brianne asked.

"I'm good. Send Marjorie in when she lands."

"You're no fun," Brianne pouted.

"I need to do more research. I'll call you if boredom strikes." Aspen bounced from the room, not a backward glance to mollify her cousin.

Her dinner pushed on her gut. She'd eaten too fast and too much. She slipped the mousse in her fridge on a shelf she reserved for food. When her gaze landed on Lucky, a flush worked up her neck. He'd dislodged the blanket. His temperature had stabilized. She pointed the thermometer on herself and noted her temperature at ninety-nine point three. Elevated, but not in dangerous territory. Aspen strengthened her spell, spritzed the cooling blanket with witch-water, and re-spread it over Lucky, her languid witch-water unable to dampen but a few spots. He slept like the dead, and she checked his pulse to ensure he was still kicking it. Again, a part of her was dying to press her lips to his forehead, but the devil on her left shoulder nixed the urge.

Before Aspen shifted to her mother's journal, Marjorie Magellan entered with crammed bags in tow. The petite older woman was all business regarding spells and healing.

"We meet again." Marjorie smiled at Aspen.

"This time my patient's a stranger. He swears he didn't know he was a warlock, or a black warlock." Aspen led the healer into Lucky's room.

"Ethan gave me the four-one-one." Marjorie opened her worn burgundy healer's bag. She set out various potions, lancets, charms, and other tools of her trade. She rolled up the side of Lucky's shirt to view his tattoo. "Let me see your back." Aspen stripped off her shirt for Marjorie to examine her. "This all started today? You sure?"

"Absolutely. After this happened." She flipped her wrist for Marjorie's inspection.

The healer gasped. Using a magnifying glass, she inspected the tiny vines growing out of Aspen's skin. "Just these two vines? Did you tear any out?"

"I dabbed a counter-spell on two and they fell off. They grew back, and haven't changed. Now they're undeterred by the counter-spell as if immune. Weird."

"I'll run tests on Lucky first. Then you next."

The witch returned to Lucky's bed, and Aspen sat to watch, donning her blouse once again. Should she just leave it off for show-and-tell?

"Then I want to see the room where you're holding your attacker. I hear there's a disaster going on there."

"I haven't seen the basement in a few hours." The least of her worries.

"Then we'll see it together. I want to witness how the plant life reacts to you." She pricked Lucky's index finger and squeezed drops of blood onto three test strips and a glass microscope slide.

Aspen drooped in her chair, her exhaustion conquering her last cache of energy. Watching Marjorie work intrigued her, but her eyes grew gritty in search of sleep. Marjorie recited what she was doing, and Aspen turned on her video. No energy existed in her body to jot notes. "Do you mind?" She positioned her phone.

Marjorie chuckled. "I'd love to mentor a young witch. There's no one in my family with the aptitude to pass along my knowledge."

"You honor me."

"You'd gain the knowledge of two great witch healers, and you'll make an extraordinary healer. Not that you aren't already."

The accolades drove a flush up Aspen's neck. "I'm still learning from my mother. I found her witch's compendium." The lure to her mother's writings was strong, but not compelling enough to eclipse her exhaustion. Tomorrow.

"I knew your mother. A healer ahead of her time." Marjorie lifted her head from her microscope and cast Aspen a pointed glare. "Did you know she dabbled in black spells and curses?"

Aspen jerked upright in her chair. "You knew? No one else in the family knows."

"We spent time together along with Ethan and Evan's mother. Lovely women."

"I'd love to pick your brain." She tipped her chin at Lucky. "Did you find anything in your research to explain the tattoos or the vines?"

Marjorie organized her tools. "He passed out from exhaustion and magic depletion. His temperature is down, but I suspect you'll both run warmer than usual from the magic. As for my research, I'm hitting walls. I've only hit the tip of the iceberg, so don't give up."

Aspen yawned, and her legs slid away from her chair. "Should I stay with him overnight?"

"Go to bed. Have your security witches check on him throughout the night."

Gnawing on her bottom lip, Aspen's mind raced with worry. Part of her wanted to stay with Lucky. The much larger part was dying to sleep. But first, she wanted to view the vines downstairs. "Let's see the basement before I crash." She drank a mild energy potion.

With one last lingering glimpse of Lucky sleeping like a baby, she left the lab. Matthew guarded her door from the hallway.

"Where to?" he asked.

"Basement. Please hang here and watch him."

"You can't go to the basement without a warlock and a trio of witches." He pulled his phone out and texted someone. "Rafael, Sage, and Ethan will meet you down there. Marina's already there."

"Marina's an earth witch, right?" Marjorie asked.

"Yep." The energy potion quickened her steps along the hallway. "Brianne's most likely hanging with her, so we'll have plenty of witches if the world tilts sideways." She engaged the eye reader, and the basement door lock clicked open.

"Oh, I'm not worried." Marjorie's soft-soled shoes followed her down the stairs.

They reached the room where they'd held Lucky first.

The purification scents of smoldering rosemary and frankincense wafted to her nose. The door stood open, and the room appeared normal, not a speck of mud or vine left behind. But a new creepy-crawly sensation slithered up Aspen's spine, and she shuddered.

Before she rounded a corner to the second holding room, she smelled the pungent flora and loam, the outdoors encroaching on the inside. She halted, bracing herself. Easing around the corner, she faced the gang standing in protective air bubbles. A mini garden had sprung up along the walls and the perimeter of the basement great room, all tracing their roots to the holding cell.

Morning glory vines with purple trumpet-shaped flowers grew in profusion over the walls. Poisonous water hemlock sprouted three feet tall from mounds of dirt on the floor bordering the walls, its white flowers stunning against its lacy fern-like leaves. Deadly nightshade, or belladonna by its fancy name, popped up in spots, the bell-shaped flowers, leaves, and berries toxic. Small toxic pink and magenta oleanders crowded the corners. Aspen recognized the stinging nettle growing before her eyes, sprouting between the other plants. The plant contained hollow hairs on the leaves and stems, which acted like hypodermic needles, injecting histamine and other chemicals that produced a stinging sensation upon contact. The nettles advanced, emerging in a green and yellow wave toward her.

Chapter 12

Sage recited a warding spell, cloaking Aspen and Marjorie in a protective bubble. The nettle and other plants squirmed and zigzagged to surround the bottom of the bubble closest to Aspen, a sea of poisonous foliage. Aspen centered herself in the warded circle as if the plants could breach the edges of the air cocoon.

"They're seeking witch-water," Sage said. "We removed Brianne once we realized. But they didn't surround her like you."

"Because I'm freaking special." Aspen scratched at her wrist, checked the sprouts. No change. No reaction to the plants in the basement. Had they spawned from the blood they stole from her?

"Did you deplete your magic today?" Marjorie asked.

"Yep. Can't raise a spitball." Aspen didn't bother trying to use her powers. Lucky benefited from her last hurrah. She rolled a tube of her frosty, pink-tinted lip balm out of her pocket and slathered it on her lips. The cool peppermint oil in the balm soothed the dryness.

Marjorie gripped Aspen's arm below her wound. "This

thing and the tattoos are draining your witch-water." The healer released Aspen's arm and shook out her hand. For all she knew, Aspen carried contagious curses.

Aspen sat on the floor and crisscrossed her legs. "Guess no sleep for me tonight. Have you looked inside the goon's room?"

"He's surrounded by morning glories, but they aren't touching him." Rafael showed her the cameras inside the room from his security app.

"Who's his mother?" Aspen asked Ethan.

"If she's the earth witch I think she is, she's dead. Andre's consorts didn't last long."

"What did he do to them?" Panic darted through Sage's eyes.

"His magic overpowers most witches' magic. One died in childbirth, one killed another in a jealous tirade, his earth magic suffocated one when he flew into a rage. The list goes on." Distaste colored Ethan's words, making his feelings abundantly clear.

The day caved in on Aspen. "Marjorie, do I need to stay awake?" She fought down a double yawn, the aridness in her body claiming the last of her energy. "Even with a no-sleep charm, I don't think I can stay awake."

"No, your magic will regenerate whether asleep or resting. But sleep in a protective circle alone. I want another witch and warlock on guard outside the circle."

"Done," Sage said. "Rafael and I will take first watch and rotate with Jessica and Ben."

Aspen dragged herself to a guest room on the second floor, Rafael and Sage following. They chose the guest room since a protective circle of chalk and salt already circled the bed. Sage invoked the protection and warding spell. Jessica charged into the room with no-sleep amulets for Rafael and Sage, her familiar cat, Pebbles, hopping a ride on her shoulder. The tabby growled at Rafael's black lab familiar, who ignored the cat in its quest to sniff every inch of the bedroom. Shadow was as protective of Aspen as she was of Rafael.

Exhausted, Aspen flopped onto the bed, its plushness enveloping her tired body. Rafael rolled her out full length and tugged her boots off before kissing her forehead, the way they liked to tease one another.

"Thanks, Dad." She laughed. Though he was only a few years older, he was wise and mature beyond his years. The warlock the coven needed to rule with Sage. The kind of warlock Aspen wanted for her own... someday.

☪☪☪

Aspen's witch-water only halfway regenerated overnight, but she could confront the day with a clear mind. Except the vines growing out of her wrist were now a half-inch longer. She'd hoped it was all a big, hairy nightmare. No such luck. *Lucky...*

"Fuck a duck." She rolled on her back and studied her wrist. "At least I rhyme well."

Sage's eyelids flapped up, and she jumped out of the cozy recliner. Rafael must've let her sleep while he played watch dog. "Show me."

Not bothering to catalog Sage's reaction, Aspen flipped up her wrist. She had her own reaction to contend with... and other matters. "Can you cut the ward? I need to check on Lucky."

Sage murmured the counter-spell and waggled her fingers in a circle above her head to break the ward. Her owl familiar lugged away the opaque threads in its beak to a negative corner of the room where the magic dissipated. Aspen sat up and dangled her legs over the side of the bed.

Rafael strode out of the bathroom, drying his hands on a towel. "Lucky's okay. He's eating breakfast."

Aspen read the time on her fitness tracker. Already past nine. "What's going on in the basement?"

"Same. With Marina's help to deflect and trick the plants, we got food and water into Pierre's room." Rafael frowned at the tattoos roiling on Aspen's arm as they sought her witch-water for sustenance.

Aspen took his frown as a sign. Not caring again who saw her in her bra—which was no worse than her bikini tops—she peeled off her blouse and turned her back to Sage and Rafael. Sage's sharp intake of breath was a dead giveaway. "That bad?" Aspen canted her head to peer over her shoulder, but the tattoo ended out of sight. That bad.

She sprinted to the bathroom. The image in the mirror icked her out. The tattoos grew and morphed, sucking on her depleting witch-water. So much for overnight rejuvenation. Leaning her elbows on the vanity, dry sobs shook through her. Not one tear breached her lower eyelids.

Sage draped a silky robe over her shoulders. "We'll solve this. Don't waste your tears."

"What tears!" Rage bubbled up from her toes. She flung herself around, her butt digging into the vanity counter. "How can I not freak out?" she shouted. "This thing is siphoning my witch-water. I replenish, it steals more water. An unknown, evil alien has claimed me. The plants downstairs are sucking me dry too."

"Maybe we need to remove her from the property." Rafael paled. Circumstances didn't bode well when even he freaked out. "Separate her from Lucky and the covenstead."

Sage didn't hesitate in her response. "You'll go to the Ravenwood covenstead."

Aspen stamped her foot on the tile floor. "No. Lucky needs treatment. I need—" She collapsed against Sage and folded her arms around her older sister the way she used to with her mom. "I don't know what I need." Documents and books were missing from her mom's belongings, and she needed to hunt clues to their location, needed to search her laptop for hidden files.

"Until we know what we're dealing with, maybe we need to separate you from all water and earth witches and warlocks," Sage said.

Gaining momentum to confront the day, Aspen stood straight. "No. Move Lucky out of my lab. I'll stay there cloaked in a protective ward."

"Didn't help last night." Rafael scrubbed his bed-tousled hair.

"Shit on a stick," Aspen railed aloud.

They hadn't heard the door open, or witnessed how long Marjorie eavesdropped, until the witch said, "Aspen comes home with me. She needs off this covenstead." The reflection of Aspen's backside in the mirror riveted her attention. "Your witch-water is feeding the curse"— Marjorie waved her right arm—"on the entire covenstead. You need to separate from the warlock in the basement and Lucky Lorenzo until we figure out how to break this curse."

"Curse?" Rafael blanched again.

"Curse, spell, bond, whatever," Marjorie said. "Pack your bags, bring all your mother's texts."

"I take it you've found no explanation." Aspen passed her fingernails over an itchy spot on her back. The tattoo moved away from her hand, creeping her out.

"Nothing concrete. A few good old-fashioned counter-spells we can test." Marjorie offered a grim-faced smile. "But I doubt it'll be that simple."

A gaggle of witches and warlocks had gathered in the hallway, watching and waiting.

"What about Lucky?" Brianne asked. "I guess I can amuse him while Aspen's gone."

Aspen threw her cousin a mad-dog look. "*Au contraire,* cousin of mine. Let him recover in peace." What she refrained from saying was, "Keep your grubby paws off him. I saw him first."

"So mote it be," Sage said, even though she hadn't voiced a spell. She released Aspen and clapped, a loud crack that echoed to the vaulted ceiling. "All of you go about your day. As we discussed yesterday, we'll have a Spring Solstice festival restricted to the Wildes and Ravenwoods. And Marjorie, of course. Let's plan some fun. Jessica is managing the budget. No more leaving the grounds." Her gaze slid to Aspen, then to Brianne and Eden. "You water witches will make do using the creek."

Surprise riddled Aspen. At least her escapade yesterday hadn't killed all the fun. Why the pointed look at Brianne *and* Eden? Eden wasn't a water witch. What nuisance had they caused in town while Aspen suffered from her smack-down of the Pierre and plant kind?

A state of excitement disbursed the small crowd, and Aspen hurried to her bedroom on the other side of the second floor. It didn't take long to pack a bag for a few days. But it took longer to pack up the things she needed from her lab.

"Jeez, moving out?" Brianne propped her shoulder against the door molding of her lab.

Aspen didn't stop cramming books and journals in her laptop bag. "What shit did you disturb at the beach yesterday?"

Brianne fake-gasped and laid a hand over her heart. "Little ole me? Who said I did anything? I swam, I waded, I sauntered along the shoreline, I took my fill of the beauty and magnitude of the ocean. I replenished my lagging witch-water. We ate like pigs."

"Cut the crap." Aspen spun on her cousin. "What'd you do?"

Brianne took a perch on the rolling stool. "Eden was reading the minds of a group of hella hot dudes who couldn't take their eyes off us. Four humans, hot as they come."

"Right up your alley."

"Except they knew we were witches. Two of the hunks were in Eden's class at high school."

Aspen shoved the last book into her bag and zipped it up. "Guys who think witches are easy?" Stories floated about how witches were nymphomaniacs when gauging a connection to warlocks who didn't exhibit warlock traits or an obvious aura. The meter usually involved sex. Rumors abounded, and they did their best to deflect them, even though true.

"Yep. Asshats." Brianne flung her hair behind her back, and a sly smile slid across her face. "They were having impure thoughts about screwing us, orgy-style."

Aspen gasped. "You're not serious? As in rape?"

"Not quite, but they didn't plan to grant us much say in the matter except for us to worship at their feet, while we traded partners. I did what any smart water witch would do." She grinned. "Can you guess?"

"Oh, goddess. You crashed a wave over their heads. In broad daylight. In front of witnesses."

"Three waves." Brianne cringed. "What would you have done? They deserved it. Besides, a few rogue waves didn't hurt a thing."

Aspen busted out in giggles. "Rogue waves my ass. Did you hightail it?"

"Eden wrapped us in an air bubble to make us invisible and we skedaddled."

"Is Sage pissed?"

"More than. After what you did and those rogue waves, we'll be lucky to leave the grounds before we die." Brianne changed her tune. "Speaking of Lucky—"

Aspen held up her palm. "We weren't speaking of him."

"We had breakfast with him. He's a puzzle, for sure."

"No shit, Sherlock." Aspen cocked her head, curiosity

getting the better of her. "But why do you think so?"

"He's hot and cold toward you, all witches and warlocks. He has something to get off his magnificent chest. We think he's afraid on one hand, on the other, he wants to blurt it out. Then on one foot, he's angry and wants revenge. He's all over the gamut of emotions. His thoughts gave Eden a headache, and she had to take a chill pill."

Marjorie appeared in the door. "Ready, kid?"

Lucky towered behind the diminutive older witch. "I still need to talk to Ethan. I invited you there as the sole Wilde witch."

"Maybe Lucky needs to join us, Marjorie. He's suffering too."

"No. You need separation from everyone here." Marjorie subtly compressed her jaw, a silent signal of her rising frustration. "We don't know if he's the cause. Let Sage and Ethan deal with him."

Lucky backed out of the doorway. "Then I'll go home."

"Not until you give up the goods." Ethan's stomping footsteps chased his words from the hallway. "You talk. Then we'll decide what to do." Ethan gripped Lucky's forearm, his long beefy fingers not quite reaching around the circumference. Lucky wasn't as muscular as the Ravenwood brothers, but he held his own. Aspen licked her lips. Damn, she loved a man's nice sculpted forearm, and Lucky's were divine.

Like they knew she was drooling over them, Lucky's arm muscles contracted, and he shook Ethan's hand off. "Fine. See ya, Aspen. Guess my warden has other plans." He straightened his rumpled shirt, the same one he'd worn yesterday. His damp hair proved that his wardens had at least accommodated his hygiene if not clean clothing.

Aspen balked. She wanted to hear Lucky's story. Where his magic stemmed from when no one knew he existed. Sage and Rafael had a good grip on all witches and warlocks in the area. An interloper always toted speculation, apprehension, and anticipation. Excitement fringed Aspen's desire to hear, see, touch, and feel everything about Lucky. Whatever was going on with him on the covenstead suppressed his aura, but what she'd experienced in the pharmacy punched all her good buttons. Could she deal with a black warlock? *Whoa. Wait.* She acted like they were already a couple. In the end, Lucky may despise her and the Wildes. Their circumstances could doom any potential relationship they might enjoy in the future. Although she harbored perceptions passed down from history against black warlocks, she couldn't help but soften toward them since Rafael's recent exposure as a black warlock and the Ravenwoods had joined the "family."

"Aspen? Get your head out of the clouds." Brianne pinched her arm. "Marjorie's ready to bounce."

Aspen drew Brianne aside. "Keep your eye on Lucky. Make sure no one hurts him." She fastened her fanny pack around her waist, making sure everything was secure before slipping in her single earbud. She craved the solace of music, but didn't want to come across as impolite in case Marjorie wanted to strike up a conversation.

Brianne licked her lips. "I'll keep my eye on him all right." The light in her eyes faded. "Don't get hung up on him. Sage isn't a fan. Rafael wants to kick his ass. Plus, he's a black warlock."

"What does Ethan think?" Black warlocks or not, Aspen cared what the Ravenwoods thought. After all, Lucky may very well be a Ravenwood.

"He's ready to welcome Lucky to the family."

"There you go!" Aspen fist-bumped the air. A fine mantle of crushed lavender and rosemary drifted off her arm to dust the floor. Sage and Rafael respected their Ravenwood allies, and whatever Ethan said about Lucky would sway her coven's actions.

Aspen and Marjorie left the house, the late morning sun striking her eyes and causing them to water. Water she couldn't afford to expend. She squinted until she dug out her sunglasses. Sage, Rafael, and Aunt Jessica waited by the driveway where Marjorie had parked her pristine Camry. Rafael took her bags and tossed them in the trunk.

Sage hugged her, and Aspen clung to her sister. "We'll figure this out, sis."

"I know."

"We'll do video chats. Learn something from Marjorie." Sage squeezed her one last time and let go. "No black magic." She waved her finger in Aspen's face. "Unless Marjorie approves."

"What if Mom approved?" Aspen asked slyly.

Sage angled her body, as if to trap secrets in the air before they escaped. "If Mom dabbled in black magic, I want to know."

"Aye, aye, *capitano*." Aspen mock-saluted her sister, letting Sage believe the best of their mother for a bit longer. Not that brewing black curses meant their mother was "bad." Just not the mother they knew.

Rafael shut the front passenger door and squeezed her shoulder. "Keep it chill. Nine-one-one me if you're threatened."

Marjorie drove around the circular drive, the wheels clicking on the pavers to the main driveway leading off the covenstead. As soon as the wheels touched the cement drive, a sharp pain stabbed Aspen's head, and every muscle froze. The stabbing radiated down the nape of her neck. An invisible claw tried to tug out her intestines. Clutching the dashboard, she cried out. Marjorie hit the brakes, jerking them both in their seats, the seat belt locking her in place. The pain intensified, and something unnamed and unholy pervaded Aspen.

Chapter 13

Despite the commands firing from her brain, Aspen's determination crumbled, leaving her frozen in place. The sun glinted off the windshield, bathing it in blinding light. The woods seemed to come alive, moving in a slow, mesmerizing dance that looked like another world. Everything appeared normal outside. But inside her, a jumble of uncertainty and panic shot normal to smithereens.

"What is it?" Marjorie's compassionate voice awakened her momentary dip into a vat of fear.

Sage and others appeared outside her car door. Aspen held up a hand to stall them, corralling her thoughts. When she'd dissected the magic, she rolled down her window. "Something's holding me here. A force preventing me from reaching the fence."

Marjorie punched the ignition off. "Try to walk toward the gate. One step at a time. Listen to your body."

Aspen opened the door, the small crowd peeling away like receding waves. She climbed out of the car, taking a backward step. Nothing changed. The dull pressure on her insides remained. "Goddess, just take me now," she muttered.

Closing the door, she lost her balance, and Rafael grasped her arm as if to stop her from toppling over the mystical ledge. She advanced a step. No change. Another step. Nothing.

Marjorie joined them as Sage recited a protective spell over Aspen. "Stop," Marjorie admonished. "We need to determine where this is stemming from."

"You mean what it is?" The sound of Sage's distress filled the air, rising in pitch.

"Does it matter?" Aspen lashed out, taking two more steps forward. A bead of precious sweat trickled down her temple. Her head thundered, and her breakfast warned of a second coming. She brushed the sweat into her hair and dug in her pocket for a pain amulet. Fresh out. Gritting her teeth, she dislodged Rafael's arm and took several more footsteps, stopping five yards from the wrought-iron gate. The pressure amplified, and air grew in short supply. She signaled Leah to open the gate.

One more step, and her head exploded. She winced and swallowed bile. Determined, she continued, fighting the rockets launching in her head and the alarming gurgling in her intestines. Each step forward was like a large rubber band attached to her ankles anchored her to the house. If she let go, would the band fling her onto the roof? *Inquiring minds wanted to know.* Each footstep turned into a slog through cement against a granite mountain.

Drenched in sweat she couldn't afford to lose, she reached the gate and banged into another impenetrable force field. The invisible rubber bands on her tripled, pulled from her thighs and upper torso, and yanked her against Rafael. Thank the goddess for his helicoptering ways or she'd have indeed splattered on the roof.

"Whoa." Rafael gripped Aspen, but the force was even

too great for his not-so-insignificant strength. They fought it, but the force dragged them behind Marjorie's car, through the scattering witches and warlocks. *Chickenshits!* Only then, did the magic call uncle, and Aspen stood steady in Rafael's supporting embrace.

"Dad to the rescue again." She straightened her skewed blouse and covered the Wicked Wrist, as she'd now dubbed the twin pests.

"Everyone hold your places." Sage held up a hand. The birds in the nearby woods trilling and whistling overshadowed the static silence, too normal on this crap-ass day.

Aspen relayed what she felt. "I can't leave the grounds."

She tried to walk through the pedestrian gate farther down the fence line. No dice. Sage and Jessica tried to float her in an air bubble over the fence and the spell disintegrated, dumping Aspen on the ground where she emptied her stomach in a planter containing her mother's early budding roses, their gorgeous red blooms killing a tiny part of her horror.

Panting, she stretched out on her back on the ground and closed her eyes. The cool mountain breeze drying her sweat calmed her, and she gave a thumbs-up. When her eyes fluttered open, Lucky's eyes locked with hers. The newest bane of her existence.

"Can you leave?" she asked.

"If you want me to." Lucky shrugged his wide shoulders. "Don't think it's in Ethan's or Rafael's cards."

"No. I mean, can your two feet walk you out the stupid gate?" She propped herself up on her elbows. His gorgeous grin dispelled her annoyance. He flung a shock of sun-bleached hair off his forehead and sauntered through the gate and returned. *Boo hiss for lucky Lucky.*

"Guess you're just as much a prisoner as me." He

reached a hand down to her. "The bed in your infirmary has to be softer than the ground, although that's not saying much."

Aspen took his firm hand, his long, slender fingers twining around hers. He hauled her up, not a strain to his arms, and straightened her blouse. The pain in her head and elsewhere receded the moment he'd stepped into her personal orbit. She wiped her mouth on the back of her hand and popped in a half dozen pocket mints. Thank the goddess she never left home without them.

"Do you live here now? Who allowed you to wander?"

"He's not a prisoner." Rafael returned to Sage's side and stretched his arm around her waist. Wistfulness roamed through Aspen's pain-ravaged body. Could she find such love and devotion with Lucky? If he wasn't public enemy number one, that is. Or a black warlock.

"The drawing board calls," Sage announced. "Guess you're not going anywhere." She locked gazes with Lucky. "Neither are you." She glanced toward Marjorie. "What's next?"

The sun ascended higher behind the eastern trees and illuminated the driveway. Light glittered off a multi-crystal pendant hanging around Marjorie's neck. Crystals for every need. The Wildes sometimes used crystal energy in a spell or two. Maybe Marjorie could teach her crystal magic to add to her expanding bag of tricks. Anything to distract the cyclone in her head.

Before the older witch answered, a navy-blue sedan drove through the gate, the Sand Dollar Pharmacy logo on the doors. Marjorie's car blocked the sedan, and it stopped, bumper to bumper.

Lucky groaned and dropped Aspen's hand, leaving behind a bereft iciness. More than a re-do of her last two days, she wanted Lucky's hand on hers again. His close presence not only stirred her hormones into a frenzy, but it helped soothe the pain and discomfort the freak show of the moment caused. As if he was the key to her internal operations. What the actual next level of hell?

Aspen recognized Dr. Lorenzo. The grim, red anger on his thin face led her to believe he didn't give a hoot if he'd abandoned his store for the day. Wasn't Lucky supposed to be working? Whatever. Dr. Lorenzo's presence didn't bode well.

All attention swiveled to the lanky man from his thick salt-and-pepper hair to his comfortable loafers. Dressed for his workday in a long-sleeve button-down shirt, sans tie, and dress slacks. Aspen saw little resemblance to Lucky in Dr. Lorenzo's facade. Maybe Lucky carried all his mother's features.

"You don't belong here," Dr. Lorenzo said to Lucky as the two faced off.

"Um, Dr. Lorenzo," Aspen said. "It's nice to see you. You have nothing to worry about."

More Wilde witches and warlocks had joined the group as the nightmare on Elm Street dragged onward. The pharmacist waved his arm at her to stifle her. A rude gesture that pushed Rafael and Sage to sandwich Lucky between them, positioning Aspen behind the trio.

Aspen gave a haughty sniff. Dr. Lorenzo had always been nice to her, maybe a little too professional. Had he buried his true feelings to accept her money? She opened her mind's eyes to study his aura. Nothing unusual. He'd never possessed magic, and still didn't.

"I think I belong," Lucky spoke with a strained, controlled fury. "Maybe not here, but among people like the Wildes and Ravenwoods."

Dr. Lorenzo's head snapped around, his gaze searching. "Steer clear of the Ravenwoods. I'm warning you, Lucky, no good will come of your fascination with witches and warlocks."

Sage extended her hand, but he shot mystical daggers from his eyes. "It's more than a fascination, Lawrence." She swished a hand toward the house, the sunlight sparkling on her diamond engagement ring, bouncing tiny diamonds off the cars. Wilde witch eyes landed on the pharmacist and impaled him with a calming stare kindled by magic. Nothing changed in his demeanor. "Shall we take this inside? Lucky, what do you want to do?"

"Stay, Dad. Ethan Ravenwood will be here soon. I'm sure you're just as eager as I am to hear what he has to say."

"No!" Dr. Lorenzo bellowed. "The Ravenwoods are evil. Traitors. They'll force you into their world, and you'll never see daylight again."

Silence enveloped the rapt group. Birds chirped in the high pines and redwoods, mocking their standoff, inciting a raucous song to compete with the discussion on the ground.

Aspen's gaze caught on a black SUV parked outside the gate. "Hello, Lawrence. Traitor Ethan Ravenwood at your service."

Steam billowing out of his ears and eyes blazing devil-like, Lawrence spun around, a small handgun suddenly engulfed in his right hand.

Aspen readied a pint-sized diffusing spell, all the magic she could muster. Fireballs balanced on Sage's, Rafael's, and Ethan's hands. Not that they'd ever toss one at a human. But Aspen knew they'd invoked the magic to get him to back off. Balthazar, Ethan's raven familiar, vaulted off his shoulder and hovered over the tableau, flapping its wings and screeching at Lawrence.

"Don't you dare come any closer," he warned Ethan, his voice glacial. "Lucky, get in the car. We're leaving. Now."

"Dad." Lucky gripped his father's forearm. "What are you doing? I came here to figure things out. I agreed to stay."

Lawrence cast a quick glance at Lucky's hand and wrist. From Aspen's peripheral vision, she noted that the vine tattoo stood out like a missing thumb, not even a sore thumb, on Lucky's bare arm. Lawrence gasped, clutching the gun tighter, then slid it along Lucky's arm before training the weapon on Ethan again.

"What atrocious matter is this?" he sputtered.

Hands in the air, Ethan stepped forward. "Let's talk. Here, inside, doesn't matter, but please put the gun down. There's no need for violence. If Lucky wants to go, he can go. You're both free to leave."

Rafael positioned Sage behind him and came abreast of Lucky and Ethan. "Lorenzo, if you plan to bully us further, get off our property. Take your son with you."

"I'm staying," Lucky announced, loud and definitive.

"Lucky?" Lawrence's gun-toting hand dipped a skosh.

"Give me the gun." Lucky stepped closer to his father. "I'd like you to stay. I bet you can fill in a ton of blanks."

"No!" Rage vibrated over Lucky's father.

A deafening boom resonated through the air. The explosive sound reverberated across the covenstead, causing the chirping birds to take flight in a flurry of startled wings and screeches. Aspen's heart pounded in her chest. The sudden eruption echoed and bounced off distant objects, amplifying the intensity. Adding a tangible weight to the atmosphere, the acrid scent of gunpowder lingered.

The gathered witches and warlocks readied their magic. The air grew humid, a breeze ruffled Aspen's hair around her face, and embers crackled above her head. Leah's ivy vines popped out of the earth and surged toward Lawrence. Sage erected a shield around him, and Eden's witch-air blew the gun under Marjorie's car. Time slowed as the batshit crazy gunfight at the O.K. Corral settled into everyone's brains.

Panicked, Aspen patted herself down, searching for a wound. Ethan gripped his left arm, and she shifted her attention to him. Sweat beads formed on Lawrence's upper lip, and he trembled as he sank to his knees. As Aspen rushed toward Ethan, Rafael and Matthew strong-armed Lawrence's arms behind his back.

Wind funneled around them as Eden's magic whipped away. The adrenaline and fear subsided, and a palpable relief washed through the crowd. Sizzling fire magic abated, a gathering cyclone spun into a trickle, and mud balls disintegrated into dust.

Aspen peeled back the ripped sleeve on Ethan's upper arm. She examined the wound, took a clean cloth from Marjorie, and pressed it to his arm. "Flesh wound. You'll live. Come to my lab, and I'll bandage you up."

"Ravenwood, I'm sorry. I lost control," Lawrence blubbered.

"He stays," Ethan said as he passed Rafael, riding Aspen's heels.

Rafael nodded. "Lucky! Follow me. Bring him."

Aspen passed Lucky holding his father in a tight embrace. Stopping him from going gangsta? Or stopping him from dumping a load in his pants?

"This day is another hellscape." She held the front door open for Ethan.

"Mind telling me what happened?" He winced as he brushed his arm against the doorframe.

"I'll tell you, but then I'll have to kill you." She attempted to lighten the mood.

"Guess you'll have to kill me too," Marjorie said behind them.

They entered the infirmary. As Aspen gathered her healing supplies, Marjorie clued Ethan in on the morning's shenanigans.

Aspen fished in her cubbies for a pain amulet and

discovered Lucky's bead bracelet. The one she'd admired. A note attached to it read, "Thank you for everything, Lucky."

A frisson of warmth calmed her frayed nerves. Out of nowhere, a memory of a similar bracelet flooded her mind. She'd loved the secret Santa gift received in high school. Never knew who'd gifted it to her. She clipped on the bracelet. Lucky had already tightened the cord to fit her wrist.

As she snagged her hoodie off a coat tree to the side of the door, something soft sifted from the ceiling onto her arm. First thought, a spider—or something equally hairy with more than two legs—and she frenetically flung it off. A purple morning glory, the size of a soda bottle cap fell onto her sneaker. Her fingers quaked, the tremors echoing the frantic dance of her heart against her ribs. Ever so slowly, eyes narrowing, she tilted her head back.

"Aspen? What's wrong?" Marjorie asked.

She pointed to the ceiling and began to hyperventilate, trying to drag in decreasing air.

"Son of a bitch." In one fell swoop, Ethan hip-bumped the exam table aside and grabbed Aspen before she splattered onto the floor.

A leafy morning glory vine grew through the vent, the leaves and purple flowers dangling from the ceiling.

Chapter 14

Rafael held the door open to a room he dubbed the "forest meeting room." The interior soothed Lucky more than he cared to admit, from a mural of the woods and a creek on one long wall to the thick padded chairs spaced around the oval table. The mural was so lifelike, he felt like he sat in the meadow opposite a babbling brook. A soundscape from ceiling speakers even brought the trickling and gurgling of water washing over rocks and pebbles to the calming room.

Shock surged through Lucky. He sank into a swivel chair along one side of the table, placed strategically to view all points of the room without his back to the door. His father sat beside him. Remorse seeped off him, but Lucky was in no mood to console his father. What he'd done was so far beneath the man he knew and loved. Where had such animosity and violence stemmed from? Before that day, his dad had possessed a gentle soul, who'd never hurt a spider. Well, maybe nothing larger than a spider. The door opened and a large white owl flew inside the room. He ducked, arms covering his head.

"Chill." Rafael handed them bottles of water from a mini fridge. "Gwyneira is Sage's familiar, checking for danger."

The owl flew from one corner of the room to the others before landing on top of a bookcase across from Lucky. It bestowed a hairy eyeball on him and smoothed its wings.

"Why's he looking at me like I'm gonna go loco and kill everyone?" He braced for impact.

"Until *she* knows you, you're a danger." Sage glided into the room.

Aspen followed, and from her red eyes, he knew something more had happened. What new twilight zone had she fallen into? He jumped up to go to her, but his father's grip on his wrist held him back. Ethan Ravenwood growled at him from behind her. He returned to his chair, grateful for the full padding hitting his ass. Another physical hit to his system would probably bury him six feet under. Ethan had a clean bandage wrapped around his upper arm, and his dad's body deflated in his chair.

The owl flew to Sage's shoulder, slipped beneath her blouse, and disappeared. Lucky blinked until he remembered how a witch's familiar developed into tattoo form. He hadn't seen Aspen's familiar, nor any familiar tattoos on her body. Had the vine tattoo covered up her familiar? Did she possess a bird too?

His dad's gaze darted around the room. "Where'd the owl go?"

"You're safe," Sage said. "She won't hurt you unless I direct her to."

Lucky surmised that humans didn't possess the same sight of magic as a witch or warlock. *I'm already believing I'm a warlock. How did I see the owl morph if I'm not? Why don't I have a familiar?* He'd already seen Ethan's raven and Rafael's lab, so warlocks had familiars.

"Time to get down to business." Sage sat at the head of

the table opposite the door in the chair Rafael rolled out for her. She caressed his hand on her shoulder as he stood behind her, guarding, watching, and waiting for several more shoes to drop.

"Give up the goods, Lucky, with all of us in the room, or you can stew on it in the basement." Rafael cracked his knuckles, slow and deliberate, the clicking sounds grating on Lucky's last nerve.

"It's fine. Everyone here has a stake. But I want reciprocation."

"Deal." Sage tapped her fingers on the table, her long blue nails adding color to the glass. "Dr. Lorenzo, do you agree?"

"Dad, I want reciprocation from you too," Lucky demanded. "I'll not go another day without the truth."

"I knew this day would come soon." His father cleared his throat and strengthened his gentle voice. "I had hoped to bury it forever. But things changed, threats made and"— his gaze bounced from Sage, Ethan, and Rafael—"We need your help. But only if you're helping us and not trying to hinder, or kill us, or drag us into your morass of evil."

"Lawrence." Ethan thumped the table. "We're the good guys here. If you've been involved with or experienced threats from Andre Charlemagne, the Black Tide, or other witches and warlocks, then you need us on your side. The Ravenwoods are not part of their numbers. We once belonged because Andre threatened annihilation of our entire line if we didn't toe the line. We grudgingly agreed for decades until we found a secure and permanent way out with the help of the Wildes."

Lucky absorbed Ethan's words. It was the first he'd heard the Ravenwoods weren't true members of the Black Tide. His mother's journals painted a different and frightening story. Hence the reason Lucky wanted nothing to do with the Ravenwoods. Once he'd heard they had aligned with the Wildes, it became clear he couldn't trust the Wildes either. Now, all bets were off if Ethan told the truth.

"I'm willing to listen." His dad sat straighter in his chair.

He'd take it. Dad listening was better than gun-waving. He had no clue his father even owned a gun.

Aspen addressed Lucky from across the table, sandwiched between Ethan and Rafael. "Pierre Charlemagne didn't single me out, did he?"

"No. He's been casing the pharmacy for a few days. I think he got a twofer with you and me, even though it backfired."

"I saw him and realized that someone had breached our cover," his father added.

"He's one of Andre Charlemagne's sons," Ethan confirmed.

"Is Lucky really a Ravenwood?" The tiny vines slashed Aspen's wrist, and she scratched at them.

Lucky positioned his chair to view his father straight on, not wishing to avoid Aspen, but the wound, the tattoos, everything about her stirred his nerves... and his desire. Foremost, he was dying to hear the secrets his father hid from him.

"Yes, Lucky's a Ravenwood." His dad twisted his simple gold wedding band. "His mother's real name is Kenley Ravenwood." He slid a dark squint at Ethan. "Her brothers Eric and Richard turned on her when they sided with Andre. When she escaped, she changed her name. We married, and she took my name. I was just a random student she bumped into at university and we hit it off. I had no skin in the game until I resolved to protect her to her dying days."

Ethan held up a hand. "Whoa. My father and uncle didn't turn on her. She joined forces with Andre and severed ties with the Ravenwoods. Kenley threatened to expose the Ravenwoods' goals to get rid of Andre and the Black Tide. She wanted no part of our plan."

Lucky pinched the hem of his T-shirt, folded it up and under, over and over. "Andre brainwashed her with both magic and herbs." He glanced at Aspen, the herbal expert in the room. "He made her believe he stood for good and that the Ravenwoods were evil, seeking the ultimate power. She made you believe it, Dad. Because she believed it once. I guess we'll never know why she didn't correct her story when she discovered what Andre had done. Maybe her head was buried in the sand even back then." He shot a pointed look at his dad.

Face awash in red, his father rounded on him. "You weren't there. How do you know?"

Lucky sat rigid in his chair, drumming his fingers on the tabletop. "I found her writings, not quite journals, possibly a memoir."

"What writings?" His father's jaw plunged. "She dreaded documenting it in case it ended up in the wrong hands."

"In encrypted files on her old laptop."

"But I scrubbed her computer and recycled it." His father wrung his hands. "I scoured it for anything that could explain *her*." He held Ethan's gaze. "She didn't tell me much of what happened at the Black Tide compound. Enough to know anyone associated with it were evil incarnate."

"I removed the hard drive before you tossed it. I know a few hackers who helped decrypt it."

"If she feared the Ravenwoods and the Black Tide, why are you living in Santa Cruz, or California for that matter?" Aspen rotated the bead bracelet around her wrist. A tenderness seeped over his heart. She touched a bowl of dried lavender on the side table, and it filled with water.

Using her witch-fire, Sage lit the candle beneath it. Soon lavender steam infused the air, fragrant and soothing.

"Good question." Ethan's eyes brightened with speculation. "We never knew what happened to her after she escaped. She dropped off the grid. We always thought Andre had re-captured her and secreted her away to one of his hidden enclaves. He owns compounds around the world. Lucky telling us she'd died was news to us. My father and uncle are grieving her and the lost opportunities of having her—all of you—in our lives."

"We wanted to blend in the community, keep our enemies closer and all that. Stupid. Yes. But she wanted to live near the Ravenwoods, despite all the baggage. She'd hoped someday the witchworld would change and calm the infighting. She hoped someone would kill Andre and end his reign of terror." He plucked a cotton handkerchief out of his pocket and mopped the perspiration off his forehead. Silence met his words, tense and thick in the room.

Ethan broke the hush, his voice hoarse, a sag to his shoulders. "She told the family she loved Andre and didn't want to leave him in the beginning. The family never abandoned her. They begged her to leave him, stopping short of spelling her the way Andre did. The Ravenwoods remained behind as surety for her to keep Andre appeased and to protect her. She escaped and disappeared. The Ravenwoods went to the ends of the earth to locate her, but she'd gone underground."

"I have a friend in the witness protection program who helped us informally after Kenley and I met."

"Wait, what?" Lucky balled his fist on the table. "Are you saying Lorenzo's not even our real name?"

"Not my real surname. I had it legally changed."

Lucky muttered a streak of blue curses. "According to her memoir, she likened the Black Tide to living in a cult, and she didn't love Andre. He bonded her, brainwashed her, used magic to control her twenty-four seven. She discovered what herbs he'd snuck in her drink and researched their origins. Once she started dumping her morning juice, her mind cleared, and she pretended to be under his spell until she devised her plan of escape. The last thing she wanted was for her family to know. Embarrassed, young, and stupid, she had stars in her eyes—her words—when the Ravenwoods warned her against Andre. But she believed if she remained behind, she'd succumb to Andre again and blurt out the Ravenwoods' plans." A crimson tide swept over Ethan's steely mask. A black raven appeared on his shoulder and emitted an ear-splitting caw.

Lawrence dry-scrubbed his face. "I didn't know any of your story. As hard as I tried to prod the truth from her, she said it didn't do any good for me to know. She quit drinking the Kool-Aid, came to her senses, and fled a cult led by Andre."

"Why did she dump the Kool-Aid?" Aspen asked, her eyes sympathetic, but glistening with excitement that set off gold flecks in the green.

Lucky continued, "She didn't elaborate. Just wrote that she needed to leave to save her family."

"This changes everything." Ethan pounded the table. Sage stroked his arm, and his familiar chittered at her. "If Andre kept Kenley—Leigh—under a glamour spell, then he assaulted her. She didn't go to him of her own volition. According to my father, he started grooming her at fifteen. It's fucking time for him to pay for his crimes."

Silent sobs shuddered through his father. A myriad of emotions deluged Lucky, and he laid a hand on his father's arm, thinner than he remembered. "She never wrote that."

"She never told me either." His dad strained to contain his outward emotions, his face screwing up and exaggerating the creases in his lightly lined complexion.

"She intimated Andre was grooming other young women—and men—and she was next to join his disgusting harem."

Ethan leaped up, shifted his wounded arm too fast and grunted. His raven familiar vaulted to the bookcase, beady eyes surveying the room. "Son of a bitch. I'll kill that warlock." He stormed around the table and headed to the door. "We have all the information out of that fucker's head we need. It's time to end him."

Rafael lunged forward and blocked him. They engaged in a force of will and strength. All brawn. No magic necessary. "No, man, not the time. We need to stop this assault on the house, Aspen, and Lucky first. Then you get first dibs at Andre."

With a red, mottled storm brewing over his face, his father stood, fists pressed to the table. "Are you saying you have access to Andre?"

"Andre is our prisoner." Sage sifted out witch-air, diffusing the lavender farther.

The flower infusing the air did little to calm his father, who rarely succumbed to plant remedies, despite his pharmacy carrying every herb under the sun.

Hands on both shoulders, Lucky prevented his father from shoving past him. "No. We follow the Wilde and Ravenwood's way." Lucky leveled a compassionate look upon Aspen. "I trust them."

"Trust!" A vein prepared to pop in his father's neck. "Your mother didn't trust any witch or warlock, least not her bio family."

"She fooled them. She lied and buried everything under the guise of Andre's manipulation and magic." Lucky believed the pieces he'd read in her scrambled writings. "Why else did she want to relocate to the Mecca of the Black Tide and the western coven leaders?"

"Dumb move, if you ask me." Rafael prodded Ethan toward his seat and returned to stand guard behind Sage.

"Not so dumb. She knew what she was doing," Marjorie contributed a crumb to the conversation.

"Speculation or truth?" The familiar scent of his dad's cologne, usually subtle and comforting, turned acrid. "You didn't know her any more than she knew the rest of this crowd."

"Oh, but I did know her." Marjorie pressed her palms to the table, emotion shimmering in her pale blue-gray eyes.

Lucky regained his seat, eager to hear what this witch knew about his long-deceased mother. "Go on," he encouraged. "Spill."

"Leigh maintained a cloaking spell on your home and business until she died. She veiled herself whenever she went out in public. The spell was so unobtrusive and powerful not even a black curse could penetrate it. She learned a lot of black magic from Andre to her and your benefit. Her magic was powerful, laced with black magic from her Ravenwood roots." Marjorie waved her arm. "She put a cloaking spell on you, Lucky, not knowing if you held magic."

"She didn't live long enough to know." He gripped the table edge so hard, his knuckles whitened.

"Leigh didn't practice magic." The shock of Marjorie's words immobilized his dad in his chair. "She always said practicing would drive Andre or his people to her."

"True." Marjorie clenched the crystals set in an elaborate antique silver pendant around her neck. "She saved her powers for the cloaking spell, which took every iota of her magic to maintain."

His father shifted his chair to address him head-on. "Is it true? You have magic?"

"He's a black warlock," Aspen uttered. "I felt his aura when he first returned to Santa Cruz when I never did in high school. It's grown stronger since then. I rarely sense warlock auras, but his is powerful."

"It's the reason he's being targeted now," Marjorie explained. "Leigh came to me, and we worked on black curses and spells together. When she passed, I continued the cloaking spell, adjusting it as needed throughout the years. But Lucky's magic has grown too strong, and he's now visible to the Black Tide."

Everyone spoke as if he wasn't the one who'd developed magical powers that disconcerted, scared, and threatened him. The truths landing on the table became too much to bear, and he rolled his chair back. "I need air."

"Is he safe here? With Andre on the grounds?" His father beseeched Sage in an acknowledgement of her leadership role.

"Yes. We've had problems since Lucky arrived yesterday, which I'll explain, but he can go outside without harm to himself, or from us." She pushed away from the table and stood, Rafael gathering her in his arms from behind, both a protective and romantic gesture. Lucky licked his lips, ducked his head to avoid Aspen's appeal. He couldn't stop looking at her.

God, he wanted to be that man for Aspen so bad, he tasted the desire in every fiber of his being. Would Aspen ever trust him like Sage and Rafael trusted each other? Could he ever trust the witchworld and the beings that inhabited it? A world he'd shunned since the moment he felt his body change in high school. The moment he'd first used his mind to light a match from a thought and smothered it with a small mound of dirt without lifting a finger. He'd never tried again, not after he'd read his mother's notes. Then this week happened and hammered his resolve to dust. He wanted to explore his magic. He wanted to explore it with Aspen.

"Can I go with you?" Aspen's demeanor held such kindness and compassion, "no" never even entered his mind. He needed solitude, he needed fresh air, earth to walk upon, water to touch from the creek. But he needed Aspen more. And he didn't know why, except for the fact that she was gorgeous, alluring, smart, and seemed to like him. And there was the intangible connection between them. He couldn't deny it any more than he could explain it.

"Absolutely."

"Wait. Are they okay together?" Marjorie asked, her meaning implicit.

"Yes," Lucky and Aspen said in tandem.

"What does that mean? Will the witch hurt you?" His father's gaze raked Aspen from head to toe, his face impassive, trying to camouflage his emotions.

"I'll explain what's going on," Sage said. "You two go. We all need a well-earned break, time to process. Stay on the grounds."

"Like I can leave. Uh, remember, sis, I'm a prisoner here."

"But Lucky's not, right?" his dad asked.

"Depends on if the covenstead lets me leave." Lucky's hands quaked as he picked at the hem of his shirt. "My magic or something brought unexplained phenomena to the covenstead. Sage will explain." He sauntered through the door Ethan had opened, following Aspen, her hair bouncing across her back like a burnt crimson tide. His gaze slid to her perfect round and firm ass, and he adjusted his suddenly too-snug jeans.

Chapter 15

Lucky's hand slid to the small of her back, so gentle that her skin tingled. Aspen led him to the marble gazebo her father had commissioned for her mother, which sat on the edge of the backyard amid the surrounding woods. The romantic spot was a favorite among the Wilde sisters, and never more so than in that moment. As they'd passed through the kitchen, she'd snatched bottles of water. She sipped from hers even though she needed to gorge on the entire bottle and more. Leaning on the gazebo's low wall, she watched two red squirrels chase each other through the woods, skirting boulders and crashing into bushes. A life of fun she may never experience again. Pine needles littered the half-wall, and she swept them in random piles to distract herself.

"I'm sorry I brought all this upon your head."

"I don't think you did." She continued gazing into the woods, the life encompassed in it, and the escape it afforded her. The sharp cedar and pine scents cleansed and purified the air. "It's not your magic."

"How do you know?" He leaned beside her, elbows on

the wall, and scooted closer until they touched.

No magic interfered, but the internal tie to him remained strong. She straightened her spine and turned toward him, so close, his cologne with cedarwood, amber, and ocean breeze notes filtered into her senses. Just like him to wear a popular cologne Rafael wore. His faint scent incited a hormonal jig in her girlie parts in a way Rafael's never had. Thank the goddess. "I have a handle on your magic. It's different. And you're not creating these tattoos and vines crawling all over yourself, me, the house."

He stood straight, his spine taut. "The house?"

"A vine dangled through the ceiling vent in my lab. I hate to think where else they're growing." Horror contorted his features, and she laughed. "Welcome to the witchworld."

"You heard about the church parking lot. Are you so sure it's not me?"

Aspen slid her hand over the tattoo trailing down from his shoulder under his shirt's neckline. A muscle jumped beneath her fingers, and his skin heated. "Are you sure you didn't know you possessed powers of any element?"

"I did weird stuff with lighting fires and mounding dirt in my teens, but I've not experimented since. When I read my mom's memoir, those actions made sense, but I loathed what was happening to me because of her fate." He rubbed his chest, his hand lingering over his heart. "I wanted to swab my insides with bleach."

"Oh." She brought her fingertips to her lips, tasting the saltiness of his skin. His gaze followed her actions, and he inched closer. "It's a travesty what happened to her and how the incident incited a toppling domino chain in your life. You need training. You need to know how to use your magic. It'll destroy you if you don't."

"I'm aware of that now." He curled his hand around her neck, her loose hair blanketing his hand in silk. "Can I kiss you?" he asked, his voice low and husky. "I've wanted to since the first moment my eyes feasted on you."

"Thought you hated me." She tried to stifle the sounds of her heart pulsing in her ears. Her eyes drank him in, thirstily tracing his every curve and angle.

"I never hated you." He slanted his head closer. His six-foot height dwarfing her five-six stature. "I feared you and the witchworld. I'm sorry for being such an ass. Sorry for avoiding you in school when all I wanted was your attention."

"When you said you wanted to kiss me since the first moment, did you mean yesterday?" She had to know the answer more than anything.

He eased closer to her until her breasts mashed his chest, and flames kindled through them. "I meant since the moment I saw you with Brianne and Marina on the first day of freshman year. You three marched up the steps like you owned the place. Everyone moved out of your way."

She stifled a giggle. "Because they thought we'd turn them into toads and add them to our boiling cauldrons."

"I know that now. Didn't then."

With every word that tripped out, his full lips beckoned. Words refused to arise, and she nodded, tamping down her desperation to feel his lips on hers. He inclined his head, and his soft and firm lips trailed up her neck, along her jaw toward her mouth. *Finally!* Then he pressed his lips to hers. Their first kiss was gentle at first, but Lucky passed "go" and it deepened into the realm Aspen only dreamed about. The taste of coffee clung to his lips, and the heat of his breath against her cheeks made her heart race. His body shuddered against her, and she pressed closer to him.

The intensity of his kiss swept her deeper into heaven. He slid his hand to her cheek and tilted her head to the side. A moan rose in her throat, and fiery desire fed her blood, igniting little fires everywhere. Her mouth parted, and her tongue met his in a frenzied dance, until air became nonexistent.

Breathless, they separated. His smile contained the entire moment. Lost in the evening ocean blue of his eyes, she dreamily returned his smile. Water spritzed off her fingers, and she waggled the drops away.

"That was..." She couldn't find the words.

"Perfect."

Everything about him and this moment was perfection. The world dissolved around them and drifted toward the infinite ocean.

He touched the water dripping from her, his fingers feathering the back of her hand. "If I create a mound of dirt and you water it, what will grow?"

"Hopefully, not a morning glory." Her mood spiraled from her own stupid thoughts. "Depends on your surroundings and where the dirt comes from. As an earth witch or warlock, you'll derive your magic from your surroundings. Hmmm." She tapped her finger on her chin. "You're an earth warlock." Trying not to melt into the lagoon of his eyes, she glanced into the woods.

"And maybe fire," he whispered.

"What?" Shocked, her face drained of heat as she twisted around. "Oh. Is that what you meant by lighting fires?"

"It was the first magic to develop when I was sixteen."

"Oh, goddess. You're a double threat. No wonder your aura is so strong."

"Is it unusual to have two innate elements of magic?" He perched his butt on the railing and crossed his delectable arms over his delicious chest.

"Rare, but not unusual. Willow wields two elements as does Evan Ravenwood. Together, they create all four elements. They're a power couple for sure. Sage and

Rafael... well, you'll learn about their magic someday."

"You and I would make up three elements. Or are you hiding air magic?"

A warm snake of surprise slithered through her gut. "You and me? Last I looked, we weren't bonded, so we don't make up anything together." A teasing lilt accompanied her words. The idea of bonding him intrigued her to the nth degree. She hadn't had a warlock of Lucky's magnitude on her mind ever, and never thought about black warlocks except as enemies to the witchworld, with recent exceptions. But Lucky presented a curiosity, a promise, a future to look forward to. If she lived beyond the week and he didn't send a dandelion army to kill her off, that is.

"I mean you're not bonded to a warlock, right? Could I be your warlock?"

"Wow, presumptuous, are you? Yesterday, you hated me. Today..." The slithering warmth traveled farther south.

"No, I never hated you. I told you that."

A playful giggle escaped her. "I'm kidding. This complicated position you're in, a black warlock who doesn't even know he's a warlock is not new. Ask Rafael. He was in the same boat."

"Do you mind if I hang with you and your coven? To learn."

She touched his arm. "I'll let you hang if you kiss me again."

Their gazes met, and they found themselves locked in a silent battle of wills. Then, he pressed his lips to hers. Again, the kiss was gentle and invited her to link her arms around his neck. Their lips parted in tandem, and their tongues flicked and danced together. He now tasted like sunshine in a dark, grim day, and she dissolved into his radiance. Time froze as their kiss deepened, as he drew her softness into the haven of his hard body. The world faded, and they existed in a void lost in each other's embrace.

When they separated, she smiled up at him, her heart racing fast and furious. "I guess you can hang with me." She winked.

His grin about made her come undone again. "Cool." He slugged down the rest of his water as if he needed to cool his desire. "Will Sage and Rafael allow it?"

"We need you here to figure out what's going on. So, I'd say yes."

"How's your tattoo and wrist?" A long visible shudder worked down his body.

"Being with you has calmed this curse, spell, whatever. My back feels normal, and I'm growing used to this thing on my Wicked Wrist."

"What do you mean normal? What does the tattoo feel like otherwise?"

"It itches as it grows, and my skin's warmer than my normal temp. The puncture on my wrist stings, and when the vines move, it exacerbates the wound. But standing here with you, I don't feel any of that." She paused, took a step back. "Do you feel your tattoo?"

"Every millimeter. Even though I've never had a real tattoo, the needle is continuously burning into my skin. It moves and tickles too."

"I'm sorry." Aspen reached into her fanny pack. "I have a pain amulet." She plucked out a round wooden disc suspended from a thin leather rope and lifted her arms. "May I?" He nodded, and she rose on her toes to slip the rope around his neck. Touching the amulet, she invoked the spell to activate it. "Give it a minute."

"Wow. Already working." He blinked up a storm and clutched the wooden disc in his hand, the magic warming his fist. "Damn. This is insane magic."

"Welcome to the weird and wonderful witchworld." Aspen paused, glacial fangs ripping through her. "Can you handle the witchworld? You seemed so against us."

Lucky hung his head. "My head's screwed up. I guess I need to talk to Rafael, see how he survived his initial confusion. My difference is all this family drama."

Aspen sifted her fingers down his arm, unable to stop touching him. "Rafael had some drama in his past. If I know you're not planning to sabotage us every step of the way, I can let you in."

He clasped her hand, ending her movements on his arm. His skin against hers set off a new fountain of internal heat. Balmy water spritzed them from above their heads. "Sorry. Sometimes my witch-water has a mind of its own."

He grinned, so devastating, her knees watered. "I don't mind. What did you mean by letting me in?" He took a half step forward until the toes of their shoes tapped.

"Witchworld secrets." The one thing she felt safe stating. "Maybe more," she added, her voice sultry and enticing.

He dipped his head, and she slanted hers back as he headed in for another kiss. The sound of footsteps crunching on the gravel path ended the moment.

"Aspen!" Brianne called.

"In the gazebo." Waggling her head, she picked up her water bottle. "You ready to confront the witch hunt again?"

"You mean warlock hunt?" He chuckled.

Aspen had to focus on her approaching cousin to avoid the magnetism of his gorgeous smile. Damn, this black warlock had consumed her. More sunk than she was the first day of freshman year when she'd gone gaga over him. Why had she let him slip through her fingers?

"Sage wants you both to return to the house." Brianne's smarmy gaze slurped them up, until it landed on Aspen's wrist, killing her teasing mood.

"Has my dad gone on another rampage?" Lucky asked as they descended the two steps to the path.

Brianne linked her arm in Aspen's arm. "I think he knows he's way over his head."

"He's been over his head with it buried in the sand my whole life."

"But did you want to know about your mom's position in Andre's cult?" Aspen did air quotes.

"Hell, yes. I want to kill the bastard for what he's done to her and countless other girls, women."

"And boys." Brianne kicked a pinecone into the woods where it crash-landed against a boulder and pieces shattered in all directions. Water misted off her fingers and sprayed Lucky's face.

"You're a water witch too?" He wiped his face on the shoulder of his shirt.

"Yes siree, Bob. Sorry 'bout that. We're more twins than I am with my real twin."

"Yeah, except Brianne rocks the blonde hair from our maternal great-grandmother. Like Sage." Talking about the mundane with Lucky reinvigorated a warmth inside her she didn't want icing over. The mundane allowed Aspen the freedom to forget her dire circumstances.

They approached the edge of the lawn, and a trio of blue jays screeched and flew into the depths of the woods, alighting in the tallest pines. The spring sun beat down on Aspen's head, and she paused to enjoy the beauty of the day, the normalcy, before entering the house mangled her good mood.

"Aspen, what's wrong?" Brianne tugged on her arm.

"Nothing. I want to enjoy this moment before all hell breaks loose and shit hits the fan and life goes to crap once again."

Lucky slung his arm over her shoulders, hauled her close, and kissed the top of her head. Life felt right, his body against hers, his arm holding her close, his lips brushing her head, the warmth of his breath on her scalp.

The closer they approached the French doors to the great room, the more Aspen's tattoo tingled with growing intensity. The Wicked Wrist stung anew, and the two tiny vines prickled her flesh. They threaded together, and barbs sprouted and dug into her skin. A pain gripped her gut so intense she doubled over. She cried out and turned her wrist to her stomach, stumbling to a standstill on the path. Vines traversed the lawn from all directions of the yard and traveled straight toward them. The creeping plants fused together into solid sheets, blocking them from moving closer to the house.

Chapter 16

Lucky screeched to a halt on the pathway, surrounded by the vines that stopped short of touching them. He held out his arms to hold Aspen and Brianne back. The vines caused Aspen pain, and he wanted to eviscerate them.

Lucky sprang toward the closest creepers snaking toward Aspen and gathered them in a bunch to prevent them from touching her. "Get her away!" he shouted at Brianne.

"No, Lucky," Aspen sputtered, unable to stand erect. The pain etched on her face destroyed him. He wanted it gone. He wanted these last two days to disappear into never-never land. Except for connecting with Aspen. He wanted that tether more than air.

Several witches and warlocks rushed out to the yard, alerted to the motion and movement of the vines. An older warlock Lucky had previously seen hovering, picked up an ax from a stack of wood off to the side of the house and raised it to strike the insidious plants.

"No! Ben. Stop." Sage darted out to the patio. "We don't

know what'll happen."

The vines Lucky held grew longer and entwined around his body. He tugged on them, but they didn't budge, clinging to him like glue. They crisscrossed the yard from some gods-forsaken root system. He couldn't tear them apart, nor peel them off. They sought sustenance and a lifeline from him. But if they wanted water, they were barking up the wrong warlock. They had no interest in Brianne, nor did they grow toward the creek cutting through the Wilde property. He'd researched the property on the county maps once he'd heard they'd allied with the Ravenwoods a month ago. If they thirsted for water, why didn't they aim for the creek?

Witch magic saturated the air, but it wasn't directed at the vines or them. Too risky. It targeted that strange alien magic the vines brought to the table. The magic, that untapped well, surging for release, opened its senses. Purple flowers popped along the branches, buds opening to full flowers, wide and colorful. Beautiful in a wild way. Attention seekers. The leaves expanded, swaying in the breeze, the stalks thickening. The plants blanketed the lawn and pathways at ankle level in a sea of purple.

Brianne hugged Aspen, a job he wanted. But not while the vines had him in their grip. He feared what they'd do to Aspen.

"Lucky?" Sage said from the patio. "Are they hurting you?"

"No. They're preventing us from nearing the house." He inched closer to Aspen. "You okay?"

"Get away from her," Brianne spit out. "None of this would've happened if not for you."

"No. No." Aspen swatted at Brianne's hands. "It's not true. I did this. I spun a black curse to open the gate."

"Yes, and we'll talk about your infraction later." Sage's dry tone carried her frustration. "For now, let's get you out of this newest jam." Her owl familiar vaulted off her shoulder and alighted on the roof gutter. A seagull sprang onto Aspen's shoulder, and with a flap of its wings, it soared into the air to join the owl, squawking and dive-bombing the vines.

Disbelief flashed across his face. "Your familiar's a seagull?"

"Don't judge." She sniffed. "Rio's a kick-ass familiar. He'll peck your eyeballs out if I ask him."

"Please, God, don't ask him." His dad shoved his hand through his hair and gripped the top of his head.

"No one's pecking anyone's eyes out," Rafael grumbled in typical Rafael-speak. "Brianne, release Aspen and try to walk through the vines."

"Are you gonna be okay, cous?"

Aspen waved her away. "Go. I don't need you dying in my beautiful disaster."

Brianne hugged her cousin one last time. "Don't say that. No one's frickin' dying. Not on my watch."

"Your watch, huh?" Aspen laughed to ease the tension.

Brianne ignored the quip and stepped away from Aspen by sliding her feet one at a time beneath the vines. Nothing happened, and the alien vegetation let her pass. She took another step, and an unobstructed path opened for her until she walked onto the patio. The path closed up, thicker than before.

"Okay. Good sign." The sun created sparkling gold flecks in Sage's eyes. Lucky gazed into Aspen's face, noticing the weariness dulling her eyes, the same green the Wilde sisters all shared. He'd kill to see the sun sparkle off Aspen's emeralds. "Now you, Aspen. Slow and steady."

She snagged his hand, avoiding a vine circling his wrist, tying his arm to his side.

"Go. They're not hurting me."

"Not yet. What if I can't return to you?" She squeezed

his hand. "Is my pain amulet still working?"

"I don't feel any pain."

"Aspen, move it," Rafael ordered. "We'll take care of Lucky. Marjorie's researching and working on a banishment spell."

"We need to use my counter-spell spray."

"We will. But we need to control the amount of magic we're using. It might be triggering and inciting this unknown magic."

Aspen backed away from Lucky. A vine reached for her, flapping in the air, depositing purple flowers on her feet in adulation. Lucky's gaze followed the creepers surrounding her, even though he wanted to feast his senses on her alone. She took a small step toward the house, sliding her foot beneath the plants the way Brianne had. The vines quivered and more flowers sprouted along their branches. Aspen took a bigger step, and one vine veered off and followed her. Two more small steps, and several more vines glided toward her.

"Stop," he said. "They're reacting as she steps closer to the house."

"Keep going," Sage encouraged, ignoring him.

She slid another step closer to the patio. The plants revolted, weaving into an impenetrable fence preventing Aspen from closing in on the house.

Uttering a frustrated screech, she balled her fists at her sides. She stepped to the left, then the right, but more living walls grew, blocking her view of the house.

"Let's put distance between us and them," Lucky suggested.

"Like minds. Obviously, the magic doesn't want me in the house." She flung up her arms, let them fall to her sides. "Why?" she growled out. "What did I ever do to you?" She slapped at a vine, and it quivered as if she'd lovingly caressed it.

As though the plants knew what Lucky and Aspen planned, they freed Lucky and slunk away, unraveling the walls they'd just made, until only one thick vine separated the lawn from the woods. A demarcation line. Lucky and Aspen strode down the path toward the woods and stepped over the creeper. She spun around and lifted a foot back onto the lawn. Gasping, she stepped back and held her wrist in her other hand. "The vines are drilling a warning into my wrist."

Concern riddled him. "We're stuck in the woods."

Sage and Rafael approached them on the path, unimpeded by the garden of evil. "Lucky, you might be able to leave the covenstead."

Before the words tripped out of Sage's mouth, a looming mother vine shot across the lawn from the woods, curled around his ankles, thick and thorny.

"Not according to this bitch." He stomped the vine down, but it cemented his feet to the pebble pathway.

"We've never had to worry about protecting the covenstead from magic intrusion. Until now," Aspen said.

"After the Helwig attack, the earth witches erected a ward against magic encroaching on the property," Sage mused, thinking. "But this magic is inside the ward."

"I did it." Aspen ducked her head. "I'm so sorry."

Lucky reached for her hand, but she pulled away. "I'm sorry for my part. What can I do?"

Sage waved their words away, her blue fingernails slashing the air, the color reminding him of the ocean and normal life. "What's done is done. If you two can stand each other tonight, take the main guest cabin. I'll send supplies."

Aspen stepped onto the path leading to the small cabins he'd spotted in the woods. "Can you grab my healing bag, pain potions, relaxation charms, and spelling supplies from my lab? Grab my bags from Marjorie's car?"

The idea of spending the night in a semi-secluded cabin alone with Aspen kindled a fire inside Lucky. He beat his desire into submission before it became obvious in his emerging erection. For all he knew, she'd not want anything to do with him. He may wind up sleeping on the porch if he didn't toe the line, or if the vines kept them apart. What else was in store for them that night? Would they even survive it? But the kiss they'd shared strangled all other thought, and he craved to touch her, hold her, kiss her and so much more. He kicked the door shut in his mind before he tripped over his own desire.

"Send my dad home." Lucky tried to suppress the huskiness in his voice. "Tell him I'll call. We can resume our discussion later."

"Don't worry, son." Lucky hadn't noticed his dad approach along the fringes of the woods. "I've heard enough to know I can trust the Ravenwoods and the Wildes. Marjorie's on our side. I never knew how she'd protected us after your mother passed." He turned to Sage and Rafael, his face pale and haggard. "Ethan has forgiven me. Do you forgive me as well?"

"There's nothing to forgive, man." Rafael snaked an arm around Sage's waist and pulled her against his body.

She took his dad's hand in hers and gave him a gentle squeeze. "Indeed. We're a force to be reckoned with, but we go to the ends of the earth for our family, friends, and allies." Sage rested her head against Rafael's chest.

The love they held for one another was epic. Something he wanted for himself. He'd witnessed so much loyalty and comfort among the Wildes. He'd pegged them wrong from the jump. It'd been him and his father for so long, he never understood what he'd missed from belonging to a large, loving family. Could he find it among the Wildes and Ravenwoods?

He missed his mother so much, and they could've been

a part of this family all along. The Ravenwoods would've protected them against the Black Tide. *If only.* He didn't harbor regrets about her decisions. God knows she had her reasons. But he'd always wanted a large family, one reason he loved university life, surrounding himself among students and faculty. But the family of college life became illusive when he'd buried his head in his studies. Oh, he'd had a couple of short-timer girlfriends and made a few lifelong friends, but they weren't blood. They weren't Aspen Wilde.

"Let's go," Aspen interrupted his maudlin thoughts.

In a pensive hush, he followed her into the woods. When he glanced over his shoulder, the vine disappeared, and relief unlocked a vise from his heart. Whoever had cast the spell on the covenstead didn't mind that he and Aspen were together. Had the magic driven them together? A renewed yearning adrenalized him, and he sidled closer to Aspen until his arm brushed hers. She didn't flinch, and a bounce buoyed his steps.

They passed by two cabins on the right, then several on the left. "Why all the cabins?"

"Used to be a campground. We updated the cabins and use them for guests. Wilde coven members occupy a few." She waved her arm toward the next cabin on the left. "Leah and her warlock husband, Ricky, live there. It's the biggest cabin, with two bedrooms." She continued striding down the pebble pathway.

"Do all the coven members live on the covenstead?"

"A few live in town, but all family, Wilde council members, and their warlocks live here." She stopped before the last cabin on the right, separated from the other cabins by a good hundred yards and privacy trees and bushes.

The path ended in a *cul-de-sac*, centering a tinkling, three-tiered water fountain. Bare hydrangea bushes skirted the foundation of the cabin, tiny bits of purplish green showing on the long stems. His mother's favorite flower. He cultivated and babied the hydrangeas in their backyard in honor of her. The purple-blue pom-poms were her favorite of all the colors. *And my brain has a mind of its own.*

He searched for electricity leading to the fountain. "You have underground here?"

"I'm powering the fountain. I just turned it on." She did air quotes. "Just needed to invoke a water spell to get the water stirring."

"Oh, snap. Nice trick."

"Solar panels feed the cabins and the fountain. When this was a campground, they used generators and overhead lines. My parents retrofitted it to underground, then solar when solar became trendy.

"I'll show you inside, but I want to sit outside for a bit." She pointed to a pair of hunter-green Adirondack chairs on the porch. "I need to think."

"No prob. I'll leave you alone. Maybe I can wander and get the lay of the land."

"You don't need to go." She touched his wrist.

Electricity nailed him when he slid his palm against hers. Before he knew it, she'd slid her other hand around his neck and pressed her lips against his. He dug his hand into her velvety, auburn hair and held her head so close, he felt like they'd melted as one. With parted lips, their tongues intertwined, and he delighted in the tantalizing minty sweetness that was unmistakably Aspen. She pressed so close, his erection poked the softness of her body, and he couldn't stop himself from rubbing against her. Damn, he needed to plant himself inside her. But it was too soon. Instead, he lost himself in the kiss of a lifetime, lost himself in the feel of her full breasts against his hard chest. She slid her lips away, but he nibbled at her bottom lip and brought her back to the kiss he never wanted to end. She whimpered, not because she needed air, but it seemed she couldn't get enough.

When he broke the kiss, he pressed his forehead against hers, his breathing ragged. "Aspen," he whispered. "Damn, woman."

"Do you have a girlfriend?" she asked breathless, moving painfully against his erection. *Tease.*

"If I was locked down, I would never kiss another woman. I've never cheated, never will. I respect you too much."

"Good. Because I'm as single as a jay bird." She planted a kiss on his lips between each word.

The statement bothered him and prevented him from taking further advantage of what she tantalized. He trusted she told the truth, but he didn't understand certain relationships between witches and warlocks or the bonding act. Hands on her waist, he put distance between them. Aspen's lips curled into a cute pout as she clasped his arms, her touch so hot on his skin he thought he'd combust.

"I need a moment to cool off."

The bulge in his jeans drew her gaze. "So I see." A tiny spritz of water sprayed off her fingers, then petered out. Her face screwed up in consternation. She tried again. Nothing. "I'm tapped out. Those blasted blood-sucker vines. I want to rip them out of my wrist so bad. They and probably every vine on the property are zapping my witch-water."

Lucky adjusted the crotch of his pants to relieve the pressure. "What can we do?"

"It's why I need to think and research. I need my laptop and my books. I need to figure out what fifth dimension we fell into." Leaning forward, she kissed him again. An unsatisfying peck. "I want to bounce ideas off you."

"Not sure how much I can help."

She trailed her left hand up his zipper, so much a

tease. "You're helping by being here." Smiling, she skirted him and entered the cabin. "But I want your chemistry and alchemy brain."

"Well, then we've got brainstorming to do."

An updated kitchen-dining-room-and-living-room combo greeted them, decorated in the latest gray and white with greens and blues adding color to the living room. The sofa-bed already had blankets and a pillow piled on it. *Ouch.*

"Wow. This is better than any five-star hotel."

"We like to provide our guests with comfort."

She showed him the bedroom, and his gaze feasted on a king-size bed. The bathroom held a shower built for four and a double vanity in marble. He shifted his focus back to the shower and readjusted his pants again. The idea of having sex with Aspen made him believe he'd never experienced the right sex. She could flip the tables on everything he knew about women or the experience of being with a woman in all the ways it counted. The idea devastated and excited him all at once. What if she'd spelled him? Or was angling for a hit-and-run?

Aspen seized his hand and drew him into the living room. Sounds emerged from the porch, and she released his hand as if he were on fire.

Marina, Brianne, and a warlock carried in bags of food, everything else Aspen asked for, and more. The beer and wine perked him up.

"Hey, cous," Brianne said. "We got you covered." She handed Aspen her laptop bag and healing tote, which secreted a myriad of herbal scents. Most he recognized, but some were suspect.

The warlock, a tall and rugged, good-looking dude who appeared a few years older than Aspen, approached her. "Do you want me to stay?"

A snake of jealousy whipped through Lucky, and he

masked his face.

"I'm good, Matthew. Go about your normal guard duties." Aspen squeezed the dude's hand.

"Gonna hang with Marina and Brianne. Movie night. We're all a text away."

Aspen's shoulders slumped. "Eat popcorn and Milk Duds for me."

"We packed you a snack bag." Brianne looped her arm through the warlock's arm. "Matthew thought you two could watch a flick if you take a break from your research."

The trio left, and Lucky's gaze met Aspen. "Is he your warlock?"

She dug into the grocery bags and pulled out containers of prepared dinner. "Sorta. We're not bonded, but he's assigned to me, Brianne, and Marina since we don't have bonded warlocks. He's my aunt Juliette's warlock. She's flitting around the world, spying on witch and warlock activities."

"Why isn't he with her? Or can you have multiple warlocks?"

"Yeah, we can bond several. Most witches have one, and it's rare to have more than three. Sage has three because it's required by witch law for a High Priestess." She folded the bags and stuffed them in the pantry. "My youngest aunt wanted to travel alone."

"Then how does Matthew derive his powers?" Lucky unpacked a bag stuffed with theater snacks and set everything on the quartz counter in a straight line.

"Once bonded, a warlock will always possess his witch's magic, no matter where she's located. But it's diminished. Juliette and Matthew meet every few months. She recites the bond again, and it tops him off."

"Can a black warlock and witch bond?" He propped his elbows on the counter. "Oh, wait. Sage and Rafael are bonded."

"So are Willow and Evan Ravenwood." Aspen grinned. "Thinking ahead?" A flush climbed up her neck.

A shivery sensation rushed through Lucky, and he had the incredible urge to possess her. He was glad the cabinets blocked the crotch of his pants. *Son of a witch's toad. What is wrong with me?* He'd never encountered a woman as beautiful, warm, and kick-ass as Aspen. Everything about her drew him to her like a moth to a flame. The reason he crushed on her in high school. He now feared the flames would devour him.

"Um, maybe. I guess if I embrace this lifestyle, I'll need to bond a witch."

"You don't need a witch for powers since you possess your own innate powers." Her lilting voice mocked him.

"Oh." He hid his dejection. "Why are Rafael and Sage bonded?"

"They're in love. Their individual powers enhance each other. Same with Willow and Evan, although it's too soon for them to talk marriage, and she needs his powers while hers are developing, late bloomer and all. Andre recently tried to kidnap her and awaken her powers for his own nefarious purposes. Then he tried to suck Rafael into his world, almost destroyed him, and this happened after we'd captured the evil warlord."

"Damn, the man's a total disaster."

"He's tenth-level devil incarnate. I'd hate to have his blood streaming through me."

"No kidding." Sobering, Lucky fought the vise clamping onto his heart. "Look at that dude who attacked you. Andre's son. He's taking his cues from Andre from behind locked doors." Lucky opened one of the food containers. Steam from the hearty beef stew spiraled up from the hot container. "Hey, this smells like the bomb. What say we eat, then hang on the porch like you wanted?"

Aspen's brows furrowed as she studied him, as if

piecing together his words against her intuition. "Yeah. There's some weird-ass crud going on with Pierre. Andre taught him well. If he instigated this plant plague upon us, how is it still active from a warded basement cell?"

She tossed aside her fanny pack and plugged her phone into a charger. She grabbed her already packed bag of hardbound books and slid them onto the dining table. Lucky dished out the stew and breadsticks.

He set their loaded plates on the table and snatched a novel off the top of the stack, third in a long series. "These are my favorite books of all time."

A flicker of joy danced in Aspen's eyes. "Have you read them all? This is my second time reading the series."

He tapped his phone. "Reading the last one published." They sat in companionable silence and ate. Man, the Wilde cooks were Michelin. Everything he'd eaten was total gourmet. "Do you like them because of the magic?"

Aspen took a long guzzle of her red wine. "I like long, complex stories. They immerse me in a world so far from my own that I lose myself, forget my problems, live vicariously through the characters. His characterization is superb, and you feel like a character in the story. It's why I read fantasy. Well, among other things." She picked up the historical romance novel Brianne had tossed in the bag. "My mom loved these romances. Sheesh. How long do they think we'll be stuck out here?" Face broiling, she hid the book in the sack.

Lucky pushed a lank of hair off his forehead and smiled. "I don't mind. As long as we get good food like this for three meals and you're here, I can stay forever."

Aspen flushed a deep red and sucked down half her wine. "What are you saying?"

"I'm not shy. I tend to be reserved when I'm out of my depth. But I want you. I told you, I've wanted you since the first moment I saw you. Your witch status stopped me from approaching you in high school." He clanked his fork on his plate and steepled his fingers. "You know my deal with witches and warlocks."

"But you're fine with us now?" Her voice had gone a seductive smoky that turned him on in ways no other voice had.

"It's the world I was born for. I know it now. Guess I need to adapt." He gloved her hand on the table. "If you don't want to help me adapt, or want nothing to do with me, then say it. I'll sleep on the porch and hit the road tomorrow."

She flipped their hands over and weaved her fingers in his. In one swift movement, she rose and straddled his lap, his erection pressed against the most perfect ass ever to sit on his lap. Unexpected but welcome desire clouded her eyes, and he froze.

Chapter 17

Lucky cupped her face and Aspen rubbed her cheek against his smooth fingers. She ignored the mossy violet scent the vines and flowers on his skin secreted.

"I've wanted you to touch me since we sat down." Lucky's lips met hers.

Aspen's inhibitions shattered as she unleashed her inner seductress on him, awakening a long-dormant part of her. *More like a dead part of me.* It wasn't like he was a stranger after four years of high school passing each other by, with the occasional "hello" and furtive and wistful glances.

Aspen ended the kiss, a long slow possession hinting at a promise. "Why didn't you say something?"

"Because I'm a gentleman. Because you puzzle me."

Shock riddling her, she drew back. "Why? Haven't I been transparent?"

"Well, there's the whole high-school-avoidance thing. I guess I'm cautious of your world. I don't know if you're gonna strike me with a wave or another spell to knock me out."

She wiggled her fingers over his head and two drops of water fell onto his hair. "You've been struck by all my uber treacherous water magic. Did it hurt?"

He laughed, then sobered. "Is it bad? Your lack of witch-water?"

"It leaves me bereft. I could fill myself with an ocean, but I'm not thirsty." Regardless, she grabbed a bottle of water off the table and sucked half down. "Guess I should keep hydrated. But that wine was too divine."

"Will drinking water help?" He steadied her at her waist. The feel of his hard-on against her rear encouraged her to shift until he pressed against her most sensitive parts. "Water anchors a water witch. The ocean grounds me and replenishes me like nothing else. The creek is so-so, but I need the ocean. I don't think I can ever live far from it." She moved in a slow rhythm on his lap, forward and backward in a little wriggle. Heat and desire exploded in her against the friction of their jeans between her legs.

Lucky banged his head against the chair and groaned. "Stop or I won't be responsible for my actions."

She leaned in and whispered in his ear, "Boot responsibility out the window. One night. Do you want me?" The lines between her morals, desire, and convictions blurred into one giant mass of raging hormones. All she'd wanted from her high school crush sat within her grasp. Fate had brought him back into her life, and she didn't think she could bury her feelings. Not this time.

"I may want more than one night."

"Ditto," she whispered, tossing all caution and the little naysayers in her head to the winds. "Let's make magic together."

In response, he trailed his soft, sultry lips down to her neck and sucked on her skin, ever so gently alternating with licks and kisses. The heat of his breath drove tingles down her spine, competing with the tickling of the vines. Rio emitted soft cooing sounds from the skin of her shoulder, more like tiny cackling, but she knew her familiar was in sync. Lucky lifted her in his arms, and she straddled his torso, locking her legs around his waist. She anchored her arms around his neck, and he carried her into the bedroom. They fell onto the bed, legs tangling.

He slipped his hands beneath her blouse and cupped her breasts, then locked his lips onto her neck again. His tongue, mouth, and teeth performed tantalizing tasks on her sensitive flesh that left no reasons to cease the pleasures ravaging her body. More shivers trailed his roving mouth on her skin. Desire swelled, causing her to squirm on the bed. She latched her hands in his hair, holding his head to her, not wanting his mouth to stop creating exquisite sensations on her skin.

He slid his hands down her sides to the hem of her blouse. "May I take it off?"

"Only if you let me take yours off."

But he didn't let her. He whipped his T-shirt over his head and her gaze met his sun-kissed chest, all muscles and ridges she wanted to touch. Again, he wouldn't let her touch, as he occupied her by ever so slowly rolling her blouse up as if unwrapping a coveted gift. With each roll, he left a trail of kisses on her torso, until he reached her neck. She helped him pull her blouse over her head, and he tossed both shirts to the foot of the bed. His gaze never left her as she unhooked her bra and freed her sensitive breasts. The longing in his eyes melted her insides into a bubbling pool of desire. His lips latched on to her right nipple, then her left, leaving her a writhing mass of gelatin.

"You're wearing far too many clothes," she gasped out, dying to see him in all his naked glory. Dying to touch that part of him she wanted inside her more than anything.

He reared back, cool air swathing her roasting chest.

"Wait. I'm not sure—" He pulled his wallet out of his back pocket, produced a condom, and tossed his wallet aside.

"One?" She squinted. "Not enough."

"It'll have to do. For now."

"I'll take what I can get."

"You sound desperate." He unbuttoned his jeans.

Arching her back, she leveraged up on her elbows. "Now that statement could land you in the friend zone." She drew the tip of her tongue across her lips and cupped a hand around her right breast.

Lucky groaned. "Okay. *I'm* the desperate one."

Aspen drew his zipper down, the rasp fueling her cravings. "I want you inside me. There's a connection between us I can't describe. Something I've heard other witches try to describe about their bonded warlocks when first meeting them."

"I'm honored to be the lucky one." Lucky shucked off his jeans and kicked them aside.

Commando. Oh, my. Aspen gasped at his magnificence, all hers for the taking. "Lucky," she chanted. "You are most certainly the lucky one." Passion burst anew, long prickles zigzagging up and down her body, to the point they overpowered the sensations from the vines or her two familiars. Rio and Rico continuously moved to avoid the vines. "Don't stop at go. Skip the foreplay." She shimmied out of her pants, toeing them off her ankles.

Gaze never leaving her face, he slipped on the condom, his erection bucking for attention. He positioned himself above her, both of them frenetic as if they'd never done the deed before. Aspen latched her legs around his hips and guided him into strike position. He slipped his full length inside her, forcing a moan to escape from deep within her. She squirmed beneath the hard length embedded deep inside. Stilling his movements, he gasped, his eyes a sea-tossed storm. His lips settled on hers, and he found his rhythm, slow and fast, so giving and sexy. They fit together more perfect than any other man she'd been with. Not that she had a high body count. The connection she felt to him intensified, and the colors of his aura burst and sang to her of his magic. Green and earthy. Crimson, amber, and orange of his fire, tinged in blue. There was no doubt of his magical identity.

His tongue followed the rhythm of his thrusts until he drew away, gasping for air. She thrust her hips up to draw him in deeper until he sent them both crashing in waves of fulfilment. With Aspen beneath him, he slumped and cradled her head in his hands. The rasping of their breaths and scudding of their hearts in unison left no lingering doubts as to how well they fit together, how much they desired each other.

Rico, her bonding seagull that once belonged to Marty, shimmied over her arm. Rico hadn't exhibited so much activity since before Marty had passed. A telling sign of her familiar's return to life and acceptance of Lucky.

"You smell so good." He buried his face in her hair, tongue teasing her ear, and trailed kisses across her neck. "Vanilla-laced orange blossoms."

"You recognize an orange blossom?" she croaked out, a sudden emptiness decimating her insides.

"My mom potted an orange tree when I was born. We planted it when we moved here, and when it blossoms every year, it reminds me of her."

"I love that. See, this moment is fate." Lucky's weight on her body became unbearable from the hollow pain in her torso to the weight of his legs entangled in hers, bogging her body down.

"Was this about sex for you?" he asked in all seriousness.

She shook her head. "It was about intimacy, forging a deeper connection." The sex was vital and life-changing, but her body continued to break down from lack of hydration and her focus shifted. "Lucky." She cleared her throat. "I'm so sorry. Can you scootch off me?" He scrambled to the side of the bed almost braining himself on the headboard. Had vines sprouted from her forehead?

"Was it that bad? Do you want me to leave?"

"No." She emitted a laugh that energized a budding headache. "My stomach hurts. My lack of hydration has worsened. Can you hold me?"

He gathered her into his arms, and she rested her head on his shoulder, twining her arms around his neck. "That was damn near epic."

"Only damn near?" Had she felt more of a connection to him than he'd felt? Had she nearly croaked from passion overload, and he thought it a hit-and-run? Her head weighed a ton, and it lolled on his shoulder. Her parched skin itched, and a bone-deep exhaustion glued her to the bed.

"One wasn't enough." His chuckle vibrated against her pounding skull as he kissed her hair.

"One, what?"

"Condom."

She giggled, wincing at the headache. "Got it. Same page."

He squeezed her close until they were one. "There're other ways."

"I'm sorry. I can't right now." A long tremble worked up from her toes. "I want to, but I don't feel so hot." Her wrist tickled, not so much a sting this time. She withdrew her arms from around his neck and gasped. "Lucky, look."

The Wicked Wrist vines had braided together. They danced limp and dull in the air and teeny flowers dripped onto the bed.

"Oh, snap." He combed tangled hair off her face. "Do you want me to get Sage, or Marjorie?"

She couldn't stop her arm from drooping to his chest, couldn't even enjoy the feel of his firm chest or his slick skin. "No. I'm just so tired. I'm so sorry. It was epic." Sleepiness overcame her. "I want more epic."

Before he responded, she zonked half on top of him, one of the most natural places in the world for her body to land.

Aspen snoozed for an hour, before brainstorming potions, curses, and everything in between jolted her out of a fitful nap.

"Lucky?" Her voice sounded raspy from a dry throat.

"Hmmm." He kissed the top of her head.

"Want to research and experiment with alchemy?"

"Thought you'd never ask."

They spent the next few hours dissecting, creating, and researching, until they both fell onto the bed exhausted. Although desire took second place to their accomplishments, falling into bed together was more natural than Aspen cared to admit. The intimacy of the act of sleeping together sated her more than the idea of making love again.

Chapter 18

Shadowy light filtered through the sheer window coverings in the guest cabin. Aspen shook her groggy head, froze when pain radiated down her neck. Every inch of her arid skin itched like crazy, her lips bone dry. The tattoo on her backside tingled in fresh places. What next level of hell invaded her body? Had epic sex with Lucky reduced her to a voodoo doll? The pins sticking in her were palpable. Speaking of… she rolled over on the bed, groaning when every muscle in her body screamed bloody murder. An empty bed met her gaze.

A slant of light leaked through the cracked bedroom door. "Lucky?" Had sex sucked so bad that he'd left her? Or had she ruined the night by wanting to do research afterward? She tried to lift up on her elbows but her dead-weight body sank to the pillow-top mattress. Maybe Lucky had been a dream. No, the slight soreness between her legs proved a different story. A story more than mere sex. The link to him filtered through her core, toying with her paltry, rejuvenated witch-water. "Lucky, are you here?"

Footsteps sounded outside the bedroom door, and it

slid open, bringing two bright rays of beauty in Lucky and the morning light. "Hey. I'm here." He carried a glass of her favorite strawberry-banana protein smoothie. "Found this on the porch with breakfast." He eased his butt on the edge of the bed and positioned the straw to her lips. "Can you sit up?"

"Not easily. Can you call Sage?"

"Already did. She'll be here in a few. She summoned Marjorie too."

Aspen sipped the smoothie, and the thick liquid clogged her scratchy throat.

"I wanted to show you something outside, but we can see it later."

"What is it? I can't take more bad."

"It's beautiful, but it's not good." He winced.

Arms languid, she swept aside the covers, not caring about revealing her near nakedness to him. He'd seen it all last night. Thank the fashion gods she kept herself groomed and wore pretty-in-pink lacy underwear. She found a pair of leggings in her overnight bag and slid them on. The juice sloshed in her hollow belly, and she didn't think she could drink more and keep it down. *Whose cup did I pee in for this revenge?*

Although desire sparked in his eyes, he snagged one of his blue pharmacy T-shirts from his own suitcase and helped her slip it on. "Guess my dad dropped off an overnight bag last night. It was on the porch too."

She sniffed his shirt, the clean-laundry smell mingling with the faintest hint of his fresh sea breeze cologne, and stored the scent in her senses. "Do you work today? Can you even leave the property?"

"I like this shirt on you." He straightened the T-shirt on her that hung down her thighs. "Remains to be seen if I can leave. I already called my dad and told him I won't make my shift. We have other part-timers who fill in."

Aspen perched on the edge of the bed, steadying her heavy legs. "I don't want to interrupt your life."

"I want you to interrupt my life. Hoped I proved it last night."

"Despite me falling asleep on you?" She covered her face with one hand. "I can't believe I did that. Please don't take it as a reflection of you."

"I don't." He sobered. "I know this magic is hurting you. We'll have other nights, right?" His back stiffened.

"Nights, days, mornings." A wan grin conveyed her lack of energy. "I'm in. I've wanted this since high school."

His large hand landed on her arm, and he massaged her skin. The vines shifted out of the way of his hand until they disappeared up the sleeve of her shirt. "Me too. That's why I'm not leaving you unless you want me gone. I'm never walking past you in a hallway again with my head up my ass."

Multiple footsteps stomped on the porch. The calvary had arrived.

"Ugh." Aspen tried to hand-comb her hair. "I'm a mess." She scanned the room. Lucky had already cleaned up the clothes they'd tossed on the floor. Didn't take a rocket scientist to glean they'd slept together, considering she wore his shirt.

"Aspen." Sage entered the room. "Marjorie's on her way." Rafael stood behind her, her ever stalwart watchdog. And now Aspen understood their absolute loving and protective devotion to one another. She wanted the same with Lucky. Damn, how, after only a couple days? Sex cemented her renewed and budding feelings for him. This time the buds had bloomed.

Sage plunked a tote bag on the dresser. "I brought more things from your lab. Wasn't sure what you'd need."

"I don't know. I don't think my potions or charms will help, except for pain."

Sage approached, knelt beside the bed, and flipped over Aspen's wrist. "The vines wove together. Your skin is dry, pale, like your witch-water didn't regenerate overnight."

"I know." She hid a smile.

"Did you two have sex?" Sage whispered.

Aspen slapped her forehead. "Why did your thoughts glom on to sex?"

"The vines are twisted, and you need to see the gardens."

"Oh, son of a lime-green donkey ball." Aspen pushed off the bed, wobbling on her legs. "Help me to the bathroom."

At least she could comb her hair, brush her teeth, and apply lip balm to her paper-dry lips. She didn't care how she appeared to Lucky, when normally she'd be freaking out and wanting to slather foundation on her pallid skin and look her best for a new love interest. Lucky had already seen her worst. He'd already experienced her most hopeful avoidance for four years, and yet he remained in the here and now.

Lucky wrapped his arm around her waist, holding her upright as they walked to the porch. Her stomach twisted, and she drew herself inward, leaning against him. The hydrangea sticks that had shown the barest hint of green yesterday had leafed out, and full purple-blue, pink, and white blooms adorned the plants. More flowers than she'd ever seen on them. They skirted the entire foundation of the cabin from the front porch and down the sides. A multitude of other shade flowers had sprung up overnight, spanning the circumference of the cabin in reds and pinks. Many flower stems coiled together, celebrating Lucky and Aspen's night. Not one morning glory vine appeared.

A clammy tendril of horror snaked its way up Aspen's throat, constricting her airway with wintry fingers. She leaned against Lucky, the horrifyingly beautiful sight a bigger eyeful than she needed that morning. The significance of the braids created havoc within her ravaged body.

"I can't with this." She retreated to the cabin.

Aspen perched on the edge of the couch, and Sage rolled up the back of her shirt. Her gasp chased the willies down Aspen's chest. Rafael's grip on her shoulder tightened.

Lucky perched on the sofa and took her hands in his. "Look at me."

Her eyelids flicked up, and she took in his high cheekbones and a narrow nose that flared ever so slightly. "How bad is yours? Let me see."

He stood to his full height and rolled up his shirt from the hem. The vines snaked around his torso and formed a heart on the left side of his chest. More flowers grew along the vines, in pinks and whites, joining the ever-present purple.

Curiosity piquing, Aspen peered inside the neckline of her T-shirt. No vines on her front-side. "I need to see."

"Later." Sage rolled the hem of her shirt down. "More flowers in pink and white. They're heart-shaped."

"Oh, joy. Putting my sex life on display." Aspen poked at the vines on her wrist, dying to poke her eyes out.

"Did you bond him or he you?" Sage rooted through the tote she'd lugged in. "Marjorie said to take these."

"I'm not ready to bond a warlock." Aspen vehemently shook her head. "No offense, Lucky." Sage handed her pain and energy potions.

"None taken. I need to learn more about bonding." He straightened his shirt and began clearing their dinner dregs off the table.

Aspen drank the potions, smacking her lips for her peppermint oil lip balm to mask the bitterness. Rafael elevated her legs on the cushions, and Sage draped a velour blanket over her. She drank more of her smoothie for the hydration and calories, but couldn't stomach anything else, not even dry toast. She hated that day, hated the attention. The only thing that made it worthwhile was the night with Lucky. It was worth all the water in the ocean.

Marjorie arrived, escorted to the cabin by all three of her cousins. They fawned over her, but Sage shooed them away. All hands were on deck to discover a solution to the magic attacking their world. Sage assigned Eden to use her telepathy to drill into the mind of Andre's son for the first time since he had arrived.

After Marjorie examined her, she drew Sage and Rafael aside. Lucky hung behind and sat on the floor beside the couch, holding her hand.

"I'm so sorry sex was such a burden."

Aspen noticed a tease in his voice, and she fixated on it for sanity's sake. "Can't wait for round two." She maneuvered onto her side to see him better, blasting through the exhaustion ravaging her from head to toes.

"Might kill you."

"You're that good?"

"I've got more tricks up my sleeve." He grinned. "Awesome tricks."

"But do you have more condoms in your wallet?"

He tipped his head back and groaned.

"Just so you know, we entertain overnight witches and their warlocks a lot. Or at least we did before our lockdown. There's a guest supply closet in the upstairs hallway of the house. Know what I mean?"

He gave her a thumbs-up. "I can wait until you're better. I still feel like I've caused all this."

"You probably did." Rafael strode back into the room.

Sage whacked his arm. "I believe it's a combination of black spells you both created with Pierre's magic. If he's

Andre's son, he may be using old black magic our spells can't fight."

"She's right." Marjorie rejoined them. "I'm positive it's black magic. What I've read so far is eye-opening, and we should've never lost this knowledge from before the war."

"It'll never happen again," Sage announced, giving Aspen the nod to continue her black magic experiments.

"Lucky and I might've found a counter-spell last night. An expansion of the first solution I brewed. We'll spray the vines on Pierre's cell door and walls and kill them off." Aspen paused. "But I might be missing something in the potion to make it permanent. I need more time to work on it. What about a tracking spell to trace the magic? Can't Ethan or Evan use their black magic weaving to reverse-weave? Rafael, can you weave?"

Rafael studied his boots, created an opaque thread between his hands, shooting off opaque rays of blue and green. The thread dissipated into a spray of sparkles dusting the floor. "That's about all I can do."

"What did *you* do?" Sage's eyebrows knitted together.

"Nothing. That's my problem. I can make one thread for a few seconds, but it doesn't do squat." He sank onto the arm of a tufted chair opposite Aspen.

"Wait. What?" Lucky gawked at Rafael. "I've been doing threads for years, then. Didn't know what it meant. Thought it was just fire play."

Sage and Marjorie rounded on him. "Show me." Sage wore a mask of curiosity and irritation.

Lucky stepped back as if Sage had grown pointy horns and planned to ram him. "Okay. Chill. Give me a sec."

"Marjorie, examine his aura. I'll concentrate on sensing his magic."

"What about me?" Aspen asked, feeling abandoned from her own life.

"You recover," Rafael ordered. "You have no magic to

deplete."

She shot him a death glare and picked at the fringe on the blanket. "You suck." Since she had a hard time even lifting her forearm, she followed Rafael's orders. Life sucked ass. It was easy to bury her head in the sand concerning her physical ailments. But she refused to think the worst, not when she had so much more to uncover. Hope existed, and she held it close to her chest.

Lucky paced the room, waggling his arms to deplete his negativity. "I need to concentrate. Haven't done this in a while."

"Prove it." Sage's sarcasm didn't fly over Aspen's head. Holy mother of the goddess. Will the guy ever get a break? If Sage pissed him off, he'd exit stage left on Aspen's life. After last night, it's the last thing she wanted. The memories of his hands, his mouth, his other body parts touching her created a new flare of desire low in her torso. She crossed her legs to keep her squirming in check, an exquisite ache radiating from her hips to her purple toenails.

Lucky shot her a questioning glance, and she waved his attention away. Oh, goddess on high, did their connection give him insight in what she was feeling? *Hello, mortification, I'm here. Steal me away.*

After focusing a few moments, Lucky drew forth an opaque thread of winding magic, a ball-shaped outline between his hands. Another thread materialized and braided the first one, both cracking and sparkling in the air. Lucky lurched toward the door as if controlled by marionette strings.

Sage clutched her neck. "Oh, my, goddess. The magic's tugging you."

"Yes." Sweat popped on Lucky's forehead, and he followed the magic to the door.

"Keep following it," she ordered. "Marjorie, are you

feeling what I'm feeling?"

Marjorie fisted her pendant as if deriving strength from her crystals. "He—"

"His aura's the same as Pierre Charlemagne." Aspen's mouth hung open.

"Yes." Marjorie nearly yanked her pendant off her neck.

Sage nodded. "Identical." She trailed after Lucky who'd tuned everyone out as he followed the threads lugging him to destinations unknown.

Aspen lifted off the couch, but Rafael's gentle hand on her shoulder pressed her down. "I don't want you hurt if this goes assbackwards."

"But I want to go!" She slapped her curled fist on the couch, such a listless, whiny gesture, it almost made her cringe. "This is my life this black curse is screwing to hell and back." But her intuition told her the magic was towing Lucky to the house. A place she couldn't go, but neither could Lucky if yesterday's events forecasted an ongoing state of being. "Son of a witch's boiled toad," she cursed aloud.

Rafael skedaddled after Sage, tossing over his shoulder, "Marjorie, please stay with Aspen."

Aspen wilted onto the couch. "I hate this."

Marjorie scooped up the top research book from the coffee table. "Let's get to work. Which ones have you gone through already?"

From the sofa, Aspen visually examined the four books. "*Ancient Witchcraft*, top one. It's all white magic. No black magic. Useless." Marjorie set it aside. Where had the middle book come from? She didn't remember having it out in her lab, nor had she packed it. "Let me see the middle one." *Enchantments and Hexes: Unraveling the Secrets of Witchcraft and Curses*. Marjorie handed her the heavy tome, and it thumped against her sore breasts, a painful reminder of her condition... and making love with Lucky. She flipped the book to the worn leather cover.

Marjorie left and returned with a bottle of water and a plate with a butter-slathered scone and bacon. "Drink. The more you drink, the better off you'll be. Then you need to eat."

Aspen scratched her arm, and dry skin flaked onto the couch. Although her appetite had fled, she needed to maintain her strength and fuel her body against the magic attacking her. "Where did this book come from?" She devoured a piece of bacon, which tasted good in her mouth, but her belly held another opinion.

"I believe it was in the stack of books Brianne packed for you last night."

"Where did she snag it from?"

"I'm not sure." Marjorie held out her hand. "Let me see it."

Racking her brain for the inventory of books in her office and bookcase, Aspen nudged it toward Marjorie. "Wait a minute. I had my great-grandmother's old copy of *The Grimoire of Moonlight and Shadows: A Witch's Spellbinding Handbook* on my desk, which I packed to take to your house. What happened to the grimoire?"

Marjorie opened the cover of the book, the binding crinkling from age. A puff of stale wind gusted out from between the pages, ruffling Marjorie's short hair. The air crackled and the book slipped from Marjorie's hands to the top of the marble coffee table.

"Someone spelled and cloaked the book." Marjorie traced the cover again, but nothing happened. "Have you opened it?"

Aspen sat up again, feeling better by the moment. She took a few bites of an orange, cranberry scone and drank the rest of her water. "No. I found it in my mother's trunk in the attic last week. Or at least I found the grimoire. I wondered why she'd hidden it."

"*Enchantments and Hexes* contains dangerous pre-war black magic. It's a highly sought-after book among the witchworld. Some want it destroyed, others want it for the long-lost spells. It's one of few copies that exist." Marjorie's gaze caught hers. "She hid it for *you*. She trusted you to do right by it."

"Is it an original?" She stared at the book, scratching her temple. The book had to be her mother's missing text. Excitement bubbled up inside her.

"There are no originals." Marjorie grazed her hand over the engraved cover, the intricate design in gold ink shifting with her movements. "Someone reproduced the original and then destroyed it. Its existence alone was a harbinger of the worst black hexes."

"How did my mom's cloaking magic last beyond death?" Aspen set her plate aside and scooted closer to the book in Marjorie's hands.

"You need to learn about everlasting spells. They're not meant to be used blithely, but in the right circumstances and the right hands, they can be effective until the intended witch breaks the spell."

"Did I break the cloaking spell?"

"Apparently." Marjorie placed the book on Aspen's lap. "You were the catalyst to your mother's spell-casting. You'll be able to reinstate the spell as well."

Aspen placed her finger on a golden thread drawn on the cover, and all the threads orbited her finger. She removed her finger and the original pattern restored itself. The cloaking resumed, and the book evolved to the grimoire. An unusual contentment hummed beneath her ribs.

She opened the book, pristine and void of any handwritten notes to retain its authenticity. But as she leafed through the light brown pages, skimming to the end, she noticed a bulge inside the back cover.

Easing a fingernail into the slit, she pried loose several sheets of papers and unfolded them. Notes with various handwritings. She recognized some in her mother's script, some in her grandmother's, and others in faded but legible ink. The ideas imprinted on the papers coalesced until they whacked her upside the brain.

She flapped the pages to catch Marjorie's attention. "I found it. We fight black magic with black magic to kill whatever curses are plaguing us."

Marjorie scoffed. "That's a given. Keep reading."

"No!" Aspen grinned, her excitement filling her parched body with newfound energy. "I mean, we use the poisonous parts of the morning glory and the other lethal plants growing in the basement against themselves. We use it to kill them. Eye for an eye to be exact. That's the permanent piece missing from the puzzle."

The speculation Marjorie gave her was all the incentive she needed. Since the magic didn't allow her to step foot in the house, she sent the healer with a list of supplies to snag from her lab. And a snip of certain plants from the murderous jungle in the basement. If they allowed her near them encased in a protective bubble, that is. Without the plant snips, Aspen's counter-spell would never be permanent, and the magic would renew and linger.

Chapter 19

Magic salted the earth, the air, and everywhere around Lucky. Innate commands broke through the buried crypts in his brain, awakened by the danger to himself and the woman he was falling hard for. The gyrating opaque threads coiled between his hands expanded like he was holding a basketball. As he hiked the path cutting through the lawn toward the house, more threads floated up from the ground and joined the first two.

"You're an earth warlock all right," Sage said from behind him. He'd all but ignored the Wildes in his concentration.

"And fire," he replied curtly as he maintained his focus on the magic luring him onward.

"Oh sure, that makes perfect sense," Sage drawled. "As if I didn't know."

"I thought the air had an extra sizzle around him."

"What do I do with these threads?"

"Keep weaving them." Rafael's footsteps crunched on the gravel behind him, attempting to distract him. "You've gathered more than I've ever seen. Something is feeding them to you. Not even Ethan can weave with such extensive intricacy."

"Lucky's untapped and untried."

"But I'm tapped, and I can't draw a tenth of that," Rafael lamented, a twinge of jealousy in his voice causing Lucky's lips to edge up in the corners.

"No, but no one was feeding you magic either." She came abreast of Lucky to open the French doors to the large great room. A comfortable and welcoming room he wanted to enjoy at least once before leaving the covenstead.

He veered to the right away from the doors. "It's pulling me this way."

"To the basement." Rafael jogged ahead, initiated the security reader, and opened a steel door. He jumped back, the color draining from his face. "The weeds are growing up the stairs."

Sage peeked around him. "Not weeds, my love. Tools of a witch's herbal arsenal." She pinched a flower off a stem and two others took its place.

Rafael whacked at a couple of four-foot-tall stems, and they whipped his leg. "I'm gonna cut this jungle down."

"Try it," Sage encouraged. "The magic hasn't prevented Lucky from coming this far. A good sign."

"Is it?" A pocketknife appeared in Rafael's hand.

"Maybe I can enter the house now, but not leave." Lucky stepped on the threshold, the opaque threads roiling in a ball shape.

Rafael sliced at a long belladonna stalk. The plant emitted a hissing scream and squirted toxic nightshade onto Rafael's pants below his knees. The stalk enclosed his leg and squeezed.

He tried to remove the plant, but it hung tight. "You had to encourage me, didn't you?"

"Sorry. I wanted to see what it'd do." Sage took a small spray bottle out of her pocket and sprayed the vine.

"Aspen's counter-spell."

Lucky winked at her. "You almost convinced me you were ready to sacrifice the love of your life and First Warlock."

"Who, me? Would I do that?" She sprayed the plants endangering Rafael.

"It's not working, Sage, love of my life. The nightshade's burning holes through my pants."

Lucky loved their banter and trust in one another. He hoped someday he'd become the love of Aspen's life and enjoy the same relationship with her. Man, he had it bad for the redhead witch in ways he never believed possible for any woman, let alone a witch. Guess he'd never stopped wanting her from his high school era.

Sage sprayed more potion on the belladonna to no avail. "The magic's expanded and strengthened." She stuck the bottle in her pocket and weaved her hands around the vine circling his ankle and calf. She chanted words Lucky didn't understand and connected both ends of the vine that Rafael severed. The ends fused together, leaving a slight scar where the knife sliced it in half. Sage soothed the stalk, and its leaves feathered her skin. The plant unfurled from Rafael's leg.

He stripped off his pants, leaving him standing in his black skivvies. Several red marks marred his legs where the nightshade penetrated through his jeans. Lucky cringed and skirted a nightshade plant.

Sage swished a hand over the marks, icing the burns, and the skin paled to pink on their way to healing. "Better?"

"Thanks." Rafael emptied his pockets and tossed his jeans outside. "Guess I'm going in like this."

A lush overgrown garden waited for them down the stairs. "Stay outside. I want no more skin-on-plant contact than we can avoid."

Rafael growled. "I don't like this."

Lucky's threads of earth magic wrenched on his core, and he stepped closer to the stairs, unable to fight it. "I need to descend."

Footsteps approached from behind, and the security earth witch Leah joined them. "Whoa, dude, you're an earth warlock. Powerful too. Nice." She licked her lips and gave Rafael an appreciative once-over. "Striptease, boss?"

"Leah, go down with Sage and Lucky," Rafael pleaded. "I don't want them alone. Who else is down there?"

"Nobody. Mr. Black Warlock Attacker is under camera surveillance. The vegetation's grown too dense. Earth magic's screwing with our wards, so we're dividing our resources."

"So he can use magic?" Sweat dripped off Lucky's face as he fought to prevent his weaving from disintegrating, fought the magic dragging him down the stairs.

"We don't know." Leah twisted a lock of her wind-blown, caramel-brown hair behind her ear. Obviously, not Wilde-witch hair. "So far, he doesn't show any signs he has access to magic. I'm hoping the wards holding him are active. This magic's unpredictable."

"I don't like the sound of that." Rafael slipped his pants on despite the holes and dried poison. "I'm going with you, or we don't go at all."

"You can't leave him forever to die." Lucky scratched the confusion tightening his jaw.

"I agree," Sage said. "We need to see where this leads us and find the source of magic. Before it gets out of hand."

"It's not out of hand *now*?" A pulsing vein threatened to pop through Rafael's neck. "Our entire basement's a breeding ground for every poisonous plant in the world."

"Maybe not every." Leah grinned. "Ward ourselves as best we can. I was down there earlier with no problem as long as I remained warded."

"If the magic killed your wards in the basement, then why didn't it kill your personal protection wards?" Lucky's mind spun. He had so much to learn.

Sage uttered a spell and wanded her arms in the air as she erected a protective spell around herself and Rafael. Leah erected her own personal ward. "Maintaining personal protective shields is easier than maintaining a ward around a room or a house, which might require more than one witch," she explained. "Let's go. If our shields disintegrate, we get out of Dodge."

"What about me?" Lucky asked.

Rafael led the way through the dense plants growing out of the stairs and the walls. Bare patches of white ceiling tiles remained visible here and there among the various shades of green.

"Lucky, you can't weave behind a ward. I need to see how your magic reacts," Sage replied.

The plants on the stairs swayed out of their way, giving a wide berth to Lucky even though he wasn't shielded. Sage's ward didn't stop the plants from touching them, but when they did, they jerked into their own lanes. After a few steps, the message spread, and the plants played nice. Lucky and the others didn't bother the jungle except to wade through it and, where they had no choice, to step on or kick plants out of the way.

Marjorie appeared at the top of the stairs behind them, a pair of garden pruners in her hand. Opaque air enveloped the witch. Lucky understood the protective ward now that he'd seen them a few times. She gave him a thumbs-up, and he ignored her to her own mission.

Flowers grew in abundance in all colors of the rainbow. Not all were poisonous to the touch. Most were poisonous if ingested or injected. He didn't plan on ingesting anything. He followed the magical threads still weaving and buzzing between his hands. They rotated and intertwined among each other but offered no inkling of what magic he'd wield if he used them. With every step he took, the magic intensified, and the threads grew brighter, heavier, the ball growing solid.

"Sage, what do I do with the threads? Do I let them go?"

The witch passed her hand through the center of the weave. "No. Each thread is collecting magic. They'll work with your innate abilities."

"I don't know how to work my magic."

"Just follow their lead."

"Don't use the magic against us," Rafael tossed in his caveman bit.

Lucky landed a do-you-think-I'm-an-idiot look on Rafael. "I may not have a choice." He shrugged. "I go where they lead." He hid a smile and continued past Rafael.

Rafael groaned and stabbed at a monster vine. "Sage, he'll get us all killed."

"You and I can shackle him if needed."

"Thanks for the vote," Lucky lobbed over his shoulder. He didn't know how his magic, such that it was, would react. It scared the piss out of him. But excitement shot through his body, and he bounced on his heels. The magic in the basement towed the magic out of him in ways he'd never experienced. He'd buried his scarce abilities for too long, and the magic wanted release. While making love to Aspen, he realized she also contributed to awakening his magic along the mysterious tether between them. *Wait. Whoa. Am I responsible for her dehydrated state? Am I also sucking her dry?* His excitement plunged, and his footsteps stuttered.

Sage pushed at him from behind. "What's wrong?"

He refused to state his concerns and admit a truth Aspen may want kept secret. But if it helped her... He motioned her away from Rafael and Leah who fought a thorny branch doing its best to adhere to Leah's boots.

"I need to run something by you," he whispered. "Aspen's condition." He paused, not knowing how to confess his concern. "It worsened overnight."

"Sex will hamper magic when a witch is already in a weakened state."

Shock jolted through him. "You knew?"

"We're dealing with an unknown here, but there's a connection between you and Aspen and both of you to this foreign magic. Plain as day." She scrutinized his horrified face. "Aspen understood the risks. She chose you. You better be worth it."

Her words floored him. More than anything, he wanted to prove himself a worthy ally to Aspen and the Wildes. And the Ravenwoods. A complete reversal from where he sat two days ago. A thread of magic slipped from the churning meld between his hands. He tried to rein it in, but a vortex seemed to unfurl it into the air above his head where it dissipated in a spray of sparkles.

"Pull it together." Sage spoke tersely. "What's done is done. I need you to concentrate on the here and now."

Absorbing her words, he stilled, straightened his spine, and concentrated before he lost all the threads. "Will she be okay? Maybe we shouldn't have left her."

"Marjorie's the best healer we know. I trust her to try everything in her arsenal."

Fury pummeled him. Before he uttered his disgust, she continued, "Family and my coven members are *everything* to me. If I don't get to the root cause, none of them will exist. So don't give me that holier-than-thou look. You left her too."

"I followed you because I believed you knew what you're doing." His fury faded.

"I do." She pushed at him. "Move it."

"Shit. Marjorie's in the doorway. She left Aspen alone."

They both looked up the stairs, but the jungle had already thickened and obscured the landing.

"Probably working on Aspen's counter-spell. They know what they're doing. Trust in them."

He had no choice but to believe in her and returned his focus to his own mission. The path from the stairs Rafael and Leah made ahead had already grown over, leaving Lucky to kick and trample a swathe for Sage to trod through.

"Thank you," she said, fighting a vine dangling from the ceiling that kept trying to grip her neck. The vine curled around his hand like a lover. "It's a Virginia creeper. The sap is poisonous if it gets on your skin." Sage used a wet wipe to wipe her neck.

Lucky slung off the vine. It hissed at him and slunk into the wild garden.

They reached the center of the basement. Not one inch of floor or walls was visible. The plants had drained all the moisture out of the arid room, the air so dry it lifted the hairs on his arms. Some were wilting, their leaves droopy, limbs and branches sagging toward the ground. Yellowing leaves dotted the otherwise vibrant green landscape. The oppressive pungency of a dense jungle on a steamy day made it hell to breathe despite the aridness.

"Keep the water witches out," Sage said to Rafael.

"What about you? Or me?" Rafael asked.

Lucky had no clue what magic Sage and Rafael carried except fire, and he'd seen her use air magic.

Leah kicked at a large red flower that fell on her black combat boot. "Not sure earth witches should be down here either."

"I don't think you're feeding them," Sage said. "But if you feel at risk, I want you out."

"Naw." Leah grinned. "I want to see this disaster to the end. Might give me fodder for new spell-casting."

"Only if you're planning on killing someone." Rafael lurched out of the way of a new bush rising from the floor, leaves budding and unfurling in seconds. "Lucky, what are you feeling?"

"I'm stuck. The magic ended in this spot." He glimpsed the door to Pierre's cell. Ten feet away. Vines snaked across the ceiling above his head in a random pattern. "What's above the basement in this spot?"

"The wall between Andre's room and the atrium." Color drained from Rafael's face. He pulled out his phone and engaged his security app. Lucky peered over Rafael's shoulder. Four cameras trained on Andre's room and another six on an atrium open to the sky behind glass panels. Andre sat at his desk reading *War and Peace*. "Normal."

"Have you surveyed the atrium?" Lucky asked. "You have quite a few plants and trees growing in there."

"We've inspected the atrium and Andre's room every couple of hours since this fiasco hit us. Plus every room and closet of the house. The vine coming through the ceiling of Aspen's lab headed this way."

A thread broke away from Lucky's meld and floated upwards. His magic faltered. He tried to recall it, concentrating so hard, his head hammered. "Then check between the walls or under the floors." Another thread separated and drifted toward the obscured door to Pierre's cell. "It's breaking apart."

"What power do you sense from it?" Sage asked.

"Nothing," he said sharply. "It's inert."

"Hmmm." She tapped her chin. "You can weave, but you don't know how to activate the magic." Sage plucked a leaf out of her blonde hair, the leaf morphing into the same golden color. "I don't know why it drew you here if you're not casting a spell."

Ice crackled beneath the surface of Rafael's gaze.

"Maybe he *was* casting and playing us for damn fools."

Lucky didn't have time to blast Rafael a new one when the rest of the threads broke apart, each whipping in the air. The threads dispersed and disappeared in the undergrowth. He dropped his hands to his sides, relief at releasing the magic loosening a knot in his shoulders, easing the hammering in his head. "That was intense."

"Hey," a muffled shout intruded upon them.

Leah thumped her fist on the door to Pierre's cell, smashing morning glories, and by the glee radiating across her face, loving it. "Shut up, asshole."

"I want to talk to Lucky Lorenzo," Pierre yelled.

"Why were you tracking me?" Lucky approached the door.

"Why should I tell you?"

"Do you want out or not?" Sage asked.

Lucky turned to her. "What has he told you?"

"Nothing." She stood next to him by the door. "We now know he was tracking you because you're a Ravenwood and he's Andre's son."

"Then why not let him go?"

"We want more info." Face coloring, Sage ducked her head. "And we can't get the door open. We can only provide food and water through the door window."

"The house wants him here, and alive." He scratched his head, hoping to spur his brain cells.

"Or he instigated this mess, and he's hit the top bullets of his agenda," Sage added.

Lucky eased closer to the door, the plants giving way to him in deference. *Freak-ass garden of Evil Eden.* A few droopy plants reverted to full health, fluttering and vibrant. Lucky didn't want to think what they were slurping out of him, Sage, and Rafael by the appearance of their pale masks. Leah didn't seem too bothered even though she was an earth witch. Or was she dessert?

"Why do you want me?" Lucky shouted through the door.

"Thought you'd lead me to Andre."

Without seeing his face or body language, Lucky didn't know if the warlock told the truth. He had no instincts where it came to Pierre.

"Why would I know where Andre's at? I've never met the man." Lucky held up a finger to silence the others. He wanted this conversation alone. After all, he was a prime victim.

"Surely you know you're on his Christmas wish list by now." The sneer was unmistakable in Pierre's tone.

"What list?" Lucky drilled through the morass in his mind. No one mentioned a list, and now his curiosity sped overtime. Sage and Rafael quieted, but they continued to show signs of distress in their listless motions and slumping shoulders. A tapeworm of terror skidded through his gut, and the oppressive plants in the basement weighed on him. The lure from the cabin to the basement still grounded him here.

"What list?" he demanded again. He'd never met Andre but had read about the Wilde coup on the dark witch web, which he accessed through a hacker friend from Silicon Valley.

"The list every black warlock wants to inhabit," the man said. "Rafael knows all about the list."

Lucky spun on Rafael and Sage. "What list?" Anger mottled Rafael's complexion. So not a good look, and Lucky took a step back.

"Special black warlocks Andre's hunted for decades." Sage placed her hand on Rafael's arm to calm him. "Black warlocks who have powers Andre wants. More powers than the usual black warlocks."

Lucky remembered the cloaking spell his mother, then Marjorie, had placed on the pharmacy, their home, him, and his father. "How did you find me?"

"Same way we find all our warlocks. I sensed your powers."

"Remember, there was a recent rift in the cloaking spells," Sage murmured. "Otherwise, Lucky would still be under the radar."

"Why am I on the list?" Lucky thumped his chest. "I'm a nobody."

"Hey," Leah called out. "Sage, I'm feeling more earth energy. Something's feeding the plants, and it's not me."

Out of the corner of his eye, Lucky spied his lost threads of magic glowing in pockets of the garden hell. They should've dissipated, but they remained intact. They coalesced into another ball of ghost threads. The glowing mass zoomed around the room, in and out of the bushes and flowers, as if imparting a message to each. Lucky felt a tug on his core so hard it doubled him over. He gripped his knees, trying to regain his composure.

The threads continued drifting, fueling the dehydrated plants. Not with water, though. They sipped earth power from Lucky, leaving a growing hole in his core. All a masterful trick from their unnamed maestro.

He stumbled erect. "The room's feeding from me."

The other three jumped toward him, and Sage waved her arms above her head, uttering a spell. "So mote it be," she yelled. The clamp on his magic lessened. "I've put you into our protective ward, Lucky."

All the plants growing from the floor in the small bubble shriveled and wilted, inert and harmless.

Mouth hanging open in awe, he watched the threads evaporate for real this time. "Better. Thanks." He tried to refill his lungs, but the air was so pungent he was forced to breathe through his mouth.

Leah kicked at a bloom of fading white petals, and the petals drifted like snow to blanket the green. If Lucky squinted hard enough, he could discern a distortion in their protective barrier. An emerald vine danced outside the bubble in front of Leah. Black flowers bloomed near each leaf. The leaves shriveled, browned, then fell off the vine in flurries of dust. Leah raised her hand. The vine followed, and with a tremor in the air, it coiled around her wrist.

Her protective ward disintegrated, the opaque air wavering for a split second. The plants sprang to life again, swishing and flapping. The flowers Leah kicked hissed, and the plants encircled her lower legs.

Chapter 20

While brewing her potions on the cabin's gas stove, Aspen took a swig of water every five minutes to hydrate. But the water didn't cut it. She needed the ocean to ground her in her magic, her crucial Zen place. Although no clouds were visible in the sky, the air remained thick and humid. The humid air hydrated her skin to a degree. Not a lick of wind blew, an uneasy calm before the storm. Foreboding set up shop in her head, and she re-focused on her potions to avoid her unease.

She knocked a beaker to the floor, and it shattered, shards of glass pinging the tile. "Goddess give me strength!" She propped her elbows on the counter and bowed her head, supporting her weight on the quartz.

Marjorie massaged her shoulders. "Take a break. I'll clean up."

"I need to hydrate. Drinking water and the humidity in the air isn't enough. All it's doing is allowing the magic to stick a fat straw in me."

"I don't feel humidity." A question mark formed on Marjorie's furrowed forehead.

"A storm's looming."

Marjorie's finger scrolled across her phone screen. "You're right. It'll hit Santa Cruz tomorrow. As long as the hydrangeas and other new plants growing around the cabin feed from you, you'll deplete your magic faster."

"Why can't the plants suck the life out of an earth witch." Aspen groaned and slapped her forehead. Marjorie was an earth witch. "Sorry, I didn't mean that. I'd never wish this BS on my worst enemy." A grim laugh escaped her. "Well, maybe a Helwig witch or two."

Marjorie bumped her shoulder against Aspen's shoulder. "Go to the creek. Water's running good after the winter rains. Between that and the rain, it'll help."

Agreeing with her mentor, she slogged to the front door and slipped on a pair of pink-and-black floral rubber waders. At least she was upright and walking. "Wonder what's going on with Lucky."

"Don't bother with him. Concentrate on you."

But Aspen wanted Lucky to bother her. Hot and bothered. Last night was the best sex she'd ever had, and they'd barely dipped a toe in the water. Or more aptly, an appendage in her wellspring. A long and thick appendage that knew exactly what to do, what erogenous zones to hit, which had her melting in his arms. She giggled at her joke to distract herself from thinking about the source of her ecstasy. For all she knew, he'd hit it and quit it after yesterday. Poor guy. But the connection they shared and the fact they both had crushed on each other in high school were enough to sweeten the pot.

When she opened the door, a floral wonderland greeted her. The hydrangeas had bloomed and expanded. Red and pink mini roses sprouted along the front perimeter and in the empty pots on the porch. Had Lucky caused this, his subconscious telling her their night had impacted him too?

As she strode past the roses, they quivered and

bloomed brighter and bigger. The plate-sized hydrangeas danced in a slight breeze. She touched a mophead, its velvety soft petals shifting and shimmering. Other blooms reached for her, and she swished her hand over them as she passed by. Petals floated in the air and showered her head. She caught them in handfuls and blew them into the air.

Hurrying along the creek path as fast as her achy legs allowed, she waved to the witches on perimeter security and jogged the last hundred yards to the creek beach, the place of many Wilde parties and picnics. A barbeque, firepit, and several wooden picnic tables dotted the grassy edges of the pebbly bank. She stopped at the smaller gazebo near the picnic area, and Rio flew off her shoulder to play guardian seagull. *Hey, he'd peck out an eye or two and drop head bombs. Who needed a warlock wingman?* But the pleasant ache between her legs refuted the question.

In drought conditions, the creek became a rivulet. Luck was on her side this spring. They'd had better-than-average rain over the winter and spring, and the creek flowed close to normal levels.

Already the enticement to the mountain spring water's purity leached into her pores, into her barren soul. It didn't cleanse the negativity like the Pacific's salt water, but it worked in a pinch. For how long? She'd never been stuck in this circumstance, never had to compare the creek to the ocean in replenishing her magic.

The humidity increased, and it felt like she was breathing through a straw. A chill worked its way through her T-shirt and hoodie. Didn't matter. She stripped off both and shivered in her bra. Next, she stripped off her leggings and slipped the waders back on to keep the pebbles and rocks on the creek bed from cutting her feet raw if she slipped off the walking stones. The Wildes had created a tide pool with a sandy bottom farther down the stream. Instead of going straight to it, she wanted to wade and beseech the goddess for healing before a full dunk into the pool.

Teeth clattering, she stuck her arms toward the sky and articulated her plea to the River Goddess who ruled the flowing rivers and streams, different from Aphrodite, the goddess of the sea. When Aspen reached the tide pool, she kicked her waders on the bank, remaining on the fringes of the water and voiced the spell, loud and clear:

> By earth, fire, wind, and sea,
> Merge your essence, flow through me.
> River's power, make me whole,
> Quench my thirst, renew my soul.
> By ancient magic, I beseech,
> Hydration from river's reach.
> So mote it be, this spell I cast,
> A witch's bond, now forged to last.

"So mote it be," she shouted, bringing her outstretched arms together and diving into the pool. Despite the frigid water temperature, she sluiced her arms to the pool's center and dunked her head beneath the surface. After a few minutes, her legs scissored stronger, the aches and pains besieging her muscles washed away, and moisture restored the aridness of her insides. The knives carving her skull receded, and her heart thudded strong against her rib cage. She swam and swam, diving in and out of the water before wading back to the shallower creek, her soul absorbing the water rushing over her feet and ankles. She returned to the gazebo and kicked herself for not bringing a towel. Shivers besieged her as she pulled her clothes on over her wet skin.

"Thank you, River Goddess." She wrung her hair and

bunched it into a bun. The meandering creek gurgled and cascaded over rocks. Water funneled above the creek and showered the surface in a waterfall. The goddess's playful response.

Stretching her arms, shoulders, and back, she walked the path to the cabin, not a soul in sight. She'd usually see a witch or three off this path at any time during daylight. Everyone seemed to be dealing with the jungle in the basement, or on Lucky or Andre duty. Just the thought of Lucky flushed her, and her shivering abated.

Marjorie stood in the cabin doorway and interrupted her delicious and sinful thoughts. "Aspen, you look marvelous."

"I feel marvelous. The only thing better would be a dip in the ocean."

"You do need an ocean dip. Sooner rather than later. It'll cleanse the negativity off you."

She laughed. "Yeah, I tried a saltwater bath once. Didn't go over so well." Teenage stupidity. Rock salt and tap water didn't equal natural elements. She ended up drying herself out from the salt, the first time she'd ever experienced a hydration event. "Wait!" Thinking, she tapped her chin, slid her finger over her lips. "I forgot to tell you. Salt will draw water out of the plants and help dehydrate them faster. We need to add it to my potion."

"Already added it." Marjorie handed Aspen a towel to dry her hair. "I read the notes you and Lucky made last night. You two brainstorming together might kill the witchworld."

Aspen flashed a thumbs-up to Marjorie. "Where is everyone? You seen my cousins?"

"Not a soul." They entered the cabin, and Marjorie stirred the potion bubbling in two pots on the stove.

As she tossed the damp towel on the counter, she couldn't help but wrinkle her nose at the bitter odor emanating from the pots. She tweaked her nostrils to halt a brewing sneeze.

"I noticed you were dabbling in molybdomancy in your lab." The spoon in Marjorie's hand stilled, and she gauged Aspen's reception of her words.

Heat traveled to her toes. "I was *sooo* bored. Thought I'd try some innocent fun."

"While brewing black curses?" Marjorie tsked-tsked.

"Yeah, well, someone's got to do it." Aspen defended her position.

"If you know what you're doing." Marjorie turned off the stove and the gas flames sputtered out. "Did you know that lead-pouring is not solely for divination? A spell-caster can use it to free people from negative energy and wicked spells."

"Wait, what?" Aspen sat on the barstool. "Could I use it on myself? Or you on me?"

"It takes a particular spell-caster. Did you succeed?"

"I foretold escaping danger, and I did at the pharmacy." Avoiding Marjorie's derision, Aspen ducked her head.

"But you aren't free. You're stuck on the covenstead. Stuck from nearing the house. Are you sure you didn't cast a black curse on yourself?"

She buried her face in her hands. "I melted lead and interpreted two shapes. No spell-casting going on." Had her escape come at a higher cost? Magic always toted a price tag.

Marjorie cleansed the spray bottles in saltwater. "Well, you're not an earth witch, so the plants didn't originate from any spell-casting you did."

"Exactly," Aspen exclaimed, a slice of relief severing a tiny knot among the million in her shoulders. Ideas on fighting the black magic cursing them spun in her brain.

A wrench on her core of magic seemed to steal air from

her lungs, and she gasped, gripping the counter edge. Her phone dinged, and she scrambled to find it buried in the cushions of the couch. She read the text from Rafael: *Stay away from the house.*

"No shit, Sherlock." She texted: *I can't get near it, anyway. What's going on?*

The plants in the basement need water. They're searching for any source.

"Oh, shit." She bit her bottom lip. *How bad?*

Bad.

How's Lucky? Rafael took too long to respond. A freezing claw ripped through her chest, as her heart took a swan dive into oblivion.

Fine.

Define fine! Aspen banged the phone against her forehead.

He's alive.

Her heart dipped farther. What did he mean? *I've brewed a potion to counteract the plants. To kill them.*

Sending Ben to pick up.

Only I can invoke the spell. A wave of revulsion deluged her as she waited for his reply.

You can't get in the house.

I'll find a way.

Aspen, it's Sage. What's your idea?

Found spells in Mom's books. Black magic. Should work.

She waited a too-long silence with her fingers poised above her screen.

What's the spell?

Sage hated dabbling in black magic. Right now, they had no choice. Aspen replied, *Fighting black magic with black magic. Potion contains all poisonous parts of the plants with a salt kicker.*

Sage's final text: *Brilliant. Come now. We're trapped in*

basement.

Marjorie packed the bottles and other spell-casting supplies. Aspen rushed into the bedroom and changed into a clean pair of black leggings and a long-sleeve T-shirt. For the first time, she realized she hadn't even thought about the tattoo still tingling and growing down to her butt cheeks. Would it ever stop growing? Was she destined to live with the mark for the rest of her life?

They rushed toward the house, a breeze carrying hints of a nightmare. Aspen drank water to maintain her hydration, but it already started dribbling away. The graying sky and muggy air did nothing but increase her sense of foreboding. At least the vines that blocked her yesterday had taken a hike.

"Will the tattoo disappear when all is said and done?" she asked her mentor.

"When the black warlock who invoked the spell is dead, most of it will fade. In time."

"Most of it?"

"He'll leave a permanent mark on you."

Aspen shored up her flagging body and the desolation waiting to submerge her. "If he's dead, how can his mark stay active?"

"It's a blood bond, from what I've read. You didn't trade blood with him—whoever he is—but it's possible another with his blood DNA could invoke the spell again. But only if he has access to your blood, and he's a powerful black warlock."

She faltered on a broken branch on the path. The insinuation sank into her brain, and she gagged and sprayed out a mouthful of water.

The healer caught her arm. "We have ways to prevent it, to veil the magic in the mark. I'm sorry, but you'll also need to bond a black warlock for protection to keep another black warlock from bonding you. Only a black warlock can accept your bond now."

"But, but…" She choked on her words and coughed it off. "If Andre's son cursed me, that means Andre could—" Her intestines twisted into a knot, squeezed by the icy fist of revulsion. "Oh my freaking God. I'm gonna be sick." She staggered three steps into the woods and tossed her cookies behind an evergreen tree.

Marjorie's hand alighted on her shoulder and gathered her unraveling damp hair behind her neck. "I'm sorry. I suspected as much as I continued to research." Aspen took a moment to recover before Marjorie guided her back to the path. "We need to get to the house."

Aspen tossed up her arms, let them drop. "I can't even approach it. How?" she snarled, slathering on her lip balm and popping a few mints. "How did that asshat even curse me?" Every curse word she knew flew out of her mouth until movement coming toward them arrested her attention.

Brianne and Marina scurried down the path. "Come on, Aspen. We're going to wrap you in a protective bubble and bounce you across the finish line."

"It'll never work." Aspen's internal Negative Nelly reared its ugly head. She drank more water, rinsed her mouth, and spat it out.

"Oh, ye of little faith," Brianne scoffed. "We spent all night researching, all of us. Don't give up now, just when we're on the cusp of breaking these shit-disturbing spells."

"Don't tell me you've been researching black magic too?" Aspen sneered. How had her life flipped into one big black curse receptor?

"No siree, Bob." Brianne's smile might've caused the ugliest toad to run for the sea. "Good ole witch magic."

It took everything in Aspen to shield her mind from the shock Marjorie unloaded on her, and not flee to the creek and drown herself, not just her sorrows. But she succumbed to her wicked task.

Working together, Brianne and Marina invoked a powerful protective ward around Aspen. They walked her toward the house, and when the black curse pressed against her invisible shield, she halted.

"I feel the curse."

"Is it stopping you?" Brianne asked.

"No. It's just obvious."

"Perfect." Brianne clapped once. "Let's get a move on, little doggie. This curse is feasting on all our magic, and I don't know how long we can hold the ward."

Each step closer to the house was like trudging through quicksand. She gnawed on her bottom lip. "How's Lucky? Rafael clammed up." Brianne and Marina traded concerned looks, and she sighed, bracing for the worst. "Just tell me."

"Sage doesn't want you to bother with him," Brianne said. "He's alive."

"Are you kidding me? You're not gonna tell me either? Who elected you Rafael's puppet?" Raising her paltry magic, Aspen shoved a hand through her protective ward. Her cousins' magic spackled the hole before the ward splintered.

"Once the plants are dead and this spell countered, he'll be fine." Brianne walked ahead to avoid meeting her gaze.

By the time they reached the basement's outer door, Aspen seethed in irritation and most of all fear. Fear for Lucky who possessed no control of his magic and was susceptible to other deadly magic. Sage and Rafael could hold their own, but not Lucky.

"Marina, did you or Leah ever determine how this spell attacked the covenstead?"

"We've used earth magic to lock down our perimeters," Marina explained. "Doesn't stop randoms entering the property or magic piggybacking on other witches."

"Oh joy. Everyone's blaming me." Aspen sniffed. Bad enough she blamed herself.

"Stop the sniveling," Marjorie demanded. "No one knows. If you brought this magic upon the coven, then you need to fix it. That's why you're here." Her irritated, motivating words struck Aspen's heart like a defibrillator. Jumpstarting her to act, to fix what she'd wrought upon the coven if it was the last thing she did before she croaked.

Aspen stopped before the doorway. "Toss the spray bottles to Rafael and Sage. Leah and Lucky if they're there."

Brianne used the eye reader to unlock the door and swung it wide open. An impenetrable mass of flowers, leaves, and stems greeted them. The top of Sage's blonde head waved in and out of view as she waited with Rafael at the foot of the stairs.

"Sage, can you blow a concentrated fire to forge an opening up the stairs?" Aspen asked. Powerful magic crowded the doorway, pressing against her protective shroud. No magic would penetrate her cocoon until her cousins discharged their magic either voluntarily or involuntarily. She fought down a twinge of hysteria to concentrate on the task at hand.

"Fire's too risky and unknown. Plus, we need to conserve our magic. We're losing our earth and water magic at a disturbing rate. Rafael will hack a path." Her sister sounded muffled from the dense field of nightmares. "Just waiting for you to arrive. What are you sending down?"

"Six thirty-two-ounce spray bottles. Is it enough?"

"It'll have to do." Rafael hacked at the jungle on the stairs, his hands and arms lethal weapons by the sound of it. Hisses, screeches, and screams from the plants pervaded the air. A frightening and haunting sound of death Aspen never wanted to hear again. Like fingernails on a chalkboard times one hundred. Rafael worked quick and reached the top of the stairs in less than a minute.

Marjorie handed him the bottles. One at a time, he tossed two to Sage, stuffing three more inside his shirt tucked into his pants. Marjorie kept one bottle to attack the plants moving up the stairs.

Decimated plants already fused together despite their lack of water. Their source of fuel seemed bottomless. Could it be the proximity to the creek? The humidity in the oppressive outside air? Aspen didn't even want to consider Lucky as their one source, even though she knew all the witches and warlocks downstairs fed the growth.

"Sage, can you use witch-wind while you spray to widen the swathe, stretch out the amount of potion?" Aspen suggested.

"Got it. I just dropped my shield."

Stray vines looped around Sage's and Rafael's ankles but didn't bind them. She suspected the plants feared the uber powerful mass of earth, air, water, and fire magic Sage and her warlock possessed along with their aether magic. Aspen craned her neck, tried to spy Lucky before the plants blocked her view. She found him standing next to Leah near the door to Pierre's room, both encased in plants.

Neither Leah nor Lucky had a free hand. The horror contorting Leah's face ratified the menace of her living, verdant cage. Vines circled her neck, lashed her body. Thankfully, she wore long sleeves and long pants. Lucky once again appeared calm and collected, the vines loose and teasing rather than threatening. He blocked some plants from reaching for Leah. Did he control the little suckers? Why didn't they threaten him?

"I'm ready to invoke the spell." Aspen waited at the threshold, far enough away where no plants could reach her through the protective ward, but close enough for the invocation to work.

"Ready," Sage yelled.

Aspen sipped more water and projected her voice, putting all the might of her magic into the spell.

> Toxic stems, stop your spread,
> By my words, your ruin is said.
> Root and stalk, relinquish hold,
> In fertile depths, your fate unfolds.
> No harm or malice shall you sow,
> With this spell, your power wanes low.
> By moon's glow and sun's embrace,
> Vanish now from time and space.
> So mote it be.

"So mote it be," Brianne and Marina shouted behind her.

The humid air smothered her last words. She held her breath until the spell caught the potion in the bottles, bound by the words she used when she mixed the two large pots. Black curse against black curse. Had she doomed them all?

Chapter 21

The clichéd saying "all hell broke loose" was never more apt in the basement plant kingdom. Sage invoked her air magic and shot out the first spray blast. The breeze aided to separate and disburse the droplets. Plants screamed, hissed, and waged their own war upon them. Soon Rafael cleared the stairway again, and Aspen could see down the stairs. Plants shriveled and died on the steps, once lush green, now dry and crinkly.

She pinched the bridge of her nose, crimping the odor of sweet and acidic plant decay from setting up shop. The potion worked, but magic came at a cost. Who would exact the cost?

"Good job. It's working," Marjorie praised her.

"You helped too." She shot the older witch a smile over her shoulder. "As did Lucky."

The former jungle transformed into a landscape of yellowing and dead plants crunching underfoot. Devoid of magic.

She spied Lucky picking dried leaves and stems off Leah. The witch kept her eyes shut as if in a trance. Lucky peeled off a disintegrating, arm-thick vine holding Leah upright, and she crumpled into his arms.

"Leah!" Sage tossed her empty bottle aside and charged the earth witch. Although not a family member, Leah had joined the coven several years ago and had quickly proved her loyalty and trust. By all accounts, she was family.

Aspen craved to go to Leah. She hadn't even brought her healer's bag, not even her fanny pack. Rafael took her from Lucky and carried her toward the stairs. Sage plucked yellowing bits off Leah. They clung for the last iota of magical life left in the earth witch.

Grim expression on his face, Lucky gave Aspen a thumbs-up. Before Rafael reached the midpoint up the stairs, the door to Pierre's cell burst open, and he barreled through, ramming Lucky to the floor. They grappled and Andre's son strong-armed Lucky in a headlock. He sprang up from the floor, using Lucky as a shield in front of him.

"I'll kill him if you don't let me see Andre *and* let us go." Leaves and twigs stuck out of his blond-spiked dark hair in all directions. The plants growing in his room were dying like the rest.

"Wards have fallen," Sage shouted.

Rafael jumped the last few steps up to the doorway and thrust Leah into Brianne's and Marina's arms. "Go." He leaped down the stairs to Sage's side.

Aspen glued her sight on the tableau unfolding in the room below. Had her potion decimated the wards on the holding cell? Or was Pierre so uber powerful?

"I'll torch this house and everyone in it." Spit sprayed from Pierre's mouth.

"Including yourself?" Sage taunted. "Because you're not leaving until you give us answers."

"What more do you need to know?" He tightened his arm across Lucky's neck. "This dude here is one of Andre's special pets. You already know I'm Andre's son. I'm not leaving here without my father. End of story."

Aspen drank the last of her water and tossed the bottle aside. Aridness deluged her body again, despite the dip in the creek. Even through her protective shield, magic sizzled around her, strong and hungry. A strange pull to the basement kept her captivated in the doorway, wishing with all her might she could do more than mix deadly potions. But with her lagging witch-water, she'd hamper their efforts to conquer the earth magic.

"You're not leaving with Andre or Lucky," Sage rebutted. "We can escort you off the covenstead since you're free now."

"If you're lucky, we might give you a ride to town in the back of a pickup, bound and gagged," Rafael ground out.

"Fuck you all." Pierre pressed his arm tighter across Lucky's neck. He tried to pry Pierre's arm off to no avail, kicking backward at his tree-trunk legs. "Andre wants Lucky, and Andre *always* gets what he wants."

A silence fell among the now quiet plants. The crunching of dead flowers and leaves underfoot remained the sole evidence of the jungle gone wild.

"We'll take Lucky to Andre. On our time and our terms," Sage said. "Let him go."

"Not without me. We're a package deal." A fireball tangoed on the man's free hand and pale fire outlined his arm. Sage tossed a sprinkle of water aided by witch-air to extinguish the fire magic. Pierre grinned. "There's more where that came from. You've blocked my magic for days and it's hungry as a horse."

Sage snickered. "Oh, I know how magic works."

"Do we look concerned?" Rafael lashed out.

Lucky's eyes beseeched Sage and Rafael. They nearly popped out of his head until Pierre loosened his hold, and Lucky heaved in air. Aspen wanted to fly down the stairs to rescue him. She wanted to kill Andre and his son for putting them all in peril from the moment the black warlocks landed in their realm at Andre's behest. The black warlock leader needed to die before he destroyed the witchworld.

She didn't know what would become of Lucky in the end of this dumpster fire. Or their relationship, if one existed. She never envisioned herself with a black warlock. Even though her sisters were both enamored with black warlocks, Willow had until recently shunned all of them. Aspen had an iffy time grappling with the idea, especially after Marjorie's assertion that she may have to bond a black warlock. The Black Tide had snared too many. Even if Andre and his son died, another leader would take Andre's place, another leader to draw any warlock to their ranks. Possibly even Lucky. Aspen dreaded any world where black warlocks ruled. Feared them running free among witches, the way before the long-ago war. In some sense, Sage wanted to return the witchworld to those days, as long as warlocks and witches worked together. Aspen remained skeptical. If any plan backfired, then which faction would benefit? The light or the dark side of the witchworld coin?

"Release Lucky, and we'll let you see Andre," Aspen projected her powerful voice, despite the anxiety gnawing on her stomach. "Seeing" didn't mean visiting.

Sage knew very well the value of words in a witch's vocabulary. "All right. We'll let you see Andre alone. After you release Lucky."

"No dice. Package deal." Fire twinkled on his hand again. This time Sage left it alone. The more magic he used, the less remained for him to use. Magic simmered off Sage and Rafael, a mix of their aether, each containing their own, but also mingled together within their bond. The aether alone made them the most powerful witch or warlock in the world. Together, they were near invincible.

Mud boiled at Lucky's feet. Fire rimmed it but died from the moisture.

"Knock it off." The black warlock slapped Lucky upside the head. "I'll kill you without risking a hair on my body."

"You're not gonna kill me," Lucky said between clenched teeth. "Andre wants me alive. He'll kill you if you hurt another hair on my head. In fact, he'll kill you once he learns what you're doing to me."

Pierre snickered, tightening his arm around Lucky's neck. "Think again, asshole. I'm his son. He won't hurt me. You're just a number on a long list."

A purple hue painted Lucky's face. Aspen brushed her arm against her ward, finding it less onerous than before since the plants had gone the way of the dearly departed. She slipped down the stairs, waving Brianne and Marina to silence. But the crunching on the plant wreckage gave away her position.

"Stop, or he's a dead man." Pierre's eyes bored into her, then softened when recognition passed through them.

"Get out, Aspen," Rafael ordered, but she saw him nod at Sage, then her, and she knew they had an ace or two up their sleeves.

"Ah. Nice to see you again, Aspen Wilde." Pierre kinked his head to the side. "You've got our boy's dick all twisted. Thought I smelled you on him."

"Yeah, you tried to bag me in town. Too bad you suck at that."

He shrugged one shoulder. "I got two birds. One stone."

"No. You got your one-way ticket to the underworld." Lucky's voice was raspy from the warlock's arm pressed to his throat.

Aspen took a tiny step backward, then two forward.

"You safe?" Sage mouthed.

"Warded." Aspen patted the boundary of the ward. A

tiny sizzle of magic prickled her hand.

Sage tapped Rafael's wrist in their personal "go" sequence. Magic vaulted into the air, sparks popping against the ceiling, then showered down upon Pierre. Mud gushed from behind Pierre and buried his boots, grounding him. The sludge bypassed Lucky's sneakers but teased the outer soles. The mud spread up Pierre's legs in a flaming river of crimson and orange sludge.

Screaming like an enraged bull, the warlock shoved Lucky out of the way. His earth magic created a cooling mud that drenched Sage and Rafael's fiery magic. Fire vaulted to his hands, and he tossed electrical bolts at them.

Sage and Rafael deflected the witch-fire with blasts of their own aided by witch-water to keep the fire from burning out of control.

Lucky found a dying rope vine and imbued it with his own earth magic, returning it to life. The magic came to him instinctively, and he logged it into his brain. He worked it into a lasso and roped it around Pierre's body, missed confining the black warlock's arms in the lasso.

Pierre tossed random fireballs to light the dead plants on fire. Aspen uttered a counter-spell to release her protective ward, the way Marina and Brianne designed it. The two witches remained safe from the melee, guarding the basement door. No way did they plan to let Pierre escape. Using her waning witch-water, she doused the tiny fires. Lightning and fireballs flew, and wind whipped up a tornado.

Lucky found another pliable plant rope and gifted it with his earth magic. It turned green and thickened in his hands, and he made another lasso. This time, he captured Pierre and locked the warlock's arms to his sides, preventing him from tossing more fire. Sparks dripped from his fingers onto the plant debris, and Sage doused the floor. Sage's dribbling witch-water and her magic overall had taken a hit because of the plant life sucking the witch-life out of all of them. None of them could maintain this fight much longer.

Lucky pulled his lasso tight around a growling and struggling Pierre. The black warlock blasted out fire magic that either Aspen or Sage doused. As Rafael approached the man, Ricky, Leah's warlock husband, stormed the basement from the interior stairway.

"I'm gonna kill that son of a bitch." Steam seemed to billow out of the neckline of his shirt, his bald head reddening. With his fists balled at his sides, he came to a standstill near the bottom of the stairs. "Leah's in a magic-induced coma. Marjorie's not sure she'll come out of it with or without her magic."

Gasping, Aspen hopped to the bottom of the stairs and crossed the room, dead plants crunching beneath her feet. The air in the basement was cloying and hot from the dead and dying plant life, from the scent of brimstone and puffs of smoke. From the oppression of Mother Nature's storm brewing outside.

"I'll go to her." As she stepped a foot onto the stairway leading into the house, she realized that the black magic no longer held her away from the house. Had all the magic stemmed from Pierre and the plant life? *Weird to the nth degree jungle magic.*

She didn't stick around to watch Ricky make good on his threat. Halfway up the stairs, thick smoke hit her nostrils. Waving the smoke away, she scanned the stairs. Fire followed her and danced around the walls of the stairwell, surrounding her.

"Oh, hell to the no." She couldn't erect a protective shield and use her diminished witch-water. "Fire!" she shouted. Sparks hit her from all directions and closed in on her. Almost hyperventilating, she tried to keep from breathing in the dense air.

Raising the last of her magic, she intoned a drenching spell to help speed along her natural witch-water. Arms outspread, she twirled like a sprinkler and doused the fire in the stairwell. By the time she soaked the stairs, she'd depleted her magic, and a blaze encapsulated the basement.

Chapter 22

Smoke swirled thick and noxious. Pierre bulldozed Lucky to the floor, pummeling him in the torso before a fist contacted the side of his head. Stars glittered in his vision and winked out as the stinging air forced his eyes closed. He fought through the muddle in his head, the lack of air, but he feared his untapped magic would go sideways against the trained warlock.

Shouts and screams echoed in the room. Fire raged in all corners, the dead plant debris perfect fodder. Witch-air swirled the fire, touching every surface until flames engulfed the room. Once the black warlock invoked a protective shield, the fire didn't touch Lucky and Pierre. Pierre hauled Lucky upright, the man's muscular arms locking his own arms to his sides. Had Aspen, Sage, and the others escaped? He couldn't tell. He didn't see water dousing the fire, just the fire and air Pierre kept releasing from inside their shield. How did the black warlock work magic from inside a protective ward? Lucky had much to learn about the craft.

The noise deafened, but Lucky spoke anyway. "Stop

this madness, and I'll do what you want." He assessed the warlock's size, an inch or two shorter, but tree trunks for arms and legs and a wide barrel chest.

Pierre tied air bands around Lucky. "Oh, I know you will." He shifted behind Lucky and positioned him facing the interior stairs. "Up the stairs. Your witch already extinguished the fire."

"You won't get in the house from there." Lucky had no desire to be trapped in a stairwell with no outlet in an inferno.

"The heat decimated the electronics." Pierre pushed Lucky hard with a hand in the center of his upper back. "Move your ass."

Stepping forward cautiously, Lucky surveyed the chaotic crackling flames and billowing smoke, hoping to catch a glimpse of a Wilde. For any sign of Aspen, who he'd last seen at the landing to the stairs. Devastation met his gaze. He toed the first riser. Sweat dripped off his scalp down his neck. He wiped his face on his shoulder, breathing into his sleeve. Too bad the protective shield didn't filter out all the smoke or heat.

Lucky trudged up the stairs, faster to escape the fire. The first drops of water from the ceiling sprinklers finally rained down upon him. Air blew downward from the top of the stairs, swishing the smoke away. Aspen and Brianne stood on the landing. Horror dawned on Aspen's face, painting it in stark shades of terror. Water spritzed off Brianne's hand, creating a clear path for Ethan Ravenwood to descend. Ethan's huge raven familiar vaulted off his shoulder, winding Ethan's opaque threads of magic around Lucky and Pierre, until Pierre's magic fractured, and their protective ward disintegrated.

"Run, Lucky." Aspen swayed on the landing. Brianne tried to catch her from taking a header down the stairs.

He bolted toward her and scooped her in his arms.

Cradling her head against his chest to avoid inhaling more smoke, he held her close. So close, he never wanted to let her go. Magic popped behind them, but Lucky only had eyes for Aspen. He carried her behind Jessica and Ben guiding them into the interior of the house.

"Wait." He stopped, Aspen's weight like a feather in his arms. "Do we need to evacuate?" Smoke stung his throat, his voice hoarse.

"No. My father built the house with steel walls and ceilings. Because we're witches. We play with fire." A smile played at her lips before she went limp in his arms.

Jessica guided him to the infirmary, and he set her on the empty bed next to Leah. Pain ravaged the earth witch's face, a startling contrast to Aspen's serene contentment. Ben opened the windows to air out the lab, and fresh air filtered in, aided by a strong breeze.

Marjorie stormed into the room. "Sit on the examination table. I'll check you in a moment." He eased out of the way but didn't leave the cubicle. She fussed over Aspen, checked her vitals, and set up an IV drip. "This needs to stop. Any more depletion of her magic in a short time frame could permanently damage her."

"I'll take her to the ocean." Emotions layered his husky voice. If he did anything to hurt Aspen, he'd never forgive himself. "Even if I have to carry her there myself."

"You're not taking her anywhere," Jessica's husband, Ben, ground out. "We don't trust you. And no one is leaving the covenstead until we have this mess under control."

Lucky fisted his filthy hands at his sides, more to vent his frustration than for using them. "I care for her, and I have no intent to harm her. I can protect her in the water."

"It's not your intent that's the problem," Jessica said. "It's the unintentional we're worried about."

"Then you all come with us. But she needs the ocean," he said through gritted teeth. "She's always needed the ocean."

"You sure know a lot about our girl." Brianne finagled her way into the room. "Guess it really was you on the beach in high school who towed her out of the ocean after thinking she was in deep doodoo. Saving her life." Her fingered air quotes didn't steal the snark from her voice. "Thought it was you."

Lucky unclenched and clenched his fists, unable to direct his anger anywhere else. "Big deal. I *thought* she was drowning."

The blood drained down Aspen's neck. "I've always known it was you. Why'd you run away?"

"Because your *cousins* tried to drown me in a rogue wave. They believed I threatened you by rescuing you from *drowning*."

Aspen snatched a sheet over her head for a second. "Sorry. We're a protective bunch."

Jessica clapped, a deafening cracking sound. "Enough. Take your petty squabbles out of here. No one's going to the beach. Now let Marjorie work."

"I'll hit the creek again." Aspen's head drooped to the pillow as if it weighed a ton. "Hey." Her eyes widened. "I'm in the house! Must mean something."

"Creek time tomorrow." Jessica shooed her daughter and Ben out.

"Today. I can't wait for tomorrow. I'm not recovering overnight fast enough."

"But the plants aren't feeding on you any longer." Jessica helped Marjorie load healing paraphernalia on a tray and rolled it into the cubicle housing the two beds.

Lucky rested a hip on the exam table and couldn't stop gazing at Aspen. His heart cricked just seeing the flakes of skin sifting off her desert-dry arms. She needed a natural body of water, and he'd make sure she got it. Sooner rather than later.

"Spraying the fire down and the plants lapping up every drop of moisture depleted me. But more than the basement jungle is stealing my magic. Remember the plants outside? As long as Pierre's still alive, his magic will keep attacking me." She glanced at the ceiling of her lab. The vine had retreated. *Small favors.*

A bustling noise arose at the end of the hallway, one set of lightweight footsteps growing closer. Sage appeared in the doorway. Soot-stained holes singed her clothing. A beautiful witch no matter how ragged she appeared.

"Pierre shouldn't be sucking anything out of you. He's dead." Sage picked at a scraggly blue fingernail until she tore it off and flung it into the trash basket. She shrugged off her short leather jacket, singed and holey and flung it in the trash as well.

Aspen's eyelids flapped up, and she tried to lift up on her elbows. Groaning, she collapsed to the bed. Lucky grabbed a bottle of water and a straw and brought it to her.

"Sip it." Marjorie waved him back to the examination table. "Let me see your tattoo. Then show me your wrist." She turned to Lucky. "You too. Strip it."

"What happened?" Lucky rolled up the hem of his T-shirt.

"Battle of wills, might, and magic. One black warlock against two didn't paint a pretty picture. He started it. We ended it." Sage plopped onto Aspen's rolling stool.

"Did he burn?" Aspen mangled the words.

"He shot fire bolts that Ethan and Rafael deflected. Two bolts of his own magic through the chest." She swept her grungy blonde hair off her face, and Lucky witnessed tears leaving trails down her grimy skin.

Alarm shot him arrow straight. "Are Ethan and Rafael okay?" Despite their original animosity, he'd grown to care about the warlocks in his short time. Plus, Ethan was family.

"They're dealing with the mess." She swiped away her tears, muddying the soot on her face. "I can't believe I'm emotional over that asshole who brought this chaos upon us."

Marjorie stepped aside to reveal Aspen's back. Jessica clapped a hand over her mouth and gripped Aspen's hand in her own.

Lucky almost brained himself on the wall turning to look. The tattoo covered the entirety of Aspen's back, the "ink" fresh and prominent. "It's like all of Pierre's magic is dancing on your back."

Marjorie shot him a curious look. "What makes you say that?"

"His magic is gone, but not forgotten." He said the words that came unbidden to him. Where they came from was anyone's guess. "She had a connection to him and is now the conduit of his lingering magic." He lifted his shirt, ignoring once again the tickling of the tattoo as it roiled and expanded. "As am I." He showed his back to Sage. "Same?"

"Same. Marjorie, is it true?" Sage asked.

Determined to kill this magic, black and white curses revolved in Aspen's brain. "What if it's Lucky?"

He held up his hand to argue, but dropped it. "What if it is?" A muscle pulsed in his temple. "I swear I'm not doing this intentionally, but what you said about the unintentional. What if I'm under a curse and it's affecting Aspen?"

"A real possibility if you didn't deliberately curse her. And yourself." Marjorie drew Aspen's blouse down, covering up the beautiful art on her gorgeous body.

"Hold on." Lucky jumped off the table and closed the distance to Aspen. He shoved up her blouse and pressed a finger to a purple morning glory in the small of her back. It seemed to wrap around him in 3-D. He withdrew, and the flower shifted on the vine. The vine whipped around her back, reshaping the entire tattoo.

Aspen squirmed on the bed, scraping her backside on the mattress. "Make it stop," she groaned out.

Lucky felt the same sensations, and a prickle worked up his spine.

"I need to hydrate before I pass out. Lucky, will you take me to the creek?"

"Not a good idea." Sage leaned her elbows on her knees.

"Because he's a big bad monster?" Aspen slammed a listless fist on the bed. "Just stop."

"I'll take you." He put Sage on ignore, slipped on his shirt, and moved to Aspen's side.

"Put her in a wheelchair." Sage relented. "I'm trusting you on this, Lucky. If you hurt one hair on her head, you're a dead warlock walking. You got me?"

He didn't bother gracing her question with a response. He was so damn tired of the insinuations and accusations lobbed at him.

Despite her half-hearted protestations, Lucky lifted Aspen in his arms, and gentle as a baby set her in a slim wheelchair designed with rugged wheels for outdoor terrain. Brianne tossed a towel and a black terry robe on Aspen's lap. Buried in the robe pocket were two Snickers bars that brought a grin to Aspen's wan face.

Not a word transpired between them until they rolled along the path through the woods out of earshot of Aspen's wardens.

Stormy clouds darkened the sky, steel and cement churning together, obscuring the sun. The wind danced through the trees, a symphony of creaking branches and whispering evergreen needles.

"Brianne will follow in an hour," Aspen said. "Like I said, we're a protective bunch."

"I figured, and I noticed." With the wind whipping about and the dense moist air, his words clogged his throat.

"I'm so over this crap. I figured if Pierre croaked, we'd return to normal."

"Is it possible for his magic to linger after death?"

"For a short time. His soul is gone, but his body's still here. The magic will deplete over time." She pointed to their cabin. Already thinking of it as theirs. Man, he had it bad. "Check out the hydrangeas and other plants. They've grown larger and proliferated."

Lucky slowed the chair to a crawl. He almost hated the flowers that sprung up overnight, but how could he when the hydrangeas reminded him so much of his mother. The unnerving significance didn't go over his head. The woods thickened and closed them in a world of their own.

"While locked up, Pierre's magic strengthened instead of weakened." He pushed her chair down the pathway, following her directions to the creek gurgling and flowing up ahead.

"That's what scares me. I really don't think he was the source of the curse. But the plants and vines didn't feed from him, so I'm torn."

"Do you think it was me?"

"No, and my coven knows it." She flicked a hand toward the Wilde McMansion. "A curse doesn't curse the spell-caster. Sage knows it's not you. She's yanking your chain because we're clueless." The chair bounced over a slight dip in the gravel path. "Argh." She clutched her head, then dipped into her robe pocket. She opened one candy bar and handed the other to Lucky. "My favorite sweet energy boost."

Lucky stuck the bar in his back pocket. "Seriously? Mine too. I'll save it for you."

"Eat it. You might need it." A playful melody wove through her words.

"Why? Do you weigh too much for me to cart into the river?" He ruffled her hair, wanting to sift his hands through the silky, coppery strands.

"You're just a cauldron of laughs." Her seagull familiar materialized on her shoulder and vaulted into the air, zinging over the path ahead. "Rio will alert me to danger. If any."

"At least he's not pecking my eyeballs out."

"Lucky you." She tittered and munched on her candy bar, the wrapper crackling in her fist.

When she'd eaten half her bar, he stopped on the path and walked around the chair to face her. "Now tell me how you scored a seagull familiar."

She laughed, and he'd never seen a more blissful face eating chocolate. "Do you remember the seagull that dive-bombed you when you 'rescued' me"—she did air quotes—"from the ocean in high school?"

His mouth hung open. "Rio?"

"Yep." She ate another small bite of her bar, licking her lips the way he wanted to lick them. "After everyone scattered, I remained lying in the sun. He kept soaring over me, dive-bombing me until he perched on a sand ridge and eyeballed me."

"But how did you know? How will I know?"

"A familiar will sense they're special with an affinity toward a magical. They'll hunt for a witch or black warlock to bond. The witch or warlock must be open, ready, and able to bond a familiar. In my case, I was kinda desperate. Seventeen and I'd been searching for my familiar for two years."

"But a seagull?" He tweaked her hair and returned to steer the chair around a rut, bumping along the path.

Rio squawked ahead, gliding in and out of the trees. "Don't knock it. You might wind up with a toad."

Lucky groaned. "Great."

"Anyway, Rio kept inching closer to me, and I sensed a weird kinship with him. He'd been protecting me when he believed you threatened me. I stretched out my arms in the sand and he waddled over and sat on my hand. He let me stroke him. And I knew."

"But how do they have magic or shift into a tattoo? I don't get that part."

"Once you've identified your familiar, you must recite the familiar bonding spell. You know the spell worked when the familiar can shift into a tattoo. Sometimes with a powerful witch or warlock, like Rafael, no bonding spell is necessary."

"What happens if it can't?"

"Then it's not your familiar. Some familiars reject a witch, some find the wrong witch, and some are just not a familiar."

"I need to know the bonding spell."

"I'll teach you." Aspen angled her head, sunlight catching the shimmer of curiosity in her eyes as she scrutinized him. "Have you ever had strange incidents with birds or animals?"

"Maybe. Now I'll be on the lookout."

"Like what? You may have already met your familiar. Not something that lives in the water, though." They reached the gazebo at the end of the path, and Aspen stuffed her empty wrapper in a pocket.

"Hiking in the higher woods last summer, I crossed paths with a mountain lion mother protecting its baby. The kit came to me, rubbed against my leg, and let me pet it. Mom cat sat there and watched as if she trusted me. The most bizarre and terrifying experience in my life."

"Oh, my, God." Aspen cupped a hand over her mouth. "I don't know of anyone other than Andre who has a large breed cat familiar. His is a black panther."

"What does it mean?"

"That your magic is freaking powerful." Aspen wiped her mouth off on the back of her hand, and Lucky wished she'd let him lick the chocolate off her lips. "We need to find that kitten."

Dampening his rising arousal, he locked the brakes on the chair, and Aspen stood on shaky legs. "I'm so glad I'm out of that thing. I'm twenty-six, not ninety-six." As she tossed her towel and robe onto a bench in the gazebo, the first drops of rain spit on them. "Mother Nature has arrived."

"Will rain help your hydration?" Wind whipped his hair back. It rustled the trees, and branches swayed above them, showering pine needles upon their heads. He skirted the chair to offer his support.

"Somewhat, but the earth, wind, and lightning will take from the rain, so it's not a significant source of hydration." She looped her arm in his, and they took slow and sure steps to the gazebo. "There's a pool farther down I want to dunk in. You game?"

"Absolutely." He set her on the step to the gazebo and took her sneakers and socks off, then took off his own. When he looked up, the world tilted on its axis. A slant of sunlight slicing through the clouds shone on her hair like a streak of molten copper. The increasing wind whipped her hair behind her shoulders, but the copper streak remained in place until the clouds coalesced and blocked the sun.

She stood with her back to him, her legs bare of her leggings. With a beaming smile, she twirled around and lifted her T-shirt up and over her head, leaving behind only a purple thong. No bra in sight. His mouth dried into cotton, and an instant erection strained at his pants. She was the most beautiful woman he'd ever seen. Is this what she meant by later?

Chapter 23

Aspen suppressed a shiver, not wanting the cold to distract her from what she offered Lucky, in her nakedness and her desire for him to strip and join her in the pool. The frigid water may prevent him from performing, but she wanted him beside her. And not merely for support and protection.

"I'll warn you now." Stifling a giggle, she inclined her head toward his erection. "You're gonna lose that magnificence once the water reaches your hips."

"Well, if you're going to tease me, then I'll wait for you here." Despite his words, he stripped off his shirt and tossed it on the bench.

Her gaze drank in his sculpted abs and chest, the arrow of light brown hair sliding beneath the waistband of his jeans. She licked her lips. "No. We both go in. Strip it and hurry." Desire tormented the vee of her legs, and she crossed and uncrossed her ankles.

"Your command is my wish." He peeled off his pants, gray underwear following, and his straining and strutting hardness sent her heart pulsing in her ears.

No commando today? He drew her into his arms, her nipples so hard, they met resistance in the hard planes of his chest. She rubbed against his erection, and when she tried to wrap a hand around him, he gripped her wrist, stopping her.

"No. You in the water." He punctuated each word with a kiss on her lips. "Now." He smacked her ass, his hand lingering and massaging her butt cheek. "You have the most amazing ass. Firm, soft, and… perfect."

Aspen licked the taste of him off her lips, relishing in the residual sweetness of his morning's orange juice. She took a step into the water, a jolt to her barren system, and she yelped. "Just my ass is amazing?" Her teeth clattered.

Shock eclipsed his awestruck eyes as his bare feet hit the glacial water. "Your ass is amazing. Your breasts are heaven. Your entire body is a stunning paradise. And your brain is a glorious thing to behold."

Aspen roasted from his praise. No man had ever used those words to describe her. Sure, boys and men had called her hot or pretty. But Lucky's praise meant more than all the others combined.

"Follow me. We added a path of flat rocks to step on, so you don't cut your feet on the smaller rocks." Her momentary burst of energy flagged, and Lucky caught her when she almost took a header into the creek. He tried to bolster his arm around her waist, but she needed to go alone, and his body was way too enticing. "Thank you." She took another step forward. "We need to go single file." Gusts of wind whipped up and drizzle plastered her face.

"Is the pool accessible from the banks?"

"Yep. But by the time we get there, the cold will have numbed us up from our feet."

"You're evil."

"Haha. For real, wading helps me hydrate faster." A few more careful steps and the bottom of the river lowered her onto the shallow edge of the pool. They departed the languid embrace of the river's current, their bodies gliding into the secluded pool. The wind created tiny caps on the surface of the water.

"What do you want me to do?" He swam close to her side, his arms scissoring through the water strong and sure. "This is amazing. And you were right. The cold isn't so bad now."

"I'll do my ritual. You swim." She splashed him. "Don't interfere until I tell you I'm done."

She treaded water, her hair floating on the surface like a burnished copper mantle. Lucky swam close enough to kiss. She closed the distance and planted one on his lips. His rain-splattered lips were firm and sought more, but she drew apart. "More afterwards." She grinned.

"I'm counting on it. You floating in this water is stirring me up."

"How stirred are you?" She reached below the surface and found him semi-erect. "A little is better than none." Laughing, she swam to the middle, using every bit of her strength to reach it, using every iota of her willpower to leave Lucky. She needed to do her ritual, or she'd never make it through the day.

Closing her eyes, she angled her head back and treaded water, her arms lethargic. Aspen recited the hydration spell to the River Goddess, rising and dipping in the water. She dunked her head backward and shot up again. The River Goddess infused her with her power, joy, and wisdom. "So mote it be." Raising her arms out of the water straight to the sky, she shouted the words, letting the water-derived energy flow from her scalp to her toes. Warmth swapped her chill and topped off her adrenaline.

A whirlpool formed, and she spun her languid arms in the water, increasing the swirling strength until she became one with the undulating water. Before she got dizzy, she laid her arm on the surface of the spinning water. The whirlpool widened and spun around the edges of the pool, around them.

"Come here." She crooked a finger toward Lucky.

"You were incredible to watch." He swam to her, his strokes confident and strong, knifing through the water. "The water followed your every movement."

She blushed. "I was channeling it up from the bottom, beseeching it to follow my commands and the commands of the River Goddess."

Water lapped over them, elevating Aspen's sensitive breasts up and down, each rise and descent mirroring the undulating water. She twined her arms around his neck, her feet not reaching the sandy bottom. He crushed her to him, her breasts mashing against his hard chest, and he dipped his head to meet her lips with his own.

The water's caress against her skin was like a crescendo of desire that intensified every nerve ending in her replenished body. Ripples of water danced over Aspen's skin, eliciting a wanton shiver down to her toes. As she wrapped her leg around his, the velvety liquid enshrouded them in its sensual embrace.

Slow and deliberate, Aspen molded all of herself against him, her yearning evident in the curve of her body pressed to his. The rhythm of their heartbeats aligned. Each pulse a reminder of their passion flowing as powerful as the surrounding currents. Curling her fingers into his damp hair anchored her to his strength. The water warmed, and Aspen's lips parted in anticipation, igniting sparks of electricity in her soul.

The hard press of Lucky's toned chest against her yielding curves generated a jolt of desire that radiated outward, causing the whirlpool to swirl faster. He gripped her waist with a controlled desperation, both seeking to possess and to be possessed by each other.

Their lips met again, and time itself ceased, as though the River Goddess held her breath to witness their perfect union in her special domain. An intoxicating blend of fire and hunger. Sparkling drops of warm water sprayed up from the surface and waterfalled from the sky, overpowering the icy rain.

Lucky's lips traveled down her neck, and she thrust back her head to grant him full access to nip and kiss her skin. She slipped one hand between them and skimmed it over the sculpted planes of his slick chest. Her hand dipped lower until she met his hardness, returned to full arousal in the tepid water.

Again, he wouldn't let her tantalize him and removed her hand. "No. This is your time."

They kissed, their tongues tangoing. His hunger for her drove every thought from her mind, and a desperation built within her. In this haven of water and desire, the world outside disappeared. Their embrace, their kisses both tender and urgent, transcended the physical realm.

Lucky was the first to ease away, gasping for air. Aspen's head lolled on his shoulder as she regained her breath, her reality. The River Goddess's hand allowed them to consume each other in her territory. Aspen couldn't ask for a better sign that Lucky wasn't the bad guy everyone believed. A sign that Lucky was her perfect warlock, regardless of his status as a black warlock.

"Aspen... that was the most intense few moments of my life. We were in another world. I could swear by it. Just you and me."

"And the River Goddess." She kissed his chest and licked the earthy and slightly metallic river water off her lips. "She wanted us together, and she made it perfect."

"No." He kissed the top of her head. "*You* made it perfect."

"Don't have any illusions I can repeat that by myself.

It was me, but I had magical help."

He squeezed her tight. "I only want it to happen with you."

"Good." She playfully pinched his arm. "Now, let's get out of here before we freeze our butts off. Or some other body part I'd like to preserve." They walked out of the warm pool, on the path to reality.

"Preserve for later?"

"Later, tomorrow, the next day."

"I can deal." He kissed her head again, his lips lingering, moving to her temple and depositing another kiss. He weaved his fingers in hers to make their trek to the gazebo. "Guess I should've asked before. Are we safe from prying eyes?"

"No one will bother us. It's a given when a water witch needs to replenish and worship the River Goddess, the coven leaves her to commune alone." She squeezed his hand. "Unless it's a group ritual."

"Do warlocks accompany their witches during their commune times?"

Reluctant, she released his hand, and exited the creek, wringing out her drenched hair. A new exhilaration guided her quick steps to grab the towel and robe she'd tossed into the gazebo, dry from the rain buffeting them. She threw the towel to him and slipped into the robe to curtail her chattering teeth.

"Sometimes warlocks join in, especially if a love bond connects the witch and warlock and not merely a guardian bond. Or if the ritual demands a warlock guardian. Or they just guard from a distance. Depends on the ritual, relationship, and need."

Lucky tucked the towel around his waist and pulled on his T-shirt. His hair stood on end every which way. He looked so cute she almost tugged his towel off. "You said love bond. Do we have...?" He reddened. "Why did you involve me in your ritual?"

Aspen gasped. "Oh, no, we don't have a bond. My ritual was already done when… when we kissed."

"But the River Goddess—"

"The River Goddess likes to play with our emotions."

"So, none of that was real?" He clenched his jaw. "Not sure I enjoy being coerced." He slipped on his jeans beneath his towel, as if she hadn't already seen his goods.

"Wait, what?" Aspen seized his wrist. "You think you were being coerced?"

"Wasn't I?" He wrenched his arm out of her grasp. "I've been nothing but used and abused since I landed on your property. I don't know which end is up half the time."

"You didn't enjoy what just happened between us?" She spat out the words like icicles.

"If your goddess manipulated us, it wasn't real," he blasted, avoiding her question.

"Welcome to the world of witches and warlocks. Nothing is as it seems." She kicked a pinecone into the woods, where it bounced against a boulder. "Magic provided a backdrop. It was real."

"I don't know what's real, what's not." He slammed his soaked towel on the wheelchair. "Does everything involve magic?"

"You're right. I manipulated you into kissing me, touching me, screwing me last night." Aspen screeched and spun away from him. "Don't get hit by lightning," she muttered to herself.

"This place is a veritable garden of evil."

"Way to ruin the moment." Aspen stomped into the woods, leaving him to deal with the wheelchair. Man, she missed her motorcycle. She needed big and growly between her legs. Something that vibrated its strength and didn't give her constant grief. He wanted to learn about the witchworld, but then threw it in her face. No wonder they never connected in high school.

He followed at a safe distance, the wheels of the chair crunching on the gravel. Anger seared her throat, fueling her cautious steps as much as her rehydration did. She passed by the cabin they'd slept in last night and slapped at a large purple-blue hydrangea, jubilant in the rain. She wanted to raze the bushes to the ground. How dare he insinuate their kiss was fake? Did he fake it? She didn't need to manipulate men to want her. Plenty men and warlocks wanted her friendship, magic, and passion. But none came close to what Lucky made her feel inside. *Asshat.*

After not caring for the longest time if she ever had a warlock, she wanted him more than anything. But not if he planned to cop a 'tude. She railed in her head until the trail spat her out at the edge of the back lawn. He reacted similar to Rafael when he'd discovered he was a warlock— not even a black warlock, a more recent revelation—and he thought Sage had manipulated him. Heck, a Helwig witch *had* manipulated him. But he came to his senses when he couldn't walk away from Sage because his dick was in a twist for her. Would Lucky reach the same conclusions despite his longtime disgust or hatred toward the witchworld due to his mother's role in it? If he fell in love with her, would he overcome his biases?

"Love, shmove." Her fingers poised above her wrist, ready to go medieval on the twin vines. "Who said anything about love?" Ravenous, Aspen rushed through the kitchen's exterior door. She had no clue where Lucky and the wheelchair rolled off to. A frisson of joy added a bounce to her steps when nothing prevented her from entering the house. "Yay for small freaking favors."

She greeted the kitchen staff, set a pot to boil on the stove, snatched cold bacon strips off the sideboard and munched on them through the kitchen to the hallway.

Bacon was her favorite go-to low-carb protein boost, and she almost returned for another handful.

Sage called to her from her large office overlooking the front yard, the circular driveway, and the perimeter woods surrounding a lush green lawn and bushes sprouting spring green. The best view in the house befitting her sister's position. "Hey, sis. Rejuvenated?"

"For now." Aspen sank into a guest chair, her robe flapping open to reveal her bare legs. "Lucky's being a prick. He needs to talk to Rafael."

Sage stilled, gnawed on a chipped fingernail. "About?"

"Becoming a warlock. Witches. Learning how to live in the witchworld."

Sage grimaced. "Oh, that convo. Sorry."

"It is what it is." Aspen finished her last bacon strip and wiped her hands on her robe for lack of a napkin.

"Will it make an impact?"

"It better."

"Because you're falling for him."

"Something like that. But if he can't meet me halfway, we're done." She said the words without a care on the outside, but they tore a piece of her soul apart. "It's not like I ever wanted a black warlock or was desperate for any warlock."

"Where is he now?" Sage rose and pushed her chair in.

"Don't know. Don't care. Send his ass home."

Pensive, Sage combed hair off her face with an exaggerated motion. "We need to determine the source of your curses and how they connect you two."

"Did Marjorie tell you about the tattoo? It might bond me forever to the asswipe who cursed me." Could she bond Lucky or vice versa if they were both marked by another black warlock? Did she even want to bond a dominant black warlock if it was her only choice as Marjorie believed?

"Yes. All hands are on deck researching how to break

the curse. I've solicited help from a couple of other trusted external coven researchers. Ethan's father is going through his wife's old books and notes, too." She delivered a sympathetic smile on Aspen. "Chill or hit the sack. We've got it covered tonight. I swear I'll be nice to Lucky."

With Sage's sage advice, her day ended. Wistfulness toyed with her ire. She wanted to see Lucky again, but he needed time. Time from her. Time to sort out his head. Time to come to grips with his true identity and how he fit within the witchworld.

Chapter 24

Refreshed and hydrated, Aspen rejoined Sage in her office the next morning. Clouds blotted the sun, dimming the eastern-facing office. They ate breakfast alone, absorbed the reports from everyone on the research ladder. Nothing spectacular came to light. After two hours of mindless brainstorming, they took a break and chilled. Aspen boiled fresh lavender in the copper bowl, using little magic to stir the water, not wanting to deplete her reserves. Soon lavender infused the room and galvanized the million thoughts roiling in her head.

The door opened and slammed against the wall, hitting the dent in the drywall that'd met too many doorknobs. Rafael marched into the office, Lucky on his tail.

"I can't leave the covenstead," Lucky announced, his fists curled at his side, one clinging to the frayed spot on his hem.

The sight of him, haggard, but showered, and wearing clean clothes, hit Aspen's buttons of desire. She needed the night without him, but she'd missed him, his enticing body, their connection filling her hollows.

"Rafael, let him go home," Sage capitulated. "We know where he lives. I'll put a tracking spell on him."

"No. That's not the problem." Rafael approached and took Sage's hand in his. Aspen ducked her head to avoid the moment of true love she'd wished to experience just once in her lifetime. "He can't physically leave. He's hitting the same wall Aspen hit."

"Oh, mother of the goddess." Sage groaned. "So much for this impending storm granting leniencies in this freak-ass garden of mysteries."

"Tell me about it." Lucky stood behind Aspen, not too close, but not far enough away that she couldn't feel the heat of his body. A body she wanted tangled around hers. *Damn him to the River Goddess!*

The day took another spin on the wheel of life or death as Brianne and Marina barreled into the room, excitement crawling over their wide eyes.

"I found something. In the basement," Marina said in a rush.

"Why were you in the basement?" Sage slapped her palm on her desk. "The air is toxic."

"Fans and purifiers are at full bore." Marina dangled a medical mask. "Post-mortem reconnaissance, sensing lingering earth magic. Trying to determine if anything's connected to or attacking the ley lines." Marina was the strongest earth witch in the history of the Wilde coven. The lines strengthened their natural security, and no other witch had ever been able to work the lines like Marina. As long as no one breached their wards by black curses, that is. Small green leaves drifted off her hands. "Whoops. Bet you've seen all the leaves you want inside the house to last a lifetime." Marina shuffled the leaves under a side table. Her cousin was the only earth witch Aspen knew who dripped plant life whenever her emotions tripped off the rails. Too much earth magic inside her to contain.

Lucky ogled her as if the leaves sprouted from her head. A pregnant pause quieted the room until he said in a huff, "Spill it, will ya."

"Yes, master." Marina bowed to him, flipping him the bird at the same time.

He held up a hand. "Look, I want off this mad merry-go-round. Is that too much to ask?"

"Maybe you should leave the room," Aspen spat out, not bothering to hide her renewed frustration.

"Knock it off. Lucky has a right to know." Sage stepped in front of Marina, swishing away a few leaves drifting in the air. "Good news I hope."

"Depends on your idea of good and bad," Brianne dropped her snarky crumb into the conversation.

Marina swiped on her phone, showed the screen to Sage. Aspen crowded in to see. "A healthy, green vine. Alive and well. It's growing by the minute."

A vine encased in heart-shaped, three-lobed, pointy leaves snaked along the charred wall between the two rooms where they'd housed Pierre and Lucky. Aspen shifted Marina's hand for Lucky to see the video.

"How?" Lucky raked his hand through his damp hair, the clean rain scent of his shampoo drifting to Aspen, softening her toward him again.

"Obviously, not everything died in the basement." Marina stuck her phone in her pocket. "It's new, tender, and bright green. Came through the baseboards. Sage, can you invoke a tracking spell? Without energy from other plants interfering with the one vine, it'll work this time."

"You can do that?" Lucky gripped the top of his head. "Why didn't you do it before?"

"We tried. Got too crowded too fast. We lost track of the source vine." Aspen forced a calm to her voice to answer his questions. He created far too much whipsawing in her head.

"But there were streams of mud where they stemmed from."

"Sure, Lucky. You're the master spell-caster. You tell us how to put a tracking spell on a shit-ton of vines that sprang from nowhere." Aspen understood his need for answers, but he was acting like a petulant child, at least in her book. She thought he was catching on to the world of witches, but his enlightenment needed enlightenment, and fast. At the moment, dealing with his lack of trust took too many brain cells she needed for other matters. *Again with the whipsaw. What is wrong with me?*

"What's gotten into you two lovebirds?" Brianne asked.

"Shut it," Aspen and Lucky said in sync. She almost high-fived him but stuffed her hands in her pants pockets.

"Enough!" Sage bellowed. "I'm going to the basement. Witches only."

"Like hell," Rafael said. "Your magic's not at peak power after yesterday."

"You heard me. I have plenty of magic to wield. Besides, I'm calling for a full thirteen." Sage strode to the door, her thumb sliding rapid fire on her phone: "Talk to Lucky. He needs mentoring, training."

"He needs a warlock brain," Aspen muttered under her breath.

"Sage. That's every witch on the compound," Rafael called before she exited. "You know this means the earth magic didn't stem from Pierre. The goon's dead."

"Correct." Her gaze landed on Lucky, slid up and down his length, then met Rafael's incredulous gaze. "Didn't stem from Lucky either."

"Bullshit." Rafael tramped over to her.

"Trust me. Lucky's a conduit, nothing more. Like Aspen. Like Pierre." She hit the hallway. Aspen and her cousins trailed behind her.

Rafael's and Lucky's solid footsteps followed, soon

joined by other nearby witches and warlocks.

A box of leftover medical masks sat on the credenza near the door to the stairway. The heat of the fire had decimated the lock on the door. No security necessary. Aspen handed out the masks.

Brianne took one. "COVID, anyone?"

Sage opened the door, the whirl of fans blowing below them. "Rafael, guard the doors, okay?"

Eden scurried down the hallway. "You rang?"

"Doing a tracking spell to expose this black curse once and for all," Aspen said.

"Wait a minute." Rafael exploded again. "If you're here, who's on Andre's guard detail?"

"Ethan and Evan. Willow's joining us. She's rounding up the outside witches."

"Did you get anything out of his head?" Aspen asked.

"Not much. His mind's a jumble most times. It's like he knows I'm reading him but can't figure me out. I get a glean or two, then bam, he shuts the gate. Maybe Ethan will have better luck." The only other psychic witch or warlock they knew. Sage was hoping Ethan and Eden would fall in love and ride off into the sunset toward the Ravenwood estate up the road. Eden had been alone too long after getting the shaft from her ex-husband, and she needed a warlock.

Willow and the other witches joined them in the hallway. It was rare they invoked the full thirteen for a spell. It represented a boatload of magic, and they didn't want everyone to deplete their magic and leave them vulnerable. Marjorie stayed behind with Leah in the infirmary. They needed an intact healer, if things tipped sideways.

Intact steel walls appeared behind the scorched drywall in spots, and soot blemished the ceiling. They'd swept up most of the plant debris, allowing access to the slightly blackened pentagram in a circle. Aspen set the pillar candles, signifying north, east, south, and west, corresponding to air, water, earth, and fire on the designated compass points. Brianne and Marina sprinkled salt to disburse negativity in the room and to consecrate the circle.

The twelve witches joined hands around the pentacle, each holding a pouch of pre-prepared herbs. The basement already smelled of scorched everything green under the sun, but the prepared herbal mixture would cleanse and soothe the senses and drive out the negativity and evil in the room. And grant the ability to see beyond the seen.

"Ready?" Sage stood in the center, holding another candle representing aether, her natural element fusing all the other elements. The twelve other witches nodded, and she began her spell-casting.

> With magic's unseen thread,
> Reveal the source where mysteries spread.
> By strong currents of earth and space,
> Guide me true to the magic's birthplace.
> Track the path where it originated,
> Follow the clues, subtle and designated.
> Let the currents of magic's birth,
> Guide me now, across the earth.
> So shall it be, this spell's decree,
> As I will, so mote it be.

As soon as Sage lit her candle, the witches sprinkled the herbs to grant enlightenment into bowls of boiling water in the pentacle. Infused steam billowed up to Sage's face and she breathed in and out several times.

"Say it with me now," she said.

"Guide me now, across the earth, so shall it be, this spell's decree. As I will, so mote it be." The witches all said the lines in unison. Eden lit the candles from north to west, the flames flickering high.

Sage blew out her candle and shut her eyes. She tipped her head back to open her senses and her mind to the goddess's guidance. Her eyeballs moved beneath her eyelids. The candle fell from her hand and rolled against a bowl of bubbling herbs.

Sparks erupted off Sage. Aspen and Brianne sprinkled water before they ignited another inferno. Wind howled, blowing their hair every which way. Gwyneira, Sage's owl familiar, materialized from beneath the neckline of her sweater and vaulted into the air, opaque threads in its beak. It plunked one thread onto the vine quivering against the baseboard, growing from under the woodwork.

Other than the howling wind, the room remained silent, the witches waiting for the images to filter into Sage's mind. Squeezing her eyes shut, Aspen concentrated. She'd never excelled at tracking spells. Sage was the best, so they left most tracking spells to her. Aspen recited the spell Sage used, memorized long ago for the right moment.

"So mote it be," she murmured, filling her senses with the infused steam. A jolt jerked through her, knocking her against Brianne. Her cousin tightened her fingers and squeezed hard. Rio squawked and landed on her shoulder, then joined Gwyneira in trailing braided threads of magic above their heads. Aspen let her mind's eye prevail.

The vine along the baseboard crept behind the woodwork. It slipped into the walls and danced between the floors like it owned the place. Morning glory flowers sprouted in the darkest reaches where the sun never shone. The flowers invited Aspen to touch each one, to give them attention. They exalted her, beguiling her along their path.

Rio's magic stirred the air, cleansed the negativity from encroaching on Aspen's mind. The braided threads unraveled one at a time. When they'd separated and drifted apart, the far end of the vine, its origins, revealed itself in

Aspen's mind.

Aspen yelped and snapped open her eyes to meet Sage's wide eyes, teeming with the same terror. Dropping the hands holding hers, Aspen sank to her knees, soft keening sobs drowning the voices rising in the room. Sage and Willow rushed to her, embracing and massaging her back. The tattoo tingled on her skin, and she shrugged the hands off her, wanting to crawl out of her own skin, like a snake making way for its rebirth.

"What did you see?" Willow asked.

"Aspen?" Sage said. "What did *you* see?"

"It's been him all along." Nausea bloomed hard and fast, and she did everything she could to temper it.

"Who? *Who?*" Brianne demanded. "I'll kill the motherfucker."

"You saw the vine in the atrium?" Sage asked. Eyes glazing over, Aspen nodded.

"Andre. It's Andre Charlemagne," Jessica uttered in disbelief.

Cries and gasps permeated the witch circle. The warlocks waiting upstairs streamed down into the basement.

"How can that be?" Willow towered over Aspen, smoothing her flyaway hair. "His room and the atrium are magic dead zones. He's triple-warded."

"And two to three witches guard him twenty-four seven. There's been no change in the wards, not even a blip." Rafael joined Sage, touched her wrist before dipping his hand to Aspen to help her stand. He hugged her, his fatherly hug. Aspen wished her own father was present to chase away the boogeyman and hold her in his protective arms.

Lucky stood helpless at the bottom of the stairs. As usual, his fists furled and unfurled. She should want him gone, but darn if she'd rather his arms held her than

Rafael's or even her father's. Rafael soothed the itch of the tattoo on her back. A tattoo born from the vilest black warlock on the planet. Maybe even the evilest man on earth. A permanent stain bonding her to him forever.

A long roll of thunder rumbled to the west, and an ominous crack of lightning followed. A twisted portent of doom.

Chapter 25

The coven council and their bonded warlocks met in the forest meeting room. Situated at the back of the first floor, the warded room was used for meeting outside witches. Connected to a strong ley line, the wards were so discreet, most witches couldn't discern them until they tried to raise magic. Downside, it also prevented the Wildes from using magic.

The council included Aspen, her sisters, aunt, cousins, and Rafael as First Warlock. Rafael made Lucky wait in the great room where lunch awaited him. Matthew and two witches ate with him, on guard duty, while Ricky guarded Marjorie and Leah in the infirmary. Leah still hadn't awakened, and he was spitting mad. Although Ethan wanted to join the meeting, Sage believed it best he remained with the witches guarding Andre. Everyone teetered on the edge and waited for instructions.

Another rolling rumble of thunder shook the house. Lightning reflected off the windows, slashes of light resembling light sabers, laying glowing stripes across the floor.

"Lucky wants to meet Andre," Aspen said. "Do you think he'd sneak off to the east wing?"

"Ethan has orders to incapacitate him if he so much as raises a finger," Rafael replied.

Sage held up a hand, then gnawed on a chipped fingernail. A sign of her agitation. "We need to decide what to do about Andre *if* he is the source of the black curse."

"If?" Aspen knocked her knuckles on the glass table. "It all makes sense. I've felt it from the jump but couldn't wrap my head around it. He cloaked his magic, and the cloak changes to divert us. The black curse I read in Mom's notes proved all he needed to create the curse was a blood bond, forged by proximity to a blood relative, aka Pierre."

"But he's warded? How did he manage it?"

"I'm gonna find out. Time for talking, researching, and speculation are over." Rio cooed at her in agreement. She ruffled his feathers, and his wings rose and dipped on her arm until the gull disappeared under her sleeve.

Aspen tuned out the witches and warlocks tailgating her down the hall to the east wing, which housed Andre and no one else. No one attempted to stop her.

"Wait by the outer door to his suite. We need to put you in a protective shield." Sage came abreast of Aspen. "How's your hydration?"

"I'm fine. Magic will stink, but I'm standing and moving." The ward on the steel door pressed against her aura, and the physical locks deterred her. "I want to see the vine in the atrium first, then we'll confront him."

"Agreed. I want to see it too, ensure what we visualized is real," Sage said.

Their three cousins entwined their magic to shield Aspen in a protective cocoon which also prevented her from using magic, as well as any other witch or warlock against her.

Rafael engaged the locks on the door, each snick and

thunk forming icicles on Aspen's spine. What answers promised to start another never-ending horror show? Would they reconcile her jagged emotions regarding Lucky and her feelings for him? Andre had a lot of explaining to do.

The group approached the two witch guards and Ethan sitting in the anteroom to Andre's suite. The chairs faced the atrium, a beautiful tranquil oasis they'd sacrificed for Andre's personal "outdoor" space. After all, they weren't ogres, even if they were jailors. Eden sat next to Ethan, across from Andre's door with a view through the bulletproof sidelight window into his domain. Andre wasn't the sole fascination for Eden's attention by her sly glimpses at Ethan.

Sage recited a spell to kill the wards on the atrium. While most atriums were a centralized focus place, joining parts of a building together, their father had built their atrium as an escape from the hustle and bustle of everyday life in the Wilde coven.

The atrium spanned two levels, inviting the surrounding natural light to dance upon its surfaces. The storm diminished the natural light, and someone flipped on the hidden lights that mimicked daylight. Aspen entered the indoor garden, gazing upon the beauty she'd missed these last few months. Lack of access to the space would hurt their coven if Andre remained on the covenstead during the colder months of the year. The tempered, bulletproof glass walls seamlessly brought the outdoors inside, which helped earth witches in the winter. Lush greenery in various hues of greens and burgundy arranged in planters, graced the corners, softened the edges and accented the sleek marble floors. Aspen had moved her herb garden out to keep Andre's paws off her most precious recipe ingredients.

A small, tranquil pool rippled and babbled, a soothing

ambiance mingling with the distant hum of activity from the building beyond. The water's reflection captured the play of light from the surrounding glass, casting shimmering patterns on the walls. Aspen would rather melt into the pool than tramp through a planter.

"I hated turning this space into Andre's playground," she said.

"Me too." Sage took Aspen's hand and motioned for the others to give her space. The pair moved to a slant of sparkling light near the wall separating the space from Andre's suite.

On silent command, they slid a rattan loveseat away from a two-foot-high planter wall. Lush plants crammed the planter, watered by an automatic drip system.

Creepy crawlies skittered across her back, outlining her endless tattoo. "I'm afraid to touch it."

"I'll do it."

"No. I need to know what it'll do to me through my protective ward." Aspen gnawed on her bottom lip, stilled to stop her heart from racing. She stepped onto the travertine planter top and into the mulch. "Do you think I'll be okay?"

"I'll raze the atrium to the ground before I let it hurt you."

"With Andre too?" She almost laughed at her willingness to kill, when she wouldn't have hurt an ant days ago.

"Yes. He's not long for our world, anyway."

Aspen's legs gelled. "What do you mean?"

"It's clear we can't keep him here much longer."

"Doesn't mean you plan to kill him. You still want to dig info out of his head, right?"

"I don't know what I mean." She squeezed Aspen's hand. "The vine's wrapped around the bottom of the ficus behind the fern, and it's rooted—"

Aspen cut off her sister. "The root's buried in the English ivy. It's vivid in my mind."

Rio remained silent and static on her upper arm. Her familiar had no ability to rise to life inside the protective ward, but Aspen muttered sweet nothings to him and Rico, anyway. More to calm herself and to normalize this strange task.

The drip system sputtered on in the planters across the room, and she mis-stepped, knocking over a foot-tall fairy statute. It plopped facedown in the planter, and Aspen fought the urge to pick it up, desperate to do a normal task.

Instead, she ignored it and waded through the ferns, spied the vine curling up the ficus trunk. She shifted fern fronds aside and tracked the vine into the English ivy, where it had hidden these last few days or even longer. "Found it." Without touching the vine, she tracked it to where another tentacle grew into the ground along the perimeter of the wall and disappeared, most likely to the basement beneath them. Aspen photographed all angles of the vine. She stood to her full height, contemplating her next action.

"What are you thinking?" Concern crackled Sage's voice, her words snapping in the air like the dried leaves. "We have our proof. Let's confront Andre."

"Not enough. I need to know what the vine will do." Before Sage could stop her, she found the root ball and pulled the vine free from the soil. The roots dangled, twisted, and threaded around each other. The vine around the ficus unwound by itself and approached her feet. It seemed to hiss at her, an almost silent sound. The roots latched on to her hand and wrist, and began extracting her witch-water, drip by drop. A slow, surprising attack since she was in the protective ward. The plant didn't have access to all her witch-water. Which meant, she needed to remain in a protective bubble until she rid herself of the clinger. The tattoo on her back roiled in all different directions. A tentacle of the vine tattoo slipped down her arm and joined the roots clinging to her. The drops of blood the vine had stolen from her days ago created a kinship between Aspen and the vine roots. Her blood tied her to Andre's magic.

"I'm ready now." She fought the urge to pass out, the dizzying sensation causing an unsteadiness. "Help me out of here."

"Why, Aspen?" Sage asked as Aspen stumbled out of the planter and fell against her sister.

"This is the mother root. Maybe it'll kill the vine on my back."

"Or kill you and Lucky."

"No. It's not meant to kill us."

"Well, hold on to that sentiment. You're gonna need it." Sage stared at the real vine intertwined with the tattoo vine. "The magic is potent if it can bypass a protection spell."

Aspen gave a gentle tug on the section of vine that'd breached the basement, an offshoot of the mother vine on her hand. It detached from the soil and the walls with ease. She brushed off the residual dirt and walked toward the door, the vine trailing behind Aspen like a slim, squiggly shadow. "'Cause it's a black curse. Not all white magic works on a black curse." The roots holding on to her prickled. They didn't hurt, and she prayed it remained so.

No one else said a word. No one came near Aspen, and she walked alone carrying her dark, twisted magic to the atrium door.

Thunder vibrated the house. Lightning splintered and scattered across the sky over the covenstead, lighting the darkening daylight. The air buzzed with an invisible current, and the ground pulled lightning toward earth, shimmering electricity above the ground. Power winked out, and the room dimmed.

"What the hell?" Rafael scanned the grounds beyond the atrium walls. The world outside dimmed under the veil of charcoal clouds.

Electricity sparkled and lit up Aspen and Lucky. Everyone backed away from them.

A handful of leaves blew off Marina's fingers. "The lightning's affecting the ley lines." A text dinged Marina's phone. "Our perimeter security's dead."

Sage wrapped her arms around herself. "Lightning doesn't interfere with our magic."

"Lightning can interfere with ley lines. Rare, but it happens. It's more, though," Marina said. "Magic drew the lightning upon us."

The electricity around Aspen and Lucky dissipated, but not the suspicions.

Again? Next-level crazy. "I didn't draw lightning from the sky. I wield water magic, nothing more, people. Carry on." Her visit to the creek seemed like days ago. She scratched her arms until flakes of skin sifted off her.

"Not me either." Lucky waggled his arms to rid them of the electricity dripping off him.

Silence hung in the air until Rafael's phone chimed, followed swiftly by Sage's phone ringing.

"All protective wards are dead on the entire grounds." Rafael read from his phone. He looked to Sage as she finished her call, her skin ghostly white, and she nodded.

A commotion rose in the anteroom outside the atrium doors. Shouts and scuffles ensued. Magic sizzled in the air, as if the lightning had carved holes through the house walls.

Chapter 26

Two witches lay knocked out cold on the floor in the waiting room. The door to Andre's room swung wide open. No one needed to tell Aspen he'd escaped. Every instinct in her warned her to give chase, but every cell in her healer's body begged her to help the witches. Rafael ran into Andre's room to search, and Aspen rushed to the two witches.

"He's bound their magic," Aspen said to Sage. "I think they're okay, though."

Willow and Brianne raced into the room. "Andre's taken Eden hostage," Willow said in a rush. "Evan and Ethan are chasing after him. Oh... he has full use of his magic."

Questions bombarded the room, and Rafael blocked the doorway, pushing them back into the anteroom to form a plan.

"Hold tight. I'm getting answers from security." Rafael scanned his texts and the electronic security system. "The lightning or magic knocked out electricity, batteries, satellites, even our wards."

Aspen sucked in her stomach. "We still have his familiars, right?"

"Yes. They're bound in their warded container," Sage replied. "Unless…"

Brianne shot from the room to check on the triple-warded containers holding his panther familiars.

"He's not at full power if he doesn't possess his familiars." A smidgen of relief trailed the frost zigzagging Aspen's backside.

"The magic came from him," Lucky mused aloud, sidling closer to Aspen. She wanted him close. Needed him close. Needed to know he was as much a victim as the rest of them and not the instigator of their epic disaster.

Sage headed toward the door, her long-legged strides devouring the distance. Aspen followed, and the room cleared. Witches and warlocks crowded in the great room. Jessica and Ben lit candles and old-fashioned oil lanterns to chase the shadows from the dim corners.

Panting, Brianne jogged into the room. "His familiars are secure. Marina's guarding the gate, and security spied Andre on the creek path."

A long roll of thunder deafened, shaking the house. Lightning lit up the room from every window, a widespread arc of electricity encompassing the entire covenstead.

The jolt hit Aspen, and she shuddered, knocking against Lucky, another conduit of electricity. Her hair floated off her shoulders, and she jumped away from him before the electricity fried her magic, if that was next on evil's agenda. The vines on her wrist and the roots wrapped around her hand lashed her skin, stinging and poking her, trying to root themselves in her muscles and bones.

"Back off," she hissed at Lucky. Everything in her core warned her about him, warned her that hooking up with him for the long term may be more problematic than his status as a black warlock. Why? Where did he fit in this mess? How had her intuition led her astray from her moments of desire and connection to him? A connection they still shared, tethered to her core of magic. "Gah," she railed, as her mind swung from one extreme to another.

Eyes softening, he held up his hands in capitulation and stepped away, the crowd opening a path for him. Electricity glowed off him, and he illuminated the room more than the candles and lanterns did.

Sage clapped her hands to gain attention. "Is there anyone who doesn't have full access to their magic?"

No one suffered from loss of magic, except Aspen's draining witch-water.

As if the storm syphoned her dry, she listed to the right and her knees buckled, depositing her on the floor. Lucky lunged for her, but a trio of warlocks barred him. Rafael picked her up and plopped her on the couch. She attempted to swirl water in a glass sitting on the end table, the simplest magic task for a water witch. Drier than a desert in a drought.

"No magic. The electricity has dried me out." She took a few sips of the water Willow handed her as she slumped against the couch.

"It's his attempt to draw her to the creek," Lucky chimed in.

Mystical hackles rose on Aspen's neck. "I need to hydrate."

"Is that true?" Sage stroked Aspen's hair. "Do you feel a pull to the creek?"

"I only feel aridness."

Lucky moved closer, and no one stopped him. The electricity he emitted tempered and didn't react again to Aspen. He held no allegiance to Andre, and Aspen knew it in her gut. Knew he had no intent to harm her. "I feel a pull. The magic plaguing us stems from the creek," he said.

"From Andre? That's insane." Aspen smoothed her

hand over the roots around her wrist, and they softened at her touch.

"A foreign magic has linked to Lucky's aura. It's causing the electricity between you two." Sage closed her eyes to feel her innate magic.

"Andre?" Lucky's Adam's apple bobbed in his throat.

"His magic's been useless, warded." Sage's wide-eyed gaze pleaded with Rafael. "No glitches, no magic detection on him all this time, right? It's impossible."

"We've detected no magic from Andre since we recaptured him during the Helwig siege," Rafael confirmed.

Lucky strayed to the door. Everyone widened their berth around him. Again. "I need to meet the man who destroyed my mother."

Aspen now knew for certainty that Lucky had an ulterior motive for gaining access to the covenstead. She'd guessed it before when he'd exposed his mother's connection to Andre but she'd buried the probability, unable to confront it head-on. Was everything between them a lie? Was she a means to an end? Had he manipulated her like he accused her of using the River Goddess to manipulate him?

Rafael grabbed at Lucky, but Aspen's words stopped him from making contact. "We need to rescue Eden. Lucky may be our bargaining chip. Andre wanted him here, clear as day." Her words punched her heart one by one.

It's what Lucky wanted, but it might be his death sentence. It might be a bigger death sentence to more witches and warlocks if they didn't contain Andre. How did they ever think they'd manage this vile being for long? Sage was right. They'd tried to bind his magic, but their spells didn't last long and it was a continuous cycle. Now this!

"We need a plan. We can't charge in and expect to all live," Sage said. "Lucky. Stop right there." Even though she didn't rule Lucky, her magic-infused tone froze him in his tracks.

Thunder growled, and a slice of lightning outlined Lucky and Aspen. The strike didn't hurt but twisted her arid core. Rain slashed the windows, buffeted by the increasing wind. A full-blown spring storm. What more could they ask for?

"We'll have a small team of warded witches and warlocks confront him. Then a team follows at a discreet and safe distance to charge in if needed."

Everyone accepted Rafael's suggestion, even though it was more an order. They gathered under the canopy on the back patio, Aspen sandwiched between Willow and Brianne. She refused to remain on the sidelines despite Sage's demands. Plus, the same magic luring Lucky also had a hook in her magic. The roots clung to her hand, refusing to let go. Knowing she'd given them what they wanted, they didn't hurt her, and she let them be. The witches wrapped everyone in protective bubbles. Sage invoked an additional cloaking spell on the entire group.

Aspen possessed enough energy to walk on her own two feet. This showdown was as much about her as Lucky, and she had no plans to sit it out. Lucky strode close to Aspen, cautious and concerned. The magic ensnaring him also tweaked at a little something in her core. If Lucky had his way, he'd already be at the creek. How would this day end? Who would live or die?

Despite the storm, the air remained balmy, the cloud coverage keeping the daytime temperatures low to the ground. The rain had ceased, but the wind continued to blow and howl, whipping the tree branches in an eerie staccato dance. Aspen snatched a lantern to guide their way. Solar landscape lights kept a charge, defining their path until they hit the woods where all the solar lights had winked out. Andre's passing caused their demise.

Although the rain had taken a breather, the thunder-and-lightning show continued for another moment until the world stilled. The wind quit blowing, and a gentle breeze swayed the tree boughs. The eye of the storm about to erupt. Distracting her free hand from touching the roots, Aspen patted down her flyaway hair. She rolled her lip balm across her lips to keep the dryness at bay.

Andre stood on the bank of the river by the smaller gazebo, waiting and taunting his audience. He knew the rest of them would come. He'd bound Eden in a ring of fire, her magic useless against Andre.

Ethan left Evan guarding Andre and joined them from behind a grove of trees. "Let me approach him first. We can hold our own against him."

"No. My aether is powerful enough," Sage insisted. "He can't kill me. He won't kill Eden until he gets what he wants. I won't let it get that far."

"Are we sure it isn't Eden?" Brianne asked. "This is the second time he's abducted her."

"He's fixated on her, that's for sure," Rafael said.

"Because of her psychic mind. It's easy to subdue her. Plus, wrong time and wrong place both times." Ethan fisted his hands on his thighs. "I'll kill him if he hurts her."

"We all will." Brianne lobbed the words at him.

"Do you still trust me?" Lucky asked Aspen.

"I don't know. Do you trust you aren't being manipulated?" As Aspen heard her words, she realized how stupid she sounded. Andre was the puppet master, and she needed to concentrate on him. She waved a hand in front of her face. "Sorry. Never mind. Do what you need to do. You have your own demons to vanquish." He didn't need her permission or her trust.

Lucky bolted from the group, breaking the protective ward Sage erected over him by his increasing distance. Ethan jetted after Lucky. The group remained silent and slow going to avoid tipping off Andre to their exact location. By the time they reached the last bend before the creek, voices drifted to them. They hid and listened.

Aspen was never so grateful to see Ethan and Evan. The Ravenwood brothers and Rafael, beautiful, powerful, loyal, and loving. Was it so bad to bond a black warlock? Her mind bounced from one extreme to another, and she buried her thoughts in a shallow grave to excavate when life returned to normal and her head stopped swinging from one extreme to another.

"Ethan, my good man," Andre purred. "You've brought my prize, Lucky Lorenzo, or should I say Luciano Ravenwood, to me. You are a stalwart lieutenant after all."

"Cut the crap, Andre," Ethan gritted out. He and Lucky stood twenty yards from Andre. "What's your ask this time?"

Andre turned at the waist toward Eden, his feet not moving. The fire ring illuminated gold, copper, and red highlights in her brunette hair, until the fire dazzled in a dozen shades of blue. The blue flames didn't touch her, and burned outward from the surrounding oval, but she'd feel the heat.

"Poor Eden Wilde, always in the crosshairs." Beneath his painted veil of sorrow, Andre's eyes held a glacial indifference as he shifted his attention back to Lucky.

Eden remained silent, lines creasing her forehead, straining as she concentrated on reading Andre's mind. Having escaped his prison, Andre was in a state of high excitement, giving her a perfect opportunity to slip through the crevices in his mind. Magic—or lack thereof—never interfered with her telepathy. The scent of brimstone, a skunky, sulfur smell, wafted on the air as Andre beefed up his fire around Eden.

"Lucky, my boy." When Andre looked at Lucky, his eyes were fixated, as if savoring every inch of his presence.

"I'm not your boy." Tension coiled in Lucky's arms dangling at his sides. "How are we connected? How did you draw me here?"

Andre laughed. "You don't know, eh? I thought by now, you'd have figured it out."

"Know what? That you raped my mother. That she couldn't escape you fast enough. Yep, know all that."

"Ah, yes, poor bewildered Kenley. One day she wanted me, the next she didn't. Back and forth, *ad nauseum*."

"You raped, poisoned, manipulated, held her captive, coerced her, you asshole," Lucky shouted, advancing a step. "I should kill you for what you did to her."

Andre folded his arms over his chest, his mouth a grim line. Listening, absorbing. Mesmerized, Aspen held her breath until forced to suck in air. A major mistake that surrendered their position, not that she didn't believe Andre already knew they'd gathered nearby.

"Sage, Rafael, come join my party," the Black Tide leader cajoled as if inviting them to afternoon tea. "You're warded. I can't hurt you."

Sage motion for them all to reveal themselves. Willow and Brianne sandwiched Aspen between them, and they stood behind Ethan and Lucky.

"Ah, the lovely Aspen Wilde." Andre beamed. "Lucky, your name doesn't do you justice. You are most fortunate to have the beautiful witch as your soulmate, your bound witch. I knew the moment I laid eyes on her. I just needed to find you." He clapped his hands, a dull whack that sounded like smacking a dead fish. "My plans may take odd turns, but in the end, I tie up all my loose ends."

"Leave her out of this." Lucky bared his teeth in a snarl. "What do you want from me?"

Andre crossed his arms over his scrawny chest, and Aspen stiffened, on guard. "I want my family with me. What's so difficult to understand?"

A lightbulb flickered brighter in Aspen's head. The blood bond between Pierre and Andre creating havoc and surviving Pierre's death. More than Pierre's blood extended Andre's magic and created holes in his wards. More than Pierre's blood survived his death and created the connection to Andre. It wasn't the drop of blood the vine stole from her.

It boiled down to Lucky.

"Speak," Lucky said. "Why am I one of your special warlocks?"

"I loved your mother. Therefore, you're special to me."

A muscle jumped in Lucky's back. "You kept her from her family. Made them abandon her to fend for herself."

"Not true, dear boy."

"I'm not your 'dear boy,' asshole."

"Are you so sure?" Smarmy smile. "How do you think I marked you? We share blood, Lucky. We have a true blood bond which defies magic."

"Doesn't mean jack." Lucky's voice was a low rumble, like thunder on the horizon, as if he already knew Andre was his bio daddy.

Aspen gasped. *He did know!* That was the reason he wanted on the covenstead, the reason he capitulated to her in so many ways. The ultimate reason she must boot him to the curb. He was too dangerous, his blood too treacherous. No way would she tie herself to any blood relative of Andre. Not even if Andre was dead. Grief wrapped her in a bitter cloak, talons digging into her chest. *This debacle keeps getting better and better.*

"I am your father," Andre said.

"Bull," Lucky blasted.

"How do you think I used the lightning to break through the holes in the ley lines to decimate the wards on this property?" Andre spread his arms to encompass the covenstead. "I need a bond to a blood relative. I am your father, believe it or not."

"Well, I'm sure as hell not Luke Skywalker. Just because your DNA runs in my blood doesn't mean you're my father. You can't claim rights to a child of rape."

"Misguided at times, Leigh came to me willingly. I didn't know she was pregnant until later. I've been hunting you for twenty-five years and you've lived under my nose for at least a decade." Andre clapped. "Well done. Well done. You must teach me your magic."

"She came to you under coercion spells," Ethan said. "My father knows the truth. He was there."

"And then you had her killed," Lucky added.

"You think so? Why would I kill a woman I loved, especially one of the few witches born to a black warlock bloodline? I didn't know her location. She hid herself and you well. Kudos." Andre pinned a triumphant look on Sage. "Accidents happen, don't they, Sage? Maybe they happen for good reasons. Do you agree? You wouldn't be in the position you're in without the result of an accident."

Sage's mouth hung ajar. "What are you saying?"

"Did you kill our parents?" Fury vibrated through Aspen, and she prepared to charge him. Willow and Brianne held her from going apeshit medieval on him.

Andre grinned, that smarmy grin Aspen wanted to smack off his face with a ten-inch knife. "Your precious mother dabbled in dark magic. She got too close and had to be stopped, or the Warlocks and Witches War happened for naught."

Willow and Aspen hugged, holding each other up. The truth after all these years hurt, like her parents' death all over again. But she refused to allow Andre to see the nerves he'd struck. "Stand tall. Don't show your emotions," she whispered to Willow. And they did. For now.

"You're aware I'll kill you for their deaths, right?" Sage strained in Rafael's arms as he held her from attacking

Andre.

They'd known all along magic might have caused their parents' car accident. But the man who'd driven the other vehicle, also drove off the Tahoe Mountain cliff and died. He wasn't a warlock. But they hadn't verified if he was a cloaked black warlock since black warlocks hadn't exposed themselves to the witchworld yet. *Shit on a murder stick.*

A syrupy silence fell over the group as the magnitude of Andre's insinuation sank deep. Lucky's eyes filled with a silent comprehension. Aspen nodded and lifted her chin to grant him the floor again.

"Why did you want me here?" Lucky picked at a ragged spot on the hem of his shirt, and Aspen felt his turmoil seethe inside her from the action. "Why are you messing with Aspen? Is the bond and the mark permanent?"

"Ah, beautiful Aspen. The woman meant for you took my mark as did you, making you equal. She's the one who drew you into the open." Andre shuffled his feet in the gravel.

"Is the mark permanent?" Aspen needed to hear his answer.

"Until you die, you are bound to the Charlemagnes." A smile curled up the corners of his lips, and he linked his hands at his waist. Did he not understand he'd never live to see tomorrow? Or maybe he did, and he didn't give a hoot.

A fresh wave of nausea engulfed Aspen. How could she have a life or bear children with a man who shared the blood of the devil himself? The sordid truth stilled the tangle in her mind. Again, parking her thoughts in a shallow grave, she signaled Eden, pointed to her own head, giving Eden the sign to read her thoughts. Eden blinked three times.

"Anything else you want to know?" Andre asked.

"What do you want from me?" Lucky repeated.

"To be your father."

"Fat fucking chance in hell."

"You'll come around. After all, you'll be the master of the Black Tide. It's your birthright. A Ravenwood and Charlemagne. And now a Ravenwood-Charlemagne-Wilde mix. The ultimate magical machine to rule the warlock world." His lecherous-old-man gaze dipped to Aspen's belly. "Who knows? Maybe the next generation is already blooming."

Sage stepped forward, her anger so tangible, she quivered. "Release Aspen from your spell."

"Charlemagne blood will always bond her to us. But I'll call a truce. Give me Lucky, and we'll leave now and never bother the Wildes and Ravenwoods again."

"Puh-lease." Aspen's snark tripped off the rails. "You just said you wanted a triad. Now you don't. Now you'll leave the Wildes alone. Your words don't mean spit to a dying plant. You are the architect of your own disaster. Live with it."

As if on cue, the dark clouds parted above them, spotlighting a giant moon glimmering off the creek in dappling white rays. Mother Nature kicked up the wind, favoring the witches' magic. Aspen signaled to Sage, and her sister cloaked her in air. She snuck behind the small gathering and skirted the gazebo, the glowing moon guiding her way on the forest floor. She recited a spell to the Moon Goddess, asking for a kicker to her powers of witch-water.

As Aspen hid in the thick of the woods, Rio broke free of the ward and decimated the protective cloak. The seagull soared toward the water. Gurgling and gushing, the creek flowed over rocks without a care in the world. The siren song of the River Goddess answered her silent call.

$$C \star C \star C \star$$

Lucky couldn't take his eyes off the demon claiming fatherhood over him. His mother didn't flat-out confess in her memoir, but she implied her time with Andre remained a lifelong remembrance and struggle. And he'd guessed Lawrence wasn't his bio father. They bore little resemblance to one another. Not that he looked much like Andre either. Now the rest of their story made sense. He hated that his mother had struggled every day seeing Lucky. But he also knew she'd loved him to the ends of the earth, despite the vile half of his parentage.

How could he ever create a relationship with Aspen? She'd not want a thing to do with a warlock of Andre's bloodline. With nothing to lose, the thought triggered his next movements. He'd save Aspen, her family, her covenstead, the entire witchworld. If he died, so be it. Maybe the world would be a better place with no Charlemagne blood left behind. At least killing Andre broke his bonds to all his bonded warlocks, and all his children floating around the world. Good would stem from Andre's death.

Vines fluttered to his right. But they weren't Andre's vines.

Out of the corner of his eye, he spied Aspen escaping to safety behind murky air, the faint flicker of a lantern fading into the distance.

"Let Eden go, and I'll go with you. No Aspen. I'll convince the Wildes to release you."

"Lucky!" Ethan's rage weighed onerous on his name. "No."

He turned to his cousin. "Back me up."

"You don't possess full use of your magic," Ethan said under his breath.

"Then help me. Cousin." Lucky added the word to prove he'd accepted his role in the Ravenwood family.

"Gentlemen. I'm over here." Andre waved and sprayed

a fresh wave of glowing blue embers to strengthen the fire circling Eden. She rested her butt against a boulder and the fire ring adapted, waving away the increased stench of brimstone.

Rivers of mud rotated around Lucky's feet and rooted him to the ground. The vine tattoo attacked him in one stinging assault after another. He shuddered and held his ground. Not like he didn't have a choice. He glared at Andre's responsive smirk. Rage so intense made him see red. A fireball rolled off his right hand and hovered in the air. The glory of his magic caused him to stutter.

"Toss it," Ethan encouraged. "Imagine it growing, hitting its target."

And so Lucky did. The fireball flew toward Andre, but the warlock deflected it, and he killed it with a water and mud bath.

The mud climbed Lucky's body, encasing him in cement-like hardness. The tattoo vines became real and created a cocoon around Lucky. No one else raised magic against Andre to avoid hurting Lucky, Eden, or Aspen. He ground his feet into the river pebbles. With each twist and turn, the mud loosened.

The stalemate lasted mere seconds before a wave of water ascended above the creek. Aspen stood in all her glory, a lantern at her feet, arm raised to direct the water. She exuded magnificence in her tight-fitting leggings and tank top. He needed nothing more than the woman whose regal presence ignited a fire inside him. The vine tattoos trailed off her arms to other parts of her body, leaving them bare as if they feared the dynamic air. Somewhere, she'd set the roots down, probably letting them gorge from the creek.

A tiny wave doused Eden's encapsulating fire ring, the blue flames sizzling out one by one. Sputtering, Eden scrambled off the muddy ground and sprinted away.

Another wave, so large, Lucky wondered if water remained in the creek, slammed over Andre, propelling him facedown onto the bank of the river. Andre fought to stand, but plants tied him down.

Vines Lucky created on the periphery of the forest, slithered to Andre, and bundled him in their green grip. Sage erected a blue fire ring around Andre, the ultimate act of his capture.

"At least you passed on your earth magic, Andre," Lucky said.

"You'll always belong to me, whether or not you want to." Andre spat out muddy water.

"I vote for not." Lucky nodded at Aspen, acknowledging her part in Andre's takedown. Rio dive-bombed Andre, wings flapping, and released his own bomb on Andre's head, a sizzling white glob. Lucky chuckled. Humor in the face of peril buoyed his soul.

Chapter 27

Rafael rang the doorbell of Andre's suite to alert him and his guards before disengaging the locks. Aspen viewed the camera monitor above the door and watched Andre obey security protocol by relocating to the far corner of the room behind a glass partition. Far enough away, he couldn't charge them while remaining visible.

Andre wore his typical dress slacks and long-sleeve dress shirt. He'd gathered his waist-length, dark hair into a ponytail. His room was immaculate, the way he liked it. Neat stacks of books and notepads lined his desk. A water flask and plastic cup sat on the coffee table, the single beverage he cared to drink between his morning tea and his brandy nightcap. Set in his ways, the man's routines may have played them all for fools. Yesterday, mud and vines covered him from head to toe, and today he was back to his same old, same old.

The spring storm had ended, and they'd restored electricity, wards, and routines on the covenstead. Aspen invoked a black curse to temper the blood bond between Andre and Lucky, a sort of hamper to prevent Andre from manipulating Lucky further. Temporary until they bound Andre's magic once and for all. Still, there was no telling what ramifications remained from the man's magic, the bond to Lucky, or her mark.

When she'd seen Lucky confronting his sperm donor last night, a myriad of emotions ran roughshod over her. When Andre raised magic against his own son, her heart had seized up. Despite his origins, she couldn't lose him for good. Her nightmares before this mess had revealed the vines and the morning glory flowers. She couldn't discount that the identity of the shadowy man was Lucky. He'd never threatened her in her nightmares... he hung on the periphery, mysterious and baffling, and confused.

Sage, Rafael, Aspen, and Ethan entered Andre's opulent prison cell. The other witches remained guarding the door in the anteroom.

"Sit at your desk," Sage ordered.

Toting a wicked grin, Andre left the space behind the clear partition and sat on his desk chair. Hands clasped on his lap, he swiveled the chair, his gaze landing on the vine and roots clinging to Aspen's hand.

Last night had been a bitch dealing with her tentacle. Part of her wanted to rip it off and burn the roots to ash. The other part wanted judgement day. As did the roots.

Andre's grin widened. "You discovered the vine much faster than I thought you would. After you killed the rest of my babies, I figured nothing survived, nothing left to lead you to the atrium."

"Because you wanted us to discover your last vine." Aspen stroked the roots. "Why else would you allow the mother vine to live?"

"How do you know it's the last vine?" His dark eyebrows puckered.

"Because it told me. All her babies are dead. She's in mourning."

Another maniacal, shit-eating grin adorned Andre's face, and he clapped. "Bravo, my beautiful red-haired, water witch. You are much more than I gave you credit for. Not sure why I didn't train my sights on you instead of Willow or your delectable cousin. But I must confess Eden was easy to coerce." He crossed his legs for the long haul. "You're a chip off your mother's block."

"How did you create the magic behind your shields?" Sage asked. Even though Marjorie let slip the information, they all wanted to hear him divulge his secrets from his blocked mind.

"Black curses are the best. Aspen opened the door when she brewed them on your covenstead, following in her mother's footsteps. Bringing Pierre here... the *piece de resistance*." He kissed the tips of his fingers. "And Aspen's drop of blood. Took you too long to figure it out. You really are stupid witches who have no business dabbling in black magic, nor holding a black warlock against his will. You can't keep me forever. Your covenstead has my magic ingrained in it, rooted to your ley lines. I proved it last night."

"The hell you say." A vein threatened to pop in Rafael's neck. "Our ley lines are intact. We know what you did. We've plugged the holes and blocked your magic."

"Are you so sure?" Andre's smirk shot a freeze over Aspen's body. Tilting forward, he said in a conspiratorial voice, "My magic's linked to one of your witches." His gaze swept over Aspen from her toes to the roots of her hair.

Even though she already knew about the bond, she'd hoped and prayed to the goddess it wasn't true. Hearing him ratify it scared the bejeezus out of her.

"And none of you linked the magic to me. Until yesterday."

"How did you do it?" Aspen adopted a defensive stance, showing no external weakness. The vine root awakened and trembled against her hand, stinging her skin in anticipation of obeying her commands. Waiting for the right moment, she ignored and absorbed the pain.

"You already know."

"Pierre and Lucky. Having blood relatives nearby aided you. Doesn't explain how you breached our wards." Sage approached Aspen's side, Rafael following.

"Maybe I'll tell you everything you want to know." He flipped up his hands, rested them on his skinny thighs. "For a price."

Out of the corner of her eye, Aspen spied Eden approach her side. Probably hoping to catch his mind off guard and drill into his thoughts. Ethan closed ranks behind Eden, so close, they appeared glued together. A strange new occurrence in Eden's man-hater world.

"Humor me," Sage encouraged. "What's your price? And there's no 'maybe' about it."

He laughed. The snively, sneezy sound grated on Aspen's last nerve. "Poor dead Pierre. He was always a hothead who didn't follow orders well. Always thinking his way was best."

Aspen gasped. "How do you know he's dead?"

Again, he leaned forward. "One always knows when an eternal bond is severed, when death arrives."

"A DNA bond is not the same as a true bonded witch or warlock." Ethan joined in the conversation, their most experienced black warlock ally.

"Ah, dear Ethan, traitor extraordinaire. So wonderful to see you again." Andre stood, stretched out his legs, shook his arms to loosen them.

"Sit down, asshole." Rafael took a menacing step forward. "Or we'll tie you to the chair."

Andre held up a hand. "No need for restraints." He perched on the edge of his chair again.

Aspen scrutinized him, the chair, the desk, searching

for anything out of the ordinary. Why had he stood? Then it hit her. The arm movements signaled the vine. She jerked her hand to dislodge the roots, but they clung to her even tighter, linking to the two small vines still growing out of her wrist. The vines twisted together, and pain seared Aspen's arm.

"He's using magic!" she screamed, and bumped into Sage to her left, the pain radiating from her arm to her shoulder and down her back, as if the roots dug into her skin to join with the tattoo.

Sage caught Aspen, holding her steady. "Cut the magic, Andre." Sage stamped her boot on the tile, raising her hands to prepare her magic.

Rafael plucked his gun from his shoulder harness. "Say the word, and I'll put a bullet between his eyes."

"No," Aspen and Sage said in unison.

It took everything in her willpower to fight the pain scalding her insides, the tapeworm of fire roving across her back, stomach, and chest. She couldn't even invoke witch-water, her magic frozen in the wasteland of lava.

"If you give me what I want, I'll let Aspen live a long and beautiful life with the warlock of her dreams. And I'll remain out of your crosshairs forever." He took a long moment to gloat. "I bonded Pierre as I do all my children and my special warlocks. Just a plain old-fashioned bonding spell for the most part." He landed a lascivious glare on Rafael. "You were one of the special ones once. Remember?"

"I thank God every day you never sunk your claws into me," Rafael retorted.

A commotion arose near the door to the suite, and they ignored it when Ethan jogged to the door.

"Tsk, tsk. I'm not so bad a master." Andre grimaced, but his attention bounced beyond their huddle. "I want to talk to Luciano alone. Then I'll tell you everything you want to know."

"No deal," Sage said.

"You can't stop me."

"A bullet can." Rafael waved the gun, then trained the barrel on Andre's forehead.

"Then Aspen will die a slow, and I might add, gruesome death."

The vine gorged on her witch-water, and her knees weakened. "Sage, I need to sit. Get Lucky. Let them talk."

Footsteps approached Aspen from behind. "I'm here," Lucky said, his voice clear and unwavering. Reconciled. The calm before another lovely storm.

"You shouldn't be," Rafael said.

"In case you didn't know, I found your private compound years ago," Lucky addressed Andre. "I've recognized all along something magical lived on the site. I offered the location as a gift to the Ravenwoods. A small recompense." Lucky moved in front of them for a clear view of Andre. "What do you want now? Thought we settled matters last night."

Tears welled in Andre's eyes, taking Aspen by surprise. Her disbelief set the roots on fire again, and her knees slammed the floor. Lucky jumped to her aid, but she waved him away. Like a crazy witch, she spoke to the vine, recited a black curse so vile, she didn't know the consequences. But her intent was unmistakable.

"I want my son."

"I'm not your son," Lucky replied, as if saying it enough made it true.

A silence so absolute smothered the room. All motion stilled. Aspen's legs ached from kneeling on the floor. The vine furled around her arm, and she tried to soothe it from her mind.

After yesterday's debacle, it made sense to Aspen what needed to happen today. All of it made sense. The blood bond alive and kicking. The reason Andre had Lucky on his radar, on his special list of black warlocks. Lucky's mother fleeing the Black Tide, fleeing Andre. Her own parents' accident and death. A fright so intense escalated inside Aspen, its potency stilled the vine. She forced her heart to level out to hear Andre's madness. A vine tentacle reached for Lucky, slinking on the floor the three-foot distance. He stomped his heel upon it. It hissed and shriveled, froze.

"Help me stand," she said. Lucky stepped back and draped an arm around her waist to stabilize her.

Drunk on newfound power, Aspen recited the invoking words of her spell. "So. Mote. It. Be," she said loud and clear, her gaze fixated on Andre's pitiful, puny-ass body. Hail to the DNA gods that Lucky took after the Ravenwoods. Tall, defined, and well-built. *What did it matter? I digress when my ass is in a bind.*

Stroking the vine, she whispered encouraging words to it and said loud and clear, "Go."

Chapter 28

The day had taken a weird-ass dive toward hell. Lucky had suspected Andre was his father, once the man had hit his radar. The date of his mother's escape and his birthdate added up. He never knew the Ravenwoods had tried to help her. It was all a jumbled mess in his head. She never wrote about it, and he believed they were in Andre's pocket, wanting her to remain behind, used and abused by the black asshole warlock sitting across the room. He couldn't stand to breathe the same air as the man who claimed fatherhood over him.

"Lucky. We have his DNA," Aspen whispered, and he bent his head to hear her. "We can run the test."

"I don't need it. I believe him. Doesn't mean I accept it."

"What do you plan to do about it?" Rafael joined their huddle. "He's still not leaving here."

"Not sure it's in my ball court." Lucky tipped his chin at Aspen.

The vine and its roots climbed off Aspen and puddled at her feet. Her skin turned sallow after the plants fed from her magic. She twisted out of Lucky's arm and stretched her arm across Ethan to jab Eden in the side. Eden grabbed Ethan's hand, and he wrapped a supportive arm around Aspen's waist. The gesture with Eden was so intimate, it clawed at a missing part of him. The intimacy of a good woman, a place of belonging, a large family to trust and rely upon. He wanted to replace Ethan's arm around Aspen again. How had everything disintegrated to dust between them?

The vine multiplied from its roots and spread out. Andre jumped up and backed against the wall behind the glass partition. A gray tint replaced his typical paleness. Death was coming for him, and it promised to be tortuous and painful, the same as he threatened Aspen. Black magic against black magic.

Magic twinkled in the air and blew a breeze through the room. Water misted the vines, and they soaked it in, growing stronger. Sage erected a shield to hold her magic in before it reached Andre. If Andre accessed more magic, they were all goners.

"What happened to the room wards?" Rafael rounded on Sage.

"I don't know."

"I'm fighting black magic with black magic," Aspen whispered. "I broke the wards."

Sage spun on her sister. "You could've warned me."

"He'll be dead before he can wiggle a finger." Aspen toed the vines.

"You can stop this, Lucky." Andre shrank against the wall. "Do you plan to let them kill me?"

Lucky's gaze locked on to Andre's terrified face. Andre had created the vines threatening him now, no longer obeying his commands. A black curse turnabout. He had no ability—or desire—to interfere in the magic. This man meant less than nothing to him. "You raped, tortured, and killed my mother's body and soul. You raped, tortured, and killed a slew of other women and men. You killed the Wilde sisters' parents."

"Lucky, my son, you have it all wrong." A last-ditch effort to dig himself out of a deep hole with no exit, no light of day. A deep hole of his own making.

The vines slunk toward Andre. The main stalk sprouted more tentacles. It didn't take long to reach the partition and slide into the small space where Andre shuddered behind the glass. He held out his arms to fend off the creepers, even as they enclosed his legs and crept upwards. Would they really destroy Andre? Or did Andre still have control over them? Lucky prepped his magic as best he knew how, just in case the magic backfired.

"Lucky, do you want this?" Aspen peeled away from Ethan and slogged to his side. "He's not fit for this earth, not even fit for hell."

Lucky touched the two tiny vines on her wrist, green and healthy, waving in the breeze. Their magic and Aspen's magic seemed to unite him, boosting his adrenaline in a way he'd never experienced. Did they truly have a bond like Andre insinuated? Something he'd felt all along.

"This is the only way to be free of him," she said.

Uncertainty set up shop in his head, and he squinted from Aspen to Andre. "That's not what he said."

"Listen to him, Aspen Wilde. You'll never be free of me. Not in life. Not in death." Andre's voice quavered. "While my bonded children may lose some magical power, they'll always have my magic. In life or in death."

"Shut the fuck up." Lucky slashed his hand through the air.

"We'll find a way for you to escape the Charlemagne blood bond." Neither Sage's nor Aspen's words convinced him. "I release Andre to you," Sage said to Aspen, nodded at Lucky. "Time to end this."

Andre tried to shake off the clinging vines, grinding them into the floor, to no avail. The vines circled his neck, and he screamed. Within seconds, the plants covered over seventy-five percent of his body, like a decaying tree stump in the north side of the forest. A loose clasp, the way the vines covered Lucky, those few long days ago. *Damn, feels like a nightmare lifetime ago.*

With a flick of his hand, Lucky gestured at Andre. Aromatic earth magic filled the air like a verdant garden turned over for new plantings. The rich scent of new soil, the green scent of young plantings. Several vines of a different sort—he had no names for them—sprouted from the roots on the floor, strewed trails of soil in their race toward Andre. Dandelions burst through the soil, open yellow flowers and puff ball bits swirling in the air and covering the floor between him and Andre. Sage surged forward to stop the plants, but they turned on her, rose up to knee height, and forced her back to the group.

"They have their mission," Lucky said. "We can't stop what Andre instigated. Not even with magic."

The vines and dandelion roots flowed toward Andre and muffled his screams. He fell to the floor, his covered legs sticking outside the partitioned cubicle. As the plants rolled him up, they drained the life out of him. His silence was absolute. The body-shaped mound stilled, a living cocoon inside the cubicle. Purple, pink, and white morning glory flowers multiplied over the mound, joining the golden dandelion heads, as if the sun shone bright on a summer garden.

Aspen buried her face in Lucky's shoulder until she realized what she'd done and dropped to the floor, her head between her knees.

Gripping her head, Eden cried out and sagged against Ethan. He caught her and carried her outside the suite.

Alarm tripped up Lucky's spine. Had Andre managed a last-ditch blast of magic against Eden?

Andre's body deflated until the vines covered a sack of clothes and bones. A living, verdant mummification.

"Everyone out," Sage ordered. "Now. There's too much residual magic."

Lucky extended a hand to help Aspen stand, but she waved him off and took Rafael's hand instead. The moment the door shut behind her, the vines withered and drooped. Movement in the atrium towed his attention to the glass walls. Half the plants in the atrium also wilted, obviously tied to Andre's magic.

Standing next to him, Sage watched the scene unfold. "It was a mistake bringing him here."

"Why'd you do it?"

"To keep him from destroying more witches and warlocks. His broad reign of dominance and terror extended decades."

"Will you be able to contain his people now?"

She shrugged a listless shoulder. "Some. But maybe you can. With his death, his bonds are all broken. I'm sure he forced many of those bonds from the jump." Her voice trailed off and Rafael pulled her away.

He waited until the vines and leaves yellowed, then browned, falling off Andre's remains in tiny heaps of death. Scanning for any sign of green life, he swept his foot through the debris until one of the witches shooed him away. Lucky jogged after the group, leaving a trio of witches guarding the suite.

"Aspen. Wait up." Rafael and Sage kept driving her forward. "Can we talk when you're feeling better?" He had so many questions, so much to say. An aching emptiness wanted nothing more to do with this witchworld, the Ravenwoods, the Wildes, and especially the Charlemagnes. How many more were there? How many half-siblings lived in this world?

Aspen glanced over her shoulder. She'd never looked more beautiful. Nor had she ever appeared so depleted or dehydrated. He wished he could take her to the ocean. For the first time, he noticed she no longer wore his bead bracelet.

"It's time for you to go home, Lucky," she said, each word a snowflake drifting from a cloud of apathy.

Her words knifed through his chest despite his own confusion, gouging his already decimated heart.

"Or go to the Ravenwoods," Sage encouraged. "You need mentoring and instruction to be a black warlock. They're family, after all."

"Aspen, we need to talk." He reached out to her, but she faced forward to avoid looking at him.

"Take me to the infirmary. I want to check on Leah and Eden." Rafael guided Aspen forward.

He watched to see if she'd glance in his direction, give him something to cling to, but she kept her feet moving away from him. The only thing that soothed him a smidgen was the tangible bond connecting them. It lived as robust as ever.

Sage remained behind. "You're in a tough spot, Lucky. Aspen never wanted to bond a black warlock. I'm sorry, but half of you contains the worst black warlock blood. And despite whatever bond Andre foisted on you that exists beyond death and has tied you to Aspen, we'll figure a way to sever it. May take time." She patted and squeezed his arm. "For now, go to the Ravenwoods. We appreciate everything you've done to help us. It won't go unrewarded."

"Seems I brought more trouble than aid."

"Everything happened for a reason. Your mother's predicament afforded me obvious proof Andre was more a monster than we'd expected. Learning he ordered the hit on my parents... I mean, we never suspected him." Tears welled in the corners of her eyes. "He needed to die for his irredeemable sins. Even though he died sooner than I wanted, it'll give us mega street cred in the witchworld and in the Black Tide. We now hold certain knowledge of black magic that exists in your blood too. I want my team to analyze the markers in Charlemagne blood." She rolled up the back of his shirt, her fingers warm against his skin. "Your tattoo's fading, growing smaller. Another matter to deal with later."

"Marjorie said it might be permanent." He picked at the hem of his shirt, wanting to rip it to shreds, matching the remaining shreds of his heart.

"Charlemagne blood has forever marked you. The tattoo may be a byproduct, enhanced by Andre's magic. An everlasting spell."

Sage followed Aspen to the infirmary, leaving him alone and bereft. The kick to the curb killed a part of him inside. The other part craved alone time to digest his complicated life.

Confusion weighing him down, Lucky drove off the covenstead. So many emotions roiled in his head and his heart, he didn't know what or how to feel, except numb. And so profoundly exhausted. He found his phone on the passenger seat and tossed it aside with a dead battery. It clinked against an object on the black leather. The gate creaked and rolled shut behind him and he prodded the seat. He picked up the bead bracelet he'd given Aspen. His heavy heart transformed into an anchor mired in sorrow.

Chapter 29

Aspen straightened her mother's notes, journals, and books on black magic, and locked the vault in her lab. Not gonna jeopardize anyone laying their grabby fingers on precious documents. Aspen and her sisters had pored through the texts and notes to learn about black curses and magic, and what their mother was working on. What Andre said about linking to a blood relative through holes in wards was all true. But they'd also found another counter-spell which might've helped if they'd known. One obvious thing: Aspen had unleashed the tempest by invoking a black spell to leave the covenstead in the first place, creating a hole for Andre to latch on to when Lucky and Pierre hit the property. Something she'd never do again in a million years. By doing so, she'd also found a fatal hole in their security. If Lucky and Pierre never walked onto the property, things might not have happened in the sequence they did. Yet she set in motion events that needed to occur for the witchworld to advance into a new reign.

"You ready?" Rafael popped his head in the doorway.

Another one of her divinations came true in the tiny cake-looking lead piece. Three weeks after Andre's death, the Wilde coven enjoyed a simple and small Spring Equinox festival yesterday. Today, Sage relented and unlocked Aspen's cage, a smidge of freedom.

Excitement buzzed through her, and she grabbed her beach bag. "I'm so ready. You have no idea."

Leah rushed into the infirmary, bouncing on her toes. "I need more pain potion." She held out the empty bottle.

"Going through the juice a little heavy, aren't we?"

"I mean, I'm better." Leah blushed. "It's not like the potion's an opioid."

Aspen rooted around in her fridge for the jug and refilled Leah's bottle. "How's the pain?"

"Still burns inside, you know. Plus, the occasional migraine. I'm also having weird reactions along the ley lines. They buzz when I walk the grounds."

"Maybe leave the ground security to Marina, or another earth witch." Rafael cocked an eyebrow.

"No. I'm not shirking my duties." Leah clenched the bottle.

Rafael sighed. "I'll talk Ricky into convincing you to chill. I already put you on a light security schedule, what more will it take? You were in a coma for a week. You deserve more time to recover."

"No, you won't convince me," Ricky's voice drifted in from the hallway, never far away from his wife. "I've lost the battle."

"It's fine." Leah waved the bottle in the air. "The elixir of life makes everything better." Whistling, she left with Ricky, their footsteps meandering down the hallway. A joyful sound of normalcy.

"Let's go before anyone else needs me!" Aspen grinned, bouncing on her sandal heels.

Rafael walked by her side, and they both waved to

Sage as she watched them leave through her office window.

"When will the atrium be ready for human usage again?" She buckled her seat belt.

"When the magic and every trace of Andre is gone."

"After all these weeks?"

"He's everywhere. I'm thinking of gutting the inside and spraying it down with bleach. Sage is ready to torch it, but I've seen one too many rooms burn in this house. Not taking any more chances with fire." Rafael started the engine, the beefy drone of the SUV and the slow roll down the driveway carried a semblance of routine, a boon to a nightmare that kicked off the day Andre tried to abduct Willow. He'd wanted one coven member or another and all the Ravenwoods on his side. His first attack against Willow became the catalyst of his undoing.

"I've got a nifty black magic counter-spell we can douse the atrium with. A spell Mom was working on."

"Different from the plant spray?" Rafael turned onto the main road leading toward the coast.

"Same base. Tweak it enough and it'll work on any black magic."

He white-knuckled the steering wheel. "Not sure I'm ready."

"It's an option." She shrugged and picked the edges of the scab healing on her wrist. The two tiny vines had finally disengaged from her innate witch-water, dried up, and fell away ten days after Andre's death. Powerful magic to linger so long post-death. She'd tossed the dried bits into their festival firepit last night, accompanying the dried residuals of Andre's panther familiars. "I meant to ask you, what did Ethan do with Pierre's and Andre's remains?"

"You don't know?" Rafael grinned at her. "Remember magic had drawn Lucky to Andre's secret compound. Ethan and Lucky took the remains there. The Black Tide is under Ravenwood control."

Shock squeezed Aspen's heart. "What the what? How did they fall so easily?"

"Because of Lucky, and most members were tired of Andre's dominance. He'd bonded so many against their will. Once they discovered what Andre had done to their wives, daughters, and others, they were ready to choose a new life. They want a leader to guide them within this new witchworld. The women—witches—under his thrall are recovering and are helping to guide the black warlocks to a new world order as part of their own revenge. Working with Sage, they hold powerful sway."

"So Ethan stepped up to the plate, huh." Aspen watched the trees they flew past, until the Pacific's aqua-blue surface expanded their horizon on the next rise in the roadway.

"No. Lucky did."

"Smoking the weed or something?" Aspen sneered. "He doesn't even want to be a warlock."

"Not that he's responsible for Andre's lifelong tyranny, he wants to make amends on behalf of his mother. He's met some of his half-siblings, and with the Ravenwoods, they're forming a ruling council. They've already dismantled the Black Tide."

"Oh. My. Goddess." Aspen covered her mouth. "Are his half-siblings for or against Andre?"

"Against. All were born from magical and forced coercion. They want freedom that Andre didn't allow."

"You mean rape." Hot and bright rage slashed Aspen's insides, trampling the grief and guilt lingering from her part in Andre's death.

"Don't let it haunt you, Aspen." Rafael stretched across the center console and squeezed her hand. "He deserved to die. He *needed* to die. For you to live. For Lucky to live in peace. For all the Black Tide members, the women, and other people he wronged. Not least, the death of your parents."

"I know." She lifted her feet on the seat and wrapped her arms around her knees, laying her cheek on a knee. "So why are the Black Tide so willing to accept Lucky, a nobody?"

"He's not a nobody. He's a Ravenwood and a Charlemagne. Andre wasn't kidding when he named those bloodlines among the best—or most powerful—in the witchworld." He let her hand go, and she tucked it between her knees and her stomach, the reminder of the tiny vines still so raw.

"But you're one of the best and you're not a Wilde, Ravenwood, or Charlemagne." She snickered.

"Thank God," he stressed the words. "But my blood will join the Wildes when Sage and I have kids. My bio father wasn't a slouch as a black warlock."

"So why else are they so accepting of Lucky? You'd think anyone with Charlemagne blood would be taboo."

"They like the guy. He's not biased, hasn't been part of the witchworld all his life. He's fresh and open to ideas for a new chapter, a new book."

A contemplative silence filled the void. Aspen rolled down her window and briny air filled the cab. Slow and deep, she inhaled sea air to cleanse the staleness in her lungs, exhaling in a whoosh. Goose pimples dotted her arms and worked across her neck and shoulders.

"Will you ever speak to him again?" Rafael asked.

"Do I have a choice?"

"You always have choices." He hesitated a beat. "Black warlocks aren't so bad. Look at me?" He grinned and wanded a hand in the air to encompass his magnificent physique.

"But you're taken." She fake-pouted. "*Dad*."

Rafael groaned at her nickname. Despite his young age, he displayed a remarkable level of wisdom. He'd make a great father to her nieces and nephews in due time.

"Sage said Andre's bloodline was once good before the war, before their warlocks fell off the deep end," Rafael explained. "His evilness came from his own skewed assessment of the war and his power struggles. Lucky is not Andre and never will be. Lucky also has Ravenwood blood to temper him. Lawrence raised a good man."

"Wow, when did you become such a Luciano fan?"

He chuckled and his cheeks flushed red. "Just repeating what Sage said." He parked the SUV in the half-empty parking lot of her favorite Santa Cruz beach.

A chill pervaded the spring air, and the weekday school and work hour lessened the usual beachgoer crowds. The Pacific stretched to the horizon and met a fog bank hovering far off over the sea.

"I'll sit on a picnic table. Hydrate your ass off." Rafael walked away, leaving her alone.

Aspen gnawed her bottom lip. It was her first time off the covenstead since her ill-fated trip to the pharmacy. The call from the Pacific grew too strong to ignore, and she tore across the sand, pulling her leggings and T-shirt off from over her more protective, less sexy one-piece bathing suit, dumping them in a heap on her bag. She ripped off her bracelet and set it on the pile.

The breeze ruffled her hair. A tendril stuck to her glossy lips, and she brushed it away. As she toed the lapping waves rolling onto shore, her body breathed an audible sigh of relief. Water pooled and frothed at her feet, compressing the sand flat. Waves lapped against her ankles, then higher. Wind gusts whispered around her, her hair haloing her head.

Without wasting another moment, she waded into the sea until the water reached her hips. Then she dove into a wave and swam, her arms cutting through the churning water, rising into the air on the other side of the wave. Her limbs vacillated from the artic chill for a second until her body sang for the salty sea. She dove in and out of waves, recited her hydration spell to Aphrodite, the Sea Goddess, and took her time giving her body the life sustenance it craved. Everything boggling her head fell by the wayside as she luxuriated in the ocean and paid homage to her goddess.

Eyes squeezed shut against the bright sunlight, she floated on the surface, rolling on top of the waves racing for shore, when she sensed a presence nearby. Out of the corner of her eye, she saw a head pop out of the water. Panic arrowed through her, and she lifted her hand into the air, ready to raise her magic against the intruder.

"Lucky?" She squinted against the sun reflecting off the surface of the ocean in veins of white light.

"It's me."

"You scared me." She returned to treading water.

"Sorry." He twisted in the water, searching. "Where're your cousins? Are you alone? Did you escape the covenstead again?"

Desire so deep and intense submerged her soul. She'd tried to bury her feelings for Lucky over the last three weeks. Thought she'd done a stellar job. A lie she told herself. Her feelings for him roared back into every crevice of her heart, her head, her soul. She'd missed him as much as she'd missed the sea, needing both to invigorate her, to take her to the next level of life. *I'm so sunk.*

"I'm not alone now." She swam closer to him, treading water through the churning sea.

He'd slicked back his burnished wet hair. Two-day razor stubble launched a new deluge of desire in her nether region.

"No, guess you're not." He pinched a wet strand of hair off her eyelash, his fingers lingering on her face.

"How'd you know I was here, *Luciano?*" She wanded

her arms through a rolling wave to keep her head above water.

"Rafael texted me. He knew I wanted to talk to you." He grinned, and he never looked more gorgeous, never hit more buttons on her hormonal switchboard.

That's the reason Rafael himself carted her to the beach. "You ever heard of a phone?"

"We both needed time. I didn't want to interfere in your life."

"Why now?"

"Because I couldn't go another day without seeing you, breathing you in."

A hot blush stole over her sun-kissed cheeks. Their separation was torture when she woke up thinking about him and fell asleep dreaming of him every day. The shadowy man of her dreams had embraced the light.

"Where's your warlock?"

"Rafael's sitting on a picnic table." She waved to him, and he saluted her, not budging to race into the sea and play guard. Which meant more than she cared to admit. Lucky was no longer the bad guy.

"That Klingon's guarding you? Sage let him leave her side?"

She play-whacked his arm, splashing water in all directions. "Sage is more powerful than Rafael and can protect herself. She just opened my cell door today."

For a beat, his gaze softened. "You needed the ocean."

"Sage knew I couldn't ignore the siren song any longer. Plus, I can hold my own against the best. A rogue wave or two." She winked. "Heard you're joining the former Black Tide and the witchworld." She diverted the discussion off her to escape her head.

"The Black Tide's dismantled. Better to confront it head-on versus walking around waiting for someone to whack me from behind." He swam around her in circles, his muscular arms slicing through the ocean water with ease. "Do you need alone time to finish your hydration spell?"

"I'm done. I was just lapping up my freedom."

"Lapping?" He laughed, stopped swimming, and faced her. "I'm sorry I was such an ass by the creek. Everything about witches, warlocks, the whole witchworld and how it affects everything in life confounded me."

She rested two fingers on his lips. "I know. The goddess didn't manipulate us. She guides what's already in our hearts, forces us to confront reality. You know Andre was coercing us together, right?"

He shook his head so hard and fast, Aspen prepared to catch it. "He may have compelled us together, but everything I felt—feel—for you is absolutely real."

Aspen stopped treading and stilled. "We're still linked by the blood bond."

"I know." He scanned the shore. "Let's swim back. Tide's coming in. Unless you need more time."

"I'm ready." She was more than ready to talk with Lucky. Everything in her told him she couldn't walk away from him. He offered her the air to breathe, the earth to exist on, and the fire to light her anew and burn away everything negative and nasty. No longer able to fight it, she needed to immerse herself in him.

When they reached shore, they sat on the warm sand, soaking up the sun rays drying them off. He picked up the bracelet from her pile of clothes and set it against the one he'd given her now returned to his wrist. Almost identical. "You kept it." Awe dropped his mouth open. "And you're wearing it."

"I didn't know you were my secret Santa in high school. Until you gave me your bracelet." She traced the beads on his wrist, her fingers tingling from connecting with his skin.

"I'd hope one day you'd figure it out. Although I made

this one, not my niece." He slid the bracelet on her wrist, caressed the healing skin from where the tiny vines had grown. His touch electrified her, and she wanted his lips on hers more than anything.

Beating down her desire, she changed the subject. "Have you talked to Rafael about being a black warlock?" Rafael hadn't spoken of Lucky to her in the last three weeks. In fact, no one on the covenstead had uttered his name. Her family understood she needed time to sort him out in her head.

"Yeah. He told me what he experienced when he first learned he was a warlock, then how he felt from that point to learn he was a black warlock." Lucky combed the sand, flicked a sand fly off her leg. "I've been spending time with the Ravenwoods, learning my history, getting to know my uncles and cousins." He tilted his head and chuckled. "My father's involved and has a major crush on Marjorie."

"He can't do better than Marjorie. But it means being immersed in the witchworld, even though she's not affiliated and stays off the radar."

"That's one thing my dad likes. I don't think he's ready for the full immersion." His gaze met hers, and she thawed in the sincere, teal pools of his eyes. "How are Eden and Leah? What happened with Eden in Andre's suite?"

"Andre's mind emptied into her head when he was dying. It's a chaotic mess, but Eden's sorting it out in bits and pieces." She canted her head. "Don't tell anyone, but she's psychic."

"Oh. Like Ethan."

Aspen swatted at a sand fly, and her hand alighted close to Lucky's hand. Almost close enough to touch his fingertips. "You know?"

He grinned. "Guess it's why Ethan has the hots for her."

"That about sums it up. He wanted Sage in his

misguided he-man thinking, whether or not Rafael remained on board in the relationship. Then Eden hit his radar and bam." Sobering, she drew images on the back of his hand. "I need to tell you something." She paused, and he nodded in encouragement. "Andre lied about your mother. At least Eden ferreted the tidbit out of his head. Guess because it was fresh."

A muscle twitched under his eye. "Go on."

"I'm so sorry. He called the hit on her head. He's known your identity since then."

Lucky gasped. "But why didn't he claim me earlier?"

"You weren't any use to him until your magic manifested. He didn't dig raising children, except to use and abuse them. He found your mother, and she refused to return with you, so he had her killed."

Lucky stroked his chin. "He's kept tabs on me," he mused. "So glad he's dead. I'd never want a relationship with such a downright evil person."

A long beat of silence elapsed. The waves rolled in and receded, the booming song of the Pacific slamming the shore, slamming the door on Lucky's parentage.

"How's Leah?" he asked.

"She's fine. When she was in the basement, she spied the mother vine that led us to Andre's suite. It's why the plants attacked and subdued her. Andre wanted to shut her up. With my newfound knowledge, I used a black magic counter-curse to reverse the damage."

Sand fell between her fingers, and she dug in for another handful. "As an earth witch she connected to the plants easier. She's got a weird magical tether to their roots. Not that it was easy since Andre veiled his magic well. But easier than non-earth witches."

They glanced out to sea, up the shoreline, at Rafael waiting on the wooden table, everywhere but at each other.

"The vines are gone." He feathered his fingers over her

wrist. "What's your back look like?"

She twisted her torso for him to see. He sucked in a shocked breath.

"What? It's fading and disappearing." When Andre had died, the vines froze in place, a snapshot that will fade with age.

"It's not that." He twisted around to show off his back, which mirrored hers in every way, every position, the same mix of vibrant and dull colors.

He straightened and twined his fingers in hers. "I know so much more about the world I've denied since I found my mom's writings. The witchworld is treacherous. It's manipulative, deadly, crazy, and unpredictable."

"You've always been a part of it." She set her gaze upon his face, highlights in his hair sparkling like strands of gold and copper under the sun. "The witchworld will always be crazy different from the human world. Not that the human world doesn't lack from its dangers. Maybe not near so bad now that Andre's gone." She scratched the scab on her wrist. "The witchworld's also an exceptional place to live within. We have love, home, fellowship. It's one extensive family. We have fun times. And did I mention we have magic?" She winked.

"I'm looking forward to the good of the witchworld."

"I guess the tattoo will be our constant reminder of this crappy time. Sometimes, despite the joy of being a witch, I wished to be a normal human."

"But you *are* a witch. Have you ever considered that everything we've experienced since high school happened for a reason? That we weren't meant to find one another until now? When the witchworld needs us the most?"

"Of course. It wasn't just Andre who coerced us together. Kismet had a hand."

"The goddesses?"

"Them too."

His face reddened and he coughed. "I have something to ask you."

Aspen's breath hitched, a trapped bird fluttering against her ribs. She nodded.

"I need a Wilde witch on my new council."

She expelled a tiny breath of dejection. "You have Sage."

"No, I need you." He scooted closer to her, sandwiching her between his spread legs.

"She'll have words to say about that. Council business is her deal."

"She already did, and she'll remain the High Priestess to the witches of the former Black Tide."

Aspen touched her lips. "What do you mean?"

"She wants you on the council... with me. If you'll accept the position."

Aspen never expected to serve on such an important council. Relationship building among the witchworld was Sage's forte. She always believed her gift to the witchworld was brewing potions, dabbling in alchemy, healing, and well, now brewing black curses and counter-spells.

"I know what you're thinking. This won't take too much time from your brewing, webstore, and healing. In fact, it's one reason we want you on the council. You possess so much knowledge of herbs and healing. I'd love to work together. You know I hold two chemistry degrees." He winked, coughed, practically hacked up a hairball. "And I won't live in a world where you aren't by my side. You give me a sense of calm, peace, and home. Something I've never felt with anyone. Not even my dad. It's scary. Without you I'm not whole, and I can't see a future without you in it."

Silence hung between them. Aspen didn't know what to say. Two hours ago, she wanted nothing to do with him and black warlocks, but everything inside her wanted him in her life. Black warlock notwithstanding. And what Rafael said in the SUV made so much sense.

Lucky built a small, dry mound of sand between their legs. The grains of sand drifted down, flattening the top. He started to swipe it away. "Leave it." She sprinkled witch-water on it, dampening the mound and surrounding sand. "Use your magic and build it up."

An opaque thread weaved off his hand, the sun twinkling on it like a trail of stars in the daylight. The thread wound around the mound until the sand peaked at six inches tall. The strands weaved up and down the sides until the mound leveled. Aspen sprinkled more water on it, and the threads dissolved.

"You're getting good. Watch."

The sand at the top of the mound shifted away, and a hole formed. A green succulent leaf poked out, and more joined it with several buds. Aspen sprinkled more water on the pile, and the buds opened to yellow ice plant flowers.

"Magic and environment." She grinned, then buried the plant in the mound. "Sorry... guess I'm not ready to grow any more plants for a while."

"Yeah. I didn't want to rain on your parade and stop you." He pulled the flowers out of the sand, bunched them, and stuck their stems in a crevice on a piece of driftwood. "Sand dandelions."

She skimmed the empty picnic table and surrounding area. Rafael had left. He knew. Sage knew. Her heart understood, but her brain had beat it into submission. Lucky was offering her a realm of excitement and challenges galore. Did he offer her love, though? Was he offering to let her bond him?

"Stop overthinking." He pulled her up into his arms. "Andre's blood doesn't define me. I'm a Ravenwood too. I'm offering you everything I have. If you don't want, then don't take. But can we take baby steps?"

"Will you stop reading my mind?" She pinched his arm and giggled. "I can't imagine a world without you in it either. Does this mean I have a warlock now?" Air lodged in her throat.

"Only if you bond me. And soon."

"You know black warlocks can bond witches."

"I want you to bond me, the traditional way."

"Charlemagne blood and black warlock be damned." Releasing her breath, she shifted closer to him. "I'm falling for you."

"Good, because I've already fallen for you." Lucky glanced everywhere but at her until his gaze fixed on her mouth. He licked his lips and Aspen wanted it to be her lip. "Can you handle kids with Charlemagne or black warlock blood?"

"Kids?" She snorted, a burst of amusement escaping her nose. "What happened to baby steps?" The idea stirred a deep-seated desire in her. Although not ready for kids, Lucky was the sole man she imagined fathering her children. The idea of mixing Charlemagne, Ravenwood, and Wilde blood sent excitement dancing through her chest, stomping away her fears. Their uber powerful children could continue and expand the changes they enact in the witchworld.

"Maybe." A mischievous grin spread across his face. "But you need to be prepared. You need to accept what our children will be."

"Ravenwood and Wilde blood will kick Charlemagne ass." She gazed toward the foothills. "Hey, how about we take a hike and hunt for your mystery kitten? You need your familiar. Now more than ever." Her eyes narrowed. "Unless you already have one?"

"No familiar yet. That hiking trail has been calling to me like mad."

"It's a sign." Dreaming of her present and her future,

Aspen focused on the water, the orange globe balanced on the still blue surface on the western horizon. She inhaled the sea air, infusing her senses with all the Sea Goddess bestowed upon her. "I love the sunrise over the creek, filtering light and shadows through the trees. It gives way to a new and unpredictable day. But the sunset over the ocean completes my day, leaves nothing unknown."

"I'll be your sunrise and sunset to start and complete your day." The hoarseness in his voice chased a shiver down her spine, whispering promises even before his words did. He dipped his head and leaned into her.

The press of their lips, a magnetic force drawing them together, ignited a cascade of sensations bursting through every fiber of her being. She coiled her arms around his neck, warm from the sun, and sandy from the ocean. Lucky drew her into the haven of his body.

With every heartbeat, every shared breath, their kiss deepened, carrying a promise of entwined destinies. In that sublime moment, the kiss declared a passion defying the constraints of time and space. Desire, tenderness, and vulnerability converged, and Aspen dissolved, unable to get enough of Lucky. Didn't think she'd ever get enough of him.

IGNITING THE WITCH

Wilde Witches – Prequel

Read *Igniting the Witch*, Wilde Witches Prequel, the first-meet story of Sage Wilde and Rafael Reyes (the main characters of *Black Warlocks Prowling*, Wilde Witches – Book 2).

ABOUT THE AUTHOR

After lamenting the lack of young adult books to read, award-winning and *USA Today* best-selling author, Erin Richards, wrote her first novel at the age of eighteen hoping to shift the tide. But the only tide she shifted was moving from high school to college. Then everyday life took its toll on her writerly dreams until she couldn't ignore the writing bug any longer. By then, she had immersed herself in reading adult fantasy and romance novels. Writing suspenseful paranormal and fantasy romance was a no brainer and she went on to publish two adult romance novels and hasn't stopped since. But her muse wanted to give that YA writing gig another chance, and Erin finally realized her lifelong dream of publishing a YA novel with the debut of *Vigilante Nights*.

Erin lives in California. In her spare time, she enjoys reading (of course!) and perpetually landscaping her yards, even though she hates digging holes...unless she's burying fictional bodies! She also confesses to a fascination with American muscle cars... and reality TV shows!

Visit Erin Richards online at:
www.erinrichards.com

Sign-up for her newsletter at:
www.erinrichards.com/connect.htm

www.ingramcontent.com/pod-product-compliance
Lightning Source LLC
Chambersburg PA
CBHW020253200626
46816CB00001BA/273